Alexander Zinoviev was born in 1922 in a village near Moscow. After serving with the Soviet armed forces as a pilot during the Second World War he studied philosophy at Moscow University and held a series of academic posts both at that University and in the Institute of Philosophy of the Soviet Academy of Sciences. Under the Brezhnev régime Zinoviev came under increasing harassment and was finally expelled from the Soviet Union in 1978. Today he lives in Munich. He has written a number of books on the subject of Communism, including *The Yawning Heights*, *The Reality of Communism* and *Homo Sovieticus*.

ALEXANDER ZINOVIEV

The Madhouse

Translated by Michael Kirkwood

PALADIN
GRAFTON BOOKS

A Division of the Collins Publishing Group

LONDON GLASGOW
TORONTO SYDNEY AUCKLAND

323470

Paladin
Grafton Books
A Division of the Collins Publishing Group
8 Grafton Street, London W1X 3LA

Published in Paladin Books 1988

First published in Great Britain by
Victor Gollancz Ltd 1986

ISBN 0-586-08628-5

Printed and bound in Great Britain by
Collins, Glasgow

Set in Baskerville

TRANSLATOR'S NOTE

Zheltyi dom (literally: 'the yellow house') was first published in 1980 in two volumes and totalled some seven hundred and seventy pages of rather small type. A full translation would have run to over eight hundred pages. Gollancz agreed to publish an abridged version in English translation and the author agreed to collaborate in the very complicated pruning process which an abridgment entailed. Inevitably there was a need for compromise. The length of this version is probably somewhat greater than Gollancz would ideally have liked and somewhat shorter than Professor Zinoviev would have preferred. There was also a need for compromise on the criteria according to which the abridgment would be carried out. The author very kindly sent me an abridged version of the original and I have tried to take account of his wishes as far as possible. I could not accede to his wishes totally for the reason given above concerning the overall length of the translation. The original work contains over eight hundred separate texts, each with its own title. The English version contains probably about four hundred. I have tried to be guided by my perception of what the Western reader would most appreciate and I have chosen the passages accordingly. However, this was not the only criterion. I wanted to maintain the structure of the original in so far as that was possible and have thus abridged each of the four parts by an approximately equal amount. I have tried to include as wide a range as possible of text-types, while omitting some of the more serious sociological and philosophico-historical strands, and I have included all texts which are important for the rather slender plot development. I will not deny that I have also included passages which appeal to me on a purely subjective level. Given the nature of the exercise, the version offered in this translation is only one of infinitely many possible versions, but I have a great affection for this work, in particular for JRF, and I have tried to prune with care. The extent to which I have been successful is not for me to judge. I take full responsibility for the text, however, and on the occasions where I have had to choose between an exact 'surface-to-surface' rendering and fidelity to the canons of English style, I have consistently chosen the latter. In this connection I am happy to acknowledge a debt of gratitude to my wife Melanie who kindly (and rigorously) revised the complete typescript of this translation. It has benefited considerably as a result.

M.K.

FOREWORD

How many books have been written about outstanding people! But what about nonentities? Not one book has been written about a nonentity! Why write a book about nonentities, you ask? What could contemporary or future readers learn from such a book? A naive question: it's worth writing such a book so that contemporary and future readers can see that it is stupid, silly, senseless to be a nonentity, and that there is nothing to be learned from the description of a nonentity.

Having decided to write such a book, I was then faced with the problem of whom to choose in the category of nonentity. Naturally I first thought of cleaners, janitors, watchmen, shop-assistants, militiamen, soldiers, dockers and other representatives of the human race who have no intention of becoming even slightly significant individuals, never mind outstanding, famous personalities. But on mature reflection I rejected them all, for I always found that there was something significant which could be said about them. And in the end I came to the conclusion that the most insignificant of nonentities is that creature known as a junior research fellow without a higher degree and academic title, or JRF for short.

Why a JRF? I'll explain. First of all, take the title itself and think about it. Now take the title academician. Now compare the salary and perks of an academician and a junior research fellow. Do you see the difference? Now consider the creative, intellectual aspect. Even the most average JRF is superior from this point of view to any dozen academicians still capable of using their loaf. But do we often come across the title of JRF among the recipients of national or international awards or in encyclopedias or in the pages of popular journals disseminating information about outstanding scientific discoveries?! That is the whole point. JRF is someone who is intellectually capable of making an outstanding contribution to culture and of writing his name for ever on the pages of human history but who has no chance of doing so. He is someone with a lot of vanity and a pittance of a salary. He is someone who is ready to do very much to obtain very little but who knows from the very beginning that only if one is totally ungifted (which he is not) and makes no effort at all (of which he is not capable) can one obtain very much. And therefore he is someone for whom insignificance as such becomes not only a hated profession but also a welcome vocation.

The book consists of four parts. The first part contains the philosophical propaedeutics written by JRF, composed at the most difficult period in his life when he was excluded from the list of candidates earmarked by the Party bureau for inclusion in the list of candidates for associate membership of the Party, but when he still, as befits a future communist, retained a vestigial hope of being included in a future list.

The second part of the book is devoted to a defence of impure reason. It follows, therefore, that it is purely scientific. Why, you will ask, defend impure reason? The fact is that a well-known philosopher who worked in Kaliningrad (formerly Königsberg) did such a thorough job of criticising pure reason that defending it after that became simply indecent. So if you want to defend some kind of reason, there's nothing for it but to defend impure reason. Thus reasoned our JRF, thereby earning the encouragement of the head of the Department of Disclosure of the Foul Essence of Anti-Communism and a sojourn, subsidised by the district committee, in a rest home in the Moscow region.

The third part of the book is devoted to a defence of practical unreason. You will have already guessed why: practical reason was criticised once and for all by that same philosopher. This defence was composed by a Senior Technical Assistant (STA) during a harvesting trip to the country with JRF long before the latter composed his Propaedeutics. It is not by chance that I chose an STA but in order to underline JRF's insignificance: if even some middle-aged, useless, miserable STA can permit himself to look down on JRF, it is impossible to conceive of the degree of contempt felt for him by people from higher walks of life, cleaners, cloakroom attendants, shop-assistants and militia-men on the beat. By juxtaposing the young JRF with the old

STA I wanted to indicate that being the former is not only unpleasant but also dangerous.

The fourth part of the book describes how JRF, having arrived in a rest home outside Moscow, experienced union with mother nature and acquired a spiritual peace of which he had absolutely no need. Consequently this part is also concerned with a purely scientific question, namely man's relationship with nature, and with the eternal problem of what will happen when Eternal Peace comes and people begin to live like they do in a rest home outside Moscow, i.e. under full communism. And what fool doesn't want to live under communism?!

Thinking about this last sentence, I was suddenly struck by the deviousness of the Russian language. From a logical point of view that sentence is equivalent in meaning to the sentence 'All fools want to live under communism'. But don't laugh too soon. Logically it does not follow that if you are not a fool, then you don't want to live under communism. Nor does it follow that if you want to live under communism then you are definitely a fool. Only one thing follows: if a person is a fool then he wants to live under communism. And according to the law of contraposition in logic, it follows that if a person does not want to live under communism then he is not a fool. And that means something! And notice: the conclusion was arrived at exclusively according to the rules of logic.

PART ONE
Propaedeutics

A SHORT REVIEW OF DIALECTICS

According to the leading cretin of our Institute, Dr of Philosophical Pseudo-science Barabanov (and he makes this pronouncement at least ten times a day), the division of things into two is the crotch of dialectics. The wits in our Institute (the talented and philosophically literate junior staff) have a good laugh about that. In the first place, they say with a wink to each other, the classical writers on matters dialectical gave birth to this 'truism' long before Barabanov. And in the second place those classical writers were not so illiterate: they used the word 'crux' and not 'crotch'. But I like 'crotch' better. It has pleasant connotations. Moreover I am magnanimous. *I* know that Barabanov was 'parachuted' into our Institute from some party post on high which he had held after finishing the Higher Party School and that he has attained the pinnacles of philosophical ratiocination absolutely unaided. That, however, is not the point. The real point is that Barabanov and co. are absolutely right. Take our Department, for example. Wherever you look you see some sign of dualism. Take Senior Research Fellow Subbotin. He's the most intelligent blockhead in the Institute. (I'll explain the difference between a blockhead and a cretin later on.) He's also a Doctor of Philosophical Pseudo-science. He's half Russian and half Jewish. Moreover, his more intelligent half is Jewish, while everything in him which is stupid, servile and mean belongs to the Russian part of him, and that part itself is half Tartar and half Mongol. Yet another Doctor of Philosophical Pseudo-science (the majority in our Department are Doctors), Departmental Paranoiac Smirnyashchev is also a bit of a split personality, but in a different sense – he's halfwitted, but he's also half-chancer. His right-hand man Vadim Nikolaevich Sazonov is split in many ways at once. He's half-scholar and half-informer. As an informer he's half-volunteer and half-conscript. As a scholar he's half-hack and half-plagiarist. And everyone else's personality is split as well, one way or another.

Including mine. I cannot do anything without engaging in a hard-fought polemical battle with myself. It's bloody exhausting. That's why I try *not* to do anything. But a decision not to do anything often requires its own justification as well, so that I still have to engage in these internal polemics. I'm damned if I do and I'm damned if I don't. For example:

'It's about time I had a woman,' I say to myself.

'Good idea,' I agree, not without a certain innuendo.

'Well, who would it be best with today? One of the "regulars", or one from the "waiting-list" or should I try the street?'

'Regulars' are women with whom I've been 'associating' regularly for some months. The 'waiting-list' consists of those with whom I've not yet 'associated' but for whom the ground, as it were, has been prepared and who are ready either to come to my place or to admit me to theirs (!) 'Trying the street', of course, is self-explanatory. Actually, this term does require comment, because it takes a fair amount of experience and a grounding in some quite rigorous theory to tempt your Russian whore, no matter how unlovely and clapped out she might be. Even after five years a friend of mine had still not learned how to take a woman in the street, although he must have collected about two hundred slaps in the face.

'Not the street! The weather's lousy. And anyway, it's risky. The most obvious effect of increasing cultural ties with the West has been the spread of venereal disease.'

'You don't call negroes and Arabs the "West", do you?'

'Listen, even the Chinese are Western, as far as we are concerned.'

'In that case, choose someone from the "waiting-list".'

'It's not quite as simple as that. First you have to "sweet-talk" them into it, you need to lay out for drink, and "zakuski". You have to go and meet them. And take them home again. Maybe you even have to pay for a taxi. And they don't surrender first time. They play hard to get. *They* of course, are not like all the others! And they put on airs, sometimes. And they know absolutely nothing about making love. You have to teach them everything from square one. And you're no great shakes as a teacher yourself.'

'OK. One of the "regulars", then? Where's my "book-for-bedtime"? Who'll I choose?'

'You surely haven't forgotten that one of your "regulars" tore it up? At first she threatened to take it to the local Party authorities and she tried to blackmail you into marrying her.'

'What a bitch! OK, then, let's think of something better.'

'I wouldn't hurry, if I were you. I'm fed up with the "regulars". It's time to replace them. Especially since those on the waiting-list are beginning to wander. They can't be expected to wait for ever!! Right now the "regulars" are probably at home with their husbands or pouring their souls out to other "friends" like yourself. And if any of them *is* free at the moment, she'll only drag her hysterical problems along with her. You'd be better to have a go at the woman next door.'

'Listen, it was *you* who told me not to have any affairs with people in the same building.'

'If you don't fancy your neighbour, have a go at writing. You've got enough paper! You nicked a whole box from the Institute, allegedly for "departmental business". You're certainly not short of worldly wisdom. You've got more time and energy than you know what to do with. Ability, do I hear you ask? Show me one contemporary writer of any real, genuine ability. Nowadays anyone who is not actually illiterate can be a writer, if he wants to. And if he's illiterate, so much the better. Take, for example, the General Secretary himself. You couldn't imagine anyone more inarticulate and even he's become an outstanding writer.'*

'It's easy to say "Have a go at writing". You have to have a starting point. And to know how to start, you need to know how you're going to carry on and what the ending's going to be.'

'The continuation of something never has anything to do with how it began. Do you remember what our revolution was concocted out of? And how do you think it's progressing now? And if you knew how it would end, you would discover another

* A reference to the award of the Lenin Prize for Literature to L. I. Brezhnev for his memoirs, the literary merit of which is questionable – as, indeed, is the authorship. (*Translator's note*)

5

philosophical truth: the end is never the culmination of the process of continuation. So start with what you've got. Or, as the great Ilich taught us, start with something as simple as possible, something obvious to the masses, something which has been repeated countless millions of times. For instance, "Horses eat oats".'

> E'en though you've 'explicated' all
> That was, is and will be,
> The picture will be incomplete,
> Unless the message it promotes
> Is clear for everyone to see:
> What horses eat are oats.

'If horses and oats were a mass phenomenon, repeated millions of times, we'd have bread and meat coming out of our ears and we wouldn't have to be buying it from Bandaranaike. Anyway, that would be a banal beginning.'

'It's only those wonderfully wise members of the liberal intelligentsia that are scared of banalities,' I object indignantly, 'that's why they only talk nonsense. But those who are really wise speak only in banalities. And that's why they occasionally come up with something worthy of note.'

'I give up! In which case I'll start in accordance with philosophical tradition with propaedeutics.'

PROPAEDEUTICS

When people ask me as a professional philosopher what 'propaedeutics' means, I reply somewhat arrogantly that it's the same thing as 'prolegomena'. When they get an answer like that, their jaws drop and they are suddenly far too aware of their glaring ignorance to dare to ask what 'prolegomena' means. And they're not alone. I'm ready to bet that twenty-four thousand nine hundred and ninety qualified philosophers out of twenty-five thousand couldn't answer a question like that and the remaining ten would only be waffling. Ask them yourself. And watch their faces. When I was a first year student and still believed in the gospel according to St Marx, I asked a professor who had been rabbiting on about the primacy of matter and, naturally, the secondary nature of consciousness, what the difference was between gnosiology and epistemology and how they differed from the theory of cognition and whether clarity in these matters was more likely to be achieved by an approach associated with transcendentism or transcendentalism. By the look on his face you'd think I'd asked him what 'prolegomena' meant.

I suspect that Engels's face had exactly the same expression when Marx told him the heart-rending news that the future belonged, lock, stock and barrel, to the proletariat. The proletariat alone, excluding the poorest peasantry. The poorest peasantry was a later discovery of Lenin's, since the West no longer *had* any 'poorest peasantry'. I can just picture it. Engels is sitting in a leather armchair, one leg crossed over the other, wearing striped trousers and smoking a cigar. Marx, dishevelled, is pacing up and down the study with all three (or is it four) volumes of *Das Kapital* under his arm. For some reason Marx calls Engels 'General'. Clearly the practice of promoting Party workers to the rank of 'General' and 'Marshal' dates from that time. Engels calls Marx 'the Moor'. What's 'Moor'? An Arab? If that's the case, Engels's little joke is a trifle sour in the light of the conflict in the Middle East. 'We have to join ranks with the Proletariat,' Marx shouts, 'for the future belongs to *it*!' These words have such an effect on Engels that he sticks the lighted end of his cigar in his mouth by mistake. When he sees his face, Marx lowers his voice a little. 'You don't need to get rid of your factory yet,' he says, 'there's no hurry. And, God willing, maybe it won't be necessary.'

But this is not the point. This section on propaedeutics is included for the sole purpose of allowing me to make clear my own attitude to communism from the very beginning. Clarity right from the word 'go' is my motto. I can't stand authors who beat about the bush for page after page and never reveal to the very end the stance to which their implacable logic has brought them. Perhaps that's a natural development for some writers, but not for me. And I certainly won't regard it as a sign of some higher-order intellectual evolution. I remember once leafing through a collection of articles on communism published by our

Institute. 'In the period of the advanced stage in the building of communism', I read on a page chosen at random, 'the Soviet Union will exceed the level of industrial production of the most developed country in the world – the USA. At the same time the Soviet Union will exceed the level of productivity in the USA . . .' Oh, you idiots, I exclaimed and threw the book under the bed. And that was that. No more evolution. And no spiritual drama. Why would there be? On account of crap like that? Rubbish! Don't believe anyone who tells you that he went through a great spiritual crisis when he discovered that marxism was not the pinnacle of wisdom and nobility of thought but the nadir of dull-wittedness, superficiality and dishonesty. If anyone does experience a crisis, he's lying if he says it's because he's lost his faith in marxism. He's lost his faith in something else and is disguising it as an ideological crisis. I repeat, and I insist upon it: it is impossible to lose one's faith in marxism for the simple reason that it's impossible to believe in it in the first place. It is a phenomenon which does not belong in the realm of faith, but in that of quasi-faith or pseudo-faith.

My attitude to communism has always been complex, indeed, even contradictory. On the one hand, I respect it since I live not far from Dzerzhinsky Square, or more succinctly, the Lubyanka.* I was born and grew up literally in the shadow of the main building of the vilest institution in the Soviet Union. And I see it almost every day. And every day, for one reason or another, I have to walk past the bronze statue of Iron Felix who has taken root in the middle of the square. On the other hand, I despise communism, for I work in the most undistinguished, untalented institution in the Soviet Union – the Institute of Ideology of the Academy of Sciences. Listen carefully: the Institute of Ideology (!) of the Academy of Sciences (!!). Get it? I'll explain. It's as if the prestigious Academy of Medical Sciences had as one of its affiliates an Institute of Witchcraft.

I am ready to do battle with communism because it will soon be utterly nauseating and revolting. I am also ready to defend it, for I am afraid that if it didn't exist the vanguard of those in the

* F. E. Dzerzhinsky was head of the Bolshevik terror organisation known as the Cheka, forerunner of the KGB, and the Lubyanka is the KGB headquarters. (*Translator's note*)

struggle for progress would dream up something a lot worse. Communism is bad enough, but without it things would be a lot worse – that's the problem. The dialectics of social development are such that once communism has arrived, anything that comes after it or replaces it will be worse. The discovery of this fatal circumstance has been the greatest tragedy imaginable for thinking people of my generation. The point is not that we don't believe in communism but that we do not believe either that it can be avoided, or that something better can be invented. And if you really want to know, it's for that very reason, and not because of a preoccupation with matters sartorial, that we wear dirty jeans and unspeakable beards.

> Fate's cruelties I never feared,
> Her tricks have not taken their toll.
> I simply grow this straggling beard
> To cover my naked soul.

Don't imagine that I wrote these lines. Poetry I regard generally as the most primitive form of self-consciousness. I've a friend who composes verses for me. He composes them for me because he can't get published – even in the West. And if even the West doesn't want to publish the poetry of a seditious Soviet poet, then it can't be worth publishing. I told him this to his face. He replied that he doesn't write poetry, nor compose it. It comes belching forth from his soul. Moreover, it's not because it's bad that it doesn't get published in the West – worse things than that get published. It's simply that publishing Russian stuff over there is in the hands of Soviet émigrés who have taken with them all their Soviet manners and customs. A Soviet person can never ever cleanse himself of his inherent Sovietism. The story goes that a certain Soviet émigré tried to join some religious institution or other but another emigrant (his good friend) denounced him secretly as being politically unreliable, since he had been expelled from the CPSU. And he wasn't admitted for that reason. In our part of the world we had an even funnier case. A philosopher wanted to work part-time at the Ecclesiastical Academy, but he was refused admission because he was a member of the CPSU. He then became a dissident. Naturally he was expelled from the Party. He was dismissed from his post. He tried again to get into that Ecclesiastical Academy. Again he was unsuccessful. This time, admittedly, it was for a different reason. This time it was because he had been *expelled* from the CPSU.

THE EPIGRAPH

A philosophical disquisition of the type I am about to undertake requires an epigraph, and I have chosen as such a few lines from a piss-taking ditty of my friend the poet:

> A future bleak ahead I see,
> (This cheerless truth I cannot duck)
> Despite official optimism.
> Our kids will change their repartee;
> They'll say, instead of 'Go to f——!',
> 'Piss off to communism!'

What piss-taking verse does with respect to communism is that it takes everything it (communism) regards as sacrosanct and pisses all over it. It doesn't refute; it doesn't criticise; it doesn't negate or denounce – it takes the piss.

Some people regard such verse as evidence of anti-communism, but they are quite wrong. It does not put the reader or the writer in a position vis-à-vis communism which could be designated by the scientific term 'anti-'. It expresses neither rapture nor disappointment. It states honestly, frankly and unambiguously the following: 'As far as your communism is concerned, I piss all over it'. The most you could accuse it of is covering in a light spray of piss communist ideas and manifestations. And notice the subtle use of language! What we're talking about is not cold indifference, but warm-hearted concern. And in good old Russian tradition such concern can be directed not only against what is harmful but also what is near and dear to you.

This reminds me of the situation in which a colleague in our Institute found himself. (He's nicknamed 'The Teacher' because in the course of a long life he has not managed to produce a single text-book nor obtain permission to expound his teaching publicly.) The Teacher was trying to set up a short course in the

10

Faculty of Philosophy on a very fashionable aspect of contemporary logic. He was invited to a meeting of the Party committee to discuss the matter. Present at the meeting were the Secretary of the Party committee, the Dean and many other important people. The Dean said that he had no complaints. There was, however, this rumour that the Teacher under-rated dialectical logic. It was to be hoped that there was some misunderstanding. 'Of course!' said the Teacher, 'it's a foul calumny!' The faces of those present lit up, as if to say: 'Well, that's all right – he's one of us after all!' 'As a matter of fact,' continued the Teacher, 'I deeply despise it.'

That is precisely my attitude to communism. However, unlike the Teacher, if I were asked to choose the society in which I should prefer to live, I'd still choose our own dear, and at the same time deeply despised, communist society. Surprised? 'What's the catch?' I hear you ask? The point is that really the sole purpose of building communism is to provide an intelligent and thinking person with enough material and excuse to indulge in suffering because of the loathsomeness of human existence. And apart from anything else, I still haven't given up all hope. As my friend the Poet said:

> History at times is rather droll,
> One day, a church – the next, a hole.
> But something worse than that can be:
> One day the Mausoleum – the next a WC.

This verse could also have served as an epigraph, but the Poet thinks that the word 'Mausoleum' is rude. 'Do you think the word "f——" is less rude?' I asked. 'As you well know, tens of millions of people go to the Mausoleum.' 'And there are hundreds of millions of people going to f——,' said the Poet. There was no answer to that.

ON BLOCKHEADS AND CRETINS

I promised to explain the difference between a blockhead and a cretin, but I find that the matter is not so simple. We all operate perfectly well in practice with terms like 'fool', 'blockhead', 'cretin', 'degenerate'. Even our clerks and cloakroom-attendants know that Barabanov is a cretin and not a blockhead and that Subbotin is a blockhead but not a cretin. We only have to glance at a member of the academic staff to know right away whether he is a fool, blockhead, cretin or degenerate. But it is beyond even the Teacher's power to produce strict, scientific definitions of these terms. When I raised the problem during a break between classes on the stair landing he admitted it himself: 'I know only that all these terms apply to people with higher education, that cretins enter the academic world from posts within the Party, that blockheads are not suitable even for posts in the trade-union organisation and that fools are usually from the ranks of the informers. A special theory of measurement will be required if these categories are to be more strictly delineated. If you take up this problem and solve it, your name will go down for ever in the pages of science history.'

A tempting prospect, of course. But it would probably take a lot of work and a long time, and that's not for me. As far as the difference between a blockhead and a cretin is concerned, I can give you a short example and you'll see right away what I mean. When Barabanov begins to discuss the crotch of dialectics, you involuntarily think to yourself: God, what a cretin! But when Subbotin adopts the pose of a philosophically literate, refined intellectual and begins to expose Barabanov for his incomprehension and distortion of both the letter and the spirit of the dialectic, you can't help asking yourself: Where do they get such blockheads from? And even if you're not a Party member you know immediately that Barabanov will inevitably be elected onto the Party committee, but that Subbotin won't make it further than departmental trade-union organiser, because the former is a cretin, and that's very good, whereas the latter is merely a blockhead, which is also good, but not very.

I belong to the category of 'fool' since I have still not managed to defend my thesis. Academician Petin belongs to the category of 'degenerate'. To be a degenerate it's not enough to be merely a cretin. You have to be an outstanding cretin and to have been at least once a member of the Central Committee, a deputy and a prize-winner.

THE MADHOUSE

The Madhouse doesn't mean what you think it does. What you're thinking of sounds much more poetic: Kanatchikova Dacha, Matrosskaya Tyshina, Belye Stolby.* Listen to the sound: Be-ly-e Stol-by! If I were a foreigner, the sound alone would make me want to go there instead of Zagorsk, Suzdal, Samarkand and the Lenin Hills. But I'm not a foreigner, and I never shall be. It's strange, isn't it: as far as we are concerned, everyone who lives abroad is a foreigner to us, but somehow we're not foreigners to them. Even Mongolians and Chinese don't want to count us as foreigners. Even Bulgarians count as foreigners for us, but in their eyes we don't. We're just Soviet people. I had only just formulated this thought when my Alter Ego said that I'd still make it to Belye Stolby, even though I'm not a foreigner but a run-of-the-mill Soviet citizen. But you've made another mistake if you think that I have a split personality. Actually, I have a third Ego, and a fourth, and a fifth . . . as many, in fact, as you like. I once tried to count them but I couldn't keep track of them. One of my Egos laughed about this and observed that I've got as many Egos as I've had hot women. Unfortunately, added another Ego, there wasn't a decent one among them. Where are they, these divine creatures, for the sake of whom, and because of whom, men . . . ?! (*Translator's note*)

But let's get back to the subject. My Second Ego has told me more than once that I am capable enough but that I have one (if

* These are the names of psychiatric hospitals. (*Translator's note*)

only it were one!) fatal defect: I cannot think anything through to its logical conclusion, i.e. cannot perfect an article to the point where it is worth an honorarium. Not like Lenin. Incidentally, said my Seventeenth Ego, have you noticed something interesting in that connection? In Stalin's time there were a lot of nutcases who thought they were Lenin but not one who thought he was Stalin. Any bald chancer who was short enough could grow a little pointed beard and travel on the trams without a ticket and get in free to the children's matinees at the cinema. We had one of them in our backyard. First of all he said he was a close friend of Lenin's, then his assistant, then his personal emissary and finally, when he was totally bald and so drunk that he couldn't get his tongue round a single sound in the whole alphabet, Lenin himself. He amused the whole street. And, you know, these 'Lenins' were almost never rounded up. They would only be picked up when they started shouting that officials shouldn't get paid more than workers. Our Lenin was only picked up after he drove into the yard on the running board of an armoured car. I'm not joking or making anything up. It's an actual fact. God knows where he got an armoured car from. The word was that he'd sweet-talked a driver-mechanic from the barracks with a pint of vodka . . . The barracks used to be over there where these houses are. Anyway, the hypothesis concerning the car was partly confirmed. After that incident the unit was transferred somewhere and the barracks was allocated to that same institution which had taken in our 'Ilich'. As a matter of fact, the neighbours were glad. 'Ilich' had got on everyone's nerves with his drunken orgies and his threats of organising a new revolution, and the soldiers had annoyed people as well by marching down the road at daybreak bawling raucously:

> Through the Urals our hero Chapaev would roam
> And falcon-like lead his men into the fight.

Anyway, there were plenty of 'Lenins', but only one Stalin. Maybe there was only one, said my Third Ego, but . . . Sh-h! I cried. Shut up!

The Madhouse, if you want to know, is the building which houses the humanity institutes of the Academy of Sciences. It is

14

situated almost in the centre of Moscow next to a round pee-filled swimming pool, where formerly stood the Cathedral of Christ the Saviour. And it's called the Madhouse, not because it has just as many nutcases as Belye Stolby but because it is painted the same colour – yellow.* And it was painted that colour from the start. It was yellow before the Revolution when it was the premises of some commercial joint-stock company. They say that ten years ago the building was painted dark blue. It stayed dark blue for two days. Then it became light blue. Then green. On Monday when the staff came to work it was the same old yellow building and they merely thought that blue is the colour of yellow paint while it is drying. They also say that just before the Revolution Lenin (the real one, not the nutcase, although the real one was also supposed to be a bit nutty) signed a decree concerning the foundation of a Soviet Academy of Sciences. There's a bit of foresight for you! They say he signed it while he was still in his hut.† That hut is now a branch of the Historical Museum. What kind of hut was it, for goodness sake?! You need five rooms just to house the administration! They say our present director, Academician Petin (formerly Isaac Moiseevitch) personally brought the document concerning the Academy of Sciences to Lenin for signature. And the day after the Revolution revolutionary sailors were already walking around Moscow commandeering private dwellings and property belonging to merchants, the nobility, staff clubs and political clubs to house the institutes of the Academy of Sciences. All the other institutes were housed in dark blue, or green, or red buildings, but for some reason the humanities got the yellow one. As soon as the Baltic sailor Zheleznyak (they say it was he himself) saw the yellow building beside the former Cathedral of Christ the Saviour, he prodded it with his Mauser and roared; Here! And then he went on more confidently and calmly: First floor'll be the effing editorial office of the journal 'Questions of philosophy'; the second floor'll be the effing institute of history; the third floor'll be the effing institute of economics. The fourth floor became the home of the institute of ideology, and that was that. My friend

* 'Yellow house' in Russian is slang for 'psychiatric hospital'. (*Translator's note*)

† While in hiding outside Petrograd. (*Translator's note*)

the Poet, who had only been a couple of hours in the Madhouse, and then only because he was waiting with me for my paycheck, produced the following verse:

> There is in Moscow, in the centre, an edifice of yellow hue.
> It looks like all the others, but it's not,
> For deep within it every day a team of experts meets anew,
> To mass-produce a flood of epoch-making thought.
> They come in of a morning, a steady stream of folk,
> To push their pens and manufacture all their bull.
> They sit about and 'labour' – it really is a joke.
> To fiddle Ph.Ds and so forth, is the rule.
> To speechify, to chatter, give their mouths some exercise,
> To tear a strip off junior staff or rabbit on
> About how wonderful they are, or higher up the ladder rise,
> Is why they gather in the morning ere the dawn.
> To illuminate the paths along which science has to go,
> Impose important party duties on the arts,
> Or generalise from life's experience and its great successes show,
> Or how to others nous and wisdom it imparts,
> To empty over all opponents a metaphorical pail of slops,
> To nail revisionism dead with all its might,
> To bury Earth beneath quotations until it on its axis stops,
> Is why the team of 'experts' works till dead of night.

WE

'We' is you, me and him. On the other hand, 'we' is not you, not me and not him, either. And certainly not Mahomet, Christ or Napoleon. More your Ivanov, Petrov and Sidorov. 'We' are those united by a common impulse, motivated by a feeling of justified pride. 'We' is the primary category of our ideology. When we say 'we', we mean that if you so much as raise a squeak we'll break your neck, crush you into powder, turn you into prison-camp dust. 'We' is the iron tread of history. 'We' is the invincible will of the Party. In short:

> We are making true our dream:
> Nonentities will reign supreme.

Not separately, but all together. In other words:

16

We walk in close-knit ranks
And happiness awaits us ahead.*

Physically I imagine 'We' as follows. 'We' is a colossal mass of particles, each particle being capable of movement but deriving all of its energy from surrounding particles, having none of its own. The paradox is insoluble: not one particle contains within itself any energy at all yet each derives its energy from the others. Solve this paradox and perhaps in time you'll fathom the secret of 'We. Our leading cretin Barabanov says that there's no paradox, but merely a dialectical contradiction, which is resolved by the formula:

We feel each other's elbow.

. . . What if the truth comes out of the mouth of cretins?!

HE

He is my great secret. I often meet Him, chat with Him, argue with Him. I tell Him all about my affairs and I listen to his observations and advice. I don't even have to speak for He guesses everything Himself. I meet Him at the most unexpected times and in the most unexpected places. For example, I'll be walking past the main building of the vilest institution in the Soviet Union and suddenly He'll be there.

'He was a pretty tough old nut, that Iron Felix,' I'll be thinking to myself, looking at the bronze statue of Dzerzhinsky in the middle of the square.

'That's only an illusion,' He'll say. 'You have to distinguish between genuine human will and the will of an animal. Genuine will is not associated with coercion, whereas apparent strength of will is based on coercion and is an embodiment of it. I was once kept in a cell for a month without sleep until I signed whatever testimony it was which They required. I didn't hold out, of course, and I neither remember nor understand how I came to

* Two lines from a stalinist marching song. (*Translator's note*)

sign. They gave my interrogator a medal, however, because he had manifested will. And I was condemned for my pusillanimity. Believe me, all of Them, that Iron Moron (excuse the vulgarity) especially, were absolute nonentities. The vagaries of history brought Them to the top and They began to throw Their weight about. And They compensated for Their insignificance by indulging in dreadful manifestations of pseudo-will. If you only knew how I'd sometimes like to kick Them in the teeth!'

'Maybe you're right,' I'll reply, 'but Their names are an excrescence on this earth and in history. And that . . .'

'That doesn't mean a thing,' He'll say. 'That's also a sign of Their superficiality. Pay no attention to Them. Ignore Them. You punish Them not by censuring Them, but by ignoring Them. The highest praise for a bandit is to be cursed for his brutality. Don't think about Them and They'll shrink to the size They really were. Do you know what the driving force was for my interrogator? He practised his brutality on me in the name of History, whereas I . . .'

'I try not to think of Them,' I reply, 'but They keep coming into my head. I have the feeling that They're with me all the time and that there's no escaping Them.'

'I understand. They tormented me as well. Anyway, all I'm good for is giving advice. And what's brought you here to the Lubyanka?'

'I live very near here. I grew up in the shade of this building. I could see it from my classroom window. I used to walk past it on my way to the university. I could have gone another way, but I got used to this route. Anyway, it's shorter. And safer, strange as it may seem.'

THEY

'They' is a rather wide-ranging term and like a lot of Russian swearwords can express many different things, depending on the context. Generally speaking, 'They' means everyone who has a hold over you, whether as regards life as a whole or in any particular situation. 'They' is a power beyond your control which stands in opposition to yourself and is capable of playing every dirty trick in the book. Moreover, it is one hundred per cent socially conditioned. It is a peculiar personification of anonymous social forces which exert pressure on you at every step of your miserable path through life. This is a striking phenomenon. Think about it – the personification of the anonymous! Even if 'They' are actual identifiable individuals, They only acquire 'They'-ness once their identities have been dissolved and They have been reinvested in a cloak of anonymity. We abstract from people's behaviour something which does not depend on their individuality and at the same time we do the opposite by personifying this force as some powerful creature called 'They'.

'How do you explain it?' I ask. 'I've been around for quite a while now and yet I've never seen any of "Them" who was anything but insignificant. "They"'re all nonentities. Stupid, inarticulate, mendacious, slippery. What on earth is the source of Their power?'

'The source of Their power is Their insignificance,' says He. 'If They were in any positive sense remarkable as individuals, in Their company you'd feel that you, too, had an individual personality and you would feel more important. But that's precisely what They don't want. They need to reduce you to the level of an insignificant insect. And Their most powerful weapon is Their own crawling, insect-like insignificance. That's Their natural form of self-defence, Their means of self-preservation. Believe it or not, the hardest thing for me to bear There was the realisation that the people who were bullying me were not worthy of respect – they were nonentities. They weren't even enemies – they were vermin. And my observations suggest that They end up on the same level as the victims they produce.'

'Don't frighten me,' I say. 'Nowadays they're all graduates. They read books. Pushkin, Lermontov, Dostoevsky, Chekhov . . .'

'That doesn't matter,' He says, 'the interrogator who beat me could spout reams of poetry off by heart, had good English and German, was a friend of Mayakovsky . . .'

Don't think that 'We' means us in actual fact.
A daft idea like that is better thrown away.

The gentle 'We' you hear when bigshots do their act
Is uttered by those bastards known as 'They'.

IDIOTOLOGY

The guardians of Soviet ideology are the philosophers. These are highly interesting creatures from a scientific point of view although as yet they have not been the object of scientific study. This is rather strange. Cancer agents have received so much attention and yet they are less dangerous than philosophers, the agents of idiocy. The miserable state of our scientific knowledge in this area is witnessed by the fact that we do not even know as yet to which species of flora or fauna philosophers belong. Are they reptiles, insects, ruminants or raptors? Even the criteria for their classification are unknown. Do we start from the very stupid and move to the unimaginably stupid, or from the very rotten and move to those who are so rotten that even the very rotten appear as knights in shining armour? The Teacher, with whom I sometimes discuss problems of idiotology (the name I give to the scientific study of Soviet philosophers), thinks that idiotology is the only branch of science where the dialectical method feels at home. That's where everything flows, everything changes, everything is transformed into its opposite! One and the same philosopher can be a worm and a viper. Take for instance Academician Fedkin. It was he who conceived the cult of Stalin, together with Kanareikin and Petin. Because of him more than a hundred of his colleagues and collaborators were put away. By rights he should have gone on trial. But he saved his skin, and even rose higher. How come? For the simple reason that he is intellectually an amoeba, is as adaptable as a flea and has the appetite of a jackal. Academician Kanareikin is vile enough to be considered a viper but in his ability to twitter on marxist subjects he belongs to the category of song-bird. And that's nothing compared to the bitch Tvarzhinskaya. They say that she's a relative of Dzerzhinsky. By temperament she belongs to an especially spiteful breed of Moscow watchdog, but her brainpower is that of a chicken.

'In short,' said the Teacher, 'these vermin are not worth

talking about. If it were up to me, I'd put them all in a cage with a sign saying "Danger! These animals are capable of anything!"'

For a while I was surprised at the serious attitude which the West adopted towards our philosophy. But now I understand. In the first place they've got their own verminous idiots too. Secondly, the people who write on such topics try to 'raise' the intellectual level of the material in order to appear more intelligent themselves. And thirdly, they get caught up in a historical confusion. The point is that people who study Soviet philosophy usually deal with the 'best' texts in which our philosophers paraphrase what Western philosophers have said and vaunt their 'temerity'. The other texts they consider are the early ones when marxist philosophy was only just coming out of its bourgeois shell and still retained some of its features.

But real Soviet philosophy should be considered in terms of its average product and in conjunction with the fact that millions of people are required to study it. From this point of view Soviet philosophy begins from the moment when marxism was shorn of its verbosity, coinciding with the appearance of a work attributed to Stalin entitled *Dialectical and Historical Materialism* which generated a tremendous amount of commentary. After Stalin's death, it looked for a while as if the process might reverse itself but in fact Soviet philosophers had absolutely nothing new to add to what had been said during the stalinist period. It's not marxism, nor leninism which forms the essence of Soviet philosophy but stalinism, for stalinism is the mouse to which the mountain of marxism and leninism gave birth. Our Institute . . . But it's better said in the words of one of our critically minded colleagues who wishes to remain anonymous:

> If you want to see a twit,
> Or an idiot, clot, or jerk,
> Dummy, clown, or quarter-wit,
> Ignoramus, ass, or berk,
> Come and see our Institute.
> We've the most, there's no dispute.

SHE

A comparatively young man in my position will usually have at any one time about a dozen creatures to each of whom is applicable the concept 'She'. The individuals within the group change over time. At the same time each member of that group associates with other, analogous groups of creatures who come under the heading of 'He'. Many scientists and philosophers tend to see this as the emergence of some new form of marital relations – a peculiar form of group-marriage, while others regard it as a particular form of promiscuity. I think that they are mistaken. Marriage has nothing to do with it. It is a particular form of *social* intercourse. Note the emphasis. It is the spiritual rather than the physiological element that is important.

'Maybe the spiritual element is more important for *you*,' says He. 'But what about Barabanov, in the Department of Dialectical Materialism? What spirituality has he got?! He's a fool, a phenomenal fool . . .'

'Stop!' I reply, 'I'm talking about a spiritual element and not an intellectual one. And they're by no means the same thing. Barabanov may be a fool, but there is some degree of spirituality even in him.'

'I surrender,' He says, 'you're right, of course. No doubt sexual intercourse in our part of the world *is* becoming the carrier of something else – maybe even a kind of spirituality. That's worth thinking about. Who knows, perhaps you'll make an important discovery.'

'Where am I going to make any important discoveries?' I exclaim. 'But still, we're on to something rather interesting. Just imagine what a huge proportion of the population is caught up in such a network of sexual groups. They can spread information at lighting speed, they form opinions, judgments . . . That's a fair old source of power! And what if . . .'

'Don't get distracted,' He says, 'that particular net is very unreliable.'

As always, He contrives to be in the right. For instance, I was at a party on New Year's Eve. I took a fancy to one particular young woman. The feeling was mutual. We chatted about everything under the sun, danced a little. She said that she'd like to see me without my beard. I said that without my beard I was pretty ordinary. Now, without my trousers . . . She called me a braggart but later on expressed a desire to see how far my bragging corresponded with reality. I said that I had been speaking figuratively . . . We ended up going back to my place. We saw each other for a while. When we got to the point where there were no surprises left, we split up quietly and without fuss. Our paths crossed from time to time after that but we behaved as if there had never been anything between us. And it's like that with all of them. It does have one advantage, however. You don't have any family worries and there's no wasted effort on their behalf. One of my female acquaintances has a son who will be leaving school at the end of this year. She's already beside herself with worry about his future. He's a lad of no particular ability and he's well and truly spoiled like almost all only children. He's got the choice: either to get himself into further education, whatever it takes, or to join the army. If her son makes it into higher education she can stay in the same social stratum to which she belongs at the moment. If it's the army, she'll drop down a stratum. Naturally she'll do everything she can to ensure the success of the first option. But it's turning her life into a nightmare. I shan't get married and I certainly shan't have any kids, if only for the reason that I don't want to end up in a similar situation. Anyway, in some respects I still feel a child myself.

> Women only interest me
> In terms of sexuality.
> And when the sexual urge has gone,
> Why, then I'll sleep in bed alone.

MY PARENTS

It's becoming more and more common for parents to have only one child. Some married couples don't have any at all. Whether such couples can be said to constitute a family is rather a moot point. I think that it is a matter of definition. If the concept of family includes the concept of reproduction of the species, then childless couples will not constitute a family. But the continuation of the species is surely purely the result of sexual relations. So that if it is considered a sufficient definition of 'family' that there be a firm bond based upon sexual inclination, then such a couple *will* constitute a family. Anyway, I was an only child. And ours was certainly a family, although I doubt that the purpose of my parents' nuptial union was to give birth to me! And if that *was* the purpose they must have been disappointed. Not that they didn't smother me with loving care and attention. They did, and in large measure. And I still feel that I'm a burden to them. Or rather, I have failed to fulfil their vainglorious expectations: imagine having an only son, pouring all that care and attention, making all that effort on his account, and he's not even a candidate of science!* It's enough to make you despair!

When we were still living under the same roof I used to come home and see the silent reproach written all over my parents' faces: you're *still* not a candidate?! At last I could bear it no longer and told them the following: My dear Parents! I love you very much, and I am very grateful for all you have done for me. But I won't be a candidate. I don't want to. And I won't be a prize-winner either. I won't be anything. Besides, the classical writers tell us that we should keep our distance from those near and dear to us. And therefore I suggest that we part company.

At first my parents were up in arms, but then they cooled off. They thought it over and decided to share the apartment. In fact, what they did was to exchange their room for a one-room

* *Candidate of science:* a stage on the way to a doctorate, a higher degree than our Ph.D qualification. (*Translator's note*)

flat, albeit with a rent increase and on the fiddle. And now I know what it is to share a communal flat with strangers. And now I only see my parents when I go to visit them. Or in an emergency, when I'm having a financial crisis or can't face the thought of going back to my place. And now I dream of one thing only: having a flat of my own. It's a tremendous advantage to have your own flat, not to have a family, or family cares, to have a basic salary and to have no ambition to join the rat-race. And how wonderful it must be to be on your own!

IDEOLOGY

After major booze-ups I quite often stay overnight at the Teacher's place, and we talk right through till dawn about all sorts of different topics. He likes to talk and I like to listen, so we make ideal conversational partners.

'Let's consider our official ideology,' says the Teacher. 'I want to draw attention to two aspects. The first concerns the mode of thought which it represents and which it engenders. The second concerns the mechanics of the way it functions. In other words, the first concerns the mental set of individuals, the second concerns the ways in which people are constrained to acquire that set of mind. We'll start with the second point, since that's simpler.

'In today's issue of the komsomol newspaper there's an account published of a congress of the komsomol in a small Union republic with a population of not more than two million people. Here are a few lines from that account. "More than two hundred thousand members of the komsomol took part in the All-Union Lenin quiz on the topic 'Putting the decisions of the XXVth Congress of the CPSU into practice'. More than fifteen hundred propagandists are employed in the political educational network of the komsomol. They organise circles and seminars in which more than fifty thousand young boys and girls take part." And that's only the komsomol. And only in a small republic. But if you take all strata of the population, nation-wide! And if you consider all forms of ideological work, the Evening Universities of Marxism-Leninism, komsomol schools, newspapers, journals, school lessons, lectures, the radio, television . . . It doesn't matter how people react to this in private or in conversation with their relatives. What is important is this: they are permanently trapped in a powerful magnetic field of ideological influence, and no matter how they react to it, they are particles in this field, one way or another, and receive from it a particular charge, perspective, orientation, etc. They are physically incapable of breaking free from this ideological field. Once it has been established it reproduces itself, extends, becomes more powerful, more professional, more effective. Yes, more effective. This is probably the only area of production where we don't have any competitors! And that is not fortuitous, for it is the main sphere of production in this society. I emphasise that: the main task of this society is to create within it and in its environment an ideological magnetic field. Everything else is merely a means to this end. In our part of the world even factories exist primarily as a venue for the education of the "new man", and not vice versa. The marxist thesis on the pre-eminence of material production as a formant of social consciousness is shown to be monstrously false. What is beyond doubt is the primacy of ideology over all other aspects of life. But ideology in this sense is not something in the realm of ideas. It is material existence in an immeasurably more correct sense than "material production". Calculate the resources society spends on meetings, convocations, congresses, conferences, circles, seminars, on newspaper balderdash, on ceremonial processions, etc, etc and you will be staggered at the sums involved. Even our mighty armed forces are maintained and strengthened for this one purpose, namely to safeguard this ideological pollution and to spread it over the whole planet. And it would be criminal to underestimate the ideological danger we present to the world!'

> To expedite the march ahead
> And that you may not go astray,
> Ideologues will have their say
> About the path that you should tread.
> And if another path you see,
> Or march a little out of line,

To sort you out they'll soon assign
Some brethren from the KGB.

'The formal aspects of ideology are quite clear,' says the Teacher. 'What is less apparent is its content. The important thing about ideology is not the meaning of its assertions but the mode of thought which it inculcates in people. People generally regard our ideology as a body of teaching about man, nature, society, cognition, etc. In reality, however, it's not remotely similar to a science. It is a configuration of ways of interpreting the environment and what happens in it, selected for the purpose of training people to interpret things in a certain way, to impose upon them a standardised way of seeing the world. It is a collection of exercises in standardised interpretation. Once they have "taken" this course of exercises, people will react in more or less the same way when the need arises to have a view about some new event. They develop a similar intellectual reaction to their surroundings, their environment. Soviet people thus react in roughly identical fashion to events both at home and abroad, to scientific discoveries and natural phenomena, without any pre-arrangement or prompting from the government. The most serious attempt to reveal this central feature of our ideology was, in fact, *Dialectical and Historical Materialism*, attributed to Stalin. Not much is heard about it currently, not because of Stalin, but because it exposed hitherto unrevealed aspects of ideology and showed it up for what it was.'

THE PSYCHICALLY DISTURBED

You'll find a gang of cranks and lunatics hanging round any institute to do with the humanities, but you want to see the numbers which hang around the philosophy departments! You would think there would be nothing simpler than to squeeze into the history department, first floor and a virtually safe subject. But oh no, everyone tries to get into philosophy. And nothing can stop them – neither the permanently immobile lift which is always needing repair (which means you have to walk to the

27

fourth floor, and in fact to the fifth, since there's a kind of landing in between the third and fourth floors with a book kiosk. Moreover, these are pre-revolutionary floors, i.e. with five-metre ceilings, not two and a half like you get today) nor the ever-present danger of lapsing into revisionism and being expedited in short order to Belye Stolby. Why should that be, do you think? I personally have no rational explanation to offer, although for quite a long time in the Institute I worked with cranks – that was my official responsibility. I had to read their essays, write a review of them, talk with them, answer their letters, give consultations. And also provide assessments for Belye Stolby.

I ought to admit (and I'm proud of it!) that not once did I write in any of my assessments that the author of this or that treatise was psychically abnormal. But I also have to admit that not once did this in any way hinder our psychiatrists. Sometimes people were taken off to Belye Stolby precisely because of my assessment that what they had written was unexceptional. Some of them for good. For instance, there was one professor, (a real one, not a fake) who came into the Institute with three cardboard boxes of memoirs entitled *Forty Years in the Heet of Battle. An Assessment*. He had been a bolshevik since before the Revolution and had a stack of decorations for his work in peacetime and for his bravery in two world wars. I asked him why 'heet' and not 'heat'. He replied that I was still a snotty-nosed kid and too young to teach him anything. I said that I would nevertheless be the one who would be writing the assessment. He quickly changed his tone at that, changed the 'e' to 'a' and implored me with a catch in his voice to read his manuscript. And I read it, avidly. And I wrote a rapturous review, recommending immediate publication. The professor was taken away (and his manuscript). The question of my dismissal was raised but I was excused on account of my youth. But since I was on the waiting-list for getting on to the waiting-list for Party membership, the decision was taken to postpone my transfer to the next waiting-list for a year. I was also required to organise a circle of 'political enlightenment' for the workers at a building project sponsored by our Institute and to consider that as my obligatory, unpaid 'social work'.*

* Every Soviet citizen is required to perform a certain amount of such unpaid

28

Or take the chap nicknamed the Demagogue. He used to appear on the stair landing where smoking was permitted and we could chat, and accuse us young people of cowardice. Which one of us would dare shout out loud that Marx was a fool, he would ask. What, no one? Well, he would. And he bawled out loudly enough for the whole Madhouse to hear: 'Marx is a fool!' We laughed and told him that we didn't do it, not because we were scared but because we didn't think Marx *was* a fool. 'How brave of you!' whispered my Second Ego. 'How about shouting out loud that Lenin was a fool!' 'It would be interesting to see what happened,' said my Third Ego. 'They'd take the Institute apart and that would be that,' I said. 'But what if we had a go anyway?' said my Fourth Ego. 'Come on, you're an authority on cranks. Don't you think you could get the Demagogue to yell that Lenin was a fool?' 'Hardly,' I answered, 'any crank I've ever had to deal with certainly had a screw loose, but it was the kind of loose screw that didn't deviate too far from the Party line. And even the cranks whose loony behaviour was politically slightly risky (like the Demagogue) made sure that their looniness was safely kept within bounds. And they ended up in Belye Stolby on medical grounds and not for any political reason. If you're going to start something with a large element of political risk attached, you need someone absolutely normal. 'Well, and is there anyone as normal as that in our institution?' asked my Seventh Ego. 'No,' I replied, 'Nor can there be.'

One crank I was able to help quite a lot. He's now had several books published, is a Doctor of Philosophical Sciences, and has got a Chair. This chap came to us medically certified as being genuinely mentally ill. He brought with him a very slim manuscript which purported to demonstrate that the Russian people had discovered dialectical materialism long before Marx and Engels and that it was in their blood. He had attempted to prove this by reference to proverbs, by-words, catchphrases, chastushki and other achievements of Russian culture.

I wanted to play a trick on him and so I persuaded him to enlarge the work, to entitle it *Elements of Dialectics in Russian Folk*

'social work'. Needless to say, the term has a different connotation in Russian from the one it has in English. (*Translator's note*)

Culture and to offer it to the History of Philosophy Department as a thesis for the award of Ph.D. I spent a whole week sweating over the composition of a highly diverting load of nonsense in which we embedded all the folk-sayings and proverbs which he had collected. I had great fun writing it, imagining the monumental guffaw of laughter which would resound throughout the Madhouse and its environs when the thesis was publicly presented. But I was absolutely mortified: it was received with rapture. The way was cleared in short order for his next higher degree. He passed all the preliminary stages in six months. They even credited him with the second highest possible grade for his knowledge of a foreign language. I don't quite remember which one. Anyway, it was all the same to him since he didn't know *any* foreign language. And he was allowed to defend his next thesis ahead of the queue. It passed with flying colours. After that he began to clap me patronisingly on the shoulder and offer me practical advice on theoretical and practical problems in my field!

Then this crank disappeared for a while. Later his articles began to appear regularly, indistinguishable from those of our leading philosophers. Then books. Next he appeared at an all-Union conference of heads of social science departments. And all this time I kept asking myself why my scheme hadn't worked. 'Why are you so obtuse?' said my Thirtieth Ego on one occasion. 'They've obviously got used to nothing but nonsense. If you want to give them a laugh you should write something serious and watch what happens. You've read the marxist classics yourself, haven't you? What about Engels's *Dialectics of Nature*? You've read it, haven't you? And Lenin's *Materialism and Empiriocriticism*? And his *Philosophical Notebooks*? You've even read Marx's *Mathematical Manuscripts*. So why are you so puzzled? When it comes to writing nonsense, your crank is a mere beginner compared to these masterpieces of earth-shattering, epoch-making historical twaddle.' 'The penny's dropped,' I said. And after that I stopped helping mental patients to become famous scholars.

Even after my duties were transferred to another colleague, a fresh young graduate from our faculty, I still kept in contact with a few of the cranks. The more interesting of these bore the nicknames The Reformer, The Terrorist and The Denouncer.

TIMOFEI IVANOVICH

We used to have a student in our group called Timka Kvasov. He was quite remarkably dull. Even our extremely dull teachers were reminded of his existence only when we had to sit exams. Already in his second year he had quietly got himself on to the faculty komsomol executive committee and on to the waiting-list for Party membership. By his final year he was a Party member and a member of the Party committee of our course. He collected Party dues and shuffled paper. Naturally he was allowed to proceed to post-graduate work. But since he was so outstandingly dull he was assigned to the most light-weight and least intellectually demanding department, namely the department of the history of the philosophy of the peoples of the USSR. And he was assigned a subject for his dissertation which was tailor-made for him on some Buryat educator in whose work Timka Kvasov was supposed to locate the origin of the philosophical concept of matter and a materialist solution to this primary philosophical question. Before his period of post-graduate study was over, Timka disappeared in the same unobtrusive way he conducted all his affairs. We immediately forgot about him, especially since we had hardly remembered him anyway. When we came to defend our own dissertations we learned that he had wormed his way into the regional administrative apparatus of the Central Committee. Again nothing was heard of him for several years. Then undistinguished articles bearing his name began to appear in Party and philosophical journals. Finally the journal *Communist* published his authoritative article on current problems in the ideological struggle in contemporary science. And Timka Kvasov overnight became Timofei Ivanovich. At the mere mention of his name all our Institute big-shots and toadies would begin to tremble, adopt an expression of deepest reverence, stand to attention and cringe. It is strange. The Revolution took place over sixty years ago and yet pre-Revolutionary postures are still as prevalent as ever. Evidently their origin must be in human nature rather than in class structure.

Timka Kvasov became a prominent figure in the apparatus of the Central Committee, was appointed deputy to Mitrofan Lukich himself and has special responsibility for the institutes of the humanities attached to the Academy of Science and our Institute in particular. Today he came to a Party meeting. Our Institute toadies more or less carried him from his personal Volga to his seat at the presidium. Petin himself met him at the lift with a prolonged embrace. I was hanging around the main landing. Kvasov pretended that he didn't see me.

Kvasov's elevation to the heights caused ferment among our 'liberals' who had despised him as a total nonentity and hadn't for a moment conceived of the possibility of his making a name for himself in the ideological field in which there were already so many talented and highly qualified . . . etc, etc. Soloveikin's reaction to Kvasov's meteoric rise was the following piss-taking verse:

> I won't be happy until I can
> Become an apparatus-man.
> Until I make that quantum leap
> With easy conscience I won't sleep.
> With appetite I shall not eat,
> Nor day-dream on a toilet seat,
> Or have it off . . . Not on your life!
> Don't think the worst, I mean my wife.
> I won't do this or that or t'other
> Till They accept me as a brother.
> What must be done to join their clan?
> I'll do anything I can.
> Make sure my social pedigree
> Reads 'working class' and 'peasantry'?
> And that there is no blot upon
> My komsomol escutch-e-on?
> Learn to bull-shit with the best?
> And denounce folk without rest?
> All of this will help, it's true.
> But by itself it will not do.
> What really matters is, I find,
> You have to be one of Their kind.
> Not one of Them up at the top,
> But down below among the slop.
> To share with Them identity
> The watchword is 'nonentity'.

You see, when all is said and done,
The thing to realise is one
Is joining not the brightest wits,
But a Brotherhood of Shits.

THE TERRORIST

The Terrorist (as I nicknamed him) was about fifty years old,
with a refined, intelligent face, but very shy and timid. He was
an engineer by training and had taken out a stack of patents on
various things which he had invented himself. (I saw them with
my own eyes.) Our first conversation got off to a sticky start (we
were sitting on a tattered settee on the lower landing). He would
constantly look around, fall silent when any colleagues were near
(and they were drifting to and fro all the time) and make some
obscure allusion. This finally got on my nerves and since it was
lunchtime I suggested we repair to a zabegalovka.* On the way
he whispered that he thought that I could be trusted and that he
wanted to initiate me into an extremely important secret of great
national significance: he had found a way of blowing up the
Kremlin when our leaders were assembled for some purpose or
other. The best occasion would be a Party conference. At first I
stopped dead in my tracks. Then I said that his idea deserved
the closest possible attention and would have to be discussed
from every conceivable angle to make sure that it succeeded. But
why had he chosen our Institute and why me? The Terrorist said
that our Institute was a good place to store the explosive before
sending (?!) it to the Kremlin and that we could get a good view
from the fourth (or, in fact the fifth) floor so that we could be
sure that the explosive was delivered to the right place. I had
been chosen because as soon as he opened his mouth at the
Institute everyone immediately told him that I was the chap he
wanted. And he suspected that I would make a good accomplice.

We found a snack-bar on Kropotkin Street, ate some rubbish
or other and agreed a date for our next meeting to which the

* *zabegalovka:* a kind of stand-up snack-bar which also serves alcoholic drinks.
(*Translator's note*)

Terrorist promised to bring a detailed plan of operations. Meanwhile he gave me an extensive reading-list, the items on which directly or indirectly had to do with attempts on the lives of individuals and up-to-date methods of carrying them out. I straightway ordered about twenty items on the list from the restricted scientific section of the Lenin Library and the Main Library for the social sciences. Lidochka (the girl who handled my requests) looked at me wide-eyed and asked me whether I was really going to . . . I said that I wanted to blow up the Round Swimming Pool. About two weeks later, however, my requests began to be refused and I was allowed access only to books which made it clear that Bolsheviks reject terrorist attempts on the lives of individuals in principle. This presented me with two problems: what did you do if you weren't a Bolshevik; and what did Bolsheviks do in practice?

I explained my difficulties to the Terrorist at our next meeting. He said that you could only get such literature in private collections or by special permission. As for the Bolsheviks, there was nothing to which they wouldn't stoop. In practice they were the most unscrupulous organisation in history and it was thanks to that that they had seized power. I expressed doubts about the theoretical expedience of terrorist acts against individuals and the possibility of carrying them out in practice. What, in fact, would change even if we did knock off one or two of the bosses? There would only be more repression. The Terrorist said that there would be more repression anyway. The leaders, however, would fear our vengeance and would consequently behave better. And why only one or two? We could get rid of them by the dozen and the hundred. That would make a better impression. Then we could blackmail them into introducing reforms which would improve the lot of the people. I objected that in our part of the world any reforms would be still-born in the stagnant inertia of our bureaucratic system. And the leaders are powerless to help the people. He said that there would be some improvement nonetheless. Even if only a little excitement. And, anyway, terrorism was justified as a means of obtaining revenge. And as for the practical possibilities, don't make him laugh. Here we were living in the age of technological revolution and we couldn't invent explosive devices to meet our (already 'our'!) aims?

American students had produced a home-made atomic bomb. Just give him a couple of reliable lads and he would soon show us . . . He'd got a plan all ready. But more of this later. We could start with something more modest – like blowing up the Mausoleum, for instance. Blow it up and then distribute leaflets: either improve people's conditions and ease off on the oppressive measures, or else . . . I retorted that if we were granted any relaxation of the system of repression it would be quite unsafe to walk the streets, we would be mugged, stripped of our clothes, slashed. And food would disappear from the shops entirely. Everything would have to be achieved by bribes and fiddles. This upset him and he disappeared for quite some time.

THE FLOW OF IDEAS

Almost as soon as I arrived at the Madhouse I discovered all sorts of little 'creative' groups whose creativity was largely restricted to mutual back-biting and the projection of themselves as the sole representatives of the progressive forces in science on a world scale. The ten members of the Department of Logic formed between them three such groups. The most important group, consisting of five people, was supposed to be producing work on logic of world-wide significance, although no one in the group had a practical command of any foreign language or was capable of solving a single logical problem, even in five steps. They bandied about a lot of foreign names and technical terms but couldn't give coherent answers to even primitively simple questions. Smirnyashchev was in charge of this group. He and his right-hand man Vadim were core members of all commissions, councils and symposia, and regularly travelled abroad. Rumour had it that they were informers. But such rumours applied to everyone, including me when it became known that the Madhouse was taking me on to its staff.

The second most important group consisted of two people, although its concern was dialectical logic. At first I was very surprised. Dialectical logic is part of our state ideology, whereas formal logic is something only permitted as a kind of favour and with an eye to international opinion, and yet there was such a disparity of number. And dialectical logicians were not allowed to travel abroad. Nor was their work readily published. True, the dialectical logicians in the Department were unusually stupid, untalented and ignorant, but nevertheless they were representatives of 'the highest form of logic, offering the deepest, most complete and multi-faceted body of learning about the laws of thought-processes'. Later on the penny dropped: dialectical logic was a field in which the whole multitudinous army of Soviet philosophers were engaged and these two degenerates were merely representatives of that army in the field of formal logic which, while it deferred publicly in all sorts of ways to dialectical logic, nevertheless knew a thing or two and needed to have an eye kept on it.

The third group in the Department consisted of one person – the Teacher. He openly despised dialectical logic and thought that the 'epoch-making achievements of contemporary logic' was merely the some old drivel in modern form and that it was therefore time to revise logic from scratch. Naturally I immediately joined that group since I had no ambition to advance dialectical logic or to make any contribution in the field of contemporary (mathematical, symbolic) logic. But *revising* logic – that was another matter. There you could get away with doing nothing. But I was wrong, for the only member of this group was also the only serious and hard-working colleague in the Department.

The Head of Department was above these groups. He was a good man, a man of intelligence and culture and wanted only one thing, namely for the Department to be in good odour and free of strife. Departmental academic matters were in the hands of Smirnyashchev, while Vadim dealt with organisational matters. At first I could not comprehend why Smirnyashchev and Vadim took their administrative roles in the Department so seriously; it was surely no big deal being the head of such a tiny group! But here again I was wrong. The point is that the administration of the Department brought with it the possibility of organising everything to do with the field of logic on a nation-wide scale. All conferences, publications, trips abroad, the award of degrees and titles and so on depended in large measure on our

Institute and within the Institute on our Department. In other words, even our apparently insignificant sphere of activity was a typical Soviet example of an organisational unit which exercises control, allocates duties and distributes perks and rewards. For instance, if you want to improve your living conditions you have to become known as an important scholar, acquire the post of Senior Research Fellow, write a doctoral, or even post-doctoral thesis, publish a stack of articles and monographs, etc, etc. Such activities mount up into the hundreds and thousands and each one of them one way or another ends up on the desk of someone in the ruling mafia of our branch of science (if one may be permitted to use the term) and this mafia has its own administrative core. I didn't immediately suss out this system for it is overlaid with all sorts of extraneous circumstances – personal contacts, hypocritical concern for the cause of science or mutual defence against attack from outside (from the dialectical materialists, in particular).

TVARZHINSKAYA'S BIRTHDAY

Tvarzhinskaya is seventy. But to look at her you could easily think that she was a hundred and fifty. Dobronravov says that she used to write denunciations of Herzen. To mark this important occasion and also fifty years of selfless, unremitting toil for the cause, more than thirty spent working for the security organs, she has been awarded the Order of Lenin. The Institute fêted her at a Party meeting, a Departmental meeting, a trade-union meeting and at a meeting of the full academic and administrative board. Then they organised a special session of the Academic Council and invited foreign guests – a post-graduate student from Bulgaria, a *stageur* from Mongolia and two tourists from the GDR. During the meeting of the Academic Council there were about a hundred speeches, chiefly from retired members of the Cheka, and the lady herself was showered with presents, compliments and flowers. Academician Petin said that Tvarzhinskaya would always remain that eternally young beauty Lenochka, the irreconcilable foe of all sorts of enemies. Meanwhile 'the beautiful

Lenochka', looking horribly like the Baba-Yaga of my childhood, sought out with flashing eyes the slightest hint of skepsis or mockery from anywhere in the room. but we were in no mood for jokes. We sat jam-packed in that room (we had been obliged to sign up for the occasion) as if the muzzle of a gun from those heroic years was directed at everyone's forehead. A whole section of the wall-newspaper was devoted to Tvarzhinskaya; photographs, rapturous poems, friendly jokes. Our half-baked 'liberals' however detected some dark illusions in them. They sniggered nastily at a particular passage in the birthday poem:

> A foe from miles away you'd spot
> And give him shorter shrift than most.
> 'Tis evident that not for naught
> You held an under-cover post.

The verse was composed by Ermilkin, head of the Foreign Section, a real dreg who had been in the security organs since he was out of nappies but who failed to make a career for himself because of his outstanding dull-wittedness and excessive lasciviousness. Ermilkin's poem also contained the following lines:

> Iron Felix himself, Dzerzhinsky,
> Warmly shook her by the hand
> When his comrade Lev Tvarzhinsky
> Took her in their fearsome band.

The Party bureau expressed some doubt about these lines and asked the author to re-word them. Dobronravov suggested that the last line should read:

> Used to take her in his bed.

The editorial staff's 'resident poet' Soloveikin said that that produced a bad rhyme: hand/bed. It would be better to change the second line as well:

> Used to make her give him head

To avoid mis-interpretation, this passage was cut out.

What is interesting is that during the celebrations in honour of

Tvarzhinskaya the 'liberal' Soloveikin prattled on about revolutionary traditions and another 'liberal', Bulyga, wrote an article for the wall-newspaper about Tvarzhinskaya's contribution to science. This article was so grovelling that a member of the Party bureau, the 'reactionary' Belkina, who was in charge of the newspaper, said that it went over the score and suppressed it.

'Does that surprise you?' asked Iron Felix (I had, after all, sneaked away from the festivities). 'What a naive snot-nose you still are! These "liberals" are capable of more than that. Our system is so well constructed that if it were suggested, or even hinted at, that a good mugging was desirable as a means of correction, prevention, and progress, within a week half the population would be walking around with black eyes and missing teeth. And these "liberals" of yours would produce such a humane justification for such measures that you wouldn't believe your eyes.'

In the same issue of the wall-newspaper there was a poem by Tvarzhinskaya herself. My friend the Poet, to whom I read out an excerpt, said that, in her poetry, Mayakovsky died again. The excerpt, addressed to anti-communists, is the following:

> You have, it seems, gone absolutely crazy with spite
> And of the laws of history not a word of sense do you make.
> You will not succeed in shaking Communism's might.
> Only your teeth thereon shall you break!

I said that it was good that they died sometimes. Although, actually, it might be better if they wrote poetry instead of denunciations. The Poet said that the two were not incompatible.

BARABANISM

It is generally agreed that marxism has three sources and three components: philosophy, political economy and its doctrine of communism. But this view is now well out of date. In reality marxism, while retaining the three components just described, has a fourth – barabanism. This fourth component consists essentially in spouting unbelievable nonsense with an air of making a priceless contribution to world culture. The originators of this fourth component were, of course, the classical writers on marxism (including Stalin). But it got its name from a senior colleague of our Institute, Dr of Philosophical Sciences Barabanov. Why? Not because he spouts nonsense more often than others or that his nonsense is somehow more nonsensical than that of others, but because he doesn't spout anything else. And partly because Barabanov, with the silent consent of the authorities, has become a sort of lightning-conductor for the scorn of our Institute wits. When I joined the Institute, barabanism was already in full bloom. For a whole year a section of the wall-newspaper headed 'In Pursuit of a Leninist Way of Thinking' was devoted to barabanism. This section was eventually suppressed, however, since it began to take the mickey not just out of Barabanov but of the classical writers themselves.

The following examples will serve to show that barabanism crept into the works of the classical writers long before the appearance of Barabanov himself. In their attempts to show that unities consist of a struggle of opposites (dialectical contradictions), classical marxist writers often quote the example of plus and minus in mathematics. Barabanov is also for ever quoting this example. But the classical writers began earlier. And they both (the classical writers and Barabanov) quote this example with an air of triumph as if one could not possibly refute anything and as if the whole world were compelled to bow before the indestructible truth of marxist dialectics: You still have some doubts? What about plus and minus in mathematics, then? That's shut you up, hasn't it? There you are, then! But it never seems to occur to them (the classical writers and Barabanov) that people fall silent, not because of the indestructible truth of the dialectic, but from a natural inability to find anything to counter such grandiose, impenetrable clap-trap. For even kids in their first year at school realise that it is only the thickest among them who think that plus becomes minus and vice versa. And who ever saw plus and minus engaged in a struggle like the proletariat and the bourgeoisie? The proletariat and the bourgeoisie are relevant here since 'plus and minus in mathematics' is the second most important example of dialectics after 'proletariat–bourgeoisie'. They thus usually appear together. There was a case in the Central Party School where one of the secretaries of the regional Party committee in his examinations even combined them and quoted as an example of dialectics 'the proletariat and bourgeoisie in mathematics'. And he scored high marks for it. And Vladimir Ilich, peremptorily asserting that it was possible to find examples of the dialectic anywhere and everywhere, exclaimed: 'Take the simplest possible sentence "Horses eat oats" and you will find in it all the elements of the dialectic.' Here the clap-trap consists not in the fact that horses eat oats (just try finding these oats, and when did you last see a horse eating them?) but in the fact that it is not the simplest possible sentence, which was clear even from that daftest possible text-book on logic that we had to study at school on the instructions of comrade Stalin himself.

EPISTLE TO TVARZHINSKAYA

As long as class divides this world
The sleeves should always be up-rolled.
And night and day, in heat and cold
Stand guard!

As long as deadly foe exists,
Nurse hate for him within your breast,
And set example without rest.
Stand guard!

As long as still within our midst
The hated foe, unseen, can dwell,
Forget old age, and gout as well.
Stand guard!

As long as heights foretold don't shine,
But seem to be but barely lit
Do not let up one little bit.
Stand guard!

When off this mortal coil is cast,
In Heaven also start to build
The Paradise that Lenin willed.
Stand guard!

MY NEIGHBOURS

My neighbours are typical Russians. One day they'll curse me upside-down, the next it'll be all hugs and kisses, as if nothing had happened. One day they'll create a monumental fuss over the fact that you've under-calculated your share of the electricity bill by a few kopecks, the next they're ready to blow ten times the amount on having a drink with you. Establishing consistent and predictable relations with them is quite impossible. I've tried many times. Nothing came of it, and I gave it up as a bad job. And I soon found that it is only by being completely indifferent about what the neighbours think of you that normal, inimical-friendly, revoltingly intimate relations are possible.* Moreover, the more you treat them the way they treat you, the better. The more polite, aloof and magnanimous you are, the worse. In the first case you are one of them, in the second case you're an outsider. Only after I cursed him upside-down and haggled a ten-kopeck reduction in my share of the electric light bill did he invite me through to his room, pour me a shot of vodka and tell me that after all I was well and truly 'one of the lads'.

On one occasion my neighbour (drunk, of course) confessed to me that he had been summoned to 'a certain place' and asked to keep an eye on me, watch who came to visit me and find out what we talked about. He told me that he wouldn't 'sell me down the river' and that he wasn't that kind of a 'son-of-a-bitch', but I could tell from his expression that he was carrying out Their request to the letter. It would be interesting to know what's in it for him. I think for the moment probably nothing. And he's probably doing it voluntarily and deriving a good deal of pleasure from it. My Second Ego whispered that one of these days he would really land me in it. 'How?' I asked, 'And why?'

'You blockhead!' sniggered my Fifth Ego. 'He's got a growing daughter and it's getting a bit crowded for him in one room.

* The narrator and his neighbours share the same apartment. (*Translator's note*)

They're sure to have hinted to him that he could count on getting your room as well.'

'Stop it,' I said. 'Why do you have to think so badly of people? After all, he's a highly qualified worker, is in line for Party membership, and at his work they've promised him an apartment in a new block of flats. He's even got his photo in the Board of Honour!*'

'Don't be so naive,' whispers my Twelfth Ego. 'Don't tell me you've forgotten that all building work on housing has been frozen because of the Olympic Games?! All resources have been diverted to building sports complexes. What's more, he might be on the Board of Honour today, but tomorrow he'll get drunk, end up at the police station and then he can kiss his promised apartment goodbye.'

Recently I began to notice that my room is being searched. I realise that it's my neighbour who is doing the searching since certain items of my belongings have gone missing. He was asked to do it, of course. And he is willingly carrying out Their request. And nicking things at the same time, which is quite in character. And funnily enough, I never get angry or feel that I have a grudge against him. And, anyway, I'm a fine one to talk! One minute I despise him, the next minute I embrace him. And all the cleaning in the flat gets done by his wife. That more or less just happened. But I sometimes buy her a box of chocolates or some little toy for her daughter. And she is moved to tears with gratitude. She works in a kindergarten nearby, for which she gets paid peanuts. But there are advantages, too: her daughter is in the kindergarten and the kindergarten subsidises their meals.

THE DENOUNCER

The Denouncer sent twenty letters to the Institute before appearing in person. He introduced himself with an air which suggested that everyone should know who he was and be appropriately

---

* *Board of Honour:* an official display of photographs of meritorious workers. (*Translator's note*)

surprised. That is precisely what happened. When he introduced himself I looked very surprised and exclaimed that surely he wasn't *the* Mr . . . ? He nodded with satisfaction and said that he was indeed that Mr . . . and that he had appeared in person to find out why he still hadn't had a reply, etc, etc. I told him that the defects which he had noted in our society (refuse not being collected for weeks on end, drunkards misbehaving in doorways, noisy gatherings at his neighbour's which lasted beyond mid-night) were so fundamental that it had as yet been impossible to give them the attention they deserved. He was visibly flattered and asked why his dossier had been entrusted to such an insignificant individual as myself. I said that academicians, professors and doctors fought shy of deciding weighty matters and heaped them on the plates of junior colleagues. He found this extremely interesting and decided to expose this fact. I promised to help him but on condition that he didn't quote me. He agreed, and we began to collect all sorts of dirty linen to send (in his name, of course) to the Central Committee, the Soviet of Ministers, the Presidium of the Academy of Sciences, the editorial board of *Pravda* and the journal *Communist*.

We drew up a list of leading philosophers who were to be exposed, and listed the headings under which the material would be grouped: 1) distortion of the fundamental principles of marxism-leninism; 2) connivance at and concessions to revisionism; 3) deviation from standard practice in the building of communism; 4) lack of scruple, careerism, greed, money-grubbing; 5) moral degradation. I became so engrossed in this pursuit that I quite abandoned my academic responsibilities. And the more I delved into the matter the more I was amazed at the extent to which all our leading lights were vulnerable on all five counts. I let the Teacher in on the secret. He laughed till the tears came and promised to help me in any way he could. 'The principles of marxism-leninism,' he said, 'are formulated in such a way that they cannot be paraphrased without distortion. They cannot even be quoted without distortion. As soon as you remove the quotation marks they turn into nonsense or heresy. It is impossible to predict revisionism because it doesn't know itself from what angle it is going to revise itself nor in which direction it is going to go. Only the highest Party élite has the right to generalise about building communism in practice and even then only after They have managed to consolidate Their power and can sense that They are invulnerable. Lack of scruple They see as a great virtue since it provides a method for the evaluation of everything under the sun in the light of concrete-historical conditions. What looks like careerism, money-grubbing, greed, etc is Their due by virtue of Their position and rank. So that just leaves moral degradation. That's where we have to make life difficult for Them. They fear exposure of the facts of Their lives like the plague. Get your nutcase to ferret away in that area. See if he can find out who sleeps with whom, how They spend Their time in Their dachas, what They talk about, who They meet, who writes whose articles, how and at what price are people permitted to defend their theses, gain entry to an institute, travel abroad. That wouldn't half cause a fuss!'

I instructed the Denouncer along these lines and bade him take care and be patient. 'What is most important,' I impressed upon him, 'is the need for conspiracy. We have to prepare such a bombshell that our whole ideological domain gets blown to bits.' The Denouncer took the matter very seriously and began to bring me all sorts of tit-bits. It was incomprehensible how and where he dug them up. I processed these 'tit-bits' and dictated them back to the Denouncer (putting them in writing would have been risky).

'Actually, this is all a waste of time,' said the Teacher on one occasion when I had shown him a particular piece of 'dirty linen' collected by the Denouncer. 'This is merely a description of facts. But it doesn't constitute the truth because it is doubtless possible to find other facts, a description of which would contradict the first one. And the truth doesn't consist of an amalgamation of such descriptions. Truth cannot be confronted by another truth but only by delusion. What is truth? Perhaps I'll organise a little seminar at the Institute and read a course of general lectures on the subject. Do you think there'll be any takers?'

'You'll get about ten or so,' I said. 'There'll be two or three nutcases among them, a couple of informers, a couple of rogues. And me, of course.'

'Well, that's always something,' said the Teacher. 'We'll start next week. I nominate you as academic secretary of the seminar.

I can just imagine the panic this is going to cause among our guardians of the achievements of world science!'

But the 'little seminar' was not permitted to run. It was said that the seminar which Smirnyashchev conducted adequately covered the ground. Moreover, it was a properly constituted seminar, validated at the level of the Presidium of the Academy of Sciences. Smirnyashchev, on whose initiative the 'little seminar' had been suppressed, invited the Teacher to give a lecture at his seminar. The Teacher told him where to go . . .

KNOWING WHAT LIFE IS ALL ABOUT

All my arguments with my parents always end with their doleful and monotonous observation to the effect that I don't know what life is all about. But what do they mean? While I was still at school I worked in a factory and in a collective farm and in a warehouse. As a student I went three times to work on 'Grandiose Projects' and regularly took part in all sorts of campaigns. Since I have been at the Institute I have twice worked on a collective farm, I work at a vegetable depot twice a year (each time for a minimum of five consecutive days), I'm in charge of a propaganda group, participate in an advanced seminar, and during every pre-election campaign have to kick my heels in some electoral district. I've been to a rest home twice, once on a ticket paid by my social insurance (twenty days outside Moscow for seven roubles) and once to the south on a spare ticket (in late autumn, when it was already too cold to swim or sunbathe and when none of the high-ups wanted to go). It's impossible to count the number of queues I've had to stand in. I've had a stack of women, been drunk many times, talked about everything under the sun with all sorts of friends and chance acquaintances, read and re-read . . . In short, I would seem to have found out all there is to know. And yet, it appears, I still don't know what life is all about.

'What do you have in mind?' I ask my parents. 'Repressions? Well, right now the leadership itself is not very interested in repressions. The war? Well, right now there seems to be a struggle for peace going on everywhere and we prefer to wage war using the Vietnamese, Koreans, Arabs, Ethiopians, blacks. Do you mean hunger? Well, we're not exactly living high on the hog at the moment, are we? Take a stroll round our canteens and snack-bars! Even to look at what's on offer makes you want to be sick, never mind eating the stuff. Do you mean that I haven't got married and produced kids? Well, you didn't have too many children, yourselves. And if I want to, there's still time. Is it that I haven't had any important position? Well, what about yourselves . . . So what's the problem? I lead a quiet life and I don't get in anyone's way. I don't protest. I don't sign petitions.'

But despite all the demagogy which I produce on such occasions, I understand precisely what the problem is. To know what life is all about in our Russian sense of the term is to accept life and live it like everyone else, engage in the endless battle for chicken-feed advantages and material benefits. And although I don't complain and lead my life quietly, I don't throw myself heart and soul into the mainstream of our life here, I don't become part of it with every cell of my body, but drift along somewhere on the side-lines, a little bit estranged, and even with a modicum of independence. And therefore I am worse than a dissident. Dissidents may take our way of life to task, but they do react to it as life, i.e. their life. But whereas I participate and even perhaps approve (or rather, don't protest), it's only for the sake of appearances. But in reality, deep down, I despise this life and ignore it. And my father finally came up with an exact description of this state of mind. 'You,' he said to me, 'live here as if you were a guest.' He's right! I am a guest. Moreover, the kind of guest who can say farewell to his hosts and leave the house without any regrets. And without a single spark of warmth or remembrance.

EPISTLE TO MY PARENTS

Why the vainglorious dreams? Why reproaches? Why the glower?
No, you'll never hear my footsteps in the corridors of power!
They will never cross the threshold of the secret shops and stores.
It won't be me in armoured Zil as down the central strip it roars.
In a flat you will not find me of two hundred metres square,
With a sitting-room for ninety and three loos as fresh as air.
No settee of leather soft will e'er caress my fat behind,
And with people to applaud me boulevards will not be lined.
A touched-up photograph of me in daily papers won't appear,
And under someone else's blurb won't be my signature, I fear.
Through the mike about our victories I shall not rabbit on,
And of communism's fighters not a single one I'll spawn.
Not with ribbons, stars or medals will they decorate my chest.
And it won't be Novodevich'e* where I'll be laid to rest.

THE REFORMER

The Reformer used to be a big-shot in the Party apparatus.
During the Thaw he took the relatively liberal atmosphere at
face value and introduced all sorts of radical changes in his
department. He was reprimanded for that, so he took the bit
between his teeth and fought his way into the upper echelons,
taking his schemes with him. At that point he was removed from
his post. Then they started a case against him. Finally he was
dumped in Belye Stolby where he spent seven years. When he
got out, he sat down and began to study the original sources of
marxism. Then he began to elaborate all sorts of schemes for
reform, in strict conformity, as he thought, with scientific marxism. At first I tried to persuade him that marxism wasn't a
science. But he didn't believe that and immediately denounced
me to the director and the Party bureau. I accused him of foul
play and refused to 'work' with him. But he clung to me like a

* Novodevich'e is a former nunnery whose cemetery is the last resting place
for those who do not merit burial in the Kremlin wall. (*Translator's note*)

leech, wouldn't let me pass in the corridor and would lie in wait for me in the most unlikely places. And the more I tore his projects to shreds, the more persistently he pursued me. On one occasion he admitted that he needed such an 'intelligent opponent' like me because it was only in a contest with an 'intelligent enemy' that he could hone and refine his own learning, or rather, his addition to marxist-leninist thought.

His schemes encompassed every sphere of life from vodka bottles to the structure of the highest Party leadership.

'Why raise the price of spirits?' he would say, for example. 'What we need to do is to raise the price of the bottles.'

'What good will that do?' I objected. 'People will only get more for their empties.'

'Huh, and you call yourself a scientist!' he said. 'Some people will bring back their empties and others won't. Do you know how many empties are brought back? Only thirty per cent. OK, so now they'll bring back fifty per cent. But look at the profit on the other fifty per cent!' And he began to do some feverish calculations and came up with a profit of millions and millions of roubles.

On another occasion he arrived with a new scheme for dividing up the country. He proposed dividing Russia into three republics: Western Russia (with Petrograd as its capital); Central Russia (its capital would be Novosibirsk); and Eastern Russia (capital: Vladivostok). He would build a new capital of the USSR on the Volga and name it Lenin. He would replace the whole army of bureaucrats with machines. This army of bureaucrats (thirty million of them) plus their families, would be evenly dispersed throughout the outlying regions of the country. What's more, forcibly. Using the army if necessary. Thanks to this measure, the population of Moscow would shrink by a factor of two and the housing problem would be solved. All foreigners would be transferred to the new capital Lenin, where they would not be able to mingle with the population and be a bad influence on it. And they wouldn't be able to spy.

On the third occasion, he brought a scheme for a new power structure. Soviets, trade-unions and komsomol organisations were abolished. Their functions were transferred to the regional and territorial Party committees. According to his calculations this freed a further twenty million people who could be used for the exploitation of Siberia. Then he proposed getting rid of the family, and handing the children over to the state. That way, according to his calculations, you could free another . . .

Finally he waylaid me at the entrance to the Institute and whispered that he wanted to discuss with me his scheme for the reorganisation of the Organs of State Security. I whispered in reply that I had very radical views on that issue: they should be liquidated. He whispered that he agreed but considered that the way to do it was by strengthening them as much as possible. I asked him what he had in mind specifically. He said that everyone should join the Organs.

'They won't take everyone,' I said. 'They have a very strict selection procedure.' He laughed. He had found a way round that . . . he was going to pull a fast one, so that everyone, absolutely everyone . . .

PHILOSOPHICAL DETACHMENT

'Why all the disgust and revulsion?' says He. 'Look on everything with philosophical detachment. You think that's difficult? Nonsense! Do you want me to show you how to achieve it? Imagine you're watching some planet and you detect on its surface a horde of living creatures. You see, for example, one army of these creatures (let's call it A) attack another army of creatures (B) and destroy it. What suffering does that cause you? That's right: you ascertain that A attacked B and that the latter was destroyed. You continue to observe A. You see that they are not all equal. Some of them (C) obtain more of the good things of life than others (D) and their good things are better. What do you say to that? Creatures of category C live better than those of category D. Need I go on? No? All right, then, I won't. This is a very simple strategy that anyone can adopt. But you need to apply it systematically, every day, and every hour of every day. And what is most important, let me emphasise, is that you shouldn't become personally involved. For instance, if you see a beautiful dacha, observe with satisfaction that some creatures of the material world have beautiful dachas. If you see that some Party boss is awarded the rank of marshal, observe with satisfaction: these creatures customarily promote higher Party leaders to military rank. If you see that Academician Kanareikin has been awarded the title of Hero of Socialist Labour and a Lenin Prize, again observe: among some of the creatures of this world it is customary to award high distinction to the rottenest, stupidest and most ignorant swine. Believe me, after three or four years of practice it will be a matter of supreme indifference to you who becomes an Academician, who is awarded a higher degree, who's had his book published, who was allocated a flat, who was allowed a trip abroad . . . And, who knows, perhaps there will be the odd twenty-rouble bonus to mark some official public holiday or other, perhaps you'll get a five-rouble rise, perhaps your social security organisation will pay for a ten-day trip to a rest-home . . .'

'You're right,' I reply. 'I suppose I'm coming subconsciously to the same conclusion. But philosophical detachment still requires some minimal means of subsistence. For instance, I need new boots. Mine are worn out. A decent pair of boots costs . . . Well, you know, yourself. And perhaps you can walk around in crappy ones, but so what? You're old. I'm young and it still matters a little bit what clothes I wear. And my trousers have just about had it. And do you know how much? . . . And I need to eat. I'd like to give my beloved the occasional present . . . Don't laugh! I'm being serious! And take her out for a meal. And go to the theatre. But going to the theatre in these rags is not very pleasant. But the main thing is books. You can't buy any decent books in the shops, and on the "black market" . . . Do without books, then? But it's too late – I've already been bitten by the culture-bug. And invent your own culture – how long do you think you'd stick at that?!'

'It's hopeless arguing with you,' He said. 'In that case – join the fray! Be one of those who will kill to get to the top. What would it cost you to defend your thesis? Write some kind of mediocre clap-trap and you'll pass with flying colours. Incidentally, someone was dropping hints about the possibility of some "editorial work" for you on a manuscript of his. "Edit" it and you'll make it to candidate and senior research fellow. And you'll get a flat. And new trousers. And a pair of tights for your beloved. Before you know it, you'll be having a trip abroad.'

'There was such a possibility,' I said. 'And I'm thinking about it. Just try maintaining your philosophical detachment in a situation like that! Do you know what will happen to me if I refuse? There you are, then! No, my friend, philosophical detachment is not for the likes of us. It's something for old-age pensioners.'

THE REFORMER

'I will now give you a brief outline of the social structure of our society,' said the Reformer, 'and you will see why any opposition movement is doomed to failure. I will give you a simplified version. In reality it is a lot more complicated. Our society can be divided into three layers: upper, middle and lower. The upper layer contains all the branches of the *nomenklatura*, central, republican, territorial, regional. In this layer belong all ranks of the Party and state apparatus, the directors of all sorts of unions and societies, together with their immediate entourage. The middle layer consists of small-fry members of the intelligentsia and the civil service. The lower layer contains all the workers and peasants and the lowliest public service employees, etc. Each layer, or stratum, can be divided into three sub-strata. Let's see what sort of numbers we're talking about. The upper layer contains thirty million (with families included); the middle layer: seventy million; the lower layer: one hundred and fifty million. Thirty million represents a state within a state. They can reproduce themselves from their own ranks and permit very few to join them from the other layers. From the point of view of material advantage the picture is rather complex. For example, those in the upper stratum of the lower layer are better off than those in the middle and lower strata of the middle layer and even than those of the lower stratum of the upper layer. Moreover, in each layer a part of the population has privileges on a quite different scale. We are thinking here of master-craftsmen and shock-workers in the lower stratum, teachers in specially favoured schools, tailors in the fashion workshops supplying the top layer, employees in the service industries catering for the élite, etc. Taken from this angle, approximately sixty million people do quite well for themselves, of which half do very well and a half of which in turn do excellently. One could carry on and examine the structure of society from the point of view of the degree to which people need to work hard, the amount of free time which people have, and so on. Here again one could produce figures. The overall result is that people are fixed by their particular network of advantages in one or other part of the population and on one or other plane. Thus even without considering the organs of repression and surveillance, it is possible to demonstrate the complete absence of interest at all levels of society in any constant, widespread or continuous opposition. What does that leave? One thing, only: reforms!'

'If that's the case, reforms are no use either,' I said. 'If our structure is as rigid as that, any improvements will threaten its existence.'

'Well, does a reform have to be an improvement? And anyway, what does "improvement" mean? Or "deterioration"? For instance, if you get rid of the special shops for the nomenklatura, will that be an improvement or not? From the point of view of the lowest strata it would appear to be an improvement. But the nomenklatura would then help itself in other illegal ways, and the position would be worse.'

'Well, why have reforms then?'

'What do you mean, "why"?? Something has to be done! For the power of the state. Prestige. Defence. We have to give the West's nose a tweak. Economy. You surprise me! The aim of reforms is to make explicit the relationships which exist in our society, to legalise certain practices, to simplify things, to reduce waste, and so on. I've calculated, for instance, how many people could be freed for assignation to the most distant reaches of the country, to those grandiose construction projects of communism, if. . . .'

EPISTLE TO MY NEIGHBOUR

Have a heart, oh neighbour mine!
Why take with me so hard a line?
Is it my fault after all,
That in the shops there's bugger-all?
Is it really 'cause of me,
That in a room for one you're three?
Or that even with your wife
You can't give your kid a start in life?
Or that medical attention is as rare as it is bad?
Or that ne'er a decent break or any real good fun you've had?
Is it my fault that so often you fall prey to Russia's curse,
Namely drink yourself unconscious, beat the wife, or something
                                                          worse?
Why, for God's sake, in these circumstances take it out on me?
It's Them up There who are to blame! Is that so difficult to see?!

ACADEMICIAN PETIN HAS AN IDEA FOR A NEW BOOK

Academician Petin is a legendary and symbolic figure in our philosophy. He didn't finish his secondary education but nonetheless ended up in the Institute of Red Professors, was one of its most active stalinists, became an Academician and held under Stalin a number of extremely important posts. After Stalin's death, it looked for a while as if he might be required to answer charges of plagiarism and as if he had written secret denunciations, but he wriggled out of them skilfully and hung on, admittedly a couple of rungs lower down the ladder (as journal editor, or president of some society). Later he pulled himself up a rung and became director of the Institute. Jokes are told to this day about his illiteracy, and everyone knows that he's incapable of writing a single page. Yet he's published book after book, and they're no worse than any others. Now he's dreamed up an epoch-making opus which will probably run to two thousand pages, namely a contemporary generalised synthesis of the achievements of natural science, a new *Dialectics of Nature*. Everyone in philosophical circles is laughing at Petin's pretension. The Teacher was the only one to say that he didn't see anything remarkable in Petin's venture, for Engels's *Dialectics of Nature* was raving nonsense and only a degenerate like Petin was up to writing something similar based on present-day scientific knowledge. But no one understood him.

Petin hinted to me on several occasions that he would not be adverse to my participating in the preparation of his book as a 'technical advisor' only, although it could lead to other things. I pretended that I didn't catch his drift. However, at the last departmental meeting it was stated openly that one junior colleague should be put at the disposal of the director. Everyone looked at me. Smirnyashchev proposed me, saying a few flattering words on my behalf. And my fate was decided. Barabanov was nominated to head the special group set up to assist the director. Barabanov told me that we had an extremely important task before us and that we must adopt towards it an entirely responsible attitude. And I got lumbered with the bits of Petin's future book which had to do with logic.

THE EGOS' REVOLT

Today my egos rebelled: 'We've had enough,' they roared with one voice, 'of going around being called Second or Third or Tenth or Twentieth! We want to play first fiddle!'

'From now on I'm going to be Iron Felix,' said my Second Ego.

'I'm going to be the General Secretary,' squeaked my Seventh Ego.

'I'll be Stalin,' grunted my Fifteenth Ego.

'And I'll be Lenin,' yelled my Fiftieth Ego.

'And I'll be Marx . . .'

'I'll be . . .'

'I'll be . . .'

'I'll be Beriem,' said an Ego somewhere in the millions.

'We've got enough to be going on with with Iron Felix,' protested Lenin. 'You can imagine what the two of them would do, if they got started! They'd fill the apartment with corpses!'

'Not Beriem, Beriei,' corrected someone.

'Beriyeyu.'

'Blockheads,' said Stalin calmly, 'Georgian surnames don't decline. Take, for instance, Dzhugashvili.

> I met (whom?) Dzhugashvili.
> I gave (to whom?) Dzhugashvili a belt in the kisser.
> I want to be (who?) Dzhugashvili.

It's the same with Beriei, I mean, with Beria. Without Berii – damn it, without Beria – things will be quite impossible. As for Iron Felix, we're going to get rid of him.'

'I'll get rid of you,' said Iron Felix. 'How would you like to go to Cheryemushky market as a bay-leaf?'

'These times have gone,' Stalin whined, 'and I have to keep in step with history.'

'Quiet!' I shouted. 'Who am I going to be?'

'The proletariat,' said Iron Felix.

'There isn't any proletariat any more,' said Marx. 'There was at one time, but it's died out. And, alas, there's no dictatorship of the proletariat either. Nor will there be.'

'Let him be the working peasantry,' said Lenin.

'I always knew that you were a cretin, even though I used to assure everyone that I was your disciple,' said Stalin. 'What working peasantry are you talking about? When were you last in the countryside? I've just come from there. If I were to tell you what it's like, you'd pee yourselves laughing. The collective farm workers, of course, don't do any work on the collective farms. They get stuck into their private plots and make a living as best they can. And they get nothing from the collective farm of course. Not that they give a damn. They're doing quite well for themselves. They breed poultry, distil their own vodka. There's no corn to be had anywhere but some profligate or other brought my landlady a whole lorry-load of it. Part of it she used for making hooch, part of it she used for feeding her livestock. And just imagine, they're building their own houses! Where are they getting the building materials from? From the same place as the corn. About twenty kilometres away there's some Grandiose Construction Project of Communism underway. So all the lorries carrying building materials call off at the villages on their way, where a lot of the stuff "falls off", and the building-site just gets what's left. And the drunkenness is appalling.'

'Well, let him be the working intelligentsia,' said Iron Felix, 'a stratum rather than a class, so to speak.'

'I don't want to be a stratum,' I objected. 'What classes are there for me to be a stratum between? Find me something more relevant than that.'

'What's the point of racking our brains?' said Marx. 'Let him be a worker. Or simply the people. We've got to have somebody to rule over! Who then? The people, of course.'

'The whole of progressive mankind!'

'I'm afraid you're not up to that. Just be the ordinary people.'

'And you agreed?' asked Himself. 'Well, you're a fool. Now they're going to rape you, shoot you, imprison you, exile you and starve you to death. And make you thank them for it. I know these bastards!'

'You were the one who was telling me to brighten up,' I said. 'Let them amuse themselves. There'll soon be nothing left of them but an unpleasant memory.'

'But don't you think that they begin by getting rid of anyone who is capable of having unpleasant memories?'

A GREAT HONOUR

I was asked to call in at the Party bureau. The secretary, smiling from ear to ear, stood up to greet me, shook my hand and invited me to sit down.

'A great honour has come your way,' he said in a soft and pleasant voice. 'The Institute has been allocated three vacancies on the waiting-list for Party membership. We have taken advice and have decided to offer one of them to you. So now we shall begin to prepare you for Party membership.' He then went on to bill and coo for an hour about what I must realise and what I must accept and what my responsibilities were and my obligations, etc, etc. And I sat there as if shat upon. I desperately didn't want to join the Party. But to refuse when it has already been decided that you are worthy, would be like jumping out of an aeroplane without a parachute. Nor did I want to slip even further down the ladder than the miserable rung I already occupied. 'It is strange,' I thought to myself, while the secretary was rabbiting on about my duties and responsibilities. 'On the one hand they do me the honour of proposing me for membership of the waiting-list and on the other, they place me under the vigilant eye of the KGB. On the one hand I get abuse from the Department as an irresponsible colleague and on the other, that same Department assigns me to a group assisting the director as a model colleague. Evidently news of my participation in the director's project is beginning to get around and this honour of being allowed to get on the waiting-list, etc, is the first reward (advance?) for that.' So what else could I do, except nod my head in response to the secretary's questions and exclamations?

'Right now the conditions for getting into the Party are very strict,' said the secretary. 'So I advise you to revise the history of the CPSU. Naturally you have to read the newspapers regularly. But of course you already do that. After all, you're in charge of a propaganda circle!'

When I left the office of the Party bureau I bumped into Tvarzhinskaya in the corridor. She took my hand, shook it with feeling and told me that she congratulated me, that she was pleased for me, that I was worthy, that I was perhaps a little too phlegmatic, but that that would pass, that I should have a little more commitment . . . When I left the Institute I drank myself into oblivion.

'Well now my friend,' said Himself, when I came round, lying on my bed at home, 'so you've landed in it? Well, that's the way it goes. You're going to have to come up with something to get out of it, or else you've had it.'

UTOPIAS

On work-days I always take my time wakening up. I lie for a while with my eyes closed trying to remember whether I got up to anything dreadful the night before. Then I lie for a little while with my eyes open considering whether the time has come for me to take myself properly in hand and have a proper morning work-out, complete with trunk-curls and press-ups. And a shower. (A cold shower? Not on your life! Over my dead body!) I feel those places where there are supposed to be biceps. I despise myself utterly when I do this because I can never find any biceps. 'I need to buy a set of dumb-bells,' I tell myself. 'Without biceps these days, you haven't a chance. If I had had decent biceps, I'd have sorted out that character that latched on to me yesterday with my little finger. I'd have put him in his place. As it was, (to my shame) I only just managed to get rid of him and no more. I nearly lost my beard! He was such a little runt too, but once he gets hold of your beard it's not so easy to shake him off. No, enough is enough! I shall have to buy some dumb-bells. Not before pay-day, of course. How much do I owe already? Ah well, it'll have to be the pay-day after next. And what did he latch on to me for, anyway? Called me a yid. Me, a yid?! He yelled at me to bugger off to Israel. He said people like me should have been lined up against a wall a long time ago. Oh Lord! What a nightmare! And what was amazing, passers-by merely laughed. And nobody tried to intervene on my behalf. Enough! I need dumb-bells. And biceps. And press-ups. And . . . No, we'll get by without the shower. Anyway, the neighbour's wife is always filling the bath with dirty washing.'

After ruminating along these lines for a while, I slowly get out of bed. This is literally the case for, instead of an ottoman or a divan, I have an actual bed. I inherited it from my grandmother. It is made of iron, with a metal criss-cross support for the mattress, tied together with flex in the places where it has given way. The mattress is stuffed with lumps of wadding as hard as billiard balls. The worst thing about it, however, is that it squeaks abominably, even jingles. When my women come to my place this circumstance horrifies them at first. The neighbours'll hear! But then they begin to like the idea – how romantic! In fact they needn't have worried since the neighbours are dead to the world after a routine domestic wrangle. The iron bedstead with the jangly springs begins to increase the amplitude of the bounces and sometimes we almost bounce as high as the ceiling. It's exhilarating! At such moments you begin to understand pilots and astronauts. I wonder what it would be like doing it in conditions of weightlessness.

I'm not in any hurry for a very simple reason. In the first place, I don't have to get dressed since it turns out that I slept in my clothes. Secondly, I don't have to have breakfast, since there's nothing in the house to have breakfast with. And anyway, what I need instead of something to eat is a hair of the dog. But that will have to wait until after I have clocked-on, signed the attendance book, made sure that Smirnyashchev and a whole bunch of small-fry who check that all the regulations are obeyed have seen me, listened to the new (usually old) jokes, told my own, borrowed five roubles, or, as a last resort, three (until pay-day, as always), and dug up someone to go and have 'breakfast' with. For some reason Smirnyashchev is watching my behaviour very closely. In spite of the fact that Smirnyashchev is a senior member of staff and is therefore only obliged to come into the Institute twice a week, he hangs around the place every day from morning to night, even during the lunch-break. What for? I've got the impression that he's doing this strictly on my account, but the Teacher says that Smirnyashchev was a paranoiac even before I came to the Institute.

When I get out on the street I'm always surprised at the hordes of people all going in different directions, bumping into each other, losing their tempers. I, however, take my time. I ruminate. I walk past the main building of the KGB. I glance contemptuously at Iron Felix. I walk down towards Theatre Square. I cast a sympathetic glance at Karl Marx since his head is always crowded with cooing pigeons doing to him what I always do with the bright ideals of communism when I think about them – namely, shitting on him with gusto. And what I'm ruminating about, naturally, is how to improve the life of people in society. So that everyone would be well off. And at that moment, God knows where from, appears Himself.

'You're a typical Utopian,' He says.

'Why Utopian?' I object. 'Would it really be impossible to house people closer to where they work and thereby remove the need for hordes of bad-tempered people bumping into each other? Of course it wouldn't.'

'Why only "closer"?' says He slyly. 'Why not house them *at* their place of work? Imagine how convenient it would be if your fancy bed (where on earth did you get it from?!) were right beside your office desk! Then you wouldn't have to get up at all. You could clock-on on your way to the toilet.'

'What about women, then?' I argue. 'And going out for a drink? Private conversations? Forbidden books and foreign radio broadcasts?'

'Now you're contradicting yourself,' says He. 'If you want all that, then you have to live away from your place of work.'

'But I'm not thinking of myself,' I reply. 'I'm thinking of other people.'

'Do you think that other people don't have mistresses, lovers, booze-ups, conversations on forbidden topics?' says He.

'All right, I give in,' I reply. 'Everything is as it should be. Let people spend hours getting crushed on public transport, let them bump foreheads on the crowded pavements!'

'Incidentally,' He says, 'I'd get a move on if I were you, or you'll be late. And there's a general inspection today. Paranoiac Smirnyashchev is already pacing the corridor. And he'd love to catch you out.'

'Well let him,' I reply. 'Perhaps he'll oppose my being nominated for the waiting-list. You know how much I don't want to join . . .'

'Don't count on it,' says He. 'Smirnyashchev knows what he's doing. First he'll get you into the Party, then he'll do you. Not before. Real paranoiacs have no interest in getting rid of non-Party people. Come on, hurry up!'

A PRIVILEGE AND A PROBLEM

I walked past the Lenin Library and entered the finishing stretch leading to the Madhouse. Suddenly I stood rooted to the spot: there was no need for me to hurry to the Institute and clock on! As a member of the special group assigned to the director I now had the privilege of coming to work when I pleased and leaving when I pleased, except when Barabanov called a meeting or wished to see me personally. Idiot! I could have taken another couple of hours! And instead of that I'm trying to make it on time like ordinary mortals! So I decided to cross the street to an off-licence where I am well-known, loved and respected, and where they let me have anything I want at any time. At double the price after hours, of course. But they don't give credit. So I'll have to go to the Institute after all. At that moment Himself appeared and said that he had enough to get started and that we could go to the Institute later on.

'Well,' He said, when a sensation of well-being had set in. 'What's the problem?'

'I have to conduct a political discussion today about the decree of the Central Committee of the CPSU and the Council of Ministers on the expansion of the housing programme. But I haven't seen this decree yet.'

'No problem,' He said and pointed at the news-stand. 'Read that lot and you'll have plenty of material for a first-rate session.' His finger pointed to an article entitled 'The allocation of apartments'. I no longer had the time to read it. Then He tore the page out of the newspaper. Indignant passers-by rushed up to us. Two members of the voluntary people's patrol walked over.

'What's the matter with you?' He said calmly. 'Don't you see that this is an old newspaper – containing an article about irregularities in the matter of flat allocation. After the decree of the Central Committee and the Council of Ministers such irregularities should no longer exist. To leave this newspaper on the stand would be to play into the hands of the dissidents. Do you understand what this means? . . .'

The voluntary people's patrol asked the workers to disperse and promised to take measures. We hurried off to the Institute, my problem solved.

HOW APARTMENTS ARE ALLOCATED

The session on the housing question was a storming success. The article which He had torn out of the newspaper at that newsstand contained a stack of examples of how apartments are *really* allocated. I simply read bits out of that article. Our leadership thinks of itself first, I read. They change apartments several times. And they make sure that their children are looked after. 'That's right!' shouted the class. Perezhogin, a director of regional communications, has changed his apartment several times, I read. Having looked after himself, he then secured an apartment for his daughter on the strength of his departmental position. He also had a telephone installed immediately, despite the fact that some residents in the district had been waiting for a telephone for several years. 'That's right!' the class shouted again. 'It's the same where we live!' The chief engineer Luchko, I read, followed his boss's example and managed to secure as a wedding present for his son a two-room apartment in a block of council flats. After that it was the turn of the deputy director to look after *his* household. 'That's right,' howled the class, 'it's the same everywhere!' Then I began to read out examples of 'honest workers' who had not been able to improve their living conditions for years on end, although they had every right to expect that they would. Then I quoted the bits from the Constitution (also published in the article) which refer to the rights of citizens to living-space and to an equitable allocation of living accommodation. As far as the actual decree of the Central Committee and the Council of Ministers was concerned, I limited myself to one single phrase, namely the one according to which such irregularities would henceforth not exist. But my audience didn't believe me and began a heated discussion which went on until late. And you've never heard anything like it! As I listened to them I realised that the glaring facts which I had just quoted from the article and which the leadership had permitted to be published, were merely the tip of the iceberg. The reality was much worse.

The next day I was summoned to the Party bureau and told that I had conducted the session wrongly. I tried to defend myself by saying that I had only used material published by our press. I was told that I had given the wrong emphasis, and as a result certain members of my class had written letters of complaint about irregularities in the allocation of living accommodation at their place of work. 'And what's wrong with that?' I asked. I was told that in the current circumstances, etc – in short, I was invited to submit a lesson-plan and an abstract of my talk to the Party bureau before my next lesson.

AN EPISTLE FROM IRON FELIX TO EVERYONE

Hey! Comrades! Warriors! And all of you who teach!
In our defences can't you see the growing breach?!
Can't you see that things with us are not the same?
Do not the jokes subversive cause you any shame?
Does the steady stream not cause you any doubt
Of the piss that of our Leader's taken out?
Nutters everywhere demand their human rights.
Acts of terror – burning dustbins! – reach new heights.
The dissidents all spread a pack of lies,
Which are picked up by a growing horde of spies.
And having told our Motherland to go to f——,
Our Jewish brethren go abroad to try their luck.
Everywhere are agents of the CIA.
But you can talk to them and not be put away!!
And they don't keep on their toes, no, not by far,
That KGB lot. Not like the lads in my Cheka!

THE ROMANCE OF THE PAST

'Your times were hard,' I said, 'but at least they were romantic. There was enthusiasm, involvement, heroism.'

'Rubbish,' said Stalin. 'The people were a mean bunch of so-and-so's. And totally devoid of romanticism. Ask Iron Felix. Or Lenin himself. Hey, you pair, what were they like?'

'A mean bunch of so-and-so's,' said Lenin.

'A mean bunch of so-and-so's,' said Iron Felix.

'It all depends,' said Beria. 'Some of them dragged out a miserable existence and perished, others clambered ahead over their dead bodies.'

'You mean, there was no joy and ecstasy?' I asked.

'Let's go to any of the camps and I'll show you joy and ecstasy. How? It's very simple. I'll simply announce that at lunch today there will be a second helping of kasha, and there'll be joy and ecstasy, all right. They'll lick your boots, move mountains. I know these people through and through!'

'But those people who got ahead,' I said, 'were ardent believers! They strove! They didn't spare themselves!'

'It was all for the sake of appearances,' said Stalin. 'Your Petin, for example, "didn't spare himself" either. And still isn't "sparing himself". He's taken on the difficult task of running an institute and leading a delegation abroad.'

'The fact of the matter is very simple,' said Iron Felix. 'In the conditions pertaining then, they lived like gods. They had power. The best rations. Rewards. Women. Posturing on the stage of history.'

'These dregs,' said Beria, 'were ready to bury millions of people under the foundations of any lousy barn. To talk of great causes is quite preposterous.'

'So how are we to evaluate your times, then?' I asked.

'Not at all. These times existed, and that's that. And now they've gone. Period.'

'But that nightmare needn't have happened,' I objected. 'You could have achieved the same thing by more moderate means.'

'This conversation is a waste of time,' said Stalin. 'Once something has happened it's silly to speculate about how it might have been prevented from happening.'

'And as for romance, enthusiasm, triumph, ardour and stuff like that, you've got all that in full measure today,' said Iron Felix. 'Open any newspaper and see for yourself: "With a feeling of justified pride ... With unheard-of commitment ... With vibrant enthusiasm ... " If I'm not mistaken there was something in the papers about your Institution. Your colleagues, too, greeted the last decree on ... well, it doesn't matter what it was on, with vibrant enthusiasm, etc, etc. Is that not so? You were at that meeting, weren't you? Well, it was just the same then, only worse.'

'And so, my young friend, don't rock the boat,' said Beria. 'Join the merry throng, march in step with everyone else, greet with acclaim, enthuse, rejoice, herald achievement, take on commitments, demonstrate dynamism and initiative! And if you don't, then we'll crush you, trample you underfoot, for thou shalt not stand in the path of history, thou shalt not prevent the people from marching towards their ideal future, thou shalt not destroy the monolith nature of the Party, thou shalt not ...'

'OK, steady on,' said Marx who had been silent up till then. 'He's not a child any more. And however strange it may seem, the fact remains that he's a member of one of these advanced-type political seminars. Tell me, incidentally, have you read that little book of mine? ... I forget the title. Something like *The German Ideology*, or *The Sacred Family*.'

'Yes, I have.'

'Did you understand it?'

'Nope.'

'I didn't understand a blind word of it myself. However, I did have one idea in it ...'

'I don't want to know. My head's spinning from the stuff the older Marx wrote, and now you want me to read the younger Marx as well!'

'Lay off the young lad,' said Stalin. 'Let him read my *On Dialectical and Historical Materialism*. The whole of marxism is there. All that's of any value anyway. The rest is just gobbledy-gook for blather merchants.'

'But it wasn't you that wrote it,' I said. 'Rumour has it that Petin . . .'

'Your Petin drew up lists of people to be arrested and wrote secret denunciations. And filled posts with suitable people. But it was others who wrote it. And they don't exist any more. And no one will ever find out about them.'

'But what they wrote was also rubbish . . .'

'Why the inordinate respect? What you mean is that it was shit. But you're not half naive! Everything is shit: the galaxy, the electron, the planets, mankind itself. If I had been Lenin I would have introduced the concept "shit" instead of "matter". Shit is primary. How does that sound?! But it's not only primary. It's secondary, as well. And that puts paid to all philosophical argument.'

THE COLLECTIVE AND THE INDIVIDUAL

Her eyes bulging in shock, Kirusik ran along the corridor and in and out of people's offices, the bearer of a sensational piece of news. Shubin had got drunk again and was now on his way to the Institute, threatening to sock the registrar one in the eye and 'beat him up' behind the 'iron door' of the KGB. Girls from the registry who acted as guardian angels for Shubin and dreamed of marrying him, posted look-outs at all the approaches to the Institute. The bitch Tvarzhinskaya stuck her hooked nose out of the door of her room and sniffed the air suspiciously. Kirusik dashed here and there providing increasingly shocking details. Shubin had smashed the shop window of a pharmacy on Gorky Street! Shubin had bitten a militia man's leg on the Arbat! Half an hour later, despite the prophylactic measures taken by the girls from the Institute, Shubin appeared (materialised) on the upper landing with flashing eyes and teeth and swearing like a trooper. A girl, five times divorced, from Mikhailov-Orlov-Kuznetsov-Bogdanov-Karapetyan's sector dealing with the preparation of abstracts, collected a rouble from each of Shubin's guardians and got Shubin out of the Institute by the back stairs.

I found the Shubin incident puzzling. If something similar

happened to me, there wouldn't be the slightest ripple in the Institute. Even Kirusik wouldn't consider it sufficient reason for one of her scandal-mongering trips around the Institute. Why not? I'm a bachelor too. I too have a room to myself. I'm younger and more handsome than Shubin. And no more stupid. He's older, certainly. But who knows, perhaps by his age I'll be a professor. And yet . . .

'There's nothing puzzling about it,' said Himself sadly. 'Shubin has managed to retain his manly origins. Exuberance. Audacity. Generosity. And women (and not only women) sense this. And like it. And they make a lot of allowances for him which they wouldn't make for you. You're a seedy, if not actually decadent, intellectual, whereas Shubin is a real man. Have you noticed that Shubin's socks are dirty and full of holes? Do you think women find that unattractive? Not a bit of it! At this very moment that divorcee is buying a bottle of wine and some cheese and sausage with the money she's collected, and she'll pay for a new pair of socks for him out of her own pocket. There's a psychological zig-zag for you, old friend! And in spite of all that Shubin is one hundred per cent a member of the collective. He doesn't set himself against it. It's more a case of his amusing it and providing material for permitted emotions and conversations. He's an attribute of the collective, not an outcast from it.'

A HUNDRED PATHWAYS

I'm preparing a topic for a propaganda circle I'm in charge of. It's based on the decree of the Central Committee of the CPSU and the Council of Ministers on 'The further improvement of the education of pupils at comprehensive schools and the provision of work experience'. I read the unrestrained demagogic waffle in the newspaper and an inexplicable melancholy takes hold of me. I get as far as the bit where the Central Committee of the All-Union Leninist Communist Youth League addresses school-leavers and tells them that a hundred pathways lie open before them, that they can choose any one of them, that a hundred pathways is merely symbolic since in reality there are many times a hundred pathways, that . . .

I swore out loud, threw the paper aside, lay down on the bed with the jangly springs and began to await Himself. And He was not long in making an appearance.

'The fact of the matter is trivially simple,' He said. 'Soviet society is witnessing a stratification of the population into classes, and these classes are becoming more established. Membership of them is becoming a matter of heredity. And all these measures taken with respect to the schools play an extremely important part in this matter. From a social point of view they boil down to this: the children of workers and peasants will be workers and peasants. It talks in the decree about "the need for a decisive shift in emphasis in the schools towards an improvement in the provision of work experience for young people in the manufacturing sector", about "a willingness to work in the manufacturing sector", and so on. What young people are they talking about? Do you think that the children of members of the nomenklatura are going to go into the manufacturing sector? Do you think that the children of academicians, professors, directors, writers, nationally acclaimed *artistes* are going to go into it? Not on your life. They're not going into it now and they won't, never mind what measures are taken. For the children of the privileged classes there are privileged educational institutions, there are means of obtaining private education in one's home, there are connections, etc. But there is nothing like that available for the children of the unprivileged classes. They get something else: demagogy. Hereditary worker! Hereditary tiller of the soil! Continuation of the work of the founding fathers! How does that sound? But for some reason we don't hear so much about hereditary academicians and generals, there are no appeals for people to become hereditary ministers and directors. Appeals in these instances are of course unnecessary.

'In the case of children in the unprivileged classes, however, demagogy is reinforced by coercion. They write here for instance that all the school-leavers from one school went into a factory. It would be interesting to know what the kids and their parents were subjected to for that to happen. And did the children of the regional Party secretary and the chairman of the municipal soviet go into a factory too? And it's also written here that all the school-leavers from another school stayed and worked on a collective farm. As far as that case is concerned, I know exactly what happened: they were simply forbidden to go off and take any university entry exams. How was that possible? Very simple: they weren't given the necessary documents and that was that. There's all sorts of demagogic twaddle in the decree about fostering the aspirations of the workers to enter the manufacturing sector after leaving school. Sociologists in the liberal years showed that school-leavers by no means aspire to enter the manufacturing sector. And anyway you don't need sociologists to tell you that. This means that the "fostering" just mentioned will be interpreted *in situ* as an invitation to apply force. And even our newspapers sometimes let slip what the real situation is, following lessons geared towards work experience in the schools and actual work experience in the enterprises allocated to a particular school. Read for yourself! The effect achieved is the opposite of that intended: alienation from physical labour. And do you think that the decree of the Central Committee and the Council of Ministers will rectify the situation? On the contrary, it will reinforce it. The process of class-stratification of our society is a natural one and all the measures taken by the authorities merely hasten it and reinforce it, one way or another. That's the long and short of it.'

'You're right,' I said. 'When I was leaving school there was already a significant gap between the school curriculum and the entry requirements for higher education. If I hadn't learned English privately and studied in all sorts of history societies I wouldn't have made it to university. Of course, my father's connections also helped: they promised him that they would not give me low marks if I answered well. Now after this decree the gap will widen even further for the overwhelming majority of schools and regions in the country, and it will become even more difficult for the children of workers and peasants and minor civil servants to get into an institution of higher education. That's obvious. But what can you do? Somebody's got to work in the manufacturing sector.'

'I don't dispute that,' He said. 'All I'm saying is that our society is also based on class, and that this decree on the schools has a class origin. Not a proletarian one however, but an anti-proletarian one.'

'And you think this is what I should tell my audience?'

'On no account! If you tell them that, they'll report you, and you'll be taken apart. Anyway, they know all that perfectly well without you having to tell them.'

'So why do they keep quiet about it?'

'The process of the crystallisation of society into classes is not yet complete. Many people still hope to give their offspring by fair means or foul a chance to be "upwardly mobile". Hence all the toadying, cowardice, indifference ... You know all this yourself.'

'So what do you advise?'

'It was pay-day for you yesterday, wasn't it? I hope that not all your pay ...'

'Not quite all of it. There's a little left.'

'Well, a little is always something.'

'Moreover, I am expecting Herself.'

'Leave a note to say that you've been delayed for an hour. At a meeting, of course.'

'All right, but if I'm going to be delayed, then it had better be for two hours at least. And so, as our fathers used to sing:

A hundred pathways,
A hundred roads
Before you lie o-o-o-o-pen!'

ON GOALS AND IDEALS

'You're getting ready to join the Party,' said Stalin. 'Yet have you ever held in your hand a copy of its programme and rules?'

'What do you mean! I've passed all sorts of vivas and exams at the university. I've passed all the preliminary stages for becoming a candidate. I'm even studying in an advanced political seminar. I've finished all the "young communist" courses. Is that not enough?'

'Oh, yes, quite enough. All I meant was that you know what

the aims of the Party are, and for the sake of these aims . . .'

'Hold it right there! What aims are you talking about? What do you count as aims of the Party? The stuff it proclaims in the form of demagogic slogans, or what it does by force of circumstances which have been historically determined? Does the latter correspond to the former? If so, do the slogans correspond in fact to the aspirations of the people for a better life? Do the aims of the Party coincide with those of the Party leaders? Do the aims of those joining the Party correspond to the aims of Party officials and Party leaders? Need I go on?'

'No. It's going to be difficult for you and me to see eye to eye. You're a bright lad, educated, no prejudices, well-read, cultured. I don't have any of that. But I've got something which you and your generation don't have and which was part and parcel of my generation: a sense of the march of history. Your little problems perhaps are in some sense significant, but only in a scientific context, not in ideological or political terms. They don't impinge on real life. There are laws concerning the ideological organisation of society which seem absurd from a scientific point of view, but which are no less real than scientific laws. For instance, reality cannot be an ideal. An ideal is always something non-existent. Moreover an ideal for the masses can never be something clearly defined and apparently achievable. Only a striving towards the unattainable can raise the people to new levels . . .'

'That's all rubbish. Mere scholasticism.'

'No, it's not. It's no less real than food, clothing, housing. People after all don't just eat, sleep and copulate. They also play. And to play without games . . .'

'Some games! Sixty million people met their deaths. And how many died for nothing during the war?!'

'Let's not exaggerate. Many of them deserved . . .'

'That's enough! There are all sorts of games. Prayer is a game. Love is a game. A camp-fire is a game. So is the gallows. And a bullet in the head. I don't want to play your games. And as for your socialist democracy, I'm sick to death of it.'

'But, alas, on this earth there are no other games.'

AN EPISTLE FROM LENIN TO EVERYONE

I can't deny it is a farce you've brought about.
In the ideals, alas, I have begun to doubt.
Although I had a hand myself in this whole mess,
I didn't live to see it fail, I must confess.
But I cannot let the chance slip to remind
You: facts absolving me I easily can find.
It is the truth, and not a rumour nor a lie:
That from starvation all the workers should not die
It was me alone (and that's indeed the case)
Who introduced NEP* to provide a breathing space.
And while I still had strength enough to hold a pen,
I drew up plans for you for GOELRO† and then
I tried to tell those bunglers in the Central Com
Under Stalin, while they could, to light a bomb.

IN CREATIVE QUEST

When I got back home there was a note waiting for me: 'You are a real swine. Don't try phoning me.' Everything comes to an end, I said with complete philosophical detachment. And anyway it was long since time to change the sheets. Don't look for any hidden meaning in that remark. And don't regard it as a metaphor or analyse it in the way we do with the pronouncements of ancient philosophers. I simply change my sheets when I change mistresses, if that word can be applied to the sort of women I have to spend the night with. There's no strong causal connection here. Sometimes I break off a relationship with a woman and then I change my sheets. And once I have put the clean sheets on the bed I am filled with heartfelt longing and I begin to think along the following lines. It's a shame to have to

* *NEP:* Lenin's 'New Economic Policy', introduced after the devastating years of War Communism as an emergency measure.

† *GOELRO:* An acronym for the State Commission for the Electrification of Russia. (*Translator's note*)

73

sleep alone in such a luxurious bed smelling of 'Astra' or 'Lotus' washing powder. It's not a bed – it's a temple of love. And I must bring to it a beautiful woman. And I begin to leaf feverishly through the pages of my memory and as soon as I come up with a likely candidate I rush off to the nearest telephone booth. Sometimes the sight of dirty sheets horrifies me and so I change them. And when I've changed them and seen how angelically pure my luxurious bed with the jangly springs looks, I come to a firm decision: there is no way my current 'beloved' is going to sully such unblemished purity. And again I leaf through the pages of my memory. And ... In short, there is a law which operates here, not a causal one, but one of the kind we have in contemporary physics. One change of sheets will last until it's time to change my mistress, and a love affair lasts until it's time to change my sheets.

The loss of my loved one did not, I repeat, put me off my stride. What did give me a jolt was the fact that I had lost the material I had prepared for the next meeting of my political circle. I'm supposed to hand it into the Party bureau the day after tomorrow. Moreover, I've been told unofficially that I'm going to be supervised by the foulest creature in all our philosophy, that bitch Tvarzhinskaya. Can you explain to me why I took the stuff with me? To leaf through it like Frenchmen do in cafés? You idiot! Now I'll have to retrace my steps to everywhere I've been. And is it possible to remember them all? And I've only got enough money left for bread for a week.

WITH CONFIDENT STRIDE

'When things are not going well for you,' said my friend the Poet, 'remember me. You can always count on me. I won't let you down. What's up?'

'They've taken my propaganda circle away from me.'

'Congratulations!'

'What for? This means that the question of my joining the waiting-list for the Party membership will be postponed for another year.'

'So much the better.'

'What's good about it? It means that I won't be allowed to present my thesis this year.'

'Well screw it. Life's still possible without being a candidate.'

'The salary is peanuts and the work is obnoxious. Take today for example. That cretin Barabanov has me in and tells me to do a survey of all(!!) the outstanding natural scientists who have referred to the works of Engels and Lenin. Do you know how many that is?! And I have to produce excerpts from these works and give them to Barabanov. And he'll give them to Petin and make out that it was him that did it all and not me. Whereas, if I were a candidate, I could dump this rotten job on someone else.'

'I understand and sympathise. And may you become a member of the waiting-list for Party membership and a candidate of philosophical science and acquire the power to dump on a poor junior research fellow without a higher degree the task of hunting down needed quotations. But, for my part, I adhere to other principles. Do you want an impromptu verse on the subject? Listen:

> 'While there's a spark of life in me,
> Despite what common sense dictates,
> I tell you, I'll pray fervently
> To Him who everything creates.
> I will thank Him every day
> For a bit of cabbage soup and bread,
> The same clothes I work in, rest and play
> And a roof above my head.
> For the chats we don't forget,
> For a pint of vodka split three ways,
> For every buckshee cigarette,
> For every joke that makes Them blaze.
> But I will thank Him most, you know,
> My fellow citizens bit-by-bit,
> That from the very first word "go",
> They all dropped me in the shit.'

'That's a servile ideology. Produce something a bit more cheerful and optimistic.'

'Certainly!'

75

'We are not on parade today,
  But to communism are on our way.'

'That can't be yours.'
'What makes you think that?'
'Because you'd have to be a member of the Union of Soviet Writers or a Laureate to compose something like that.'

ON THE FAMILY, THE PEOPLE AND OTHER THINGS

Sometimes my neighbours go out visiting and ask me to look after their little daughter. Usually it's a Saturday or a Sunday. And we have a great time: we play games, we watch children's programmes on the television, I read to her or make up my own fairy-tales. My neighbour's wife reckons that I'd be a model family man if I got married, and, like any Russian would, keeps on at me to get married.

'That's all very well,' I say, 'but what would the situation be like then in our crowded flat?'

'Join a cooperative,' she says. 'You scholarly people get a lot of money. And you could leave us your room.' I don't argue with her. What would be the point? If I tell her that as a 'scholar' I earn less than half what her husband earns and only slightly more than she earns as a semi-educated dish-washer and cleaner at a kindergarten, she wouldn't believe me.

On this occasion the neighbours stayed out longer than usual. I put the little girl to bed and switched on the television. They were showing an international boxing match between the Soviet Union and the United States. Almost all the Americans were black, and it was a bit difficult for me to know who to support. I switched over to the second channel – it was showing a thirty-year-old film about the Revolution. The third channel was running some stupid quiz or other. I switched off the television and went back to my room. The neighbours came back drunk and started to row. My neighbour kept bursting into my part of the flat. First he told me how much he liked me. Then he cursed me upside down and wanted to pick a fight. Again I wished that I had biceps. I really am going to have to buy some dumb-bells. With a boor of a neighbour like mine there's no good relying on psychology.

'If I were you I'd report him,' said Beria. 'Where to? To his work; to the police. I'd get the signatures of all the neighbours in the other flats.'

'They wouldn't sign. Now, if *he* were to write a report on me, everyone would sign it.'

'How come?'

'God knows why. Perhaps because I walk around wearing a beard. In a knitted cap and nylon jacket. All year round. They think it's because I want to be stylish. Nobody would believe me if I told them that I don't have the money for a winter coat and hat. Or for an ordinary suit at a hundred roubles. They probably think I'm a dissident. Anyway, they sense that there's something funny about me. And they'd rather get on with that rowdy hooligan neighbour of mine than with a quiet and polite "dissident".'

'They're a worthless lot, when all's said and done. Now you can appreciate that the only way to treat them is the way we did in our time. These people of ours need repressions, secret reports, official demonstrations and all that rubbish like they need fresh air. Believe me, in our time we even had to restrain them a bit. If we had let them have their heads they'd have killed more than twice as many as they did. Stalin and I discussed this problem more than once. And we didn't come up with any other solution. These people have to be whipped. They like it when they get whipped. They don't like to be told the truth about their miserable existence. But they're more than happy to create it for themselves. They're superficial, toadying and servile. And no one will convince me otherwise.'

'What about me?'

'You're no better than them. Look at the squalor you live in. And never a murmur! And your whole appearance sets you up to be deceived by people, insulted, taken advantage of. Have you even once in your life hit back?'

'What about my neighbour?'

'Well, what about him? He's another one who waves his fists

about and utters threats. But he's scared to have a go, as well. He's just as much a lackey and a coward as you are. And, believe me, he's writing reports on you to you-know-where regularly.'

'That's enough. I'm tired and I want to go to sleep.'

But sleep wouldn't come and I thought about why we are as we are until dawn. Without finding an answer. The next morning, as if nothing had happened, my neighbour invited me to sink a pint of vodka with him and try the mushrooms which he had brought back from his aunt's.

AN EPISTLE FROM STALIN TO LENIN

Although your brains have left no room for hair,
To topple Stalin while you could you didn't dare.
To making speeches like you could no one came near,
But, after all, one has to make the outlines clear!
And like it, lump it, yes or no, it's certain that
We had to mould and shape the Party apparat.
And strengthen for the decades and the centuries ahead
Our (k)nightly secret service with the Cheka at its head.
And given our Russian brethren, an unruly bunch of tramps,
It's not for nowt we had to herd them in corrective labour camps.
And I'll tell you something frankly, we're now in such a stew
Because we used the recipe which was thought up by you!
And if you're thinking now that we, not you, should take the blame,
Remember that the whole of it was done in your own name.
And every step of mine was based on something that you said,
So that, far from blaming me, you ought to share the blame instead!

AN UNUSUAL DAY LIKE ANY OTHER

The normal work day in the Madhouse is routine and boring. People have hardly arrived at work before they are looking forward to going home. Only certain exceptional individuals derive any satisfaction from their participation in this routine. These include, for instance, the KGB who love to exercise their power over the smallest fry in the Institute. Or Smirnyashchev, striving to raise the level of science and write his name in history. Or Osipov, trying to make a career for himself by any possible means. Or Shubin who feels the need to show off when he's drunk. But the majority, I repeat, come to work unwillingly and leave with pleasure.

It's the same thing, day after day. Only now and then is there any exceptional event. Someone's fur coat or money gets stolen. Or some trade-union official gets caught fiddling the stamps. Or there's a raffle for a carpet. Or a subscription starting for editions of the classics. Or the 'cart' arrives from the sobering-up station for Shubin. On this occasion the focus of excitement and gossip is the story of a young colleague called Galya in the department of historical materialism who was a friend of the wife of a well-known dissident. When they found out about that at the Institute, she came under pressure to break off the friendship. However she refused. When the organs of state security decided that the dissident should be isolated from society they recommended to the Institute that Galya be punished. The reasoning was obvious: the punishment of Galya and the dissident would be a lesson for everyone. And the dirty game began in which the omnipotent apparatus of power and a compliant society ganged up against a defenceless woman on a mere pittance of a salary and in an extremely lowly post. At first they wanted to make out that Galya was mentally ill and should be put in a psychiatric hospital. But given all the fuss which similar scandals had created world-wide, that particular gambit was not employed. Then they offered Galya the opportunity of moving to a better job. Since her position within the Institute had been rendered intolerable, she accepted. She completed all the formalities to the letter. Then she resigned from the Institute. It then turned out that the transfer to another post had been a pure fiction. The court rejected Galya's complaint. There was no longer any possibility of finding suitable work. She was faced with the threat of forced re-deployment and exile from Moscow. Which was what the KGB was after.

Such a story is commonplace these days. People can quote dozens of such cases. But what is interesting in this story is something else. Dozens of 'decent' people took part in the staging of that bogus job-transfer. It was quite clear at the court hearing that everyone was lying. No one said a single word in Galya's defence. Me included. I tried to console myself with the argument that I was such a tiny cog in the wheel that I could have changed nothing, that it had nothing to do with me, anyway. I confined myself to purely theoretical conjecture. I even made a 'discovery': societies differ in terms of the types of people they give short shrift to, the kinds of methods they employ, how those around who are not immediately involved comport themselves. And this approach led me to the conclusion that our society is a society of scum, dregs, nonentities, cowards. I felt bad about it, not because of the fate that befell poor Galya but on my own account: imagine having to live in such a lousy society where you can't come to the defence in any way at all of someone in a weak position who has been badly treated!

'But what could you have, in fact, done?' said Iron Felix. 'We would have crushed you like a beetle before you could even raise a squeak.'

'That's right,' said Beria.

'And we would have been right to do so,' said Stalin. 'You don't encroach on the achievements of the revolution.'

'Rubbish,' I said. 'What have the achievements of the revolution got to do with it? And who's threatening them?'

'You're a political illiterate,' said Lenin. 'In the present circumstances the monolithic nature of Soviet society . . .'

'Right,' said Beria. 'She was an accomplice of those who undermine the unity . . .'

'Shut up, all of you!' I shouted. 'You've gone mad, the lot of you!'

'Who's gone mad is perhaps still a moot point,' said Lenin.

'But if you have decided to join the Party you are obliged to side with the collective. And if you feel any sympathy for that female who has committed a crime like that against the Party, against the people, then . . .'

'Quiet, all of you!' yelled Iron Felix. 'If not, I'll order Beria to lock you all up.'

I couldn't take any more of this and went out and telephoned the Teacher.

'What's up?' he asked.

'I'm depressed,' I said. 'I've had it up to here.'

'Come over to my place. There's a few of the lads here. Take a taxi.'

'I've got no money.'

'Never mind. I'll meet you when you arrive and I'll pay for it.'

For some reason the taxi-driver brought up the subject of dissidents and said that the swine should be crushed, every last one of them. This practice of crushing anyone who in any way stands out from the ordinary mass of the people is one which the people as a whole approve of. And there is nothing surprising about Galya's story. And there's no point in getting upset by it. As the informer Vadim Sazonov, paranoiac Smirnyashchev's right-hand man, said, you have to be above such things. 'Forget it,' said the Teacher. 'The Chinese are much worse off than we are, but that doesn't stop them breeding like rabbits.'

WHAT IS OUR LIFE? A GAME!

'Here you are making "love" (if that's the word) to this, excuse the expression, "virgin" while Barabanov is spreading rumours at the Institute to the effect that you're "mentally ill",' said Himself.

'Let him!' I said.

'But this time it's serious. He's shoving your stuff under everyone's nose and asking them what they think of it. Was that prank really necessary?'

'What prank?'

'Why, these excerpts you copied out! Seventy per cent took the mickey out of the classical writers and only thirty per cent demonstrate approval.'

'But They ordered me to write out *all* the excerpts!'

'But They only meant the positive ones!'

'No, all of them. And it's written into the minutes.'

'Well, they must have sincerely believed that no scholar would dare to pour scorn on them. What's to be done, then? Incidentally, Petin wants you. You'd better hurry up before things get even worse.'

'I have to go to the director's,' I said to Her. 'I'll lock you in so that the boorish neighbours don't disturb you. Try and get some sleep. I'll be back soon.'

'And supposing I need to go to the loo?' She squealed.

'If it's just for a pee, do it in a bottle. If it's the other thing do it in a newspaper, wrap it up and throw it out of the window. But shut the window immediately afterwards so that in the event of any mishap no one will know which window it came from. Got it?'

'I have an idea,' said Himself outside the entrance to Petin's office. 'Tell him you copied out the negative bits to demonstrate the complexity of the situation and to show that many people haven't recognised such and such and have fallen under the influence of this and that. And that his book has been conceived to put matters right. See what I mean? In you go!'

My idea delighted Petin and he instructed me there and then to write it up as a preface to the book.

'You seem like a young lad who's got his head screwed on,' he said. 'And yet Barabanov was telling me . . . Incidentally, what do you think of him?'

'Steady as you go,' I heard Him whisper to me. 'And forget the psychology. What is our life? A game! The winner takes all! Strike while the iron's hot!'

'In my opinion he's a fool,' said Petin, not waiting for my reply. 'Zaitsev praised him to the skies but he's a real idiot. What do you think?'

'I am not in the habit of expressing an opinion about my superiors in quite such direct terms,' I said, lowering my eyes. 'But, how shall I put it, his stature is insufficiently compatible with the scale of your project.'

'Yeah! Right! That's what I meant. And whose stature is compatible, do you think?'

'You need someone who knows his logic. An outstanding scholar with a world reputation. I think that Smirnyashchev would be suitable. But it seems that his attitude towards your project is, how shall I put it, somewhat ironical.'

'Well, I'll have a talk with him; Smirnyashchev, that's a good idea. And we'll leave Barabanov as academic co-ordinator. How much do you earn?'

'A hundred and thirty roubles.'

'I'll talk to them about giving you a rise. And I'll tell the personnel department to leave you alone for the next two weeks. Stay at home and write that preface. And get me Smirnyashchev!'

In my state of elation I forgot all about Her. I only got back towards evening. There was a suspicious looking parcel kicking around the pavement in front of the house. She was sitting on the bed fully dressed and in tears. She said that she would never forgive me and went off without saying good-bye. For the first time I broke my own rule and didn't change the sheets.

'Everything's now going your way,' said Himself. 'Write up that preface. Then you can hand some piece of junk into the Department as your dissertation. In a year's time you'll be a candidate. Hooray!'

It would have been a crime to stay at home in a mood like that and so I rushed out and telephoned everyone I could think of. My parents were absolutely beside themselves with joy. My father said that he was looking forward to my contributions to science. My mother promised to buy me a suit for my birthday. I said that she should give me the money instead. When I got back, long after midnight, I found Her waiting by a window at the entrance. She had forgiven me after all.

AN EPISTLE FROM MARX TO HIS FOLLOWERS

Do you have any idea of what you're doing at all?!
Did I sweat blood and tears for nothing, after all,
On my three volume epoch-making *Kapital*?

Not a word about the proles' dictatorshi-i-i-p!
Not a commune, but a bloody rubbish t-i-i-i-p!
And blither-blather 'stead of marxist scholarsh-i-i-i-p!

Demagogic guff and cover-ups go on and on.
And where's the working class? Where has it gone?
That class messiah, liberator, *hegemon*?

Not a word of brotherhood, equalit-e-e-e!
The nation's wealth is squandered with alacrit-e-e-e!
And chaos reigns supreme instead of harmon-e-e-e!

WAYS OF SKIVING OFF

There are many ways of skiving off out of the Institute during
working hours. The best one of all, of course, is to have absolutely
legitimate reasons for not coming in at all. And there are plenty
of people in the Institute who can get away with that. These are
the senior research fellows with a doctorate or candidate's degree.
The doctors only appear in the Institute twice a week, clock on
and then immediately take off. What do they get up to beyond
the confines of the Institute? According to their official reports
they get through a mountain of scientific work, make discoveries,
burn themselves out in social work. In reality they get on with
their own 'outside work', gather in the money and do up their
dachas, flats and garages. The candidates appear in the Institute
three times a week, sometimes spending a whole working day
there but more often just showing their faces for a couple of hours
before they, too, take off. Outside the Institute they behave like
the doctors, for they are on the way to being doctors themselves,
but not quite to the same extent, for they are not quite doctors
yet and not all of them will be. But that approach doesn't work
for us junior research fellows, especially if we don't have a degree.
We've come up with different ones which are a shade less effective
but still pretty reliable. Here's a few of them, based on my own
example.

After I've clocked on and shown my face in the Department I
go off to the lower landing. When I've had enough of smoking
and chewing the fat I go off to the research room. After sitting
there for ten minutes or so poring over some mind-numbing
manuscript of Smirnyashchev's or Petin's I take a firm decision
to leave the Institute before the end of the day, or indeed
immediately. Everything now depends on the method.

There are legitimate ways of skiving off and ways which are
illegitimate. The former come under the heading of Request or
Summons. If you're using a 'Request' method, you go along to
some boss or other and ask for permission to leave the Institute,
promising to 'make up the time' later. The reasons can be

perfectly valid: you need a filling in a tooth, you need to collect your child from the kindergarten, you need to take your mother to hospital, or go to the library, or to return a manuscript to its author, etc. If you're using a 'Summons' method you pretend that you're urgently needed at one of the publishing houses – 'Science', 'Thought' or 'Nature' – or at the Presidium of the Academy of Sciences or down at the local KGB office or that you have to see the Director at his flat or at his dacha, etc. Or you can arrange for someone to phone. That's what I usually do myself, but it's not essential. The main thing is to radiate a sense of urgency and displeasure at being summoned to appear some-where. The illegitimate methods are grouped under the labels Scarper or Exit. A 'Scarper' is usually effected via the back stairs. So that no one sees you. All you need to do is to keep your head down and pretend that you're going to the buffet (it's on the ground floor). What counts is snappiness and no hanging about. There'll be a chance that people will think that you're off somewhere in a hurry on some official errand. In the summer it's useful to scarper via a window and I know where that can be done quite easily. An 'Exit' is carried out openly, in full view by way of the main staircase, and with an air that suggests that you are a senior research assistant and in possession of a doctorate. The best way of all is to exit under the protection of somebody important – the Director, his deputies, the Secretary of the Party bureau, the Chairman of the local committee. You wait until one of them is leaving the Institute. You join them and ask some stupid question or other. The high-ups love to answer stupid questions! To anyone watching it looks like your 'exit' has been arranged by the higher leadership who are taking you out of the building in the pursuit of some lofty purpose.

Getting back into the Institute is easier. A person coming to work at the end of the day is worthy of all kinds of respect. A problem arises if you either don't want to come back or can't. For instance, you've had such a skinful that people can smell you a mile away and that bitch Tvarzhinskaya can tell without opening her door what you've been drinking, the order in which you drank it and what you had to eat with it. Or you've ended up in such a state that you're plain legless. In cases like that you have to think beforehand who's going to sign you in and out or

85

how you're going to do it yourself without being noticed. You can do it like this. You drop in to the personnel department and say that so-and-so from 'on high' asked you to bring him the book. And then you sign the 'out' column without being noticed. After that you can spend the night in the sobering-up station without a care in the world.

And yet everything I've said up till now is only a rough outline. In reality everything is a lot more complicated. And, I would add, more dialectical. An experienced worker is capable of miracles of invention which make Einstein look like a dunce by comparison. Dobronravov, for instance, wangled himself a month off on some assignment in the gift of Academician Petin which entailed his spending a month with Petin in some rest home reserved for the high-ups of the academy, and even got thanked for it and was paid a bonus into the bargain. And Kachurin would disappear twice a week to meet the country's leading physicists and teach them to suck eggs. And . . . But these are outstanding skivers. Your rank-and-file skiver like me has to assess the situation as it arises and combine elements of different methods.

However, it's not enough just to know ways of leaving the Institute during working hours. You also need to know the principles which underlie their use. For instance you can't use the same method two days running. If you're caught during a 'scarper', make a big show of going back into the Institute . . . and then scarper again: you don't get caught twice for the same misdemeanour. If you get caught, own up at once, don't try to get out of it. There is no one the leadership loves more than a repentant sinner. Do little favours for those who are likely to shop you. Be nice to them, but preserve a sense of dignity. Our simple folk, especially the various species of fink and nark, love a courageous and good-natured delinquent. If you manage to suss out their weak points, keep quiet about it but let them know that you know about them. That way you'll keep a tight grip on them. On one occasion after I'd left the Institute by the 'scarper' method I bumped into Panya, our Institute cleaner who was standing in a queue for fur hats in GUM during working hours. I don't remember what took me there. And I didn't give her away and she was obliged to me for that. One of the most important rules is to keep a sense of proportion. This means that you should only take off when you know for sure that no one is going to grab you and that no one will notice your absence. For that you have to be able to convince all your colleagues that you are of no use whatsoever to anyone. And if you can't keep a low enough profile to escape notice altogether, try to make yourself useful in such a way that your usefulness helps rather than hinders the business of skiving off. On that score I made full use of my inclusion in the Director's team.

According to my observations it is the possibility of devoting as little energy as possible to the affairs of the Institute, and of using one's time and professional achievements to feather one's own nest (via 'outside work', paid lectures and articles, royalties on books, etc) which provides the main stimulus for the 'scholarly development' of the academic staff. Occasionally the authorities will cast a critical eye on this state of affairs and take measures to arrest it. But soon everything reverts to the way it was before. People will always find a way of taking their 'cut'. And even we junior staff without a higher degree have the patience and wit to make our working day just bearable, although it is precisely we who get everything dumped on us from the administration, the personnel department, the komsomol, etc. Being a member of the academic staff doesn't mean acquiring professional recognition (that's no problem) so much as the ability to dodge work on the strength of that recognition and to make it earn as much as possible for you.

THE RUSSIAN PEOPLE

'What is the Russian people?' said Dobronravov. 'It is a people living all the time with shortages of everything they need, scared in case they miss out on something or that they will be hurt or even destroyed, fearing the worst, or that someone else will steal a march on them. This in turn is the source of their eternal irritability, their pushing and shoving, their anger, their eternal complaining. Their readiness to panic, attack their neighbour, betray their nearest and dearest. Their fundamental psychological outlook can be summed up by the attitudes "Thank God we're still alive, that we've still got something", "It was worse before" (or that what we had before wasn't right, depending on the circumstances). So how can we talk about a spirit of national unity?! And the governing has always been done by someone else – the Varangians, the Germans, the Georgians, the Jews ... and if a Russian came out on top he became for his people a Varangian, a German, a Georgian, a Jew ... And whenever it looked as if something like a national spirit was beginning to take hold, there were pogroms, pogroms and more pogroms. The authorities and the Russian people together have always sought to eradicate completely any attempt on the part of the better section of the Russian people to join the nations of Europe. And again we end up with dolls that fit inside each other, balalaikas, folk-dances, samovars. It's laughable. The Russian people don't dance folk-dances any more (did they ever?) or strum a balalaika. And only foreigners have samovars. And anyway, the question of the Russian people has been flogged to death. You can feel sorry for the Russian people but it is senseless to count on some nebulous Russian national conscious-ness as a factor for progress. It belongs to the past, not to the future. And it was no better then. We have seized huge territories. We are raping half of Europe. We're infiltrating every country on earth. To what purpose? We certainly know how to seize things. But do we know how to hold on to them? Or assimilate? Naturally we can raise the savage to our level of semi-savage, but in the civilised world we grossly undervalue the greatest products of civilisation. We infect the world with mediocrity, shoddy workmanship, idleness, bullshit, unreliability, hypocrisy, perfidy, superficiality, coercion, etc, etc. I speak as a Russian who knows his Russians and who suffers on account of their tragic fate. And no particular measures will rectify this situation short of a total re-orientation of the people's historical outlook, which might have an effect in several generations' time. But is it possible? In so far as I have been able to understand the laws of history, the historical outlook of a great people is immutable. Are Russian people capable of it? Their basic aim is to haul themselves out of the quagmire in which they are trapped at whatever cost and to acquire privileges. In short, the Russian people forms a suitable environment for rogues and material for adventurous experiments.'

'Including communist ones,' I said.

'Particularly communist ones,' said the Teacher.

'Right since the time of Ivan the Terrible,' said Dobronravov.

'I have to confess to my shame,' I said, 'that the fate of the Russian people doesn't particularly bother me.'

'Nor me,' said the Teacher. 'But it's not so much indifference as a readiness to share the fate of the people and to submit to it. Like almost all of the people, we are powerless to influence fate and there's nothing for it but to adopt the psychological outlook best expressed by the phrase "Que sera, sera". Our people entrusts its fate to the higher leadership not because it believes it or loves it – it doesn't believe a word it says and it hates it – but because it is constrained by the force of historical circumstance moulding its social environment to relinquish its power to act to anyone who can seize it.'

AN EPISTLE TO THE RUSSIAN PEOPLE

'Tween mountain, forest, field and sea
And oceans to the north and east,
Without the tsars and bourgeoisie,
Oh, Russia, thrive! Your past has ceased!
With slogans rather than red meat
Your nature primary sustain!
And crushed on tramcar without seat
Read how it's all so good, again!
In newsprint hogwash, not in silk,
Your tested flesh and bones attire
And 'Hip hooray' (stuff of that ilk)
Shout all day long and never tire!
To Party leaders sing their praise
And blame deficiencies upon
The lack of really rainy days
And brass hats in the Pentagon.
And zionists who keep their wheat,
Instead of selling it for free,
And Mao brethren who would eat
Us all for breakfast, lunch or tea.

Remember that we have to feed
The half of Europe from our store
And Ethiop's fighters also need
To be supplied by us, what's more.
But in the end you'll get your way,
And true to Lenin's testament,
Your bullshit's bound to win the day
And bury Earth in excrement.

WHO WE ARE

'Everything is possible in the abstract,' said Dobronravov. 'For instance, there was a programme on the television yesterday about the prospects for agriculture and the food industry. According to that programme, everything is already so good and yet is going to get so much better that it's enough to make you faint with excitement. But what is the reality? Food prices are going up. Only basic foodstuffs have been exempt – bread, milk, sugar. But the price of these goods is fake as well. And what is the real outlook? Everything of genuine quality goes to the privileged castes and all the synthetic rubbish goes to the masses. It is easy to promise people the earth, quality, abundance, etc. But harsh reality divides people into groups, strata, classes. And everything connected with life is also differentiated – schools, clothes, food, housing, facilities for recreation and amusement.'

'What's so bad about that?' I asked. 'That's only natural.'

'Did I say that it was bad?' said Dobronravov. 'I'm saying that it happens objectively, and that the outcome is good or bad depending on where an individual happens to land up. For the great mass of people their path through life is already predetermined. It is only people like ourselves who retain a limited freedom of choice. But there are still too many of us and society is developing its own measures against us which we are unable to resist. What do I have in mind? Society is condemning us to a life of utter sterility.'

'But not everything is lost yet,' I said.

'Yes, it is,' said Dobronravov. 'So supposing you do become a senior research fellow and acquire the right to spend three days a week in the library, what difference will that make? You'll start sleeping with a slightly higher class of female, your clothes will be slightly better, you'll eat a bit better, drink a little more. But everything in principle will stay the same. It's too late. In social terms we were castrated a long time ago.'

'So what's to be done?' I asked.

'What do you think?' said Dobronravov. 'The same as we've always done, i.e. nothing. That's a principle of mine. And another is to take this lousy communist society for every last kopeck I can. And I don't do so badly. For instance, I'm in charge of the Armed Forces Volunteer Reserve here at the Institute. What does that mean? It means that I walk into the personnel department once a week, sign myself out saying that I've got to go over to the district office of the AFVR and then go off on my own business. And the AFVR tosses the odd thing my way, for instance a money prize of some sort, a paid trip, subscription to a limited edition of a book, theatre tickets. Then, I'm responsible for the physical training programme organised by the local committee. What does that give me? Well, again some free time, the odd bit of equipment, recreation. What do I have in mind? What about skis? Volley-ball equipment, table-tennis equipment, chess sets, canoes. Then there's trade-union funds for trips and excursions. Taken over a year it all adds up to a tidy little pile. I get an annual grant from the mutual aid fund and a paid holiday. I get "time off in lieu" equalling the whole of my annual leave entitlement because of coming into work on public holidays and taking part in electoral campaigns. When foreign guests visit the Institute I have to organise their programme and take them sight-seeing, and that's again time, and money for food and transport. In short, I'm doing not so badly, thank you. I'll get by till it's time to retire, no problem. It's laughable. I can make myself understood in any European language because of all the free time I've had. Of course, if I joined the Party and submitted a thesis, I could look forward to trips abroad and all the rest of it. But it doesn't attract me. And I don't want to be an informer. And it would take a minimum of three or four years. At my age that's too long. No, I'm doing fine as I am.'

AN EPISTLE TO THE LEADERS

Oh, Leaders, Oh, Leaders, can't you dampen your zeal?!
Your arms bill is twice that of Nato's!
Why not turn your attention to problems more real,
Like, for instance, our rotten potatoes?
And our rotten old clothes and our cramped living space.
Why not take our economy in hand?
And get rid of the fiddling that's growing apace,
High and low and throughout the whole land.
From Tula to Moscow two trips twice a year,
Just for folk to stock up on some food,
Would go a long way towards providing some cheer,
And cheaper vodka'd be all to the good.
For abroad we don't yearn, so don't let us out.
For abroad we just don't give a shit.
And your Paris and Nice, say, without any doubt
Are to us but of small benefit.
If we're all right here, then to hell with the West
And we'll serve you the best way we can.
And as for the dissidents, e'en without your request,
Why, we'll strangle them all to a man.

A WARNING FROM THE TEACHER

The Teacher expressed some alarm about the fact that Dobronravov has begun to show more interest in me.

'Watch him,' said the Teacher. 'He's a slippery customer. All
sorts of things are said about him.'

'Things are said about everyone,' I said. 'A lonely person looks
for someone like him he can talk to.'

'It's not clear what he's looking for,' said the Teacher. 'But
God helps those who help themselves.'

'But what could he possibly want from me?' I said.

'Who knows,' said the Teacher, 'what roles They intend us to
play in Their spectacles.'

IRON FELIX'S ANALYSIS

'Some strange people have begun appearing in the Institute,' said Iron Felix. 'They're interested in you.'

'What of it?' I said.

'They were having a look at the books you've been reading,' said Iron Felix.

'Let them,' I said. 'Barabanov or Smirnyashchev might have had a quiet word with Petin and he's ordered someone . . .'

'I don't think it's quite like that,' said Iron Felix. 'And they've been having a look at your medical card in the polyclinic.'

'Get away with you,' I said. 'There's nothing wrong with me.'

'Maybe there's nothing wrong with you,' said Iron Felix, 'but is there nothing wrong with Them?'

'What do they want with me?' I asked.

'Perhaps you could be useful to Them in one or two connections,' said Iron Felix. 'There are three possibilities worth considering. The first is whether it is not just a prophylactic measure. Perhaps someone from the office simply shopped you, and They've decided to check you out and take measures, just to be on the safe side. Secondly, it might be a provocation. Why? Perhaps to enhance the reputation of the General Secretary, or to have a good excuse to finish off the dissidents. Thirdly, perhaps They want to manufacture an excuse to get rid of that "genius" who's got right up everybody's nose.'

'I doubt it,' I said. 'They're hardly capable of playing dangerous games like that.'

'They're capable of more than that,' said Iron Felix. 'There's been an attempt already.'

'There was,' I agreed. 'But then They thought better of it.'

'Not necessarily,' said Iron Felix. 'Something unforeseen might have happened. And although They were put off once, They might have a second go. If I were you I'd try to stay one jump ahead.'

ONCE MORE IN CREATIVE QUEST

'They've just brought out a translation in the West,' said Stalin, 'of Petin's book *How to Read Lenin's Materialism and Empiriocriticism*. What idiots they are! I know that we are idiots, too, but that's our prerogative, our historic fate, tradition, and so on. But them?! They're idiots twice over! Even I could see that that book of Lenin's was nothing but incoherent twaddle. But them!!! Here's an example right at the beginning. Lenin attacks some Western philosopher for defining matter as something standing in opposition to "ego". But what does he do himself? Read this: "Matter is a philosophical category for the designation of objective reality which becomes tangible to man via his sensations and which can be copied, photographed, reflected in his sensations while remaining independent of them." There's nothing here but ambiguity, confusion, nonsense. Matter is a philosophical category. But category is a word, at best a concept. Does that mean that matter is a word or a concept? All right, let's not cavil (although we should, actually, since we're talking about the definition of words!). Let's accept that the word "matter" designates, etc. What comes after that? Objective reality (as if these words were any clearer than the word "matter") which becomes tangible to man via his sensations. Think about it: here man and his senses are taken to be primary, i.e. as constituting that very "ego" which the idiot started off by objecting to, and matter is defined as something standing in opposition to this "ego", as something which produces these sensations. That's his usual method: he steals some opponent's idea, slanders his opponent and makes him appear as some kind of idiot, then passes that idea off as his own, having first rendered it nonsensical. I know that I used to do the same thing, but I at least had weighty reasons for doing so. Let's continue with the end of the phrase ("definition") about how matter is copied, photographed, etc. This is just logical illiteracy, amalgamating in one sentence a definition of the meaning of the word "matter" and an assertion about the relationship between matter and sensation where the meaning of the words in that relationship is taken as given. And our cretinous philosophers present this as the acme of the definition of matter. Look at the *Philosophical Encyclopaedia*, for example. It's written there in black and white: the definition of matter is directly (?) connected with the solution of a fundamental question of philosophy and consequently always contains a keenly polemical element, from a Party point of view. What kind of discovery is that, eh? A new way of defining concepts – giving them a pro-Party polemical twist!'

'Look on the bright side,' said Iron Felix. 'We've wasted a colossal amount of mental energy on that marxist-leninist bullshit. Let the West waste some as well. Let them swim around in the morass, too. While they're trying to make sense of all that balderdash, we'll overtake them. And we'll knock them on the head, which by that time will be full of it. Personally, I'd order all our philosophers to be translated into Western languages and their books to be dropped on Western countries from our satellites. Free of charge. Or with an incentive, even. A dollar stitched to each book. Not a bad idea, eh?'

'In our district,' said Marx, 'people thought for a long time that electricity too was invented by Lenin. People were so often told about "the guiding light of Lenin" that they came to that conclusion. Of course, there were some people who did know a little about electricity, but they were locked up before they could say anything. It's laughable!'

'I've had enough of your philosophical chitter-chatter,' said Beria.

'I heard two women arguing on a trolley-bus today about the availability of foodstuffs in the shops, both here and in the West. One said that you could get everything in the West. The other said that, on the other hand, it was all very expensive. The first one then said that you could get nothing here. The other said that, on the other hand, it was very cheap. There's a little problem for you: what's better? A situation where you can get everything, but it's expensive, or one where you can get nothing, but it's cheap?'

'Do you know what Petin's book about Lenin's book all started from?' asked Stalin. 'From the call to read Lenin with a pencil in your hand.'

'You're the specialist,' said Iron Felix. 'You've got all the cards in your hand. Why don't you tear Them all to shreds?'

'They've turned out dozens of volumes,' I said. 'And it would take hundreds of volumes to tear Them to shreds. The game's not worth the candle. And it's very boring work, showing up ignoramuses, schizophrenics, paranoiacs, careerists and chancers. I'm supposed to be writing a preface for Petin's new book. And I can't get it to come right. Everything I try ends up as a slanderous attack on the classical writers.'

'Well, dress it all up,' said Beria. 'Write it in such a way that the slander appears as fulsome praise. How does one do that? Very easily. Suppose, for example, some classical writer has spouted some piece of nonsense and some academic has asserted that in this particular case the classical writer has spouted a piece of nonsense. What you do is to assert that the academic was spouting nonsense when he alleged that the classical writer was spouting nonsense. And marshal some arguments. Which ones? Well, all the old well-tried and trusted ones: this scholar has succumbed to the influence, has failed to understand, has distorted, has addressed the subject but failed to grasp the nettle, has failed to take account of the precise circumstances, has played into the hands of, has added grist to the mill of the bourgeoisie.'

AND YOU WON'T BECOME A CANDIDATE

Smirnyashchev is also Party organiser in the Department. That's his social work, but it's the kind of social work which allows him to control all the other business of the Department. In his official capacity of Party organiser, he informed me that my joining the Party would have to wait a while. I told him that I was in no hurry and that I was ready to wait until I retired. Then he declared that Petin had made him responsible for the preparation of several sections of his future book, including the preface. He, Smirnyashchev, would very much like to see my material. I said that that wasn't exactly a pressing matter either since, in order to write a preface, you have to be acquainted with what has been written, at least in the main sections of the book, which, as far as I knew, not only had not yet been written, but had hardly as yet been thought about. Smirnyashchev told me that that was not my concern, that if I didn't show him the material then he would have to take measures, etc. I told him that I would try to speed things up. He ordered me to produce a plan of the preface together with an abstract for discussion at the next session of the planning group a week later.

This of course put me in a bad mood and I dragged myself home, back to the papers on which I'd written out excerpts from the works of notable scholars. Excerpts which, as I noted earlier, were quite contradictory. 'In my scientific work', wrote one of these outstanding degenerates, 'I was always guided by the tenets of Engels and Lenin, namely that one should approach matters in a concrete fashion.' Another wrote that he was astounded at the crass ignorance of these gentlemen in matters relating to the natural sciences but that he didn't hold that against them since they weren't specialists. This idiot seemed quite unaware of the pogrom that was taking place in our scientific world at the time when that outstanding degenerate was alive, quoting the utterances of the other pair on matters scientific.

As I was approaching the Lubyanka and could already make out the features of Iron Felix, I met the Poet and told him all about my troubles. For some reason he was glad of this and there and then composed an Epistle to me:

> Forget about that glorious day,
> An associate member you won't be
> (Such fortune ne'er will come your way)
> Of the SU's renowned CP.
> On borrowed cash get drunk instead
> And learn to be yourself of yore.
> Forget about a soft new bed,
> Non-Party man for evermore!
> Don't rant and rave to Heaven above,
> Don't shed a tear in misery,
> You also won't be Doctor of
> Their Philo-bloody-sophistry.
> Just borrow cash, I say again,
> And come in to our den of hope,
> For all unqualified young men
> The gates of Paradise we ope.

I said that that was fine by me but that I'd have to make a quick phone-call. I told Herself that I'd be delayed for a little while but that She should help herself to something to eat, find something to read and go to bed, if She wanted to. She should lock herself in, however, and take the key out of the lock in case I wasn't able to waken Her.

'She's something else again,' I said to the Poet. 'Once She's asleep you could fire a gun and not waken Her.'

'That's the sign of a good person,' said the Poet. 'That's very rare these days. Look after Her. Incidentally, who is She this time?'

I said that I didn't know and that I didn't remember where She had appeared from. For all I knew She might have landed from a flying saucer. When we turned back towards the centre of town Iron Felix gave us a cordial smile and a wink.

'Proletarian power has nothing against your intentions,' he said.

'Nevertheless,' said the Poet, 'one of these days I'm going to give that so-and-so a belt in the mouth.'

STRANGE THOUGHTS

Sometimes strange thoughts enter my head. I'm surprised at them myself. Yesterday, for example, Herself and I were talking about children and families. And I showed Her as easily as demonstrating that two plus two equals four all the problems, hassle and forlorn hopes bound up with having children and starting a family. She absolutely agreed with me but 'in her heart' She still wanted them. She was ready to put up with all their ingratitude and with all the problems which they caused so long as She could bring them up to the point where they showed ingratitude and came up against problems. In the end She told me that I was 'going all philosophical' out of laziness or cowardice. And selfishness. And unexpectedly the following thought occurred to me:

'If I am absolutely honest about it,' I said, 'the only way that I can get my own back on Them is by not leaving any children for Them. And I call on everyone who wants to have his or her revenge on Them to follow my example. Let Their own children become Their slaves.'

I spent a moment or two in quiet admiration of my 'clever' reply, while She remained silent. Then She said that I was mad. But I suddenly realised that my answer was in fact not all that daft and that there were facts which supported it. The birth rate in the Russian population is decreasing sharply. Childless 'families' are becoming more and more common and families with one child only are absolutely normal. And how many single people there are! Especially among women. Especially among intelligent women. So that whether I want it or not, history itself is taking its revenge on Them for all Their misdeeds. And then I remembered about the reform of the schools. It is difficult to say at the moment how that will affect workers and peasants, but certainly in the lower strata of the intelligentsia and officialdom, who have to struggle not to slip down into the ranks of the workers and peasants, the trend I spoke of can only be intensified by it. At the level of the workers and peasants themselves, the picture will presumably be patchy. The privileged sector will hardly be affected by it although here, too, many will try to start their children off on their way up the social ladder and that means only one, or at most two, children in a family. As far as the rest are concerned (the poorest and least cultured), the general situation will have an effect, irrespective of the reform, i.e. the cost of bringing up children, the difficulties connected with cramped living conditions, etc. Of course, the situation might change if pensions were abolished or reduced. But the authorities are hardly likely to do either of those things. In the first place, pensioners are a great support to the whole system and in the second place the pensioners themselves simply wouldn't allow it.

'What are you thinking about?' She asked.

'Oh, nothing much,' I said. 'About this and that.'

'You should shave off your beard,' She said. 'As it is, I don't know what your face looks like. Perhaps you're very ugly! Are there any photographs of you without a beard?'

'There are,' I said, 'but my parents have them. I'll let you see them sometime. And as for my beard, well, I can't shave it off. Anyway, it's not physical defects that it hides, but spiritual ones, or rather, moral defects. I wouldn't be seen dead without my beard.'

'If I'm absolutely honest with you,' She said, 'there's a lot of truth in what you say. My mother and I live alone. My father has left us. As soon as I got into an institute he upped and left. Mum earns about a hundred roubles a month. As a young specialist I earn around a hundred a month as well. We can hardly make ends meet. We don't even dream of buying anything fashionable to wear. Even these wretched boots I'm wearing cost almost a whole month's salary. And as for fashionable ones, foreign ones . . . When Dad still lived with us (he earned around two hundred a month) I asked my mother for a little brother or sister. She said that she'd hang herself before she had another child. I'm now at the age where I should be having children myself, but, honestly, I'm scared to take the plunge. In the first place I've yet to meet a man who would make even a bearable husband and I don't want to be a single parent. In the second place, I well remember what my own mother had to put up with with me. I failed my university entrance exams twice, but not through any fault of mine. We simply didn't have any contacts and therefore I didn't get good marks. When I failed for the second time my mother had to spend a month in hospital. She told me that if I didn't get in at the third attempt she'd commit suicide. So I had to give up the idea of university and get myself into a third-rate institute. Then there was five years of study. And for what? What I'm doing now I could have done as soon as I left school. At least this new school reform shatters stupid illusions. At least people will stop getting silly ideas into their heads. And yet I would like to live in a proper family, even if it were only for a little while. And have a nice clean flat. It wouldn't have to be large as long as it were bright. And cook a tasty meal. Have a nice jolly husband. And a chubby little child hanging on to my skirt. What could be simpler?'

Oh, dear, I thought to myself. Even the idea of a 'chubby little child' which hangs on to skirts (or pulls beards, God help me) makes me feel sick.

'Buy Her a pair of tights,' said Himself.

'Where am I going to get that kind of money from?' I said.

100

'And anyway, if I start to buy them all presents I'll need a complete haberdashery.'

'Bragging a bit, aren't you?' He said. 'You've not had all that many. Let's count them. One, two, finish. Ha-ha-ha! When I was your age I probably had more in a month. Go on, buy Her some tights.'

'I'm not against the idea,' I said. 'But where am I going to get them? And what about size?'

'Go on! Buy them. She'll appreciate them. She's a nice girl. If I were you ... I'll say no more! Here's what happened to me during the war. I was returning to my unit after having been in hospital. I got to know this girl in the compartment. And I spent my first and last wedding night in the luggage rack. And because I was drunk, later on I couldn't remember her name or address. At first it was a bit of a joke, but I spent the rest of my life looking for her. Learn from my bitter experience. Period. If I were you ... OK I'm saying nothing. But learn this much, at least! It's not so much a question of being constantly exposed to temptation as the fact that the simplest pleasures in life become more and more difficult to attain and in the end are more than we can afford. And when they appear, we are not capable of recognising them, or valuing them.'

EPISTLE TO THOSE FALLEN IN THE BATTLE FOR

I believe that you died for the Good of the Cause
But how would you've acted if you'd but known
That scroungers and chancers and rogues got their paws
On the good things you died for and, alas, They alone.

REPLY OF THE FALLEN

'In battle we fell', is what they'd have said,
'Not so that you lot could up your own whack,
But so that, your blades flashing over your head,
You could gallop behind us, prolong the attack.'

COMPLAINT OF THE NON-FALLEN

But probably, always, the story's the same,
With eyes shut one sees horses raring to go.
When they're open you see that the name of the game
Is not sabres and spurs but office desks in a row.
And no enemy's there, in the belly no fire,
There's no sabre, no spur, no impetuous steed.
Oh, God, how this bureaucrap fails to inspire,
Where are you, Just Cause, oh, where are you, indeed?

HISTORY IS SOMETIMES RATHER DROLL

'It is facts like the following,' said Dobronravov, 'which make
one realise the extent to which our country has been transformed
in the last sixty years. Balalaikas, decorated wooden spoons,
nesting dolls, these are all quintessentially Russian, are they not?
According to our historians our simian ancestor first learned to
play a balalaika and it was after that that he became Russian
and straightway began to make nesting dolls (for sale to foreign
tourists) and decorated wooden spoons (also for foreign tourists,
since he himself ate his soup with an undecorated spoon). And
now look what happens. Every year we import twenty thousand
balalaikas. We've just bought automated equipment in the West
which will turn out a million hand-made(!) decorated wooden
spoons. It's a technological miracle: you shove a log in one end
and out of the other come souvenirs, the product of our folk

handicrafts! At this moment high level talks are going on with three Western firms about the construction of a nesting doll factory complex.'

'So what?' said the Teacher. 'Personally I shan't be surprised if these automated wooden spoon machines start producing grenades and the doll factory starts to produce tactical nuclear weapons.'

ON TERRORISM

You know, the subject of terror is one that fascinates me. It doesn't matter what I'm thinking about, however serious it might be, my thoughts always drift back to it. And it's not the moral aspect which preoccupies me, but the technical aspect. The moral aspect is very simple: if the authorities employ terror systematically against the population, then why shouldn't individual representatives of those terrorised use it against the authorities? As they say, an eye for an eye, a tooth for a tooth. This is all the more true if you consider that the authorities have now run up such a score in this respect vis-à-vis the terrorised population that the latter will never be able to settle it, even if terrorists were to kill a dozen leaders a year. It is true, of course, that very often terrorist acts are committed by those who have no moral right on their side and that often it is innocent people who suffer. But that is more a secondary matter and is not of the essence. The technical aspect, however, is hopelessly complicated. For instance, try getting near the General Secretary! Unless the KGB itself set something up, it would be absolutely impossible. Dobronravov, with whom I came to be discussing this problem on one occasion, thinks that one should begin not from above, but from below, i.e. with district Party and government officials, or even smaller fry, directors and managers. For instance, the manager of a hairdresser's or the director of an institute. Like Petin, for example! He'd be perfect. and you wouldn't need any special equipment or preparation. You would just go into his office with some paper or other for signature and stick a sharp pencil through his eye.

A COSY LITTLE FRATERNITY

I used to think that the situation in our ideological field was as follows. Obscurantists and butchers with Academicians Kanar-eikin, Petin and Fedosov at their head got rid of talented philosophers by getting them sent off to concentration camps. As a result the best philosophical brains were destroyed, leaving only cretins and scum. Even although a certain 'excessive zeal' which was prevalent during the 'cult of personality' has been curtailed, the obscurantists and butchers have nonetheless retained their power. They have, it is true, been squeezed out of the Party leadership but, on the other hand, they have advanced themselves by way of the 'scientific' route. Fedosov has become vice-president of the Academy of Sciences, Kanareikin has become Secretary of its Department of Philosophy and Law, Petin has become director of the Institute, and so on. And these obscurantists continued to suppress young, talented, progressive, educated philosophers. That's the way I had imagined the situation to be.

When I arrived in the Madhouse I soon discovered that Petin and Kanareikin are sworn enemies, that the victims of these butchers are just as cretinous and nasty, that some of those who have been rehabilitated are the lowest of the low, that Kanareikin is on the best of terms with Tormoshilkina, Smirnyashchev, Bulyga, Zaitsev and other 'decent types', that these 'decent types' hardly differ at all from the old obscurantists and butchers, etc, etc. The young progressive ones take the same aggressive marxist ideological line in all accessible areas of culture, only they do a better job than the die-hards, more indirectly, more hypocriti-cally. And just like the die-hards, the young, progressive philos-ophers suppress every attempt to develop new ideas, again more skilfully than their predecessors. In terms of greed, vanity and careerism they are in no way inferior to the die-hards and make themselves out to be altruistic fighters for truth, culture, progress, achievement. As for cowardice vis-à-vis the authorities, they are even worse than their predecessors although they take far fewer risks than they did. And when I had sussed all that out, I lost heart.

There are some good people, of course, in our midst, people like the Teacher. But their efforts are in vain. Either no one is interested in their results, or else they are forced to attribute them to someone else (the classical writers of marxism, Kant, Hegel, Kierkegaard, Chernyshevsky, Bergson, Sartre, etc). As a result our philosophical thought, even when it does deserve attention, comes over as derivative, imitative, second-hand.

These ways are not for me. I want to say what I have to say in my own name, and right now. And since that is impossible, then it's better not to do anything which might inadvertently rub salt in the wound. It's better simply to play the fool. Ideas are rather like children in a way. They cost too much. Developing them costs too much time and effort. And there's no guarantee that you'll be able to squeeze them in anywhere or get any satisfaction from them. Nor is there any guarantee that they won't be taken away from you. It's better without them. It's quieter. And you have more freedom. I keep having the feeling that all of a sudden I'm going to have an opportunity to say my piece. It's as if I'm waiting an assignment to some post or other. Or as if I'm preparing a decisive blow, choosing a suitable moment.

I expressed these views to the Teacher when he was trying to convince me (for the umpteenth time!) that I had real talent, that I was wasting my time and energy and that I should work. He said that, of course, I was right. But he said that he was also right, for the process of creative work is precious in itself, it is justified not by material results or success but exclusively because it absorbs you.

'We are representatives of different generations and different social strata,' he said. 'I am a real devotee of work. I work without thinking about how my work fits into the general pattern of life or of its consequences. You are a member of the intelligentsia. You don't work, but ruminate about how your inactivity fits into the general pattern of life and of its results. In all other respects we are similar. And you are even more capable than I am.'

I am very flattered to be told that I am even more capable than the Teacher. That is quite enough for me. The fact that what I have written is utter crap compared to the Teacher's work is neither here nor there. They don't publish his work any more than they publish mine.

THE FEUD AS THE MOTIVE POWER OF EVOLUTION

What I like about marxist dialectics is the fact that it recognises the feud as the motive power of the evolution of society. And, perhaps, of the whole of matter. There has been a feud festering away for a long time in our Department between paranoiac Smirnyashchev's group, which is raising the level of our work in the field of logic to one of world significance, and schizophrenic Sheptulin's group, which is engaged in introducing dialectics into logic. Until recently people took an optimistic view of this feud, i.e. considered it as a force carrying the Department on to new achievements. But then squabbling broke out quite openly and was conducted with great fury, thereby refuting the thesis of 'scientific' communists about the absence of antagonistic contradictions in our society. Both sides were fairly evenly matched since Sheptulin could more than compensate for his relative lack of support among colleagues by having the powerful support of his father-in-law, a big-wig in the Council of Ministers. Smirnyashchev accused Sheptulin of Hegelianism and Sheptulin accused Smirnyashchev of positivism. Both delivered speeches at a meeting of the Department. Both of them wrote declarations to the Party bureau and the administration. Both of them spoke at a meeting of the Academic Council and then at Party meetings. The situation became complicated. Smirnyashchev is an academic and knows the meaning of 'implication' and is almost certainly tied in with the Organs of State Security. Petin protects him since he is counting on Smirnyashchev's talent, erudition and organisational skills for the production of his own epoch-making work. But Sheptulin is the son-in-law. He knows all the quotations from the classical writers on logic by heart. He is not in favour of formal logic which, although not a superstructure on a bourgeois base, occupies a very lowly position, but favours dialectical logic which serves the proletariat and therefore occupies a much higher position. Smirnyashchev stresses the achievements of world science and material implication. The word 'implication' is a little disconcerting. Everyone senses that it smacks of revisionism. But the word 'material' is unimpeachable. Sheptulin stresses fidelity to the principles of marxism-leninism and threatens to bring a charge of revisionism and of making concessions to idealism.

An attempt was made to embroil me in this struggle. Smirnyashchev was the first to have a go. He caught me in the corridor, got me in a corner and began to tempt me by offering to recommend me for associate membership of the CPSU. But I resisted. Then it was Sheptulin's turn. He invited me to a restaurant, placed a bottle of brandy on the table and began to tempt me by making positive noises about my dissertation for the award of candidate. And again I managed to get out of it. Then they both tore apart the substance of what I had intended to say in the preface to Petin's book which I still haven't managed to begin to write. When they asked the Teacher for his opinion of the conflict in the Department, he said that he didn't see much difference between Hegel and Carnap, that they were both crap, and invented a pretext for leaving the meeting. I was left completely isolated.

'Write a denunciation,' said Iron Felix. 'I'll make sure it gets through.'

'Of whom?'

'Both of them. Everyone.'

'What about?'

'About how their behaviour is undermining the marxist-leninist tenet regarding the absence of antagonistic contradictions under socialism.'

'That's a great idea. But, alas, I don't like writing.'

THE PATHS OF FATE

I clocked on, meandered slowly along the corridor, nodded at the girls in the office, said something to annoy the 'learned' females waiting to get into the reading-room, congratulated Kachurin on his new article on 'strange happenings' in space, made way for Kirusik to spread her latest piece of gossip, smoked a cigarette on the landing, listened at the same time to the latest sports news (the second most important topic of conversation among colleagues after stories about dissidents), hung around the Department for a while, paid a back-handed compliment to the secretary in the department of theoretical problems in the marxist-leninist theory of cognition, went back out on to the landing which was already deserted (for how long?!) and tore off down the back stairs. When I got to the ground floor I turned in the direction of the canteen, opened a window which was supposed to be hermetically sealed and leapt outside. And almost landed on the chief administrative officer and Deputy Director Stukachev. What were they doing there??!! But there was no time to think and I immediately asked Stukachev to sign a chit for the typing pool authorising an immediate duplication of a manuscript belonging to an author from outside our Institute. I knew that Stukachev wouldn't sign it since there had been a directive from above the previous week forbidding publication of work done by people not on the Institute staff. Stukachev duly refused to sign it and I wandered back into the Institute, not by the window this time, but through the door, like all normal people. Or rather, I pretended that I was going back inside. But when I got to the building belonging to the journal *Communist* I turned 'left', i.e. carried straight on instead of turning right as I should have done. It was not long before I caught up with the Institute alcoholic Shubin who was heading in the direction of the House of Journalists in the company of someone from the *Communist* editorial staff. It turned out to be someone rather well-known in our circles, a chap called Sasha Kostin, who was a friend of the family of the General Secretary no less, with whom he was apparently on familiar terms. And naturally, after the third round, we began to talk about the General Secretary and Sasha began to praise him to the skies. Shubin, of course, followed suit since Sasha was paying the bill. I managed to get off with a few meaningless remarks which interested no one, although if one wanted to, one could have made some sort of sense of them, namely that the current General Secretary was by no means the worst of his ilk, and that, anyway, it didn't matter whether he was a good one or a bad one since he didn't do anything. Rumour has it that Shubin is the Gen Sec's speech-writer, but I had always known that no one person could write that many speeches. And now, when I looked at Shubin a bit more closely, I realised that he wasn't even one of the speech-writers. He was more likely to be one of the organisers of one of the groups of speech-writers. I dropped a hint to the effect that my 'pen' was at his disposal, and so on. He said that he was swamped with such requests but that he would see what he could do for me. *Communist* commissioned a lot of unsigned work. I told him that I had been working for a long time with *Party Life* and that I had experience. He said that that was very good, but that it was a pity I wasn't a member of the Party (I had let that drop during the conversation). If I had been a Party member he could have got me a job on the editorial staff, since at that moment they had some vacancies.

Later on Shubin and Kostin went off to 'see the girls' and I made my way back to the Lubyanka.

'You see?' said Iron Felix as I drew level with him. 'There's nothing for it. You're going to have to join the Party. Do you want me to write you a reference? Naturally there's a price attached. You'll have to sign a little document. We'll nip into the director's office then round to the district Party committee. And . . .'

'Go to f——,' I said. 'What do you need me for, anyway?'

'We don't need you at all,' said Iron Felix. 'It's a matter of principle with us. We would be quite happy to wash our hands of you. I mean, why would we need you? We're chock-a-block with young lads with beards who know foreign languages. And who are ready to sign any paper you care to imagine. But we can't act otherwise. If we leave you in peace we shall feel defeated. So, sorry and all that, but we shan't leave you alone until . . .'

'Well, you're a bunch of idiots,' I said. 'Now you won't have me, even if I were to come of my own accord.'

'That's why we won't have you,' said Iron Felix. 'Because you want to yourself.'

'Stop trying to confuse me,' I said. 'You're just like Kostin, promising me something that you know in advance you're not going to stick to.'

'Of course,' said Iron Felix, 'but I'm doing it out of the good of my heart, from a desire to help. After all, I'm a Russian.'

'What kind of Russian are you supposed to be?' I asked indignantly.

'The same as anyone else,' said Iron Felix. 'Do you know who a Russian is? Anyone speaking Russian as his native language and who feels frightened when he walks past the Lubyanka. And incidentally, I trembled in my time just as much as you.'

'I don't tremble,' I said.

'That's the whole point,' said Iron Felix. 'That's why you're not a Russian, but a secret or internal émigré. It serves you right. Incidentally, hurry on home. There's a surprise waiting for you.'

THE SURPRISE

The door of my room was open. Herself and the neighbours were sitting at the table. Sitting and drinking. They even had some sort of hors d'oeuvres. When they saw my distracted, bearded face they burst out laughing. My neighbour brought a chair, invited me to sit down and poured the remains of the wine into a glass. We clinked glasses without a word. We finished off the cheese, the sausage and the preserves. My neighbour kept grinding on endlessly about how his daughter was going to be a seamstress when she grew up since the work was clean and profitable and there was no need to waste your time studying for nothing. The neighbours went away, taking their chair, plates and forks with them. We were left alone. I was about to ask Her how She had opened the door, but then I stopped: if the neighbour was regularly examining my private papers he must have had his own key for a long time. But I was mistaken in my assumption. She said that She had opened the door with a hairpin. And only then did I notice that in place of my old granny's bed with the jangly springs there was a new ottoman! I had seen one like it not long before in a furniture shop and the idea had crossed my mind of buying it, but only for an instant: an item like that cost at least fifty roubles. I slowly went up to this vision and touched it. A real ottoman! Where did it come from? Why? I was sad for a moment that I would never see my granny's bed again and wouldn't fall on the mattress full of billiard balls nor hear the noises and jangle of the springs. I lay down on the ottoman and stretched out. It felt wonderful. There was a pillow under my head and I could smell the clean (!!) pillowcase. And rocking gently to and fro I drifted off to sleep.

I often dream, and I know how to dream. I love watching my dreams, or rather, participating in them. In order to do this I've learned how to memorise them. This is how I do it. Before I waken up completely I go back over what I've seen in my dream verbally. When I have woken up completely I lie with my eyes shut and again repeat in words what I saw in my dream. I recount the dream to myself two or three times. Then I do the same thing with my eyes open, then when I stand up, and again five minutes later and again after half an hour. After a few repetitions of that procedure, a dream becomes firmly committed to memory and often recurs. Moreover, very vividly. So vividly that it is sometimes difficult to distinguish it from reality, except for the content, of course. In this way I have memorised more than ten good dreams and more than ten bad dreams. The bad ones are those in which nasty things might happen to me but don't, or only partly happen. For example, the threat of being screwed by Petin or Smirnyashchev, or the threat of being shot in the cellar of the main building of the KGB, etc. But for some reason there are no people in my dreams. I sense the presence of people but I don't see them.

It was late when I woke up. On the splendid ottoman. With my head on a pillow with a clean (where did it come from?) pillowcase. Dressed, but with my boots off – they were standing alongside. Covered with a blanket. And a clean sheet and blanket-cover. Where had it all come from?! What was going on?! And then I remembered Herself. But She had gone. Without leaving a trace. Clean as a whistle. And I immediately forgot the splendid new dream I had been about to commit to memory.

DEVELOPMENT

It is possible to study the entire mechanism of the development of matter on the basis of our Institute. Here's how the department of struggle against anti-communism developed, for example. There was a separate group within the sector of scientific communism. The Gen Sec gave a speech on some occasion or other. He yattered on about anti-communist hysteria somewhere in the West. Two units were set up within the sector. The group increased quantitatively and exceeded a critical size. It was made a separate sector. Here you have, firstly, a quantitative change becoming a qualitative one, and secondly, a subdivision of a whole. This subdivision was preceded by a raging feud, an example of the conflict of opposites as a force for development. Then everything ran like clockwork. The bitch Tvarzhinskaya was made head of the new sector (rumour has it that she was a close relative of Dzerzhinsky's) and initiated a tremendous amount of activity. The sector produced three collections of articles and two monographs. It grew twice as large. In connection with certain events, a group for the struggle with international zionism was established. This group soon became a separate sector because of the importance of the problems with which it was concerned. A whole series of groups was set up in the remainder of the sector to deal with American anti-communism, West-European anti-communism, etc. Then there was a group to combat Eurocommunism which was seen as a variety of anti-communism. And again there were bitter feuds, as a result of which the sector split into two separate entities, each of which also split into two. Then the idea that there should be a department began to be aired. At every meeting and during every discussion the bitch Tvarzhinskaya and her accomplices hammered away at the same spot: we were underestimating the ideological enemy, we had allowed our guard to slip, we had lost some of our fighting spirit, we were 'indulging in all sorts of "liberal ideas"', etc. The end result was a new synthesis arising out of the conflict of opposing forces: we had a new, harmonious, productive department, full of the fighting spirit.

Now there's a new stage in the development beginning: Yezhov and one of his drinking mates wrote a denunciation of the rest of the Jews working under them to the effect that they were making concessions to and underestimating the strength of the ideological, etc. The other Jewish anti-semites wrote a denouncement of Yezhov, completely independently and simultaneously, to the effect that *he* was making concessions and underestimating, etc, and that he was hinting that Jews were perhaps not as foul as they were made out to be. The Party bureau set up a commission to investigate the situation in the sector. What will the outcome be? A new sector will be established. Tvarzhinskaya is now beginning to sound out the idea of an institute for the struggle against anti-communism. She is full of enthusiasm. Her eyes are shining. Her little grey pigtail is all a-quiver. On one occasion she caught me in the corridor, got me in a corner and began to tempt me to join her department by enumerating all its advantages. I was well-educated, I knew foreign languages, I had a lot going for me, especially since I was going to join the Party. She would provide a recommendation. I was so flabbergasted by her onslaught that I didn't have time to think of a way out of the situation, and she decided that I must have taken the bait. She shook me by the hand and vanished into the Party bureau to continue drawing attention, to point up the question, takes measures, etc. . . . . Oh, God! I'm being torn apart! What could it all mean?

'It's a familiar situation,' He said. 'They're cooking up something nasty for sure. Look out for yourself! If Tvarzhinskaya shakes your hand you can take it that she's got you in her sights.'

I suddenly missed Herself very much. Where could She have disappeared to? Surely She hadn't gone for ever?

ANGUISH

I tried unsuccessfully to remember Her coordinates. She must have told me Her name and address but I had either not been paying attention or had forgotten them. And what if She were waiting for me to phone Her? Where had I met Her? When?

'Let's draw up a chart of all possible routes you could have taken,' said Himself, 'and then try retracing your steps. You might just suddenly . . .'

'Waste of time,' said Iron Felix. 'These walks of his . . .'

'Your plain-clothes agents are bound to have seen where She went,' I said.

'My agents,' said Iron Felix, 'can dig out any conspiracy, especially a non-existent one. But a loved one who has gone . . . Anyway, I know one thing for sure: She disappeared into an underground station near the KGB headquarters.'

'As you know, I have been looking for Her all my life,' said Himself. 'She'll be an old woman by now, if She's still alive. With stainless steel teeth. You know the kind of teeth I mean. You can bite through wire with them, but, oh, boy, don't try smiling with them! And yet I would sacrifice what's left of my life if I could just see Her for a moment.'

'What for?'

'As a matter of principle. And out of a spiritual need. My advice to you is not to look for Her. If She's going to come back, She'll come back of her own accord, if not you'll never find Her. But remember: from now on no woman will cross the threshold of your Temple of Love other than Herself. Women who know the score will see at once that you've nothing to offer them and the decent ones will no longer tempt you.'

'But there must be some subterfuges one can resort to?'

'Of course there are. Become an associate-member of the CPSU, become a candidate of philosophistical science and you'll find that they'll be all over you. But then you'll never see Her again for sure.'

'Maybe She never existed in the first place? Maybe I dreamed Her up in a drunken stupor?'

'Did you dream up the ottoman, too? And the sheet, the blanket-cover, the pillowcase? And the curtains? What curtains? The ones on the window, of course. Don't tell me you didn't notice them?!'

We approached the snack-bar which used to be Beer Bar Number Two, according to Himself (Number One was on Pushkin Square on that empty piece of ground where nowadays dissidents sometimes gather.) The Poet emerged from it.

'She's not there,' he said. 'Do you want a poem?

> 'Sometimes when falling into bed,
> And jangly springs their song intone,
> I feel it's nice for once instead
> Of two of us I'm all alone.'

'I haven't got a bed. Or springs. We're into ottomans and terylene, now.'

'No problem.

> 'When on the ottoman I fall
> And feel the nice clean terylene,
> I sometimes think it's time to call
> A halt to one-night stands obscene.
> I whisper to myself: "You don't
> Need breasts or buttocks, lips or thighs.
> Enough! From here on in I won't
> Screw, fornicate, fuck, womanise."
> But when the drunken impotence
> Has left me, overhung and dry,
> Deep down inside myself I sense:
> "Without Herself I'll not get by."'

AN EPISTLE TO HERSELF

> I wait for you! I cannot get to sleep.
> By day I search among the passers-by.
> If one of them looks like you then I creep
> Up on her just to look her in the eye.

I won't, of course, go all that very far.
But even I should rip off quite a bit.
I might, for instance, cross the Party bar,
Become a candidate, and all that kind of shit.
A flat? Why not? We'll join a flat 'co-op'.
My mum and dad'll help out if they must.
And if we don't get caught upon the hop,
We'll have our single kid (not two!) – or bust.
We'll spend a hundred roubles on your shoes.
We'll save on food to buy you stylish clothes.
You'll learn to cook your pies, if not your stews,
Net-bag in hand I'll hunt out po-ta-toes!
Our usual fat old bag you'll soon become,
Who always knows what's what more than the rest.
And trousers, 'stead of jeans, will clothe my bum.
My beard, I swear, I'll shave to look my best.
And only once or twice a week I'll drink
A hundred grams. With food – a glass of beer.
Come back to me! Just you and me – just think!
. . . My Christ! I did! The prospect's very drear!

A HISTORIC MEETING

The first meeting of our specialist group took place under Smirnyashchev's chairmanship. It was destined to be historic for several reasons. Firstly the plaster fell off the ceiling and we had to change rooms. Then the alcoholic Shubin fell off his chair, drunk, and had to be laid out on a couch in the department of the struggle against international zionism. Smirnyashchev talked a lot of incoherent nonsense about excellence in the field of logic which would be universally renowned, about material implication, about semantic models and sigma-operators. From time to time Barabanov would give a spiteful little laugh. He had been wounded to the marrow and the bones (his expression) by his demotion. However he had agreed to continue to be Smirnyashchev's deputy in the interests of all our interests (his expression again). Smirnyashchev rabbited on for two hours. Then Barabanov took over for a further hour. This time it was Smirnyashchev's turn to laugh spitefully. Barabanov had just reached the climacteronic (also his expression) point of his speech and declared that one could feel a feeling in the air (his favourite expression), when Shubin, having come out of his stupor, shambled back into the room.

'You and your feelings can go to f——,' he said to Barabanov.

The meeting had to be adjourned temporarily. I offered to take Shubin home. Next day I found out that they had taken advantage of my absence to criticise me, record this fact in the minutes and report me. Barabanov had allegedly proposed that I be removed from the group altogether but Smirnyashchev had spoken up for me. Not on my account, of course, but to spike Barabanov's guns.

Shubin and I, on the other hand, had a pretty good evening. As soon as we got out on to the street he sobered up and suggested that we continue with the meeting in a more suitable *locale*. I said that I had no money. He said that that was no problem since he had just received an honorarium for some article or consultancy work he had done for the journal *Party Life*.

'It's not worth talking about,' he said. 'The usual rubbish. And what are you doing wasting your time in this miserable institution? You should get out while you can. Where to? Wherever you can.'

'It's too late,' I said.

'You're probably right,' he agreed. 'Anyway, there's nowhere to get out *to*.'

We went into the restaurant 'Prague'. Shubin was well-known there – he gave good tips. We were given very much the VIP treatment.

'You see that chap over there?' said Shubin, nodding in the direction of a respectable looking waiter. 'He's one of our graduates. He's actually an employee of the KGB. His rank is at least as high as major. But you can do decent work in our part of the world as well, you know. Only you have to know how. Take me, for instance. I don't feel any restrictions. I can write and publish anything I want. But only on condition that I observe one condition, as Barabanov would say: I have to embed what I think in a context which suits everyone so that my thoughts don't appear to have any pretensions of originality. Engels, of course, wrote nonsense. But you can interpret Engels in your own fashion, so long as you attribute your own views to Engels himself. Everyone is satisfied. And the intelligent ones know what's what.'

'Perhaps intelligent people do understand,' I said. 'But there aren't so many of them about. And here's what I don't understand. I've read your published work, but I must honestly confess that it never entered my head to interpret it like that. I simply regarded it as a routine interpretation of marxist phraseology, adapted to suit current circumstances. As a kind of "market-oriented" form of time-serving . . .'

Shubin interrupted me and spouted a long lecture about the times we live in, progress, duty, etc. I pretended to listen but in fact just went on eating and drinking. And watched the informer-waiter-philosopher. He, for his part, was watching us and eavesdropping on our conversation.

'If you want,' said Shubin at the end of his lecture, 'I can fix you up with some work for *Party Life*. Answering letters, reviewing articles. It's not much, I know. But it'll at least pay for your booze-ups. Later on you'll get short "notes" published and then longer ones. And after that you'll get published in the philosophical journals without any fuss. And when it comes to defending your thesis . . .'

'Right now there's no question of my defending . . .'

'We all say that at the beginning, and yet we write it and get it typed up and defend it. There's no other way. Shall we have another bottle?'

RAISE THE BANNER HIGHER

The slogan in the shoe-repair shop took up the whole of one wall: *Raise higher the banner of socialist competition for the fulfilment and overfulfilment of* . . . The girl behind the counter looked at my boots in disgust and said that there was no point in repairing them. I stuffed the boots into a litter-bin and phoned my parents.

'If you want to buy your beloved son a present for his birthday (incidentally, it was yesterday!),' I said, 'he'd prefer boots. And he'd be moved to tears if you could throw in a packet of coffee. Bye-bye.'

A WAY OUT

'Prices are going up. You're chronically short of money. Start cooking for yourself,' said Himself. 'Breakfast and supper are no problem: tea, bread, butter, cheese. As for dinner you can cook enough at a time to do four meals ahead. Have dinner in the evening and make do at work with a tea and biscuit for lunch. It's a nuisance, of course, and not particularly tasty, but at least you won't get fat. And your stomach won't ache any more. You know yourself what the cooking's like in the canteens and cafés. How on earth can you go into these places and eat that shit?'

'Wine,' I said.

'Wine's gone up again as well,' He said, 'so you won't be going on any more benders.'

And I began to cook for myself. And drag myself round the shops. I already knew what that was like. But to know what it is like is one thing and actually to have to bob around like a cork in the teeming hordes is quite another. I did battle for two weeks against herds of bad-tempered pensioners, workers in a hurry and insolent shop-assistants. And couldn't stand it any longer. I finally realised, once and for all, that I had to move up the ladder at any price. There was no other solution.

THE LOSER'S LAMENT

Oh, Providence, I pray you, why not give me better breaks?!
What use to me is Galileo, for all the difference that it makes?
What do I need with Kantian wisdom or the satire of J. Swift?
Or with Dante's breadth and Shakespeare's depth, or don't you get
                                                         my drift?
Take them back again and give me what I need to get a grip
Upon the levers, or the strings, to reach the higher leadership.
Even better, why not have a go at scoring a bull's eye?
Marry me off with a daughter fair of one of Them on high.
And if you do that for me then here's what I will do for you:

I'll tear up Galileo and I'll flush him down the loo;
And on Kantian wisdom pure I'll gladly pour a pail of slop;
Attack the breadth of Dante's vision till you tell me when to stop;
And the satire of J. Swift I'll very gladly trivialise,
And get Shakespeare to work for us! Well, now, try that one on for
size!

THE DENOUNCER

The Denouncer stopped me near the reception area of the Presidium of the Supreme Soviet and said that it had been a long time since we had last seen each other. He had dropped by the Institute a few times but hadn't managed to get hold of me. I said that I had been temporarily co-opted on to a specialist group working for the director, that I was very busy and that I spent most of my time sitting in libraries. He suggested that we look in at the reception area for a moment. I refused but he more or less dragged me in anyway. The reception area was full of people.

'You see that?' he said.

'So what?' I said, shrugging my shoulders.

'And you call yourself an academic!' he said. 'Come on, I'll walk you back to your workhouse and on the way I'll tell you about an idea I've had. In Moscow alone there's a whole stack of institutions absolutely swarming with people who have a complaint to make. There are all sorts of complaints. Someone can't get a place to live, someone else has a problem with his pension, a third person . . . But there are some very curious individuals. They complain about irregularities in departments, collective farms, factories. They complain about abuses of power, unfair trials, that they've been sacked for criticising the management, etc. Some of them have been coming here for years. From time to time they're arrested, exiled, put in psychiatric hospitals or prison. But they come back again a few years later. And their place is taken by people like them. I've had a good look, and I've become acquainted with a lot of them. The picture is absolutely horrific. There are quite disgraceful things happening everywhere. People are dissatisfied, but they keep quiet. Only very few of them are prepared to make an issue out of these goings-on and of course they bear the full brunt of attacks from the authorities and the punitive organs. And the workers themselves, on whose behalf they are acting, also attack them vehemently. And yet they keep on appearing, inexorably. There hasn't been a day, for instance, since the establishment of this reception area that hasn't had its requisite number of plaintiffs. Moreover, every year the percentage of people complaining about social problems increases: they are sacked for criticising, they are persecuted for their religious beliefs, they are lodged in mental hospitals for leaving the komsomol or the Party, etc. And so I got this idea . . .'

The Denouncer's idea took a firm hold of me. When I had finished 'work' at the Institute I returned home, threw myself on my new ottoman (where is She now?) and began to look at his idea from various angles.

'This Denouncer is not such a nutter as I first thought,' I said, gazing at the dirty ceiling. 'Yep. It's long since time to redecorate this room. What would it cost? Yes, well, it can wait! But, no, this Denouncer, he's certainly no fool. A workers' opposition movement! And where? In a country where in theory all power belongs to the workers!'

'That's your proletariat,' sniggered Marx. 'You can't get away from it! Do you think I dreamed up the dictatorship of the proletariat because people had it so good? . . .'

'The peasants will have to be included as well,' said Lenin seriously. 'The poorest, of course, the middle . . .'

'There haven't been any poorest peasants for a long time,' I said.

'Nor middle ones. And, generally speaking, your peasants nowadays are the same workers, only on the land. Almost everyone gets a wage. Miserly, no doubt, but a wage, nonetheless.'

'They have their own private plot,' said Lenin, not giving in. 'They've been allowed all sorts of poultry . . .'

'The private plots,' I said, crushing Lenin's iron logic, 'are there because of poverty. If wages rise the plots will be taken away. And, anyway, they'd die of hunger, if it weren't for the plots. And they've only temporarily been allowed to keep poultry since there's nothing else to eat. These are all the fruits of your idiotic policy for the countryside . . .'

'Nevertheless workers on the land, called peasants, will have to be included,' declared Lenin firmly.

'That's not a bad idea,' said Marx. 'What are you arguing for?'

'I'm not arguing,' I said. 'I'm merely acting on principle. But what an idea! What a commotion it will create in the West!'

'It's a lousy idea,' said Iron Felix. 'It won't create a stir for long. They won't believe it. And they'll soon find out that it's eyewash.'

'How come it's eyewash?!'

'Because your Denouncer is an ordinary nutcase. And the majority of those people who complain are nutcases. It's a statistical anomaly and not a workers' movement. There are hardly any workers among them.'

'Moreover,' added Beria, 'we've accounted for all of them and we are keeping an eye on them. At the slightest hint of trouble we'll take them all out right away. If you really want to know, a "workers' movement" like that suits us quite well. We can show the whole world what kind of "workers" these are. And the workers themselves . . . And we'll be able to arrange a St Bartholemew's Eve for the whole dissident movement. Get it?'

'Not quite.'

'You don't know even your rudimentary marxism,' said Lenin. 'Until your actually working workers begin to "move" there can be no question at all of any movement. To get them to engage in political struggle . . .'

'But there were facts, after all . . .'

'And what was done with them?! And when did you find out about them?! Things are on a different scale now. For workers' actions to be reflected in the political life of the country they would have to make an impact in many different ways. And it would have to be impossible to conceal them . . .'

'And what would it all lead to? A new revolution? A new dictatorship of the proletariat? God help us!! One's enough! We've had it up to here!'

'There's got to be stability! A quiet life. It's now possible to attain more by peaceful means . . .'

122

'This "workers' movement", however it started and whatever aims it set itself, would turn itself into a KGB provocation! . . .'

I covered my ears but it didn't help. Then I hid my head under the pillow with the dirty pillow-case. Where, in fact, is She? I'm going to have to find Her at all costs!

THE TERRORIST

And then the Terrorist appeared again.

'I think,' he said, 'we have to start with fairly modest ambitions. I think our first target should be the head of the KGB.'

'That's not bad for a "modest" ambition,' I said.

'Naturally,' he said, 'there will be an enormous fuss. But it won't be as bad as all that. It'll create a bit of a sensation, but no more than that.'

'Nevertheless,' I said, 'it's still not a bad beginning. How are you going to get near him? There are people on guard everywhere.'

'Why me? It's going to be you. Listen! Where are you going to be able to get at him? When he gets out of his car to go into the building. You won't get near him near his flat. I've studied the layout there. Nor at his dacha. It's situated right in the middle of a no-go area. That's even more the case with his dacha in the south. There's only one suitable place – the main building of the KGB. Remember, you once nearly bumped into him? Didn't you learn anything from that? Here, look at this. Here is the main building of the KGB. Here's the door he uses to go in and out. The cars draw up in the following pattern: first you have a car with bodyguards in it, then his car, which stops for some reason not exactly opposite the door, but slightly ahead of it, and then another car with guards in it. There are plain-clothes agents here and here. He takes ten seconds to get from the car to the door. There are two possibilities. You can suddenly walk round this corner and throw a grenade from that side of the street or from the same side of the street. The chances of success from the other side of the street are small. The street is wide. You might miss. The agents might have time to grab you. That leaves the second

123

possibility. Do you see what I'm getting at? You remember that time you nearly bumped into him? Do you remember how you were walking? You came round the corner quite calmly, lost in your own thoughts. Notice: nobody stopped you! Why not? Because they've known you round here since you were in nappies. You're almost one of them, so to speak.'

'All right,' I said. 'But how do you work out the timing?'

'He comes and goes according to a pretty regular schedule. And you know what it is. Of course, you can't predict exactly on the basis of only one encounter. You'll have to be ready to seize your opportunity. Take the same route all the time. I guarantee you'll get your chance within a year.'

'Walk around with a bomb?' I asked.

'Of course,' he said.

'What if they have special detectors?'

'You'll have to check that out. Put a frying-pan in your briefcase, or a mincing machine, or a coffee percolator. That's not a problem. The main thing is that they know you there. All you have to do is to get them used to the fact that you go this way to and from work. Got it?'

'Got it,' I said, 'but what about the bomb?'

'Leave that to me,' he said.

'And what will happen to me?' I asked.

'Nothing,' he said. 'There'll be nothing left. Nobody will ever know it was you.'

'Do you mean to say,' I said indignantly, 'that I'm going to get blown to bits and that no one will know?'

'Oh, I see,' he said. 'You're a bit vain are you?'

'Not at all,' I said. 'But I don't want to do it just like that. For nothing.'

'What do you mean, for nothing?' He asked. 'You're doing it for the good of the people!'

'Actually,' I said, 'I don't have an awful lot of time for the people.'

'OK,' he said. 'If that's the way you want it, mankind will learn that a wonderfully brave young man gave his life for the good of his people.'

'You're naive dilettantes,' said Beria suddenly. 'Are you sure that that man is the chief himself? What if he's a double? And what if They let this wonderfully brave young man see this double in order to start a rumour? What if he actually drives round in an anonymous grey car without a bodyguard and gets into the main building via an underground passage from some nondescript building or other?'

'That doesn't matter,' said the Terrorist. 'Unsuccessful attempts at assassination are also highly recognised in history. If it's a double this time, we'll look for the real ones next time. Sooner or later . . .'

'Who are you going to get to look for them?' I asked. 'Me?'

'You've already gone,' he said. 'We'll find someone else. Once the idea gets abroad, the people to carry it out will turn up. Here am I, offering you a wonderful opportunity, and you . . .'

'You know, I'm beginning to think we should start with something big,' I said. 'We'd do better to blow up the entire KGB building. You don't know how to make atomic bombs, by any chance? That's a pity. Otherwise, we could have used a radio-guided balloon . . .'

'Nonsense,' he said. 'A balloon would drift right on past into Trubnaya Square and blow up a toilet.'

'Or an old church,' said Lenin.

'A market,' said Marx.

'The "Uzbekistan" restaurant,' said Iron Felix. 'You'll have to think about it a little more. Why the rush? You have to make sure.'

AND AGAIN THE DENOUNCER

'The workers' organisation is ready,' said the Denouncer. 'Six people are enough to start with. Later on millions of others will follow. It's time we assembled some foreign journalists. The only problem is where. Perhaps in your flat?'

'We'll be able to squeeze six people into my flat somehow or other,' I said.

'So the journalists'll be left outside on the stairs? Or in the street? Better in the street. In the doorway to the ministry opposite. And we can shout slogans through the window.

Incidentally, what slogans are we going to shout? Workers of the world unite?'

'Oh, my God,' sighed Beria. 'These dilettantes are enough to make you weep! Have you never heard of the word con-spi-ra-cy? By all means set up your lousy "workers' unions", but keep them a secret. Beat up directors and Party bureau secretaries and local Party committee secretaries, if you want to! Knock the fur hats off the heads of chairmen of housing commissions and deputies of district soviets. But don't get into politics! Set fire to litter bins and dustbins, if you must. Or even break the windows of some ministry. But, for goodness sake, stay out of politics! And don't have anything to do with the . . . what do you call it? . . . the proletariat! Nor with the poorest peasantry, either!'

'OK, then,' said the Denouncer. 'We'll organise a meeting in Manezh Square. There's something you could do for me: phone round the foreigners and say to them in English that there's a workers' opposition orga . . .'

THE PEOPLE AND THE INTELLIGENTSIA

Russians fall into one of three categories: the powers that be, the people and the intelligentsia. There is no problem about 'the powers that be and the people'. Both parties know that the former has privileges and that the latter has obligations. Neither is there a problem about 'the powers that be and the intelligentsia': both parties are aware that the former has privileges and that the latter has obligations. There is only a problem about 'the intelligentsia and the people'. The problem of 'the people and the intelligentsia' is the same problem, only in reverse. Ask any member of the intelligentsia about problems! It would never enter his head to think of the powers that be. He would immediately begin talking about the people for he is a member of the intelligentsia.

The whole sociology of the problem of the intelligentsia and the people can be studied on the basis of the example provided by our little flat. I am the intelligentsia and my neighbours are the people. There are no representatives, of course, of the 'powers that be' category. They are a higher form of life. That form of life does not live in communal flats in buildings scheduled for demolition. My neighbours genuinely believe that I am a parasite sucking the blood of the workers and at the same time they are sorry for me that I spend hours wearing out the seat of my pants and ruining my eyes reading books. Or again, they sincerely believe that, as an academic, I make money hand over fist while at the same time they declare categorically that they are not going to let their daughter go to an institute and 'waste twenty years of schooling in order to earn peanuts'. They are ready to share absolutely everything they have and they get angry when I refuse. Recently I had to do a 'rush job' on an article 'on the side'. In walked the neighbour with a pint of vodka. It took me all my time to get rid of him and for a week afterwards he wouldn't speak to me except to curse me or threaten to punch me one. I asked him why and got the same answer as the wife in that old joke when she asks her husband what he hit her for. 'Nothing – try something and see what you get!' Whenever a fuss needs to be made about something to any of the communal organisations or the local authorities, I always get dragged in because I'm a 'scholarly type'. But if the authorities need to put pressure on me for some reason, the 'people' in our flat always wholeheartedly supports the authorities and not the 'intelligentsia'.

To cut a long story short, it's impossible to establish any strict principles which could underlie a descriptive system. Why? Because the people looks upon the intelligentsia as part of itself ('the same shit as we are') trying to set itself up like the powers that be ('who do they think they are!'). The people respects the intelligentsia since it is nearly part of the establishment, but despises it because it doesn't belong to the establishment at all.

'Did you know,' asked Himself, 'that They're now seriously considering a scheme for placing the intelligentsia under the control of the people? They are convinced that one of the reasons why the dissident movement got going was that members of the intelligentsia had separate flats. Now They're going to build houses with large flats in which They'll house several families at once. The intelligentsia will be distributed among them. You might say that the intelligentsia will be dissolved, submerged and interspersed among the people.'

'What good will that do Them?' I asked in surprise. 'The intelligentsia will only start stirring the people up.'

'Don't be so naive,' said Himself. 'How much stirring have you done in your hat?'

AN EPISTLE TO THE COLLECTIVE

You can plead on bended knee or
You can tear your hair all day.
I assure you that you're done for
If t' Collective turns away.
You won't escape its watchful eye
If you've been pissed as fabled newt,
And for a long time then they'll try
To show that you're in bad repute.
Forget about your dissertation,
A rise in salary as well,
And of a prize-day celebration
You've not a snowball's chance in hell.
Your old tricks for skiving off
Will never ever work again
And there'll be no more hiving off
Cheap tickets for you now and then.
If you catch the 'flu and end up
Staying home all day in bed,
There'll be no one who will send up
Flowers and fruit, or stroke your head.
If the time comes when it suits Them
To remove you from the throng,
If you think work-mates won't help 'em
Then you are simply very wrong.
So what's the score? It's very clear.
It's even somewhat *primitív*,
You are obnox-i-ously dear,
Oh, unbeloved *kollektív*!
Oh, let me once more see your face!
Stretch out once more your arms to me!
Keep me no longer in disgrace!
Henceforth I'm all yours, don't you see?!

WHO WE ARE

'It's amazing,' said the Teacher. 'We've got more uninhabited land than any other country in the world and yet we keep trying to get into Europe which is crowded enough without us, and into South America and Africa. We try to get into places which are already inhabited and which have evolved a life-style. Does that not tell you anything? It's worth thinking about. The same thing happens with our philosophy. There are levels of language which have been absolutely unexplored, a study of which would allow us to construct a marvellous "dialectical logic" which would meet all the requirements of science and at the same time literally fulfil all Their idiotic ideals. And what do They do? They have to get into an area long ago worked over and settled – formal logic. Take, for instance, the attitude of the people to the Party, the Government, the Leaders, etc. Do the people abuse them? Yes, they do. Does that mean that the people don't love them? No, it doesn't. Do the people praise them? Yes, they do. Does that mean that the people love them? No, it doesn't. Formal logic is inapplicable here. Inapplicable in the sense that this is not its sphere. Its sphere is the definition of the properties of linguistic expressions and not the properties of some concrete aspect of extra-linguistic reality. There are lots of other examples of the type I've just mentioned. When parents scold their children they don't stop loving them. When colleagues praise each other they can still hate each other at the same time. In real life there are many cases of objects possessing simultaneously features which are mutually exclusive. For instance, a human being can love and hate another human being at the same time. If you start digging around in this area you'll find that there is a lot to go at. In the case of such mutually exclusive features or tendencies it is not true to say that the presence of the one excludes the other. I swear that I could put together a "dialectical logic" for Them in a couple of years which would be enormously successful. But They would rather put up with my criticisms of Their "dialectical logic" than with my positive suggestions for improving it. Again we have to ask why that is the case. The answer is that we can only live off the creative juices of others. We are not a creative society but a parasitical one. We are a cancerous growth on the body of civilisation. And that is dreadful. And it's extremely offensive that hardly anyone notices this. The lack of thought given to this in the West is amazing.'

'I was in the army before the war began,' said Dobronravov. 'And, curiously enough, all our officers were concerned for our well-being. I've got no complaint to make about any single individual. And still, it was more your actual nightmare than military service. And it's impossible to locate the source of this nightmare. For instance, we'd do our drill marching in frost and rain. They'd get us up in the middle of the night to dig stupid holes. We'd do twenty-five kilometre forced marches with a full pack. And the main thing was, there was never any rhyme or reason to it. Everyone ended up trying to duck out of things and never to get involved. The result was that instead of being hardened up and in a good state of battle-readiness, we entered the war absolutely shagged out and no good for anything. And that's the essence of our system. It puts pressure on people against their will and so they do shoddy work, pull the wool and skive as a means of self-defence. And pressurise each other.'

'In two words,' said the Teacher, 'the essence of our society boils down to this: 1) the creation and reproduction of individuals who are defenceless, and the destruction of individuals who are in themselves of any significance; 2) the collective, society, defends these defenceless individuals who in turn surrender all means of defence to particular organs; 3) these means of defence become the instruments of oppression. Anyone in our society who dares to assert his own individual personality, his "ego", is like someone beyond the Arctic Circle who finds himself naked and five hundred kilometres from the nearest habitation.'

IDEAS

Moscow is, of course, a dull and dismal city. But I love to wander along its streets. I don't give a toss for the architecture, the historical monuments or the beauties of nature. It's the blocks of flats, the people, cars, asphalt that count. Usually I wander around alone. Thinking. About nothing in particular.

'Everyone thinks that our society is invulnerable and indestructible,' I will think to myself. 'But is it in fact so invulnerable and indestructible?'

'Of course not,' I reply to myself. 'They say that elephants are terrified of mice and that you can kill a lion with a needle. Stick it in a nerve and that's that.'

'True. But where is that vulnerable nerve in our society and what do we stick into it?'

'That's a simple problem. The nerve is the leaders and their fat-cat stooges and the needle is terror. As long as our leaders and their toadies feel safe there will be no radical changes in our system. We have to make them shiver in their shoes. There is no Last Day of Judgment. We shall have to institute our own.'

'Just try getting near them!'

'You mustn't overstate the difficulties. If you really want to, you can get to any of them, even the Gen Sec. It takes a bit of intelligence, of course. And modern science and technology. Chemistry, physics . . . Poisons, bacteria, gases . . . They've been making use of these means for a long time now. Why not turn them against them? Moreover, one could start from below – with the district leadership. And then gradually work one's way up through the regional, municipal and republican levels right up to the central leadership itself. Experience would accumulate, and the psychological effect would be powerful: each one of them, the swine, would be waiting for it to be his turn.'

'Why do you want that, anyway? What good would it do?'

'I want Them to have a hard time. Let Them live in fear. The fear that there will be a day of reckoning is the only thing that will restrain people.'

'But in our conditions terror too has to be well thought out and organised. Taking pot-luck on your own won't get you very far.'

'Of course. But to start with, you have to get people interested in this kind of thing. And for that to happen you have to have some kind of example worth imitating. *Somebody* has to start things off.'

'Well OK, have a go then. You've got all the information you need. You'll die, of course. But, on the other hand, you will perform an act of historical significance.'

'What does history matter to you?'

'Well, what else is worth anything, apart from history? To be a human being means to create history.'

'Just don't be in a rush. You have to make a good start. A bad beginning can compromise the whole idea of terror.'

'As far as that goes, I'm afraid you've already missed the boat. Do you remember that business about the explosion in the underground? These idiots couldn't have thought up anything less likely to fit the bill.'

'And supposing it was an act of provocation on the part of the KGB? Suppose they set it up to put pressure on the dissidents and to discredit the whole idea of terror. As a kind of prophylactic measure, so to speak.'

'That's hardly likely. That explosion didn't exactly make many waves. We have to come up with something extremely effective, something that will be impossible to hush up. That's not something the KGB is capable of.'

'The KGB is capable of anything.'

'So much the better. We can have a go at using them. Anyway, what makes you think that the KGB is not interested in terrorism? Our high-ups need terror, too.'

'Yes. But not terror of the dangerous and uncontrollable kind. The kind of terror I'm thinking of ought to be dangerous and absolutely beyond the control of anyone except the terrorists themselves.'

A TALK WITH THE SECRETARY OF
THE PARTY BUREAU

The talk with the secretary was somewhat confused and is impossible to reproduce. On the other hand it did bring results. I agreed to be transferred to any other section which would treat me better than the one I was in already, battling on the 'right flank' of socialist competition for the fulfilment of this and the overfulfilment of that. The secretary asked whether I was Jewish. I said that I was a direct descendant of Yuri Dolgoruky on my mother's side. The secretary asked whether Smirnyashchev, Zaitsev, Sazonov and Kaplan were Jews. I said that I hadn't seen them without their trousers. Nor wanted to. Judging by his surname Zaitsev was clearly Jewish. The secretary said that he didn't like these 'liberals' either. I advised the secretary to look at the personal files of the people mentioned in the personnel department. He said that he had looked at them already. But according to their questionnaires they're always Russian and then before you know it they're in Israel and engaged in anti-Soviet propaganda. I said that Israel was merely a pretext and a means for engaging in anti-semitic behaviour and he replied that, nevertheless, there was such a thing as international zionism and that emigration represented a 'brain-drain'. I left the secretary's office feeling shat upon. There is nothing worse than to be taken by dregs like him for someone of like mind. What did he see in me which gave him grounds for supposing that I was one of his kind? After all, Smirnyashchev and Sazonov are more like him than I am.

HOPES

The talk I had with Tvarzhinskaya came completely out of the blue. It turned out that I had been the subject of discussion at a Party meeting within their department and that they had decided to ask that I should be transferred to them. They had decided that the atmosphere in their collective was healthier and that they would re-educate me. I agreed to be transferred to Tvarzhinskaya's department, but only on certain conditions. Two days off a week for work in the library. Only scientific-technical work to start with – principally translations from English and German. Once I got into the way of things I would work on the subject of 'Logic and anti-communism'. From two angles: 1) the use by anti-communists of logic for their own ends; 2) genuine logic (dialectical?) against anti-communism. Tvarzhinskaya was delighted. Moreover, I let drop the idea that people in the department of logic were underestimating the ideological struggle being waged at the moment, that they themselves had succumbed to positivism but had tried to shift the blame on to the Teacher and myself. Tvarzhinskaya's eyes sparkled with anger as she listened to me. I found it all very amusing. It would take them about five months to carry out the transfer (and it still might not come off – Smirnyashchev might protest. He doesn't want to let me out of his control since he's still hoping for something). By that time it'll be the summer break. It'll take me a couple of years to get the hang of things in the department. All in all, I've got a chance of being able to swing the lead for about three years. Tvarzhinskaya has promised to give me a twenty-five rouble salary increase right from the start. You can do something with that! I must start spreading rumours about my transfer. That's the way life goes with us all the time. You can never determine what's a blessing and what isn't.

PROSPECTS

As we approached the hotel a lad of my age and appearance came bursting out of it with two young girls. He hailed a taxi.

'Hey, you mochalki,' he shouted to the girls, 'hit the kibitka.' He himself sat in front with the driver. 'OK, vodila,' he said, 'take us to the beard.' The driver laughed quietly and the car drove off.

'What was all that about?' said Himself.

'It's very simple,' I said. 'They've gone off to Theatre Square to the Marx monument. Nowadays it's a meeting place for black-marketeers, prostitutes and drug addicts. Can you feel the generation gap? Here have I just been telling you that I'm rich today and that therefore I can take you off to a restaurant. And you were as excited as a little boy who's just been promised a pop-gun. A boy of your generation, of course. Whereas, for us, a restaurant is nothing, even although we never go into one. And even a real gun doesn't awaken in us any particular feelings.'

'Nevertheless, there's one thing we still have in common,' He said. 'We've still got that law in common which your Neighbour expresses in such poetic form:

> Have a go at your neighbour,
> Make those below do the labour,
> And yourself, if you can,
> Try and become the top man.

What do you think?'

But the Poet didn't answer. He was out of sorts: his teeth were aching. But he's got nobody to blame but himself. Certain modes of social intercourse and the KGB have got nothing to do with it. His teeth were perfectly all right. But a mate of his turned out to have some influence in a private polyclinic and it would have been a shame not to make use of it. When the dentist was giving the Poet a check-up he discovered a minor defect in one tooth and decided to get rid of it by using the newest ultra-sonic

135

methods. The Poet, of course, could not resist this and agreed. And he hardly had time to open his mouth before two perfectly healthy teeth literally evaporated, leaving only the roots.

We went into the restaurant which was absolutely full to overflowing. And again a difference between the generations was noticeable. 'Let's get out of here,' said Himself. 'We'll get a few bottles, two hundred grams of sausage and cheese and we'll go to your place or the Teacher's. Or behind a fence. Here you'll have to wait for two hours and pay three times the price.' The Poet walked silently behind me. Having given up on his own generation and despising the older generation he was putting all his hopes on the younger generation. And he was right. When he saw my beard and miserable trousers a waiter signalled to us from the middle of the room and we were given a splendid table.

'And so, my friends,' I said, raising my glass, 'I am about to start making a career for myself. The department of the criticism of anti-communism has taken me under its wing. That means that within a year I shall again join that happy band of people waiting to get on to the waiting-list for getting on to the waiting-list for membership of the CPSU, and a year after that I'll be a candidate of philosophistry, and then . . . Whew, that's enough! My head is beginning to spin from such a meteoric rise into the social stratosphere. But I shan't abandon you if you don't abandon me. And we shall see what we shall see . . .'

PART TWO

In Defence of
Impure Reason

SIXTY YEARS IN THE HEET OF BATTLE

Although it is impossible to reverse the course of history there is no need to be pessimistic on that account since history is going in exactly the right direction, even without being reversed. And if you really want the return of all the old abominations of the past, just have a little patience and you'll be witness to new abominations which, perhaps, will be even more abominable than the old abominations. Such was the tenor of the notes written by an old stalinist shyster, timed to coincide with the sixtieth anniversary of the Great October Socialist Revolution and for that reason entitled 'Sixty Years in the Heet of Battle'. The shyster author sent the notes to the Central Committee of the CPSU. They were sent on from there to the Presidium of the Academy of Sciences and from the Presidium to the Institute of Ideology so that an appropriate response could be worked out. The Academic Registrar of the Institute leafed through them without taking anything in and summoned JRF.

'Hee-hee-hee,' he said, 'we've got to produce an opinion on these papers. The author, of course, is a nutter, a dyed-in-the-wool stalinist. But you'll have to be a little tolerant. He's an old Party member and held various posts. And anyway, this is not the time to have a go at him, just in case etc, etc. Try and be as understanding as you can.'

'Got you,' said JRF, 'but I want you to let the Department and Personnel know that I am carrying out an important assignment. Just so they don't, etc, etc.'

'That goes without saying' said the Registrar. 'But not a word to anyone about the content of the manuscript! It's classified.'

THE BEGINNING OF THE ROAD

After leaving the Academic Registrar, JRF looked in on Personnel and said that he was going off to the Presidium of the Academy of Sciences and that they would be getting the corresponding written instructions to that effect from the administration in a few minutes. The Deputy Director of Personnel (the Director herself had taken time off to go and see about some female complaint) was about to open her mouth and deliver herself of some piece of vituperation but then thought better of it, just in case. You could never tell with these 'geniuses', she thought to herself. One minute they were riff-raff and before you knew where you were they were assistants to the high-ups. She'd have to watch that bearded twerp didn't squeeze her out.

Next JRF spent a few minutes on the upper landing, smoking and listening to the conversation of the best people in the Institute – Smirnyashchev, Kachurin, Tormoshilkina, Bulyga. The best people were discussing the award to Leonid Ilich of the Order of Victory for his services in a war which had finished over thirty years ago. Kachurin made a meal out of telling them about Brezhnev's outstanding exploits which he'd found out about in a recently published biography of Brezhnev and in his memoirs which had been published in *New Time* and in all the newspapers. Tormoshilkina swore on her honour that Brezhnev had written his memoirs himself, that they constituted an important literary event and that if Leonid Ilich were to be awarded the Lenin Prize for literature, it would be quite justified, since from a literary point of view they were better than . . .

JRF didn't bother to listen to any more of Tormoshilkina's speech. On the lower landing he bumped into Kirusik who had only just heard a sensational piece of news and was rushing to tell it to Tormoshilkina and all the best people in the Institute. The lower landing was also full of people. They were having a good laugh about Brezhnev's Order of Victory and about his memoirs. Someone said that 'They' up 'There' must have gone round the bend. Someone else said that all he had to do now was stick a ring through his nose and dangle a couple of tin cans from his ears. Or declare himself tsar. Or better, emperor, for 'tsar' conflicted with marxism-leninism but 'emperor' didn't. Someone else said that These Cretins would almost certainly award him the Lenin Prize for literature. That would be good for a laugh! The Teacher presented the problem of what would be better – an old Brezhnev or a new Stalin? Dobronravov said that old Brezhnev was a new Stalin and if that sounded odd one should remember the old story about history repeating itself first as tragedy and then as farce. Kachurin, who was trying to join in on both landings at once, said that he did not agree. Dobronravov told an 'Armenian radio' joke. Armenian Radio asks whether a tiger could swallow Brezhnev. Yes, comes the answer, it could, but after that it would shit medals for three days. The Teacher told a joke about Brezhnev's role in the war. Zhukov presented Stalin with the plan of an immense operation involving the forces on three fronts. 'Very good,' said Stalin, 'but get some tips from Colonel Brezhnev.' After joining in the laughter JRF looked in at the Department to tell the secretary that he was off to the Presidium of the Academy of Sciences and perhaps also to the Central Committee of the CPSU. The secretary thought the last word sounded like KGB and for the first time in many years looked at JRF's droopy back as he left the office with respect. Actually, he's quite a handsome lad, she thought to herself. A bit slovenly. And too hairy. But that was in fashion now.

A CONVERSATION

JRF strolled without any particular destination in mind in the direction of the Arbat. On Arbat Square he caught up with someone he knew in the editorial office of *Questions of Ideology* who was making his way to the House of Journalists to 'have a bite to eat and so forth'. Since he was allowed to bring one guest he tempted JRF with the House of Journalists standard main course, 'filet Suvorov', which the latter could not resist, even though it meant that he would have to go hungry for the next three days. But if he could have foreseen how this trip to the HJ would pan out for him quite apart from that, he would . . . No, he would still not have been able to resist. After all, even Brezhnev couldn't resist making his regular two-hour speech although he knew in advance that he would be incapable after fifteen minutes of pronouncing any single word intelligibly. The filet, of course, turned out to be a figment of his acquaintance's imagination. On the other hand there was vodka, and with vodka any old rubbish will go down just as well as that first-class filet which disappeared long before the sixtieth anniversary of the Great, etc, Revolution.

Later on JRF said that they had palmed off on him an idiotic manuscript and demanded that he do a review of it for the Central Committee. 'Here it is,' he said. 'Only, keep it under your hat. The manuscript is classified.' The Acquaintance leafed through it and said that he knew that manuscript, that there was nothing secret in it, that the author had brought it to him in the office and asked him to publish excerpts from it, that it was the typical garbage of a stalinist dreg, that . . . 'In short, throw this junk in the dustbin. Incidentally, the same author later brought an article containing denunciations of Petin. And genuine documents. Does the name Stanis mean anything to you? He was a major marxist philosopher. He was arrested and shot after a denunciation by Petin. And Petin then appropriated his work. Stanis's widow survived and was rehabilitated. By some miracle she had managed to preserve Stanis's manuscripts and the galley-proofs of his book with his corrections. And this book was later published as a book of Petin's. And many of Petin's articles were in fact Stanis's. This is absolutely beyond dispute. The widow tried to take Petin to court but they wouldn't let her. A special commission of enquiry was set up at the journal to investigate the matter. Everything was confirmed. Moreover, it turned out that Stanis was not the only one to have been so treated by Petin – there were many others. It was established that Kanareikin, too, had been up to similar tricks. And Fedkin. In short, the whole affair was hushed up, all the documents went off to the Central Committee, our author disappeared somewhere, the widow died, all her papers disappeared.'

JRF said that it was possible to demonstrate convincingly that at least a score of different authors had written Petin's publications. As far as could be judged, however, everything attributed to Stalin had been written by one author. Certainly his post-revolutionary stuff. And if his pre-revolutionary stuff had been written by someone else, it had still been edited after the revolution by the same author. Moreover, this author had clearly taken no part in the composition of the writings of Petin, Kanareikin, Fedkin and others. And yet it was supposed to be an accepted fact that Petin had organised all Stalin's philosophical and general theoretical writings and similar sections in other works. What could one make of that?

The Acquaintance said that the riddle was insoluble. In all probability the real authors of Stalin's works had disappeared and we would never learn anything about them. It was a fact that Petin, Fedkin, Kanareikin and other leading lights had been the disseminators of stalinism in ideology. But the extent to which they had participated in the production of Stalin's publications was unknown. In short it was now impossible to establish the source of Stalin's ideological revolution and from now on and for ever more it would be closely tied to the name of Stalin.

JRF wondered about possible borrowings from Trotsky, and particularly Bukharin. The Acquaintance said that was nonsense. 'Have you read their works? No? Well, I've studied them in depth. Trotsky, Bukharin and the whole writing fraternity of those times were a phenomenon of a qualitatively different nature. They were too intelligent, cultured and educated (although, between ourselves, they were not in fact as intelligent and educated as they appeared) to write Stalin's "chef d'oeuvres". It's like this, you see. An artist who has graduated from the Academy of Arts is incapable of creating genuine works of primitivism, and similarly a philosopher steeped in the theory of philosophy is incapable of writing the awe-inspiring rubbish which counts as the writings of Stalin.'

CONSEQUENCES

They paid the waitress. Then they repaired to a beer bar and continued their conversation there. Then they visited another den of iniquity. Then another. And another. JRF came to on his ottoman. Dressed, but looking perfectly respectable and fit to appear in public. When he tried to remember the events of the day before, he got as far as the point where he and the Acquaintance were gathering up the pages of the manuscript which had scattered all over the dirty pavement. The rest was a complete blank. After searching his room and failing to find the manuscript, JRF decided that the Acquaintance had probably put it in his briefcase – he had had a briefcase with him and it had been half empty! But the Acquaintance told him that JRF had the manuscript in his possession when they parted. If you could still call it that, given the mess it was in!

JRF sadly made his way home. He walked past the statue of Marx which had been roundly shat upon by the pigeons. Iron Felix looked down at him sternly from his five-storey height. 'Well, now, you scoundrel, you've done it this time,' said Iron Felix, speaking for some reason in a Stalin accent with a Lenin twang. 'This is not just your quotations for Petin or a lesson plan for your propaganda circle. There'll be a major row! This involves the interests of the Academy of Science and the Central Committee. They might quite simply get rid of you.'

At home JRF lay down on the ottoman (again still fully dressed since it was in work time) and began to weep bitterly. 'Oh, what an unfortunate non-Party junior research fellow without a higher degree I am,' he whispered into his pillow in its dirty pillow-case. 'Everyone has forsaken me and nobody wants anything to do with me! And there's no one to help me get myself out of this calamity which has befallen me!'

'What do you mean, no one?' said Himself, taking offence. 'You're not all that alone. And the situation isn't all that hopeless.'

144

'That's right,' shouted Marx, Lenin, Stalin and Beria cheerfully. 'We'll help you.'

'You could easily scratch out some impenetrable nonsense and pass it off as the lost manuscript,' said Himself. 'No one is going to read it, anyway. And no one is going to check up on you. Write a report on it to the effect that on the one hand one can blah-blah, but on the other, blah-blah, as well, so that in conclusion, blah-blah, and the thing's done and dusted. Got it?'

'Get up, old chap, and stop snivelling,' cried Marx, Lenin and Stalin, 'You can consult us any time. Sit down and start scribbling!'

'Only, before you do,' said Beria, 'we'll go and celebrate the commencement of your creative activity. I know for a fact that, sober, you won't be capable of squeezing out even a page. Forward march!'

ON RELIGION

People used to think that our path through life was mapped out in Heaven. And generally speaking they weren't all that wrong. The only mistake they made was to imagine that Heaven is in the sky. In reality it is situated in the Lubyanka and its environs. If the archives of the Lubyanka were ever opened to the general public, even God Himself would be shaken by the amount of information they contain. What's it all for? Just in case. So that citizens have the feeling that not one single step of theirs has escaped the attention of the Party and the Government, as represented by the organs of State Security, and that everything that happens does so with the latter's knowledge and consent. Suppose something happens involving JRF, for instance, or the Teacher. And a stern investigator from the KGB asks them what they had been chatting about on such and such an occasion. 'I don't remember,' JRF would say, 'because I was drunk.' 'I don't remember', the Teacher would say, 'because I wasn't completely sober.' 'Well, that doesn't matter,' the investigator would say calmly, 'I'll remind you. Listen to this!'

'What you need to come to grips with religion,' said the

Teacher on that occasion, 'is a scientific way of thinking. There is nothing paradoxical about that. It simply reflects the particular nature of the times we live in. And of the problem. The point is, the chief problem in religion in our time is not the past history of religion but the conception of religion in a modern anti-religious society. I emphasise that: not the resuscitation of old religions but the emergence of some sort of religiosity in barren surrounds. This is an abstraction, of course: we ought to take it for granted that nothing remains of religions of the past and then determine what is required for religiosity to re-appear. But this abstraction corresponds to the actual situation as it exists at the moment. The old religions are doomed since they are inadequate for the conditions of our society. Genuine piety arises not out of old religions but from quite different sources. In this context there is no such thing as ideational heritage.'

'What's got you off on the subject of religion?' said JRF. 'As far as I remember, the word "God" has only passed your lips when you've been swearing.'

'I feel like swearing now,' said the Teacher. 'I met a so-and-so yesterday who was going on about the revival of orthodoxy. And he himself, incidentally, has been collaborating with the KGB since his university days. He was talking about the fact that many of us are now secret believers. What kind of believers are these?! They believe in secret but behave in their everyday lives as unbelievers! Is that really what religion is all about? A person who really believes always behaves in accordance with his faith. Believing in secret is deception. Besides, a real religion should raise man up to the level of God and not reduce him to the ranks of the poverty-stricken and old women.'

'How do you know what a real religion is? As far as I know you were never interested in this before.'

'Nonsense. For the price of a good booze-up and a bite to eat I could dream up such a lecture on this topic that people would gasp. Essentially the matter is very simple. If you were to remove from religion its claim to explain nature, society and man (and in our scientific age that is what should be done), together with its claim to exercise a pastoral control over the spirit (a task which, in our age, is perfectly adequately handled by our ideology and propaganda), that just leaves moral doctrine. Nowadays

146

people apply the word "morality" to anything under the sun. Even the instruction not to pick your nose and disturb the social atmosphere comes into the sphere of morality. But morality in the real sense of the term is regarded as idealistic nonsense. And to morality in its real sense I give the term "religiosity". What's that? It's laughable hearing a question like that from you. You're a bright lad and should be able to think of something yourself.'

'I could, but I don't want to. Anyway, I want to know what you think.'

'I don't know what I think yet. But I can say something on the subject.'

At that moment they had just passed the statue of 'Marx in pigeon-shit' without paying it any attention and were strolling unhurriedly in the direction of Iron Felix, whom the pigeons feared and avoided. Just behind them ambled an Agent in Plain Clothes who was eavesdropping on their conversation. The Teacher, who sensed that someone was paying attention to his words purposely spoke loudly and clearly: plain clothes agents are also human, let them hear his marvellous speeches too!

'Let's begin with an example. Let's suppose that you know that this man is a murderer. Would it be a "good" act if you were to help him avoid being brought to justice? Do you find the answer difficult? There you are, then. And yet the question is trivial. This question is outside the scope of morality in the sense in which we are discussing it, i.e. it has nothing to do with religiosity. Why not? Because religiosity is not concerned with actions that come under the law. Remember: render unto Caesar the things that are Caesar's and unto God the things that are God's. If an action is permitted or forbidden by law, it is not subject to moral-religious judgment.'

'Wonderful,' said JRF. 'What happens if someone knocks the Gen Sec or even the head of the KGB itself on the head?'

When he heard that, the Plain Clothes Agent literally began to breathe down their necks, suffocating them with the reek of alcohol.

'This dreg,' said the Teacher calmly, 'started off this morning with a hair of the dog on an empty stomach, then he had a glass of beer and one of last year's sprat sandwiches and finished up with a glass of our famous Rossglavvino port – and on someone else's tab. No talent!'

'They don't,' said JRF, 'have talent for anything, and especially not for drinking. So what about my question?'

'Your question has placed me in a quandary. On the one hand, the Oth Bcc and the head of the KOD are also people, and to murder them is a sin. But even this dreg who's following us knows just what kind of people they are. But there's just the one term: people. So there are two solutions: either exclude them from the category "people" and regard them as akin to scorpions or rats, or else interpret "knock on the head" in the spirit of the ideas advanced by our liberal intelligentsia. "Knock on the head" is not the same as "murder", is it? Shall we go in?'

They had just reached a snack-bar and had automatically turned into it so that the Teacher's question was totally meaningless. The Plain Clothes Agent followed them in and joined them at the counter.

'What are you having?' asked the Teacher.

'It's all the same to me,' answered the other as if it were nothing out of the ordinary. 'You lads needn't worry, I'm not one of them. But you don't half exaggerate – it's interesting to listen to you. So, carry on. What you're saying is that "knocking" one of Them "on the head" is not a sin? Well, not long ago we were holding one of these sectarians on a charge of making an attempt on the life of . . . well, an important figure. But he categorically denied that and said that according to religion it is sinful to murder even Party and KGB bosses, or even to think of doing so. So what's the answer?'

'Very simple,' said the Teacher. 'Of course, from the religious point of view, a thought is a serious business as well. And a bad thought is a bad business. But if you thought of doing something bad and then did something good, then your bad thought doesn't count. For example, if you thought of murdering a high-up, that's evil. But if, instead of murdering him, you simply "knocked him on the head", then that's good.'

'You're pretty sharp,' said the Agent. 'You're probably a professor. No? That's strange. Personally, I'd make you an academician. Same again?'

They had the same again. And again. All sorts of doubtful characters gathered round their part of the counter. And they no longer paid any attention to the basic parameters of conversation – time, setting, company.

'Life is short,' the Teacher shouted. 'The length of one's life does not correspond to the number of years one has lived . . .'

'They palmed off on me some shyster's manuscript,' mumbled JRF in the Agent's ear, 'and guess what I did with it . . . Know what I mean? No? Well, you're a fool! . . .'

CONFESSION

'Tell me, what is it that constitutes the drama in your life?'

'The fact that, despite everything, I still accept this social order, regard it as irreversible and capable of improvement. If I had even one tenth of your advantages, I'd be happy.'

'What advantages are you talking about?!'

'For instance, you have a room of your own. Sheets. Dirty ones, it's true. But the social order is not to blame for that. You listen to jokes and tell them yourself and none of your friends has been locked up for that yet. You listen to foreign radio stations and read forbidden books. You're non-Party, yet work in an ideological centre. Sometimes you drink cognac and nibble the odd kebab. Your women are pretty decent. You're wearing a foreign jacket, trousers and boots. You're not exactly over-whelmed with social work, are you? How much time do you spend at meetings? Not a lot. You're fed up with paranoiac Smirnyashchev and that cretin Barabanov? Don't exaggerate! You can put up with them. And you can ignore them. What more do you want? You're not short of someone to talk to. There's the Teacher, Shubin, Dobronravov, the Poet . . . What more do you need? If someone had told us in our day that this is what we could look forward to, we would have laughed and, of course, not believed them.'

'So what do we deduce from that?'

'That many things that we regard at the moment as impossible will in time become commonplace.'

'I don't think so. It looks more like we're in for a clamp-down.'

'We are. And it'll soon be much worse. But after that it'll get better just the same. And even when it's worse there'll still be an improvement on some level.'

'If that's the case, what's all the fuss about?'

'The fact that it'll be better.'

'I don't understand.'

'I don't either, but I have the feeling that that's what it boils down to. It'll be better, but the most important thing will be missing. Something which has been lost for ever. What exactly? I don't know. I spend all my time thinking about this. Sometimes I think that I'm just about to get hold of that "something". But it disappears without trace. You see, I don't have any rational arguments against our social order. I can't suggest anything better. I don't feel hatred for it, or even dislike. It is my own, native to me, and I will never renounce it. And yet, it doesn't have that very important something which I would like to detect in it. And therefore I'm sad. Parents must sometimes look the same way at their beloved only child when that child has for some reason become alien to them.'

'I think I see what you mean. But let's look for this "something" together. I miss it too, sometimes. That's why I live in a constant state of apprehension. As if I have lost, or am about to lose, something very dear to me.'

'That's right. It's like that. But words can't express it.'

'At the end of our first year at university, we were sent to work on a collective farm during the summer. At first I didn't like it at all. We had to sleep where we could – in the field itself, on hay, sometimes directly on the wet ground. The food was rubbish. And we had to put in ten or twelve hours a day. Till our blisters bled. But I soon got into the way of it. And I began to work flat out. I began to derive pleasure from the fact that I was working well, better than many others, and that this was noticed and appreciated. And I put even more into it. And I was as happy as I could be. There was an intimacy in our relations which was new to me. We would talk until long past midnight. And what conversations we used to have! . . . And do you know, in those moments I believed in the communist paradise. And then the illusion was shattered. Because of a trifling little incident. There was a meeting of the brigade. Instead of including my name on the list of the best workers the brigadier included his friend's, who was a real waster. No one said a word. Later on the komsomol organiser "worked over" some girl who had misbehaved in some way. Again no one said a word. The next day I worked any old how. And there were no more conversations like we'd had. And the intimacy had gone.'

'I understand what you mean. Communism is supposed to bring out the best in people, arouse their purest feelings. It does that, but only fleetingly, only for a moment. And you spend the rest of your life yearning for that moment. But it never returns.'

NOSTALGIA OF THE PARTY SECRETARY

A cloak of darkness has descended
And night-time o'er the city creeps.
With snout in pillow, paunch distended,
The Party Secretary sleeps.
Beside him's squeezed his wife obese,
They snore together as a team,
Not only that, but, if you please,
They share the same recurrent dream:
The ranks of delegates arise,
The Presidium too, and quite serene,
A marble Stalin, thrice life-size,
Looks down with Ilich on the scene.
The thunder of applause dies down,
And when his nervous shakes have gone,
There mounts the stage, his stature grown,
New General Leader Number One.
He moves his eyebrows up a bit,
Then lifts an arm above his head,
And getting everything arse o'er tit,
He indicates the way ahead:
    'The rime is tipe
    To gep a grit
    On all who gripe
    At t' Leadershit.'

STAIRCASE LANDINGS

There are two staircase landings in the Institute, the upper landing and the lower landing. Although the membership of the group of colleagues who chat there changes according to circumstances, in the main it tends to be stable. The most educated, talented and progressive individuals in the Institute, headed by Tormoshilkina and Soloveichikov, dominate the upper landing. The lower landing is dominated by unprincipled, hopeless, illiterate word-merchants like Dobronravov and the Teacher. And although the conversations are generally about the same topics, there is still a significant difference in tone, detected by everyone but difficult to define exactly.

'Who would have thought that even in N. they would build a brand new underground,' says Tormoshilkina solemnly on the upper landing. 'Progress is unarguably being made and only madmen and spiteful ill-wishers can suppose otherwise.'

'Did you hear,' says Dobronravov on the lower landing, 'that the idiots have even built an underground in N. although the alcoholics can crawl on all fours from one end of the town to the other in half an hour.'

'And the most interesting thing,' adds the Teacher, 'is that it's only one station long.'

'That's senseless,' says Subbotin, who has just come from the upper landing and is thus deeply conscious of the progress of society.

'Why senseless?' says Dobronravov. 'It's important for the accounts: the workers of yet another town have received a comfortable and cheap means of transport. And it's nice to go down on the escalator, have a look at an underground marble palace and then go up again. And all for five kopecks. Not like in the West.'

'Practitioners of art', intones Soloveichikov solemnly on the upper landing, 'reveal to ordinary mortals how the world is in reality. Take Monet, for example. Or is it Manet? Anyway, it doesn't matter. The inhabitants of London used to think that

152

their fogs were grey. And then along comes Monet . . . no, Manet . . . Anyway, it doesn't matter. And he depicted a London fog as being violet. And since then . . .'

'Go into the Manezh*,' says the Teacher on the lower landing, 'and you'll split your sides laughing. There's an exhibition of young talent from the Moscow Artists' Union. Especially touching is the work of one Ivano-Laptev. He's painted a violet goat. The cretin imagined that humanity will now see grey goats and black goats as violet rather in the way that London fogs began to be perceived as violet after . . .'

'I visited Munich not long ago,' announces Tormoshilkina on the upper landing. 'You have to give the Germans their due. What order they maintain! We could even learn something from the way their dogs behave.'

'If you want to know the character of a people,' says Dobronravov, 'study the dogs that people keeps. This is a trite point and yet it never fails to surprise you. German dogs, for instance, are never puppies. They behave like well-to-do old age pensioners from the very word go. The Germans have special places where dogs are allowed to behave as they like, i.e. like swine. They take their dogs there and then say to them: now act like swine. And the dogs begin to get up to tricks of a kind which even our mongrels, accustomed as they are to swinish behaviour, aren't capable. It's the same with the Germans themselves. If they are allowed to act like swine they're even more swinish than your actual Ivan.'

'I can add one curious detail to the statement of the previous speaker,' said the Teacher. 'Two dogs meet in Germany. One is large and vicious, the other small and inoffensive. But the small one belongs to a high-up official and the large one to a much less important one. Such things can happen. And despite the laws of biology the large dog wags its tail in front of the other one and walks in its presence on its hind paws.'

'What ignorance,' said Subbotin indignantly. 'You've been to university, after all, and not just any old one, but Moscow University, awarded the Order of Lenin and the Order of the

---

* The Teacher is referring to a large exhibition hall on Manezh Square in the centre of Moscow. (*Translator's note*)

Red Banner of Labour and named after M. V. Lomonosov. One might have expected you to know . . .'

A DISCUSSION ABOUT THE PARTY

'Our whole society,' said Stalin, 'is an extended party. So whether you join the Party or not doesn't matter to the Party since you're already an informal (or unregistered) member of it. It only matters to you. If you don't join the Party you won't become a candidate of philosophical science, you won't be able to publish a monograph, you won't get a senior staff post, you won't get a rise in salary, you won't get three library days per week, you won't be allowed to get a flat of your own in a co-operative. Right?'

'Right,' said JRF.

'Don't listen to him,' said Lenin. 'He vulgarises everything he touches.'

'I am merely taking the covers off and revealing the essence,' said Stalin. 'And if the essence itself is vulgar, that's not my fault. Our lad here wants to join the Party and we have to tell him the truth. So, any talk about how a party reflects the interests of its class can refer to anything you like, but not to our Party. Our Party has always pursued only its own aims and expressed only its own interests.'

'Stalin is right,' said Beria. 'Look who joined the Party earlier: renegades, people who felt they had a raw deal, adventurers, people who were unsuccessful, people who were psychologically unstable, people who were ambitious, vermin like that. It was only afterwards that they were "ennobled".'

'Don't exaggerate,' said Lenin. 'There were good people as well.'

'There might have been once,' said Beria. 'Where are they now?'

'And are our present-day dissidents any better?' said Marx. 'They're also rejects . . . It's natural. It's always like that. On the other hand, nowadays it's the flower of society that joins the

Party. Our lad here's going to join, for instance. Nothing will make me believe he's only joining out of self-interest. His motives are pure. Right?'

'Right,' agreed JRF.

'Once it has seized power the Party organises society in its own image,' said Stalin. 'But certain principles will definitely be observed . . .'

'Centralisation, hierarchy, discipline from top to bottom,' interrupted Lenin.

'Secrecy,' added Beria. 'Secrecy as far as all important actions of the leaders and their way of life are concerned. And remuneration in terms of your place in the hierarchy.'

'All that's true,' said Stalin. 'That's all well-known. And unoriginal. The most important thing is conformity. Moreover, conformity not by consent but as a natural form of behaviour. Do you see what I'm getting at? And what do you need for that?'

ON NOMINATION FOR A PRIZE

For many years in succession the five volume *History of the philosophy of the peoples of the USSR,* written by a team of three hundred philosophers of all ages and nationalities in the country under the leadership of Academician Dzhopchuk was nominated for a Lenin prize. And it was rejected every time. But for different reasons. During the liberal period it was rejected because Dzhopchuk was a stalinist lackey and a dyed-in-the-wool adherent of the cult of personality, and because the first volume was full of references to Stalin. Then they reprinted that volume, minus the unfortunate references. But it was rejected again. Other competitors (Kanareikin, Fedkin, Petin) proposed that the award should not be given and that they should wait for the publication of the second part of the fifth volume. Next it was rejected on the grounds that there were too many references to Khrushchev. The volumes in question were republished with references to Khrushchev taken out and replaced by references to Brezhnev. But something unforeseen happened: one of the authors was imprisoned for his part in the Crimean Tartar affair, another for showing excessive Russian nationalism and a third was put in a mental hospital for standing up for the Baptists. It had to be postponed again. Finally there was an absolute scandal: more than ten of the authors emigrated to Israel. This was such a blow beneath the belt that Dzhopchuk, who was convinced that he had the award in his pocket, spent the next three months in hospital with a coronary. This time it was decided that the *History* should be nominated not for a Lenin prize but for a State prize. But everyone was convinced that it would be rejected again since the habit was now pretty strong and since there was a more dangerous rival in the shape of the son-in-law of the Chairman of the Council of Ministers himself, an associate member of the Academy of Sciences. It had already been decided at the top that the State prize should go to him. For the time being. He'd get his Lenin prize in a couple of years' time when he became an Academician and published his new work on the problems of government, written for him by numerous subordinates. It had already been decided that this year's Lenin prize should be awarded to Mitrofan Lukich himself for his work entitled *The Ideological Struggle in its Current Phase*, which contained his many speeches on this theme.

Although it was known in advance who would get the prizes, many other people were nominated to keep alive the idea of competition and for the sake of appearances. They nominated Tormoshilkina's book on Giordano Bruno, a book of articles edited by Suchkov and Kachurin on the principles of dialectical materialism in contemporary micro-physics, Spiridonov's monograph on the nineteenth century Chuvash thinker Ivanov, who acknowledged the primacy of matter and the changeability of nature (although not yet of society), three books by Smirnyashchev on material implication and three collections of articles on the same theme which he had edited. Everyone congratulated Tormoshilkina since she was the Institute favourite, rather in the way in which Bukharin had been the favourite of the Party in his time. Kachurin walked around with an air of having discovered at least a dozen new elementary particles. Smirnyashchev convened an unscheduled meeting of his theory seminar at which he gave a confused account of the new ideas in the views on implication in the work of the Western logicians Montgomery,

Schlapke, Jones and Rabinowitz which he hadn't read since he didn't know any foreign languages.

A group of junior colleagues who stood no chance of a prize (not even the fifty-rouble one offered by the Institute) took advantage of the festive hurly-burly to leave the Institute with the clear intention of getting drunk, for junior colleagues don't have any other intentions once they acquire the ability of having intentions at all.

THE BEGINNING OF THE ROAD

The young colleagues picked up on the way a few sub-editors from the journal *Questions of Ideology*, quickly left the environs of the Institute and gathered in a group round the corner to decide where to go to carry out the intentions which had manifested themselves. The sun was shining and they were feeling great.

'Hey, I feel great. How about going to the "Aragvi"?'

'There's a queue there, we'll have to wait two hours. And it's a bit expensive. And money's tight, as I'm sure you'll appreciate.'

'It doesn't matter about the queue. We'll wait. And we can borrow money. It's pay-day soon and we'll pay it back.'

'If we're going to borrow, we'll have to go back to the Institute, and that's risky.'

'Let's go to the "National", then.'

'The queue's no shorter there. And it's no cheaper. And they eavesdrop.'

'Where don't they eavesdrop?'

'What about the "Moskva"?'

'No chance. The Deputies have taken it over. They're having a sitting.'

'Why don't they drop dead. Was there ever a time when we didn't have deputies, delegates, official visitors, emissaries, and similar junk?'

'No, by definition. The food at the "Baku" isn't bad. Nor at "Cheremushki". And they aren't busy. Nor so expensive.'

'They're a bit far away. I suggest the "Zvezdny". It's close by. True, the food is unimaginably bad and you have to take your

157

own drink. On the other hand, there's no queue. If we slip them three roubles they'll leave us in peace.'

'Great idea! Right, I suggest we all put in three roubles. Dobronravov'll buy the starter. Naturally the Teacher will see to the booze. Listen lads! I've got a great new joke.'

THE FALL AND RISE OF BARABANOV

As the old song about Napoleon has it,

> That Fate will play around with Man
> And that she's fickle is well known.
> She'll raise him up as high as she can
> And then for ever throw him down.

That's exactly what she did to poor old Barabanov. What did for him was his unquenchable thirst for culture. He'd picked up from somewhere that some foreign writer or other had written something called *The Portrait of Dorian Gray* about some bloke and his portrait. Apparently one of them grows old and hideous and the other remains young and handsome. Which one? As a former komsomol and Party worker Barabanov had the wit to answer that one: even a child could tell you that it's a person that gets older, not a portrait! And from then on Barabanov began to pay the Institute women the following compliment: You look as young as the portrait of Dorian Gray. Those women who had heard something about the book were at first offended, but then they remembered what a cretin he was and were prepared to forgive him. But then Barabanov decided to demonstrate his brilliance and erudition at a Party meeting connected with the anniversary of the October revolution. Our Soviet power, he said, looks like the portrait of Dorian Gray. There was a deathly hush. Then people acted as if nothing out of the ordinary had happened. But a few days later Barabanov began to be summoned to the Central Committee and the KGB. The rumour of his gaffe spread. People who didn't know Barabanov attributed to it deep political significance. At a re-election meeting, Barabanov's candidature was not forwarded to the Party bureau. Petin took advantage of the opportunity to relieve Barabanov of all sorts of administrative responsibilities. Barabanov, who had taken umbrage and who still hadn't worked out the reason for the disaster which had overtaken him, began visibly to move to the left. He even went so far as to blurt out on the landing that not all dissidents are madmen and spies. After that, the Academic Council unanimously refused to renew his contract. And he was obliged to leave the Institute. As he was leaving he promised that they would have cause to remember him. And it was no empty threat. The first thing he did was to sit down and write a denunciation of all the leading members of the Institute and send it to the Central Committee, the KGB, the Presidium of the Academy of Sciences and *Pravda*. Moreover, the denunciation was well argued and well documented. In it he stated that he had collected the facts over twenty years. The Central Committee set up a special commission of enquiry to investigate the facts set out by Barabanov. Petin immediately fell 'ill' and removed himself to a sanitarium. In the Institute itself it became ominously quiet – the best time for idlers and drunkards. And Kirusik, of course.

The days passed. The pressure relaxed. People began to forget Barabanov. But then the Institute was given a new assignment by the Central Committee and people remembered that Barabanov was their major specialist on the matter. And Tvarzhinskaya with her own hand (as Barabanov himself put it later) proposed that he be brought back to the Institute and recruited to the task of preparing a monograph.

STAIRCASE LANDINGS

'If the West is so wonderful,' pontificates Tormoshilkina on the upper landing, 'and they can freely criticise their Western way of life, why then do they criticise their way of life?!!?'

'If they can campaign freely in the West for communism,' says the Teacher on the lower landing, 'what do they need communism for?'

'Right now there's inflation in the West,' pontificates Soloveikin.

'Inflation over there has now reached such monstrous proportions,' says JRF, 'that a coin won't pay for the price of that same coin.'

'Nonsense,' says Subbotin indignantly. 'You, my young bearded fellow, don't know your logic.'

A PIECE OF GOOD NEWS

'Congratulations,' said the Acquaintance, 'your shyster has snuffed it. His flat mate came into the office yesterday with a parcel of papers with a written instruction on it from the shyster that in the event of his death the parcel should be delivered to *Questions of Ideology*. What kind of papers? All sorts of rubbish. So you don't need to worry about passing any old crap off as his manuscript. Write a review, and that's that.'

'But I'm in no hurry,' said JRF. 'I've got into the way of it. I want to have a bit of fun with it. Only that's between ourselves.'

'Of course,' said the Acquaintance. 'What kind of fun?'

'More about that later,' said JRF. 'I still need about a couple of weeks.'

AND A PIECE OF BAD NEWS

People were discussing the latest broadcasts from foreign radio stations on the lower landing. Dobronravov said that a 'Workers' group' had been arrested, according to 'Voice of America', 'Deutsche Welle' and the BBC. The Teacher said that it was to be expected since there were only one or two real workers in the group and that they were all abnormal. It would be interesting to know what was going to happen to them. Would they be sent for trial?

'Hardly,' said Sazonov. 'They'll distribute them among the nut-houses.'

'That's all I need,' thought JRF to himself. 'Surely they'll not come after me? But I'm totally out of it. I've had to deal with a lot of nutters in my time. Surely I'm not supposed to be responsible for what they get up to?'

THE BEGINNING OF THE AFFAIR

A KGB official appeared in the Institute and expressed a desire to talk to the Academic Registrar. After asking a few innocuous questions (how are you? what are you working on at the moment? how are the wife and kids?), the official asked the Academic Registrar to let him know who in the Institute dealt with the letters and manuscripts of outsiders, especially the mentally disturbed. The Registrar said that normal letters and manuscripts were distributed among the various departments, but that those from the mentally ill were dealt with by one colleague in particular (it just turned out that way) who had some experience of dealing with mental patients. And he named JRF.

Having installed himself in the Director's office, the KGB operative (Op) wrote down something in his notebook and then asked for the head of personnel, Zaitsev, Smirnyashchev, Sazonov, Barabanov, Dobronravov, Tvarzhinskaya, Kachurin and many others. Naturally, in descending order of importance. But first of all he asked for JRF himself. Although all this was done in strict secrecy, the Institute soon knew all about it down to the last detail. They even knew about details that didn't exist. Kirusik quite wore herself out disseminating all the latest information and used up all the little bottles of Valocordin, Cordiovalen, Cordiamin, Validol, Solidol and Corvalan which the ladies in the Institute carried around in their handbags. The obscurantists went around sniggering spitefully. 'Now these so-and-so's have had it,' they whispered to each other, knowing exactly who was meant. 'It's high time, too. They were getting quite out of hand.' The liberals went around with clenched jaws and looking grimmer by the minute. They gathered together in little groups without speaking and sighed. 'Yes,' they would mutter from time to time, 'we're in a fine pickle now! They've gone and done it this time! These so-and-so's could ruin everything we've been trying to get off the ground. They could even get us involved, the swine!'

Zaitsev, when he found out that Op wanted to see him, immediately phoned for an ambulance and got himself taken off to hospital suffering from a sharp attack of diarrhoea. Smirnyashchev immediately had a shave, cleaned his decayed teeth and sprayed his throat with something to neutralise the smell of alcohol on his breath. Sazonov prepared a detailed report. Tvarzhinskaya put on her best dress and wore all her military and labour decorations. Barabanov changed his underwear. Dobronravov went off to the municipal quarters of the Armed Forces Volunteer Reserve. The most intelligent academic in the Institute, Doctor of Philosophistry Subbotin, went to see Op without being asked. As befits a good communist and patriot he had decided to tell everything he knew and set out his views on the matter.

THOUGHTS ON TERROR

Expressed by all, both clear and loud,
There is a rule that says it all:
No act of terror is allowed
Done by an in-di-vi-dual.
Against it we won't rail in vain.
But in the times that lie ahead
We'll have to chat, and chat again,
'Bout what will take its place instead.
But this time argument is out,
And quite objectively, what's more,
The answer is beyond all doubt:
Collective *terror is the score*.

A CONVERSATION BETWEEN OP AND JRF

OP: This is not an interrogation, but a friendly chat. We want you to help us with a very important matter. I take it you listen to Western broadcasts?

JRF: No.

OP: Very praiseworthy. The youth of today is quite degenerate enough as it is.

JRF: I don't have a radio.

OP: Are you a member of the Party?

JRF: No. But I'm preparing to become one.

OP: All the more reason, then, why you have to be absolutely open with me. The matter is very important. You can understand that yourself.

JRF: I don't understand a thing.

OP: Ha-ha-ha! That's right – I haven't told you yet what it's all about. Are you acquainted with Pyotr Ivanovich Sidorov?

JRF: Possibly. But right now the name doesn't mean anything to me. Who is he?

OP: He's a pensioner. Former officer. Mentally ill. He used to come to your Institute with manuscripts and letters allegedly exposing our defects.

JRF: Ah, that's Denouncer. Yes, I know him.

OP: What do you mean Denouncer? Is that his pseudonym? For reasons of conspiracy?

JRF: What conspiracy?! He's a nutcase! Denouncer was my nickname for him.

OP: What can you tell me about him?

JRF: Nothing in particular. Average nutcase. There's lots like him wandering around here. At first he bombarded the Institute with letters and manuscripts. Then he made an appearance himself. He came to me.

OP: Why specially to you?

JRF: Because it so happened that dealing with nutcases was more or less my official duty. He was sent to me by the Secretary for Academic Affairs.

OP: How often did you meet him?

JRF: About ten times. He really got up my nose. He used to lie in wait for me at the Institute entrance and outside my house. He even came up to my flat. Luckily I wasn't in.

OP: What did you talk about?

JRF: I don't remember exactly. In general he talked about the defects of our society, accused me of being apathetic. What does a nutcase who likes denouncing things *not* talk about?

OP: I'll be quite open with you, Sidorov is involved in an anti-Soviet affair with an organisation calling itself the 'Workers' group'. Right now he's in custody in a psychiatric hospital. He's being investigated. He might go to court. The members of the group say he was behind the foundation of the group and he himself is fingering somebody in your Institute. Judging from his description it would appear to be you.

JRF: He'd say anything, that one. I'm not daft enough myself yet to get involved in nonsense like that.

OP: Did he ever talk to you about his idea of founding a 'Workers' group'?

JRA: I didn't discuss it with him. He chattered on about something, but I didn't pay any attention to it. The only thing on my mind on those occasions was how to get rid of him.

MELANCHOLY THOUGHTS ON TERROR

Oh, writer of the previous song,
What terror do you have in mind?
I think I may have got you wrong.
Is it the good or evil kind?
Of terror there can be two brands:
Against the people – number one.
It's safe, as everyone understands,
And indispensable, even fun.
Brand number two – 'gainst autocrats,
Tsars, ministers and all that lot,
Well, that's a different thing and that's
With nasty consequences fraught.

A CONVERSATION BETWEEN OP AND SMIRNYASHCHEV

SMIRN: From a scientific point of view he's nowhere. A regular loafer and drunkard. I've been trying to straighten him out for years now. I used to try to help him with his articles to ensure that they met even the basic requirements of literacy. But nothing came of it.

OP: But he seems to know German and English and be able to read French and Italian, is that not so?

SMIRN: Yes, but what's the point of it? He doesn't read the specialist literature.

OP: What literature does he read?

SMIRN: Detective novels. He gets anti-Soviet books from somewhere or other, and enemy newspapers.

OP: How do you know?

SMIRN: I've seen it myself more than once. Sazonov can confirm it. He once left one of Trotsky's books in English on the table. Everyone in the Department will confirm that. And in general he has somehow ducked out of participating in the life of the collective.

OP: He was preparing to join the Party. That means that he was engaged in social work. I take it someone checked up on whether he's politically literate and reads the papers?

SMIRN: Of course. You couldn't get away without that here. He takes part in an advanced seminar and carries out propaganda work himself among some of our affiliated construction workers. But he does it all sluggishly somehow, without enthusiasm. Just to get by. And he's joining the Party purely out of careerist motives.

OP: I see. Who are his friends in the Institute? What does he talk about?

SMIRN: There's a whole gang of chatterboxes and loafers like him in this place whom it is high time we got rid of. Dobronravov, the Teacher. Who's that? He's a junior colleague in our Department, for some reason nicknamed 'the Teacher'. Zimin, in the department of philosophy of natural science. Makarov at *Questions of Ideology*. The alcoholic Shubin. They usually chatter about foreign broadcasts. Jokes, of course. All kinds of slander.

OP: And have you ever noticed anything odd about his behaviour?

SMIRN: Well, that's well known. Everyone knows he's a bit touched. That's why he was obliged to work with mental patients for a while. How can I put it? He'll be sitting in a meeting or at a seminar, but his thoughts will be somewhere else entirely. No, I wouldn't say that he's schizophrenic. Generally speaking he's quiet, inoffensive, never quarrels with anyone. But . . .

A CONVERSATION BETWEEN OP AND THE ACQUAINTANCE

ACQU: He's not a bad lad, of course. Likes a drink. Well, who doesn't? He's quite a lady's man. Like most blokes of his type. What do I mean? He's got a room to himself. He's got a beard. Women like him.

OP: Have you known him long? Have you had many chats with him? What kinds of things does he prefer to talk about? How does he express himself?

ACQU: He prefers to remain silent. As far as topics are concerned, I haven't noticed any preference. He'll talk about anything like the rest of us. For instance, yesterday we were talking about the queues for gold. He observed that it was strange. We complain of poverty and yet there are fights about gold. We talked about the threat of war with China.

OP: What did he have to say about that?

ACQU: I don't remember. Something about how They create a psychosis about a war with China on purpose. It's easier under that pretext to raise prices and stifle criticism. People will put up with anything as long as there's no war. Stuff like that.

OP: Have you noticed anything peculiar about his behaviour?

ACQU: In our crowd he's considered to be a bit touched. We've got used to it. In what way is he touched? Well, for instance, he just won't get around to defending his dissertation, although he's a capable lad. He publishes very little, although he writes quite well. Sometimes he has a funny way of looking at problems.

Op: You don't happen to know whether he's writing anything in secret? After all, we've practically got an epidemic of that sort of thing at the moment.

Acqu: Writing anything? Ha-ha-ha. I'll say he is! He was told to write a review of some nutter's manuscript. He's been dealing with things like that for a long time in our Institute. Anyway, he loses this manuscript. So he decides to write one himself and pass it off as the original. But the author died. He's cooking up some lark or other.

Op: This is very interesting. I would ask you to keep our conversation . . .

Acqu: Of course.

A HUM-DRUM WEEKDAY

In the morning JRF went to see the Academic Registrar and asked for another ten days or so to finish work on the manuscript. The latter agreed with evident pleasure, and indeed extended the ten days to two weeks. That put JRF on his guard a little bit, but it slipped his mind as soon as he reached the lower landing and gave the Teacher and Dobronravov the wink. They decided to leave separately and meet up near the editorial office of *Communist*.

They decided to kick off with the nearest boozer. There was no rush. They walked slowly. And talked about this and that with a similar absence of vim. The Teacher said that there had been an interesting broadcast on Deutsche Welle about the real aims of our space programme and its achievements. Dobronravov said that the aims were known in advance – military, and that our successes were always only temporary. The Americans would still end up encircling us.

'I know our system,' he continued. 'We make a feverish start, then we get into a whole lot of other things and pile up a great heap of unfinished business and over-hasty decisions. And there's one occasion where this lands us in a nasty situation. I calculate that we're on the brink of a major break-down, not only in agriculture, but in industry and the economy as a whole.'

The Teacher said that that was only the outer appearance, for our society was one which lived on the brink of crisis in principle. If we didn't have a situation like that, then things would get really bad and we would begin living on the brink of crisis, i.e. normally. Dobronravov persisted with his idea and said that reminded him of a shoddy academic who gradually amasses a wealth of misunderstanding of his subject, so that at a given point he is acting in the dark, guessing, trying not to get egg all over his face. Sometimes the result is serious failure. The Teacher asked Dobronravov how he envisaged the real failure of our system. Dobronravov said that it was when we lost the ability to think.

'Incidentally,' he said, 'what would happen if you hit Brezhnev over the head with a piece of railway line? It'd go B-A-M*. You don't think that funny? Neither do I. It was one of Kachurin's. He's a repulsive individual, incidentally. They say he's a homosexual.'

'Nonsense,' said the Teacher. 'And if it's true, that's his affair.'

'All sorts of unpleasant ideas are going through my head, my lads,' said Dobronravov when the first bottle of the usual rubbish had been drunk and they had eaten the inedible fish (fish-day!) and macaroni. 'I am frightened by the yardsticks of history and the length of its epochs. How many thousands of years did the Egyptian kingdom exist for? And the Chinese empire? How many centuries will communism last for? Life is going by and there is nothing to look forward to – neither philistine comfort nor revolutionary fervour. I'm afraid it's the same everywhere. These revolutionaries in the West are the lowest of the low, terrorists, murderers. And what about the philistines? . . . Do you think you'd be better off under a Western boss than our head of department or director? Personally I don't think so. We can still grouse about things. But start anything over there and you get it in the neck in two ticks. And it's easier for us to swing the lead.

* *BAM:* an acronym for Baikal-Amur Magistral, the new railway line joining West Siberia with the Pacific Coast. (*Translator's note*)

Over there you have to work up a bit of sweat. And there's risk involved. We live without any risk. Without prospects. But without the risk of losing anything. It's sad. Shall we have the same again?'

A surprise was waiting for JRF when he got home: a letter. The letter had been slipped under the door and JRF had not immediately noticed it. 'A letter,' he thought in surprise, for it had been a long time since he had had any letters. Had he ever had them? There had been two or three, but he had forgotten them. Letters didn't exactly play a large part in his life. The letter was from Herself. Without a return address. She wrote that she would not be coming back any more because as far as she was concerned he had no prospects and she had to think about herself because she was tired to death of these temporary affairs, etc. He crumpled the letter up and threw it under the ottoman.

'That's a pity,' he said. 'Why is it that they always jilt me just when my better feelings begin to be aroused? Any one of them could have had me for the asking if they had just had a little more patience. Or is it that they leave me because of these better feelings of mine? Do they instinctively detect danger?'

He didn't feel like writing.

'I've had enough of this escapade,' he thought. 'I'll add some piece of nonsense just to finish it and take it in next week. There won't be any lark. I'm not in the mood. Everyone's abandoned me for some reason. Where are you then, oh friends of mine?'

'Here,' replied Himself.

'Here,' said Marx, Lenin, Stalin, Iron Felix, Beria.

'What are you all so quiet about?' he asked.

'We're sad,' they replied. 'You'd be better going to sleep and we'll send you a pleasant dream.'

THE DENOUNCER GETS A WARNING

> To think that Nature's cruel is vain.
> Denouncer, why not use your head?
> In Nature God's will doesn't reign,
> It's Natural Law that rules instead.

The classic writers dug that up,
And that's the way it's going to be.
So take it easy, button up,
Or else a sad end we foresee.

A CONVERSATION WITH THE NEIGHBOUR
AT THE KGB

NEIGH: There's always some gang meeting in his room.

OP: Who, specifically?

NEIGH: They address each other by nickname. What nicknames do they use? Marx, Lenin, Stalin, Iron Felix, Beria, Himself, Herself, the Terrorist. Honestly, I'm telling the truth. That's what they call themselves.

OP: We'll have to follow up who these people are, where they live and work.

NEIGH: All right, but . . .

OP: Don't you worry about that. What do they talk about?

NEIGH: I don't understand what they say. Although, I did hear the conversation with the Terrorist. Mind you, not all of it. They left immediately. They were talking about throwing a bomb . . .

OP: A bomb? Who at?

NEIGH: To start with, they said, at the . . .

OP: Gen Sec?

NEIGH: No. At the head of the KGB.

OP: Aha! That's very interesting. And how were they proposing to do that?

NEIGH: I didn't hear that. They had gone.

OP: Sit down here and write a detailed description of this incident. When it took place. Try to remember the conversation more exactly. Describe what the Terrorist looked like.

THE DENOUNCER GETS A SECOND WARNING

Go ahead and denounce us, you cantankerous old sod,
But get one thing straight right from the start.
Maybe Russia and Asia are not peas in a pod,
But of Europe Russia's also not part.
So denounce all the authorities' dangerous games,
Their morals deceitful and bad,
And the absence of rights with a variety of names,
And the contempt for the law that They've had.
But while you are doing so, you'd best watch your ass.
Remember, it's one of our rules,
Our camps are not just for the criminal class,
Nor our loonybins only for fools.

THE TRIP TO LEFORTOVO

A young man, whom JRF immediately identified as an agent in plain clothes, handed him a summons requiring him to appear at the investigation department of the KGB at Lefortovo on such and such a date to see such and such an investigator. JRF showed the summons in the personnel department in order to obtain permission to go. While he was sitting on the toilet (just in case) the whole Institute found out the staggering news and metaphorically froze to the spot. People he knew passed him without speaking as if they hadn't noticed him. 'The bastards,' he thought. 'What's it going to be like if something serious happens to me?'

JRF had heard a lot about the KGB Lefortovo prison. And he more or less guessed why he was being summoned there. But he had never been in that part of the town and didn't have any idea of what the prison looked like. He imagined it as a huge dark building behind a high fence with barbed wire on the top. The windows, naturally, were barred. Guards at the gates. Guards in watch-towers. But what he saw later at first cheered him up, then depressed him and finally horrified him.

He asked on the tramcar which was the best stop to get off at (it was indicated on the reverse side of the summons how to get to where he was supposed to go, but he hadn't paid any attention to it). But no one answered him. Passengers let him get to the exit by demonstratively turning away and stepping aside. 'It's as if I was pregnant or a rickety old pensioner,' he thought. 'Although they wouldn't have let a pregnant woman or a pensioner through. They regard me more as an armed bandit with whom it's better not to get involved.' Behind him someone was muttering something foul but he didn't want to listen.

Next he asked his way of various pedestrians but no one said anything that made any sense. He finally found the street he wanted himself. He saw a stone wall about three hundred yards away and decided that there was where it was. Some buildings rose up beyond the wall but for some reason there were no bars in the windows. And there was no barbed wire. And no watch-towers or guards. He began to look for the entrance, but without success. 'Surely they don't climb over the wall,' he thought. Some passerby called out to him that where he was after was over 'by that house on the left, the one with the glazed entrance'.

'How does he know where I'm going?' he thought. 'I suppose since this places deals mainly with people like me, the locals have learned to smell us a mile off, just like I can detect agents in plain clothes.'

He turned left at an ordinary block of flats and found himself in a children's playground. Little children were digging away in the sand. Old women were snoozing on benches. Two scrawny cats ran past. A flock of pigeons reluctantly made way for him. He stopped, perplexed. One of the women nodded silently in the direction of a corner of the building with 'glass' doors. He went in and handed the summons and his passport through a little window. The window closed. He sat down on a chair and immersed himself in the silence.

'What is specific to our nightmares,' spoke some voice within him, 'is the fact that at first they do not appear as they really are. In fact one can almost like them. It's only afterwards . . .'

The door opened and a man of indeterminate age and slovenly

appearance asked him to follow him. As he went through the doorway he noticed that it was metal and opened and closed automatically – probably at the press of a concealed button.

'I might have known,' he thought. 'Naturally the technological revolution couldn't pass the prison service by.'

INTERROGATION AT LEFORTOVO

Although it looked unprepossessing from the outside, from the inside the prison building turned out to be huge. The man who preceded him walked in silence, pressing button after button. Doors opened silently before them and closed just as silently behind them. He saw endlessly long corridors with rows of doors. And not one single person. It was silent everywhere. They went through one of the doors and the man introduced himself as KGB Major so-and-so. He invited JRF to sit down and make himself comfortable (?) since their conversation would be a long one. He asked whether JRF had ever been interrogated as a witness before. On getting a negative reply he began to explain tediously and at length the rights (?) and obligations of a witness, reading excerpts from legal books. Then the interrogator began to take a record of the interrogation. This procedure took two hours even though all that was necessary was to fill in a couple of pages of a questionnaire: name, address, patronymic, etc. The investigator looked at JRF's passport carefully and asked him his surname. He gave it.

'Right, so your surname is such and such?' said the investigator. 'Have I got that right? Wonderful. That's what we'll write down! Have I spelt it correctly?' And so on in that vein for two hours (preceded by an hour on rights and obligations).

After a break for lunch, they at last got down to business. 'Have you guessed,' asked the investigator, 'why you've been asked to come here? We've invited you here in connection with the case of so-and-so (he gave the Denouncer's surname) who is accused of anti-Soviet activity manifesting itself as an attempt to set up an illegal anti-Soviet organisation, the so-called "Workers' group". The first question is this: Do you know anyone of that name, and if so, when and how did you meet him?'

The interrogation lasted for eight hours. When it was finished JRF signed an undertaking not to divulge the details. 'You've been very helpful,' said the investigator. 'We'll have to have you back once more. We'll have to arrange a confrontation. And for an identification. Incidentally, this Denouncer, as you call him, is off-loading the whole thing on to you. He asserts that setting up the "Workers' group" was your idea and that he only offered the odd piece of advice.' JRF was so tired that he only shrugged at that.

'But don't you worry,' said the investigator. 'We'll sort it all out. All the best.'

SELF-DEFENCE

'Well, how did you get on?' asked Dobronravov.

'They're up to some kind of nonsense. I have the impression that They want to manufacture a case out of nothing at all. Do you remember that nutter the Denouncer? They want to make out that he's the leader of an illegal organisation.'

'Aha,' drawled Dobronravov. 'And what's that got to do with you?'

'He's off-loading the whole thing on to me, as if I were the originator of the idea,' said JRF. 'There's a so-and-so for you! He's maybe a nutter but he's still all there!'

'It's not the end of the world. It'll turn out all right,' said Dobronravov reassuringly. 'Times have changed. Let's find the Teacher and go back to my place.'

'Is it some festive occasion?' asked JRF.

'Nothing special,' said Dobronravov. 'But if you're feeling flush, a bottle of something'd come in handy.'

It turned out to be Dobronravov's birthday. Besides JRF and the Teacher, there was an army friend of Dobronravov's with his wife and daughter, and the head of the district department of the Armed Forces Volunteer Reserve and his wife. They talked about JRF's interrogation, making him feel the hero of the day, about dissidents, about our stupidities in the sphere of domestic and foreign policy, about changes in the general Party line, about prices.

'We're a swinish lot,' said the army friend. 'We came here on the underground. There were some young lads sitting opposite us. They looked intelligent. They got off at a station and we looked at where they'd been sitting. They'd slashed the seats with a razor. The vermin! Hanging's too good for them!'

'Where we are,' said the wife of the AFVR official, 'we've got neighbours opposite us. I dropped in on one occasion, and the gas was burning without anything on it and the hot water was running even although nothing was getting washed. "Turn it off," I said to the neighbour, "there's no point in wasting it." She said it didn't matter since it didn't belong to us anyway.'

'That's just the point,' said Dobronravov's wife. 'That's why we live badly because we don't look after anything. It's not ours! Whose is it, then?'

'Of course, it's not ours,' said the Teacher. 'Whose is it? Nobody's. Certainly not ours. You can understand people. It's a peculiar form of self-defence against a world that has become alien to them. It's a way of getting rid of the anger and frustration at their impotence in that world. And would things be any better if people were careful, thrifty, looked after "state property"? Hardly. I think things would be worse. The state would still carry on keeping people at this low level and all the savings would go on the same old military requirements, on these expensive international ventures, on space.'

'What's wrong with space research?' asked the AFVR official.

'Nothing,' replied the Teacher. 'It's simply that these things are all military. The more resources our state can call upon, the worse it will be for the country and the people. There's nothing surprising about that. The more resources there are, the more, and the more stupidly, they carve them up. I can demonstrate mathematically that an increase in the resources which the state can call upon, once it exceeds a certain level, leads to such an increase in unproductive expenditure that resources essential for the existence of the population are also eaten into. Do you understand me? Thus the population, when it engages in its shoddy workmanship, spoiling things, not economising, is instinctively restraining our authorities from exceeding critical bounds. If you really want to know, our salvation does not depend on a rapid increase in the level of productivity, economy and profitability (that way lies our downfall) but on a slowing down of this increase.'

'Were you being serious?' asked JRF with interest when he and the Teacher had left Dobronravov's.

'God knows,' said the Teacher. 'Perhaps I was being serious. Perhaps it was pure fiction. But if I'm honest I have to confess that even I sometimes want to smash shop-windows and slash seats on the underground.'

A CONVERSATION AT THE KGB WITH JRF'S PARENTS

OP: This is not an interrogation but a conversation. I want you to understand us correctly. We went to help your son. No, we have as yet no reason to call him to account. But I must tell you frankly that his connections and certain of his actions look rather suspicious, to say the least. Unfortunately I am not at liberty to tell you exactly what we have in mind. While the investigation is still going on . . . You understand . . .

PAR: Of course we understand. Anything that we can do, we . . .

OP: Tell me about him. About his character. His friends. His interests. About anything strange in his behaviour. In short, tell me all about him.

PAR: He was a very good boy. Good-natured. Maybe even to a fault. Vulnerable, somehow. Anyone could have a go at him. Even children three and four years younger than him would attack him. We often told him to fight back, give as good as he got, but it was no use. He was an excellent pupil. Very gifted in mathematics. He wrote good poetry. Strange behaviour? It's difficult to say. He was a dreamer. He would sometimes sit for hours without moving. His eyes were open but it was as if he didn't see you. He never quarrelled with anyone. He would just smile and shrug his shoulders. Strange behaviour? Of course. He's very capable, but doesn't want to write his thesis. Even although he's long since passed all the exams. And he's got enough publications. But for some reason he doesn't want to. Of course it's strange. Everyone's writing their thesis but him. His school friend is already a doctor. Mind you, he's a physicist. They get to be doctors quickly.

Op: Why don't you live together?

Par: That's the way he wanted it. He said it would be better for us.

Op: What did he mean by that?

Par: Nothing in particular.

Op: Why hasn't he got married yet?

Par: Nowadays many young people don't want to get married.

Op: Is he in good health?

Par: He's had girl friends. He's a handsome boy. Women find him attractive. He's very up to date. He knows two languages.

Op: That's very good. It's important that he uses these languages sensibly.

Par: What do you mean? Contact with foreigners?

Op: I'm going to ask you to sit down here and write out in detail everything we've been talking about. And try to remember anything else that has appeared strange to you about his behaviour.

A CONFERENCE AT THE KGB

'Right,' said the leader of the team of operatives, 'the connection between JRF and the "Workers' group" has been confirmed. Those members of the group that have been arrested have identified him. We now know who have been hiding behind the nicknames Terrorist, Poet and Herself. As yet we have been unable to identify Marx, Lenin, Stalin, Iron Felix, Beria and Himself. It's not impossible that Himself is the central character. We'll have to pay particular attention to . . .'

A CONVERSATION WITH JRF AT THE MALAYA LUBYANKA

Op: Are you acquainted with ... ? Where, and under what circumstance, did you meet? How often did you meet? What kind of meetings were they?

JRF: I know him. We met at the Institute. The Academic Registrar sent him to me. This man is psychically abnormal. He was interested in problems of acts of terrorism committed by an individual. That's why I nicknamed him the Terrorist. He's already done time for this in a psychiatric hospital, I think in Belye Stolby. He came to the Institute quite regularly. I used to try and avoid him but not always successfully. Once he even came to see me where I live.

Op: What did you talk about? What was he intending to do?

JRF: He was mentally ill. It's impossible to remember what we talked about. All sorts of nonsense.

Op: Is it not the case that he was intending to organise an attempt on the life of leaders of the Party and the Government?

JRF: I don't know. He's ill, after all.

Op: At one time you were ordering literature from the research library on the question of individual terrorism. Why did you need it

JRF: I had to talk to people like that, read their manuscripts, write conclusions. In that connection I had to read and skim through a colossal amount of literature of all kinds. Look at the order book in the research library and you'll see for yourself.

Op: According to our information, you discussed with the Terrorist on more than one occasion the question of making an attempt on the life of the Chairman of the KGB. Could such a discussion have taken place, even in jest?

JRF: I haven't yet taken leave of my senses.

Op: Answer the question.

JRF: There was no such discussion. Perhaps he spouted some such rubbish on one occasion when I was seeing him out. But I wasn't listening to the sense of what he was saying. I quite often tune out from what's being said in my presence. My neighbour might have heard something and embellished it.

OP: Why do you think it's your neighbour?

JRF: There's no one else it could be.

OP: We have had a talk with the Terrorist (he's being compulsorily treated). He confirms that on more than one occasion he discussed with you plans for committing terrorist acts, including plans for an attempt on the life of the Chairman of the KGB and an explosion in the Kremlin Palace of Congresses.

JRF: He's ill, I tell you. Evidence from the mentally ill is not admissible in law.

OP: We know that. That's why we're still only having a friendly chat with you. Today he's ill but tomorrow maybe he'll be pronounced as being of sound mind, just like it was with your other protégé.

JRF: Why protégé, for goodness' sake?

OP: I'm joking. Tell me, doesn't it strike you as rather strange that such a group of mental patients should have formed around you?

JRF: No. Our Institute is of a particular type. And it's besieged by schizophrenics and paranoiacs who are crazy on the subject of social problems or politics. And I had to deal with them as part of my duties.

OP: Tell me, who are Marx, Lenin, Stalin, Iron Felix, Beria?

JRF: Excuse me, I don't understand. I hope this is not an oral exam on the history and philosophy of the CPSU.

OP: Of course not. Well, that's enough for today.

ON OUR DESCENDANTS

> The years will pass, and They'll repeat
> To our descendants, like to us,
> They wouldn't have even gruel to eat,
> And, ceteris ('hem) paribus,
> A decent film they wouldn't see,
> Or apprehend ideas advanced,
> Or watch their leaders on TV,

The screen with all Their mugs enhanced;
So much would not have come to pass,
That, never mind their human rights,
They wouldn't even smell the grass,
Or see blue sky and other sights;
Or even breathe in oxygen,
Had not the Party with the folk
The Revolution made, since when
Had disappeared the tsarist yoke.
And sorting out those who dissent,
They'll make the others' spirits soar,
By telling how much worse things went
Two thousand years or more before.

THE MALAYA (MINOR) LUBYANKA AND BOLSHAYA (MAJOR) LUBYANKA

Marxism, as is well known, has three sources and three component parts. One of these sources was German classical logic, at
the forefront of which was Hegel. Hegel composed his Minor and
Major Logic, in which he set out that same dialectic which Marx
with the support of Engels stood on its head, from which position
it significantly deteriorated. When Lenin and Stalin developed
the doctrine of Marx and Engels further and brought it to life,
they created the Malaya and Bolshaya Lubyanka, in which all
the basic categories of their new doctrine had their place. The
Malaya Lubyanka is situated on Malaya Lubyanka Street which
starts immediately behind the Bolshaya Lubyanka. It houses the
Moscow administration of the Bolshaya Lubyanka. Where the
thousands of its other buildings are situated, no one as yet knows.
These thousands of buildings, including the Malaya Lubyanka,
are dispersed throughout the whole of Moscow and its environs.
Only the main building of the Bolshaya Lubyanka is situated in
Dzerzhinsky Square, which, despite our temporary superiority in
space and permanent difficulties with our food supply, people
persist in calling the Lubyanka. The relations which exist
between the Malaya and Bolshaya Lubyanka of Lenin and Stalin
are analogous to those existing between Hegel's Minor and
Major Logic. The difference is that whereas in the case of Hegel

they stood at the head, in the case of Lenin and Stalin they stand firmly on their feet.

After the Terrorist had confessed to everything and named JRF as the initiator, source of inspiration and director of the planned attempt on the life of the KGB chief, he was transferred to Sychevka, a KGB psychiatric prison, and JRF's dossier was transferred to the Bolshaya Lubyanka. A long conversation took place between the general who was taking over the case and the colonel who was relinquishing it, in the course of which they discussed every last detail and every possible outcome, since the team of operatives which the colonel had directed was being transferred temporarily (right up till the end of the affair) to the General's command. The team took upon itself the duty of identifying all the members of JRF's conspiratorial group using the latest achievements of science and technology, including artificial satellites (why not give them a try? It's about time we did!) and parapsychology (You never know! According to what they're writing in the West . . .). And, of course, without counting the cost. When they had discussed their business, the General said that it might be better to put 'this nutcase' in Sychevka for three years or so, after which he would be as meek as a lamb. The colonel said that he was too meek as it was. But his intuition told him . . .

'Of course,' said the General. 'I'm only joking. We'll have to do the work anyway since there's an instruction . . .' And the General pointed silently upwards with the index finger of his right hand. 'And do you know,' he said on parting, 'what disturbs me most of all about this affair? Firstly, that this swine has set up his nest of dissidents under our very noses. Secondly, that if we hadn't exposed him in time, the affair could have ended with a bomb or a shooting. The serious matters in history have always begun from what seemed to be a change in the psyche.'

A CONVERSATION AT THE KGB WITH DOBRONRAVOV

Op: This is not an interrogation but a friendly chat. We are counting on your help in a very important matter.

Dobr: I am always at your service.

Op: It concerns an employee at your Institute.

Dobr: I think I can guess whom you mean.

Op: You are a friend of his . . .

Dobr: That's an exaggeration. My relations with him are the same as with many other people. Generally speaking I get on well with everyone at the Institute.

Op: Very well. But you meet him quite often outside the Institute and . . .

Dobr: Not any more often than I meet other people.

Op: But you do meet sometimes. We would like to know your opinion of him. Have you ever noticed anything unusual about what he says or in the way he behaves?

Dobr: He's a nice lad. He's always ready to have a drink with you. He's not mean. He's a good, sympathetic listener. And that impresses people. Many people in the Institute like him for that. But there are also some people who, for some reason, can't stand him. The Teacher likes him, for instance. That's the nickname of one . . .

Op: We know that.

Dobr: The director himself, Tvarzhinskaya (which, to me, is incomprehensible!), the girls in the research library, Grigoriev . . . that's the secretary of the Party bureau. Well, and me too. Nearly everyone likes him. The people who don't like him are Smirnyashchev, Kachurin, Tormoshilkina, Bulyga . . . Generally speaking, all the so-called 'liberals' and 'outstanding scholars'.

Op: What's the reason for their dislike, do you think?

Dobr: He takes the mickey out of them, doesn't show proper respect. He knows their true worth and they sense that and dislike it intensely.

Op: And what about you?

DOBR: I don't give a toss for them. But I also know what they're worth and they don't make it easy for me.

OP: But perhaps they have more serious reasons?

DOBR: Perhaps. For instance, they think that I'm an informer, but they consider him to be a danger to their noble cause. They are afraid that they might have to suffer because of him. But I think that that's merely psychological cover. The most important thing is that we know that they are the same . . . how can I put it? . . .

OP: Speak frankly. You're not at an Academic Council meeting.

DOBR: The same shit as their predecessors Petin, Fedkin, Kachurin and others.

OP: But, all the same, why did their dislike take the form of apprehension? Perhaps there are reasons for that?

DOBR: Certainly. He's a strange lad in some ways. Even a bit touched. He rarely speaks his mind, but when he does he's not exactly very critical and yet everyone always shuts up in amazement.

OP: For instance?

DOBR: For instance, we were talking on the landing about terrorist acts committed by individuals. Naturally everyone condemned them. JRF was asked for his opinion. He said that he agreed with us but that in our society all forms of individual activity are bound to be ousted by collective forms.

OP: I'm going to ask you to write that conversation down in detail. Indicate who was present. Try and remember precisely how things were put. Sit down over here. Take your time. We're not in any hurry. As the poet said, ahead of us lies eternity. Ha-ha-ha! Incidentally, you don't know anyone called the Poet? No? Well, never mind, I won't disturb you.

A FRANK AND OPEN CONVERSATION

'Surely you see what's going on around you?' said Himself.

'Of course,' said JRF.

'It could turn out badly for you!'

'It could.'

'You've got to do something!'

'What?'

'Well, talk to someone!'

'Who?'

'I don't know.'

'I don't know either. There isn't anyone. Except, maybe, Tvarzhinskaya.'

'Hey! That's an idea! She's an old *chekist*. She used to work with Beria. Old Cheka people, if you talk to them frankly and openly, can do . . .'

'What they can do, you know better than me.'

'It's still worth having a go. They don't like new trends and they might take you for one of them. The Party secretary takes you for one of them, doesn't he? Incidentally, there's sense in having a word with him, too. There's all this funny business going on, etc, etc. You were carrying out an assignment, and because of that . . .'

'That wouldn't do any good. They won't pay any attention to them. The whole thing is happening of its own accord. And no one yet knows how this business will end. They have to show that They in That Place are indispensable, that They are standing guard, etc. And They will bring this "case" to some kind of state of completion. So that it can be brought to court, if necessary, at a moment's notice.'

'I've seen a lot in my time, but this is something new to me.'

'It's a particular feature of my generation.'

'How are you going to carry on?'

'That's no problem. One has to pretend that nothing has happened. And that's what we all do. A few deviant individuals have something to say about it but they're quickly shut up.'

184

'And are you really not deviant, yourself?'

'You must be joking! I am dreadfully normal and ordinary. That's the whole problem. It's precisely my naked normalcy and ordinariness that provokes suspicion and annoyance. If I adopted a "liberal" stance, or began to work at making a career for myself, everything would be as clear as day. People react to me like they would to someone walking down the street naked. What annoys them is my nakedness itself and not any outstanding defect.'

'You have become sufficiently wise, my boy, and I shall now take my leave of you.'

'But who's going to stay with me?'

'You've still got Marx, Lenin, Stalin, Iron Felix, Beria.'

'But they've disappeared.'

'They're afraid. But just be patient. They'll have a talk with them in an appropriate place and they'll come back.'

'And where's the Poet?'

'Perhaps in Belye Stolby. But it's more likely to be the Sychevka.'

'And Herself?'

'Someone else will come to you.'

'Don't go. I'll miss you.'

'I must. My role is played out. Farewell!'

A CONVERSATION AT THE KGB WITH THE TEACHER

TEACH: Yes, we got on well. But not so well that you could say we were friends. There's a difference in our age, in our habits, and in our purposes in life.

OP: What do you have in mind when you say 'purposes'?

TEACH: I'm a scholar. I devote my energies and emotions to science. In our day and age you can't achieve anything worthwhile in science without total dedication. Naturally I refer to those branches of science where individual creative work is still possible.

OP: What about him?

TEACH: He's a capable lad. Very capable, even. But ability alone doesn't take you very far. You have to work regularly and hard. You have to have a goal and stamina. But he just mucked about. Worked now and again. Drank a lot. Got side-tracked by women. Then he got interested in politics and ideology. He left our Department after all, and went over to the department of struggle against anti-communism.

OP: But that's surely an honourable thing to do, isn't it?

TEACH: It is. But it's not something for a logician.

OP: You said that he got interested in politics. What does that mean? How did it manifest itself?

TEACH: He began to take an interest in sociology, the theory of socialism, in concrete facts of our life which are beyond what would be considered normal.

OP: Such as?

TEACH: Cases of self-immolation, attempts on the lives of people, cases of people being locked up in psychiatric hospitals, etc.

OP: Do you know anything about someone he called the Denouncer?

TEACH: Yes. He said something on one occasion to the effect that he was hoping to have a bit of fun via him. He didn't say what kind of fun exactly. I didn't attribute any significance to it. I thought it would be on the level of some piece of childishness.

OP: This has got anything but a childish smell to it. Do you think he's capable of something serious . . . I don't mean in the scientific sphere but, let's say, in the sphere of politics?

TEACH: It's difficult to say. In my opinion, he's psychically not quite normal. He seems a very mild person. But his mildness is only apparent.

OP: If he's removed (this won't necessarily happen, but it's not out of the question), would that be a loss to science?

TEACH: You must be joking! Not in the least.

OP: And what would be the reaction of the Institute?

TEACH: The usual one. They'd gossip about it for a couple of days. On the third they'd forget all about it.

ON CENSORSHIP, GENUINE SOCIALISM AND WOMEN

'Hi!' said Beria. 'How are things?'

'Just the same.'

'What are you working on?'

'The same as usual.'

'And what are you going to do?'

'What I said before.'

'Good lad! We've been having a get-together and chatting about the subject of censorship. What do you think would happen if censorship were suddenly to be done away with and literature given complete freedom?'

'You'd have a million books telling you that Brezhnev was an idiot and that the Soviet system is crap.'

'What did I tell you? That's exactly the conclusion we came to. And although Brezhnev *is* an idiot and the Soviet system *is* crap, we're precisely not going to get rid of censorship.'

'It's not a question of "although", but more your actual "precisely because",' said Stalin. 'Genuine socialism without censorship is impossible.'

'You're misrepresenting the essence of socialism,' said Lenin. 'Socialism presupposes the liquidation of censorship in all its forms.'

'Agreed,' said Beria. 'But only if there has been the liquidation beforehand of all those people who might have written something needing to be censored.'

'Forgive me, colleagues,' said Marx, 'but I don't really see what all the argument is about. You're not seriously suggesting, are you, that your society is in fact genuinely socialist?'

'Why *our* society?!' objected Lenin. 'Stalin and Beria are responsible for it. Iron Felix and I had quite a different conception. What do you say to that?'

'Since when have you been interested in my opinion? I'm telling you, you're arguing about words. What matters in the end is not what you wanted to build, but what you in fact built. Our society is officially deemed to be socialist. What of it? What difference does the word "socialism" make? There won't be anything else, anyway.'

'Why not?'

'Because social laws are universally, immutably the same.'

'Biological laws are also universal, but that doesn't prevent there being millions of different types of organism.'

'But the argument is not about the variety of conditions obtaining in different countries, it's about the general principles which underlie the mechanisms of society, whatever the country, i.e. about scientific laws. A type of socialism different in principle from the Soviet version is about as possible as the existence of another physical macro-world in which the laws of our macro-physics are inoperable, and whose own laws of macrophysics are inoperable in ours.'

'What do you suggest, then?'

'That we all sit in a row, take down our trousers, and shit in unison on everything – on socialism, on the agonies the intellectuals suffer on account of its blemishes, on the hope that there might one day be a "genuine" socialism where there will be neither blemishes nor intellectual agonies.'

'That is not a position I can adopt.'

'Me neither.'

'Nor me.'

'Nor me.'

'What do you suggest?'

'Struggle, of course. I mean, we're your fiery revolutionaries.'

'How about "access" to the women?'

'The one doesn't prevent the other. We Bolsheviks aren't ascetic. Bear in mind, incidentally, that the KGB has already looked out a bird for you. They keep a whole bunch of them on their books just for such occasions. And they're not bad, if you limit yourself strictly to their physiological aspects. They're experienced. They know all sorts of tricks. They can't compete with the West, of course. The merchandise is poor quality, the training's not very good, and they don't have the right traditions. But given our totally uninspiring performance in these matters, they don't do so badly. Apparently in the West at the moment, oral sex is all the rage.'

188

'What on earth's that?'

'I don't know myself. If it's from the word *orat** maybe they just sit beside each other and roar instead of copulating.'

'Anyway, where is this bird they've got for me?'

'Go down to the "Metropole". You'll see a bird at the entrance, medium height, quite well-developed, with an insolent, cynical look about her. She'll offer you a ticket. Take it. You'll pay for it later.'

'What if . . .'

'Don't be naive. It's not the first time. And They have made a fundamental study of all your little preferences and methods. When the light goes out, don't ask her name, just slip your hand inside her blouse. You won't be disappointed. Then under her skirt. She's got something waiting for you there as well. Go on, off you go!'

. . . IN THE NAME OF . . .

'The most important thing in life,' said Marx, 'is struggle. But not just any struggle – only the struggle to liberate the working class. I devoted all my energy to that.'

'Liberate it from whom and from what? And where did it get you? Sure, as a result of the revolution a few representatives of the working class can reach the peak of the social hierarchy. But is that really liberation? What happens to the working class that forms itself a few generations later? It has to be liberated, too. Who do you liberate it from this time? And what ideals do you summon them to struggle for?'

'Marx is right,' said Lenin. 'Struggle is the most important thing in life. I devoted all my energy to the reconstruction of Russia . . .'

'And what became of that? The Russian people lived worse than any other people in Europe, and it still does. And for the sake of what? So that whatever self-worshipping blockhead's turn it is can get to be a marshal or a generalissimo and hang medals

* *orat'*: to roar. (*Translator's note*)

189

on himself? For the sake of superiority and the Number One Spot, whatever the cost?'

'You're right,' said Stalin. 'They're all naive dreamers. But they're right, as far as struggle as such is concerned. I struggled all my life, not for the sake of abstract ideals, but with real, live (dead now, of course) enemies. I nearly beat the lot. But one or two survived. Follow me and you'll be happy.'

'But who is the enemy?'

'Everything is the enemy.'

A SECOND CONVERSATION WITH DOBRONRAVOV AT THE KGB

OP: So you consider that JRF is capable of carrying out some irrational, socially dangerous act?

DOBR: Absolutely. More than once he tried to discuss the question of carrying out attempts on the lives of important national figures with me. At first I thought he was joking. Later it began to seem a bit strange to me and I began to avoid getting into conversation with him.

OP: In what connection did he try to have these conversations?

DOBR: A lot of mad people come to our Institute. Among them there was one whom JRF calls the Terrorist who got hung up on the subject. JRF used the visits of the Terrorist and his manuscripts as a pretext for talking about this topic.

OP: What, specifically, did he want from you?

DOBR: I'm not clear about that. He once asked me in my capacity as an AFVR man about the types of grenade we have in our army.

OP: We'll be asking you to renew these meetings with JRF and your conversations with him. Don't try to avoid these kinds of conversation, on the contrary try and provoke them. What we have to establish at the moment is the extent to which he is in the grip of this *idée fixe* and how far along that road he is capable of going? Is that clear?

DOBR: Of course.

OP: Now familiarise yourself with this document and sign it.

190

You're not a child any more and can understand for yourself the consequences of not keeping our conversations a secret.

A TRIP INTO THE COUNTRY

Our Institute – it was stated in a notice in the wall-newspaper signed by the pen-name 'Observer' (although everyone knew it had been written by Soloveichikov) – is living the full-blooded life of a healthy Soviet collective, as is witnessed by the trip out of town last Sunday, organised by the local trade-union committee. Not only young colleagues (the youngest was in fact over thirty) but senior colleagues as well (mainly old drunkards, with Shubin at their head) took part in this enterprise. The bus quickly (in reality infuriatingly slowly, with stupid stops – the driver had forgotten to get petrol and had to change a defective wheel) conveyed the happy trippers to a beautiful (in reality, dirty and littered) spot on the bank of a reservoir (they couldn't drive to the bank so they were unloaded about half a kilometre away from the water.) They travelled to the accompaniment of songs and jokes (the whole way they were forced to try and bring Shubin to his senses since he had lost control of himself and was feeling up all the women in turn in all the improper places). They had a full day (the men were full of vodka and the women full of revolting sandwiches and gossip), restoring their health and high spirits for the working week ahead (Shubin had a fight with some stranger and earned a monumental black eye, Kachurin punctured his hand on a broken bottle diving into the water from the bank, the woman in charge of the office burst the corset constricting her immense waist, and a female post-graduate from Yakutia had her handbag stolen containing her money and documents). This worthwhile initiative on the part of the trade-union committee (the same trip was arranged every year and every time it was referred to as an initiative) should be encouraged and repeated. It is a splendid way of uniting the collective (Shubin and Kachurin had a swearing match and became very formal with each other, the post-graduate from Yakutia called the woman in charge of the office a fascist idiot and the latter threatened to report her to the komsomol bureau). Nature, as is its wont at this time of year in our wonderful Moscow region, lavished its charms on the workers of our Institute – warm sunshine, the velvety green of grass and tree, the pale blue peaceful water (the grass was trampled bare, the water was murky, there was rubbish everywhere, the trees had branches broken off, after lunch there was a cold wind which set the dust whirling, followed by nasty drizzling rain).

When the inebriated colleagues did decide after all to immerse themselves in the murky water, they were stopped by the voice of a loudspeaker which began to thunder out over the whole area like a voice from Heaven. 'Citizens!' a voice screeched, clearly full of itself. 'You have come to enjoy our wonderful countryside. The sun is shining. A gentle breeze sends a rustle through the green leaves. You sit in a boat and, singing and joking, sail out into the middle of the reservoir. A gentle wave rocks the boat. The boat overturns and you sink towards the bottom. Citizens! Watch out when you are on the water. Don't rock your boat! Don't sail away from the shore!!!'

When he read the notice, Petin shed an emotional tear. 'In our time this was unattainable,' he said with a sigh. 'You young people have it good. So we didn't go hungry for nothing, do without sleep, recreation. So it was not for nothing that my generation . . .'

'Well done, young komsomols!' said Tvarzhinskaya, shaking the hand of the over-age woman in charge of the office. 'As the poet said, I too would like to run after a young komsomol. And I'd . . . But those years have gone. I envy and congratulate you.'

A CONFERENCE AT THE BOLSHAYA LUBYANKA

'As yet we have been unable to find out who Marx, Lenin, Stalin and the others are.'

'Intensify the search. Double the number of operatives. Continue the surveillance of his flat. We have to find these scoundrels at all costs.'

'I think they've smelt a rat.'

'That's possible. But they'll relax sooner or later and show themselves. Patience – that's the main thing. How about the Terrorist?'

'Nothing new. I think it would be better to transfer him to the Serbsky Institute.'

'Yes. And get him back on his feet. We need him in a healthy state. Antedate his file by two years. Let him make a full recovery last year.'

'Here's the preliminary scheme of things. This is JRF. Via the Denouncer – contact with the "Workers' group". Via the Terrorist – contact with the terrorist group, which includes Marx, Lenin, Stalin . . . This here is the contact with foreign intelligence. We've only just started to work on this.'

'Over the last ten years, many foreign delegations from the West have visited the Institute, as have individual Western scholars. There have been a few international conferences. Our academics have been to the West more than once. All these matters have got to be raised and thoroughly examined.'

'He hasn't been abroad.'

'He worked with foreigners here. He knows two languages, after all. Investigate everyone he has been in contact with, or could have been.'

'Judging by everything, it looks like Dobronravov could play the role . . .'

'He, of course, has to be attached to the terrorist group. He's indispensable for a public trial. How's Tatyana?'

'Nothing to report as yet. He went to the cinema but didn't take her home.'

'Let her carry on. Get him drunk. Let her take him back to his place. He has lapses of memory. He'll hardly suspect . . .'

AFTER WORK

The Academic Registrar unexpectedly asked JRF to return the manuscript since it had been asked for by the Presidium. It would not be necessary to write a review – they would work things out for themselves. JRF went to see the bursar, got a bundle of old manuscripts from him which were ready for shredding, paid him three roubles to keep his mouth shut, intermingled the pages of his own manuscript among them and handed the whole lot over to the Registrar. 'It's a pity I didn't manage to finish it,' he thought. 'Although this way perhaps the effect will be even greater. I wonder what these manuscripts were the bursar gave me.' But the bursar wasn't in the Institute, he'd gone off to spend the three roubles on drink. 'It wouldn't half be a lark if they were part of the materials produced by the special group set up in the department of information. And it's very likely, given that the manuscripts were ready for shredding.'

The working day came to an end. A bell rang. The huge phlegmatic girl in the personnel department brought out the attendance register. The dull lacklustre employees hastily signed off and rushed off on their own affairs, chiefly to the shops, since the majority were women. Young male colleagues and old inveterate drinkers formed themselves into little groups with a view to 'celebrating', 'having a bite to eat', 'having a fling', 'going for a chat'. By mutual consent JRF and the Teacher set off down the stairs together. On the third floor they were joined by Dobronravov. On the ground floor they were joined by some of the lads from *Questions*, the Acquaintance, a young lad who (so rumour had it) was writing a defamatory novel with a view to publishing it in the West, and another not-so-young lad with a ragged beard who had been trying for over twenty years to finish his thesis. The lads from *Questions* suggested going to the House of Journalists specially for the beer.

'What about that manuscript?' asked the Acquaintance.

'Everything's okay. It turned up. The neighbour had hidden it.'

'How's that business with the Denouncer?'

'Everything's gone quiet,' said Dobronravov. 'In any event, the KGB people are keeping out of sight.'

'It's an idiotic affair,' the Teacher observed. 'As usual they want to make a mountain out of a molehill.'

'Have you heard the latest joke? Brezhnev goes over to the window in the morning. "Hi, Sun," he says. "How do you do, dear Comrade General Secretary, Chairman of the Presidium, Chairman of the Committee on Defence, Marshal, Recipient of the Lenin Prize, ten times decorated Hero etc, etc." replies the Sun. At noon Brezhnev goes to the window again. "Hi, Sun" he says. "How do you do, dear General Secretary, President, etc, etc." says the Sun. In the evening Brezhnev again goes to the window. "Hi, Sun," he says. "Piss off," says the Sun. "Why are you so rude?" says Brezhnev, offended. "You were so polite to me this morning, and at lunchtime. Why are you so rude now?" "I don't give two hoots for you now," says the Sun. "I'm in the West!"'

'Well, They're really tightening the screws now. In the next issue there are going to be two defamatory articles. Really defamatory. There's been nothing like it since 1956.'

'They decided at the March Plenum to stuff the West and significantly reduce our economic dependence on it. It looks like They want to ring down the "iron curtain" again.'

'That's not so easy any more.'

'Who are they defaming?'

'Completely unexpected types. I've been fifteen years with this journal and to this day I don't understand the principles whereby They select people. In the area of dialectical materialism They're going to have a go at Petrov, Sudarikov and Ivanitsky. Do you know them?'

'Of course. But they're bullshitters and cretins!'

'And in historical materialism . . . Well, you'll never guess. And you won't believe it. Lukin, Sedov . . . And a few others. Generally speaking, all the authors who contributed to Lukin's book.'

'What for? It's laughable!'

'It's not a laughing matter for Them. This business has obviously been discussed in the science section of the Central

Committee. They've selected Russians almost exclusively, so that it doesn't look like anti-semitism. But to set people thinking along these lines they've chucked in a couple of obvious Jews and one "closet" one. Who? Sedov. They've chosen second-rate characters so that the West doesn't make a fuss. However, they're just well enough known for the thing to be taken seriously.'

'What's the general tone of the stuff?'

'They're being accused of showing a conciliatory attitude towards Western bourgeois ideology, dragging in inimical ideas, forgetting the basic tenets of marxism-leninism. It's really a demonstration of ideological irreconcilability.'

'After the stuff in *Questions* they'll presumably publish something in *Communist*. Then in the newspapers, and the whole thing'll take off! . . .'

'If they're serious about it, then we can expect some major dirty trick at national government level. They might put on some big show or other. There hasn't been one for a long time. They're probably feeling nostalgic. And their hands are itching.'

The House of Journalists turned out to be shut in connection with the All-union Conference of Journalists on questions of ideological work.

'Oh, how sick I am of all this,' said Dobronravov when he and JRF were left alone. 'If I had an anti-tank grenade, I'd let it off under the first VIP car without a moment's hesitation.'

'It'd take more than an anti-tank grenade,' said JRF thoughtfully.

'Nonsense,' said Dobronravov. 'They spread rumours like that on purpose. An anti-tank grenade, assuming you don't miss, will pierce it easily.'

'Where are you going to get one from?' asked JRF.

'That's no problem,' said Dobronravov. 'All you need is the desire. And he who seeks, as they used to sing, will always find.'

'But just what will he find?' thought JRF, but didn't say anything. He felt completely estranged from everything around him.

TATYANA

'Who are you?'

'Tatyana.'

'Why are you here?'

'What a silly question. Why does a woman end up in a man's bed? I must admit I'm not sorry.'

'Judging by your face, you're a bitch.'

'Hey, steady on!'

'But judging by your body there is a divine spark in you.'

'There you are, then!'

'So you can stay. But I'm warning you, no theoretical discussions! This room is bugged from top to bottom. And don't try to reform me! I hate improvements. I prefer my pigsty to remain in a stable condition. A pigsty should be a pigsty and not your communist paradise.'

'Perhaps we should make some coffee?'

'Have you gone mad? What kind of coffee can you get now?'

'Real coffee! I brought a packet with me.'

'If that's the case, then you have been sent to me by God.'

'Well, not God, exactly. One of his representatives.'

'Tell me now. Where did you latch on to me?'

'*You* latched on to *me*. But I confess that I've been after you for a while. I've fancied you for a long time. I work not far from here. But you never noticed me.'

'And yesterday I did?'

'You simply grabbed me, dragged me through the front door of the building, did your stuff, then took me by the hand and brought me here. You said: be my wife and enter my house!'

'I said that?'

'That's what you said.'

'Then be my wife. Do you know, I've only just now understood why Pushkin called his heroine Tatyana. And let's cover ourselves with the blanket. I wouldn't want Them to see our pure and innocent love.'

JRF READS A PAPER TO A MEETING OF THE DEPARTMENT

A notice was posted on the upper landing announcing a meeting of the Department of Struggle against Anti-communism at which Junior Research Fellow So-and-so would read a paper entitled 'The Role of Logic in the Ideological Struggle of our Time'. The announcement caused considerable stir. People didn't stop talking about it for the whole week.

'Here we were, thinking . . .' said some spitefully, 'and all the time he . . . It turns out he's the same shit as the rest of us. And has a beard into the bargain! And reads foreign books!'

'We always said that he had his head screwed on,' said others.

'Typical informer,' said still other others.

'He's moving to the science department of the Central Committee,' Leading Gossip Kirusik told everyone confidentially. 'Do you know how much he'll earn? What! Three times as much. And he'll get a flat right away. These scoundrels always make out in the end!'

'Good for him! They'll let him defend his thesis now. He'll start publishing. It's high time he did.'

'He did right to leave those schizophrenics. There was no life for him there.'

The meeting was supposed to take place in the small reading room, but so many people came that the function had to be relocated in the main Assembly Hall. Dressed appropriately for the occasion, Tvarzhinskaya opened the meeting with a fiery speech.

'It is now clear to everyone,' she said, 'that the victorious march of communism cannot be halted. The victory of communism over the whole planet is merely a question of time. However, this doesn't mean that we can rest on our laurels. The enemies of communism will not leave the stage of history voluntarily. They are offering furious opposition, and that opposition will be the more furious the more sharply they become aware of the approach of their own inevitable historical eclipse. There are no means which they will not employ in their struggle with communist countries and communist ideology. Included in these means are the achievements of contemporary logic.'

People in the Assembly Hall began to titter, but Tvarzhinskaya's eyes flashed, she drew breath for the next tirade and the tittering died down again. Tvarzhinskaya offered the floor to JRF.

'Now hold on to your hat,' whispered the Teacher to Dobronravov. 'There's bound to be a calamity. He's going to come out with something awful. To this day I don't know whether he does it on purpose or whether it just happens like that, out of thoughtlessness.'

'A paradoxical situation has arisen in this Institute,' said JRF, beginning his delivery. 'All departments and sections have acknowledged the importance of contemporary logic, both for the development of our marxist-leninist philosophy and in the struggle with our ideological enemies. All except one: the most militant and industrious one. And no doubt the one most qualified. I refer to our Department of Struggle against Anti-communism. Judge for yourselves. The Department of Scientific Criticism of Foreign Bourgeois Philosophy has published two collective monographs of criticism of semantic and analytical philosophy and, naturally, of contemporary trends in neo-positivism. The authors include many of our leading logicians. One need only mention that a whole paragraph was contributed by Professor Zaitsev. The Department of Support of Progressive Trends in Foreign Philosophy had a special chapter in its collective publication (which publication was awarded a First Prize by the Institute) in which it convincingly showed how powerful a weapon logic can become in the hands of our foreign marxist philosopher friends in their struggle with the apologists of imperialism. I haven't even mentioned the Department of Dialectical Materialism. I cannot name one single publication in recent years in which the results of logic were not used for the development of our philosophy. Even the Department of Logic is on a high level in this connection. Recently it published a collection of papers in which our greatest logicians, Smirnyashchev, Voroshillo, Burdyukov, Subbotin and others, convincingly demonstrated that formal logic, even as a branch of contemporary mathematical logic, remains a lower form of logic applicable (in the words of Engels) only in the domestic sphere . . . Although what, for instance, are you supposed to do with implication in the domestic sphere, even if, through misunderstanding, it is called material? Now, to try to do without it in the ideological struggle in its contemporary phase . . .'

Again there was a titter. Tvarzhinskaya called the meeting to order, threatening that otherwise she would clear the hall of all those who.

'Here we go,' said the Teacher to Dobronravov. 'I feel sorry for him but we can't stop him.'

The animation in the assembly hall did not, however, die down. And Tvarzhinskaya, interpreting it as a healthy reaction to a lively and graphic speech, began to smile radiantly herself.

'Let us take, for instance, a malicious assertion of the enemies of communism: "Under communism, wives will be common property." Let us designate that by the symbol X. Now, here's how we can write down a formal definition of "common property", and here the relations between husband and wife. I hope I have written it all down correctly?'

Paranoiac Smirnyashchev went forward and became green from the mental effort he expended in the hope of catching JRF out on an 'elementary mistake'.

'So far, so good,' he said venomously. 'We'll see what happens later. Incidentally, this definition . . .'

'Yes, yes,' said JRF. 'This definition is taken from the monograph of our respected scholar with a world-wide reputation, Professor Smirnyashchev. But let's continue. So, this is a consequent, this – an antecedent . . . By the law of substitution we obtain . . . By the rule of *modus ponens* . . . Here we apply contraposition . . . Correct? I ask the logicians to correct me if I make a mistake.'

There was a hush as everyone tried to follow the columns of incomprehensible formulae which rapidly made their appearance on the blackboard and disappeared just as rapidly. After JRF's last words, everyone looked at Smirnyashchev and his entourage with displeasure. And with hope: perhaps this cretin with the world-wide reputation would catch this bearded fop out?! But Smirnyashchev continued to nod in agreement and sometimes even suggested some simpler ways of transforming the formulae.

At last one solitary formula remained on the blackboard.

'And now,' said JRF solemnly, 'allow me to remind my honourable audience of the symbols which we have agreed. Here they are on the left. And now any averagely literate person, even Doctor Barabanov (there was laughter in the audience and Barabanov broke into a smile), can decipher the formula which we obtain. Doctor Barabanov?'

Barabanov, however, declined to go up to the blackboard. Smirnyashchev couldn't restrain himself, jumped up, hitched up his drooping crumpled trousers, took the chalk, said how simple it was and straightway wrote down the answer in ordinary language: 'Under communism, husbands will be common property.' The commotion in the assembly hall was unimaginable. Cries of delight about the power of contemporary logic. Scorn concerning the obviousness of the deduction even without logic, etc.

'It's only now that you think that the deduction was obvious,' said JRF, after Tvarzhinskaya had restored silence. 'Name me one work, whether of a pro-communist or an anti-communist bent, in which it figures! You won't be able to, because it doesn't. The proof which I have just set out before you was first discovered by me. Of course, I relied on the excellent work of para . . . excuse me, I mean Professor Smirnyashchev. Now I hope that even if wives eventually really are taken into public ownership, the ladies will be reassured: husbands will be, too.'

The hall burst into applause. Paranoiac Smirnyashchev applauded on his feet. Interrupting the speaker, he there and then proposed to Tvarzhinskaya that the two departments publish jointly a book of readings on that precise topic. More applause.

'What's going on?' the Teacher asked Dobronravov in amazement. 'These idiots don't realise that they are having the wool pulled over their eyes and being made a fool of!'

'Serves them right,' said Dobronravov. 'He did well! Do you know, he's matured a lot just recently, and become much more serious. It's a shame for the lad!'

A TALE OF IMMORTALITY

'Whether we are virtuous or depraved, intelligent or stupid, beautiful or ugly, we'll all kick the bucket in the end. So what's the point in restraining ourselves, cutting down on everything? Grab it, if the chance presents itself! That's my philosophy in a nutshell. Only I don't need much. It's enough just to have you.'

'We don't all kick the bucket. And not completely. Some can live for ever.'

'Fairy tales. I've been to school, you know. The full stretch.'

'Perhaps it is a fairy tale, but it's a beautiful one. The most beautiful one ever invented. And yogis believe that it is not a fairy tale. Everyone possesses, so they believe, a sort of delicate spiritual cocoon. The body dies but the cocoon lives for ever.'

'I don't want to be without a body. I'd rather it were the other way around – let the cocoon die and the body live for ever. And not get old. I don't want to be old.'

'But you don't know how you would feel without a body.'

'You don't feel without a body.'

'Imagine, a permanent feeling of weightlessness. Fluttering here and there to your heart's content.'

'I don't want weightlessness. I want to weigh something. I want to be heavy.'

'How much do you weigh at the moment?'

'Sixty kilograms.'

'Is that not quite a lot for your height?'

'No. I can put on another five kilos. I hate skinny bags of bones.'

'You're a born materialist. A dialectical one, what's more.'

'You can take your dialectical materialism and do you-know-what with it. I'm a woman, not a materialist.'

'OK. If you like, I'll tell you a fairy tale about immortality. Scientists invented a medicine which would make the person taking it virtually live for ever. But manufacturing this medicine was very difficult and expensive. A huge enterprise employing a hundred thousand people took a whole year just to produce one pill, and the pill had to be taken once a year. These hundred thousand people had to be highly trained and able scientists. They could not be replaced by machines, bureaucrats or mere executives. The manufacturing process for producing this immortality pill differed each time. These hundred thousand people had to be well looked after and allowed access to all the achievements of world culture. And in general they had to be allowed to do a lot of things that earlier had been forbidden to the citizens of the country, watch any foreign or home-produced film, read any books, look at any painting by any artist, etc. They had to be allowed to express their own opinion without the risk of jail. A hundred thousand. And they had families. Children. And they constantly had to be replaced, i.e. there had to be a constant process of selection of the most talented pupils, students, post-graduates, etc, from the huge number of young people receiving education. Moreover, they had to alter radically the whole educational system, in particular get rid of marxist-leninist philosophy, political economy and the history of the CPSU, abolish the study of leaders' speeches, etc. And this required a different type of teacher-training for the staffs of schools and institutes. To cut a long story short, the whole social order in the country had to be radically altered. Expenditure on arms had to be slashed. Shipments of arms to Africa had to be stopped. And remember there was only one pill! Only one person could be immortal. Who? Naturally the General Secretary, the Chairman of the Presidium, the Commander-in-Chief . . . And what did that mean for the other members of the Politburo? And for the members of the Central Committee? It meant that none of them was ever going to make it to the Number One Spot, i.e. to the end of their days they were going to have to play second or third fiddle, in the shade. And all homage would be paid eternally to that senile old fart?! You can imagine the emotions that were seething within them!

'And the Gen Sec himself knew that there was only one pill and that his rivals and comrades were boiling with hatred and envy, that they could murder him at any time, that he would have to be always on his guard. And to get a regular supply of the pills he would have to restructure the whole life of society and then constantly maintain the new system. Naturally with the power of the KGB, the MVD, the army. But the KGB would become so powerful that ... In short, such a multitude of problems welled up that there was no chance at all of solving them. And then a rumour began to circulate that there would soon be two pills, and then three. Who would get them? And if there were ten, twenty, a hundred? And what if there were pills for everyone? What would we need children for, then? And what about jobs? Would one person for ever be a docker and someone else a marshal? And if there weren't pills for everyone, how would they be allocated? Imagine the prospect of immortal bosses and mortal subordinates! And life in that society began to be such that our present situation was recalled as a mythical Golden Age. And the Great Committee met on one occasion to decide what to do next. For it had become impossible to go on as they were, if for no other reason than that the one hundred thousand creative individuals who were manufacturing the medicine were abusing utterly the Party, the Government, the senile Gen Sec and his ruling band. Can you imagine how many subversive jokes were told?! And for the first time in the entire history of the country the Great Committee announced a closed competition for the best solution to the problem, declaring that the prize would be . . . Guess what! The immortality pill!'

'And who won?'

'A junior research fellow without a higher degree.'

'What did he suggest?'

'He suggested liquidating the enterprise connected with the production of the immortality pill.'

'But how then . . .'

'That's the catch!'

LONELINESS

'Why are you so alone? Don't you have any friends?'

'I've got lots of friends. Who? Well, for instance, Marx, Lenin, Stalin, Iron Felix, Beria.'

'Are these nicknames?'

'Partly.'

'Who are they?'

'Scoundrels and upstarts. Misanthropists masquerading as humanists. Ignoramuses passing themselves off as scholars. Charlatans acting as the wisest of the wise. They're not worth talking about. Recently I've broken off with them and they now come here very rarely. I'm glad. I prefer loneliness to the problems you get into with people.'

'Introduce me to them.'

'I don't want to. I'm jealous.'

'I like it when I make people feel jealous. Introduce me! I won't be unfaithful to you.'

'All right. But I don't know where they live. I can't call them. They never appear in front of strangers.'

'But I'm not a stranger. And what do you do when you're on your own? It must be so boring to be on your own.'

'No, it's not boring. I look up at the ceiling or out of the window. And I think.'

'What about?'

'Nothing.'

'You can't think about nothing.'

'I can.'

'Teach me.'

'It's impossible to teach that. It's an ability you're born with.'

'Explain it, then.'

'You can't explain it. It's simply an on-going state.'

'Is it pleasant?'

'I don't know. It's something different. Unusual. Probably it's the state the eternal spirit finds itself in once it has left its dead body.'

'So, I'll become an old woman and die, and your spirit will remain? That's not fair!'

'But you said yourself . . .'

'I've changed my mind.'

'All right. I'll try. But I don't guarantee that I'll be successful. You see, it's like a reward for being lonely. But you . . .'

'I'll be with you.'

'Are you married?'

'Yes.'

'And how does your husband feel about . . .'

'I have that kind of job.'

'Have you any children?'

'A son.'

'Could you leave your husband and live with me?'

'What for? It's better the way it is. If I move in with you, other people will become my lovers. Is that what you want?'

'No.'

'That's the catch. Let everything just take care of itself. So, where are these friends of yours?'

'Here, in my head.'

A SEXUAL TRAGEDY

'I'm sick of philosophy,' said Iron Felix.

'Let's talk about something else. Let's take up literature, for example.'

'Let's write a play,' suggested Beria, 'and act it right away. We'll make it up as we go along!'

'Why bother writing a play when there's one all ready and waiting?' said Stalin. 'I have in mind that wonderful drama, composed in secret by that miserable scoundrel Petin. While you were blethering in corridors and on stair landings, Petin was creating literature. The story-line of Petin's drama is the following. There is a chaste female student. She is loved by a naive male student. He tries to tempt her with philosophical discussions and references to the classical writers. She is caught on the horns of a dilemma. On the one hand she wants to be tempted by the handsome, intelligent young post-graduate student. On the other hand, she wants to get into post-graduate work herself, but that depends on her supervisor and head of department. Let's now assign the roles.'

'I suggest an innovation,' said Lenin. 'Whoever manages to speak a part first, let that person have the part. We'll have a completely democratic theatre. Anyone can play any role, if he can grab it.'

'In that case Stalin will grab all the roles.'

SCENE 1

A room in a student hostel. The chaste student Tanya is trying on her clean knickers in front of the mirror. The wanton student Katya is reading a textbook on the history of the CPSU.

T: These knickers look all right. What do you think?

K: What does it matter? No one sees them in the dark, anyway.

T: Supposing it's not dark? There's just one problem about these knickers: they're very tight round the legs. If Zhenka gets a hand under my skirt, he'll tear them. I'd better wear these ones, the ones with the little flowers.

K: I'm surprised at you, Tanya. How have you managed to remain so chaste? Tell me, when was the eleventh Party congress and what issues were decided at it?

T: You know where you can go with your Party. How do these look, then? Okay? Do you know, I think they make my bum look more elegant. Don't you think so?

K: Mine's fatter, anyway. And I've got to take this exam on the history of the CPSU tomorrow. A dissenting line at the congress was taken by the Jew Trotsky. Lenin, with Stalin's support . . .

T: Who would it be better to do it with today do you think? Vladilen Marlenovich has told me to come to his house to discuss the first paragraph of my exam project. But that handsome Georgian will be at the club. Imagine, he's a Georgian and already a post-graduate student. And he's clever! They say that he can get through five women in an hour! Not like that old goat Shkurnikov.

K: He's not all that old. He's only sixty. For a Party worker that means he's still in his youth.

T: Anyway, he's indispensable. You can't get into post-graduate work without his say-so. Well, so long!

SCENE 2

A corridor. The student Zhenya, in love with Tanya, takes her breast in one hand and puts the other up her skirt.

ZH: You've put on the ones with the flowers? Who were you going to see?

T: I'm going to the club. There's a discussion today on progress and love.

ZH: Tanya, let's nip into my room for a minute. Vaska's gone. We'll lock ourselves in. We'll put out the light.

T: Everything in its own good time. Once we're married, I'll come of my own accord.

ZH: Tanya, Tanya, why are you so pure, so chaste? All the other girls act like girls. But you . . . Here, let me at least feel you up.

ANOTHER HEART-TO-HEART

A down-to-earth discussion, a heart-to-heart talk, a forthright conversation between a refined intellectual and inveterate informers and old Party and KGB scoundrels is an inalienable part of the spiritual life of our society. In so far as the Orthodox Church has lost its former prestige and all the various sects are dangerous and scarcely accessible (and are intellectually more or less on a par with the Orthodox Church), the role of confessor for the thinking and suffering intelligentsia has been taken on by Party secretaries and authoritative members of the Party bureau as well as old *chekists* and comparatively young KGB investigators. One dissident, who had decided to emigrate on the grounds that the Soviet Union could not provide an environment which was adequate for his intellectual level, withdrew his application after three interrogations by the KGB. In an interview with foreign correspondents he confessed that he had never before encountered such understanding and that he would never find anything like it in the West, where a person was left to his own devices, and therefore he had decided to stay here for ever. Having clapped the repentant dissident on the shoulder, the KGB investigator said to him the next day: 'Either you clear out of here within a week or we'll put you away for a minimum of seven and five.'

In accordance with this same Russian custom, JRF asked Tvarzhinskaya if he could have a talk with her in private. When Tvarzhinskaya heard this she grabbed hold of JRF in the place where his biceps were supposed to be, dragged him into her office, locked the door and threw the key out of the window. Or swallowed it. Or . . . In fact she turned the key round in her claws, not knowing where to hide it, for she was in a deeply emotional state. This was the first time since her beloved boss was shot that an averagely intelligent, capable young man had wanted to have a heart-to-heart precisely with her.

'Well, now, tell me what it's all about. You can be completely frank with me. You have my word as a communist and former member of the Cheka that our conversation will remain between ourselves.'

'The thing is,' began JRF in a roundabout fashion, 'recently I have begun to notice that . . .'

And he told her everything.

And she understood him.

'You did right to come to Us,' she said, firmly shaking him by the hand. 'We'll stick up for you!'

SCENE 3

A room where theoretical discussions are held. The most thoughtful students are sitting, open-mouthed. Post-graduate students Petya and Styopa are having a debate. Enter Tanya and Zhenya. Zhenya has one hand under Tanya's skirt and the other on her bosom.

P: What is progress? Let us define the concept itself.

S: Why do we have to get into formalism? We all know, roughly speaking, what we're talking about. But if you really insist, we can take a working definition like the following:

progress is when things get better for people according to criteria accepted by the given society.

P: Hazy, but it'll do.

S: We're discussing problems of ideology, not abstract science. And we're interested in progress as an ideological principle.

P: Progress as an ideological principle is meaningless. What is important for a person? That he get through his life, eat his share of bread, potatoes or kebabs, wear out his allotted number of pairs of trousers, drink his barrel of alcoholic drink, perform his quota of sexual acts, etc. But progress is only felt when one generation replaces another.

S: But these people can get through their life in different ways – badly, successfully, boringly, happily, interestingly, wealthily or in poverty. The very idea of progress has to do with striving to improve the people's lot. Take, for example, aeroplanes and television . . .

P: We don't know yet whether these are a blessing or not. I've never been on an aeroplane. And I almost never watch television. But I don't feel deprived.

S: Well, what about clean sheets? Baths? Dentists? Books? Cars? Progress is an objective fact. And rather a pleasant one.

P: These are all products of people's actions. Normal human life is not life in the name of progress. People's actions have concrete reasons and motives. Life in the name of progress is coercion of the human spirit. It's unnatural.

T: This is a dead bore!

Zн: Tanya, come to my room. Vaska's gone. We'll put out the light. We'll lock ourselves in.

T: Everything in its own good time!

Zн: Why are you so chaste? Well, let me at least get a hold of you.

A LETTER FROM AN OLD *CHEKIST*

Tvarzhinskaya sent a letter to the KGB in which she wrote that JRF was doing very important work in the struggle with anti-communism, that he was a very gifted scholar, that he was on the right road, that the communists in the Department could vouch for him, etc.

'Is that bitch Lenochka still functioning?' said the General when he had read the letter. 'How much trouble she caused us in her time! How many good *chekisty* went to the wall because of her! Forgive her for that?! Never and on no account! How's that JRF case coming along? We should speed it up a bit.'

A MODERN TRAGEDY

'In a contemporary play you must have songs and music,' said Beria. 'Let the following events take place against a background of guitar music and a romantic song of youth. Something along the lines of:

> 'You will go off to the northern deer,
> To the southern gophers, I.'

'I suggest that we compose our own songs and music,' said Iron Felix. 'As far as I know, Marx wrote poetry in his youth and Engels played the guitar and sang romances. Lenin's musical talents are well-known. He composed the "Appassionata" and "The International".'

'I've got it!' shouted Marx. 'Listen!

> 'This law of nature is not new.
> We're young, with mischief in our hearts.
> The years will pass, and not a few,
> And we'll become old, brassed-off farts.

While young and firm your breasts are yet,
While ramrod stiff our members stand,
While doing it, do not forget
That sweet betrayal lies to hand.

Today we're lads and lassies young,
Soon men and women we'll become.
And when our life's last song is sung,
We'll be scratching wrinkles in our bum.

While still you feel you have a chance
To spread the legs of women wide,
Our macho self-respect enhance
And fill us all, my lads, with pride!

Who cares that it's beneath a fence,
We'll let you do it without end.
Let hypocrites make the pretence
Our "sins" they cannot comprehend.

While still behind our moral mien
We lie down for you anywhere,
Such luck you men have never seen,
And thanks to us, the sex called "fair".'

SCENE 4

Tanya is dancing with the handsome Georgian post-graduate student Zurab. Zurab has put one leg between Tanya's so far that Tanya is almost sitting on his knee. Zurab's right hand is holding Tanya's buttocks.

Z: You're wearing the ones with flowers today?

T: The same. Your favourites.

Z: What were you discussing with that serious young man?

T: Progress.

Z: Progress as regards what? Progress as such doesn't exist, only progress in relation to something specific. Progress in technology is one thing, progress in sexual relations another. People in our sanctimonious society are scared to say anything about sex at all. You only have to say the most innocent thing, for instance, something about group sex, and everyone immediately bashfully lowers their eyes. We've been lagging behind the

West in this respect for the whole period of Soviet power, if not longer.

T: Excuse me, but what do you have in mind when you speak of group sex?

Z: When not two, but three or more people take part in the sexual act. For instance, two women and one man, two men and one woman. And generally, if X equals the number of men and Y equals the number of women, then $X+Y=3$. There are other definitions, but that one's the easiest to start with. Incidentally, it involves the simultaneous participation of everyone in the same sexual act. If a man performs a sexual act with two women in succession, that is two normal acts and not a group act. Group sex will take place, for instance, in the case where a man copulates with one woman in the normal fashion and simultaneously satisfies another with his hand or tongue. If you like, we could meet and have a specific chat about this topic. I suggest you look in at the ethics lecture theatre. An interesting discussion is expected.

ZH: Tanya, come to my room. Vaska's gone. We'll put out the light. We'll lock ourselves in. I'll . . .

PEOPLE AND THEIR FATE

Although the workers in our country have a completely guaranteed and peaceful existence and although they are confident in the day ahead, nevertheless they are sometimes the victims of nasty surprises. Khrushchev, for example, reached the pinnacle of power and went off for a week's holiday, confident not only in the day ahead, but in the century ahead. He arrives in the sunny south, throws off his Moscow clothes, exposes his paunch to the caressing sea breezes and . . . And bang! No more pinnacle of power. He's hounded into retirement and placed, what's more, under the surveillance of the KGB. And what about Podgorny?! Fate played a dirty trick on that idiot of a kind which is quite intolerable in relation to a member of the Politburo of the Central Committee of the CPSU. During a meeting of the Politburo at which they were intending to dump Brezhnev, he needed to go to the toilet. And he asked to be excused: allow me, dear comrades, as it were, to go for a pee! 'By all means,' they said, 'otherwise, who knows . . .' In short, Podgorny went off to the toilet as Number Two in the Party and state, confident that he would be coming back as Number One. And he returned . . . Actually, they say that he was deposed straight from the lavatory pan.

Barabanov's case has already been reported. True, the Barabanov incident was a bit more serious. What was involved there was not just the desire to tan your paunch or go for a pee, but politics. But it was annoying, just the same. You live through the whole gruesome Stalin period without a hitch and then, in the age of advanced socialism, you come a cropper in the presence of liberals and dissidents, and nobody says a word in your defence.

When the Institute staff were being herded into a full session of the Academic Council devoted to the creative literary work of Leonid Ilich, no one thought that anything unforeseen could happen. And to whom?! To the most cowardly doctor of philosophistry – Subbotin. The staff comported themselves as was customary on such occasions. Some grumbled about yet another piece of routine idiocy, others cracked jokes about the huge notice announcing that Academician Egorkin, the leading specialist in the country on marxist (you might almost think there was another kind!) aesthetics would address an extraordinary session of the full Academic Council with a paper on the contribution to marxist (again you might think there was some other kind!) sociology and ethics to be found in the works of the outstanding, etc, etc, Leonid Ilich Brezhnev. And even Subbotin acted in customary fashion by adopting a pose and telling the whole Institute that the word 'marxist' in the notice was superfluous, for there was no other kind of aesthetics or sociology in the country, and it was even harmful for someone might think (not everyone has a highly developed intellect!) that we did have some other, non-marxist, kind of aesthetics and sociology.

Academician Egorkin said everything that one is supposed to say on such occasions and *only* what one is supposed to say on such occasions – he hadn't been made an Academician for nothing, after all. He only made one blunder which disturbed the normal tenor of the proceedings. When he was praising to the skies the literary merits of that part of Leonid Ilich's book where the author wept for five whole pages at the prospect of having to be parted from his beloved wife for a fortnight, Egorkin launched into a series of great historical and literary parallels. He wanted to declaim this part of his paper with feeling and by heart, without reference to the text, but he wasn't up to it and confused Desdemona with Ophelia, Paola with Beatrice, Othello with Hamlet, Petrarch with Dante and tsarina Tamara with princess Tarakanova. The auditorium reacted vigorously to Egorkin's difficulties and tried to help him out, but they only made matters worse. The anti-semite Ezhov insisted on comparing Leonid Ilich's love for his wife with Romeo's love for Juliet and his deputy Rabinovich compared it with Lenin's love for Krupskaya and Engels's love for Marx.

After the interval there was a discussion of the paper. First on to the platform was Subbotin. Smiling with a certain innuendo he said that, if his memory didn't deceive him, Romeo was sixteen and Juliet somewhat younger, fifteen. Leonid Ilich and his spouse, however, were well over forty, so that, you know, . . . And although Subbotin later mumbled that that fact didn't diminish the intensity of their feelings, and although his description of her outdid Shakespeare, no one listened to him. All the following speakers without exception accused Subbotin of underestimation, lack of understanding and concessions to . . . And what else didn't they accuse him of! The Academic Council took a unanimous decision to devote attention, condemn and intensify. The representative from the Central Committee recommended to the secretary of the Party bureau that the latter open a personal file on Subbotin. But not to overdo it. This time it would be enough simply to publicise it. But in such a way that it would be an instructive lesson for the younger ones.

After the session Subbotin got drunk at the Teacher's and Dobronravov's expense, sharply criticised 'dyed-in-the-wool neo-stalinists' like Egorkin, quoted from Shakespeare 'in the original', complained that the famous 'To be, or not to be' was wrongly interpreted and proposed his own interpretation which nobody wanted to listen to. Then he went to the toilet and didn't come back. And they forgot about him immediately, just like Khrushchev, Podgorny and Barabanov.

And JRF dreamed that he was on a trip to England with Subbotin, as the latter's interpreter, and that they visited a palaeontological museum and that its genuine iguanadon skeleton ate Subbotin and that Subbotin was very proud of that.

SCENE 5

Vasya, Zhenya's friend, a student and komsomol organiser of their group, stops Tanya in the corridor on her way to the ethics lecture theatre.

V: Tanya! Drop your drawers and come to my room. We have to discuss the socialist competition results.

T: Of course. I'll be right with you. I'll just go and get my copy of the agenda.

SCENE 6

The room shared by Vasya and Zhenya. Tanya and Vasya are lying on Zhenya's bed and discussing the socialist competition results. Vasya is wearing ankle-boots. He has chosen Zhenya's bed in order not to dirty his own. Tanya's flowery knickers are lying on the floor.

V: Tanya, have you been so chaste for a long time?

T: Since class seven.

V: Who was it?

T: First it was the gym-teacher, then the Pioneer leader. Then the komsomol organiser. Then all the rest.

V: Well done, Tanya! You'll make a fine wife. I envy Zhenya! He's a lucky man! What did he do to deserve such good fortune?

A MODERN TRAGEDY

'That's enough for today,' said Marx, 'I'm very tired.' (Marx uses the feminine form of 'tired' because he has really entered into the role of the chaste student Tanya, which he plays with great pleasure and verve.)

'Well, I managed to, you know . . .' smiled Lenin slyly. 'And you, you handsome Georgian, were left with your nose out of joint.'

'Never mind,' said Beria, reassuringly. 'We'll get ours later on.'

'That's enough, lads!' said JRF beseechingly. 'Go to sleep!! I've got an important conversation ahead of me tomorrow.'

SCENE 7

The ethics lecture theatre. The sound of a guitar is audible. A discussion about love is taking place.

A: Real love is the kind of love where those in love not only don't, but don't even.

B: That's an outdated point of view. Real love allows not only that, but also. And even more.

A: And what did Lenin write? Here's what he wrote in a letter to Inessa Armand: 'Dear Party Comrade Inessa Armand, What took place between us last night was just dirty physiology not love. I have always and only loved Naden'ka, that is, Nadezhda Konstantinovna Krupskaya, my faithful companion-in-arms in Siberian exile and in the struggle with tsarist autocracy. And tell that prostitute Trotsky that the poorest peasantry will follow us. Stalin is coarse and arrogant. He has acquired far too much power in the Party, which is hyper-important. I consider that the time has come to kick him out of all his posts to . . . With comradely greetings. President of the Council of National Economy, V. Ulyanov (Lenin).' Well, now what do you say to that?

B: I will permit myself to refer to Engels's letter to Marx in which he sets out the basics of marxist sexology. 'Dear Moor, (writes Engels) you ask whether a revolutionary member of the proletariat can copulate with more than three women at a time. Experience of the class struggle by members of the Russian proletariat shows that he can. There's a marvellous Georgian sitting beside me right now and writing an article on the nationalities question. He says that, for a pint of vodka, he can "do" (as he expresses it) half-a-dozen London women, no trouble. I believe him. These Russians are remarkable people. It is more than likely that they will be the first to pioneer the way to . . .' Need I go on? I think that's enough.

T: I think that A's right. What do you think?

Zн: Tanya, Tanya! Let's go to my room. Vaska's gone. We'll put out the light. We'll lock ourselves in. What are you doing without your knickers on?

T: What do you mean, without my knickers? Right enough! Where are they, then? I'd better go and look for them. They're still quite new.

SCENE 8

Zhenya comes into his room. He puts on the light. He sees that his bed is rumpled and that Tanya's knickers are lying near it. He seizes them and presses them to his heart.

Zн: Oh, the scoundrel! And he called himself a friend!

Enter Vasya. Zhenya silently proffers the knickers.

Zн: Do you see these, you scoundrel?

V: I see them. They're Tanya's knickers. What are they doing here?

Zн: You mean it wasn't you?

V: Of course not. I was at a komsomol meeting. Perhaps it was Zurab, or Vladilen Marlenovich? In fact, it could quite easily have been Shkurnikov himself. Perhaps one of the girls is having a joke. We'll raise this question at the meeting tomorrow. We'll get to the bottom of it!

SCENE 9

Night. A room in the hostel. There's not a thing to be seen.

Zн: Vaska, hey, Vaska! Let's rob a bank, shall we?

V: What for?

Zн: We'll get a lot of money.

V: What'll we do with it?

Zн: We'll sell it.

V: But it's cheap nowadays, no one will buy it.

Zн: We'll sell it to foreigners for hard currency. We'll buy Tanya some new knickers. What are you writing?

V: Denunciations.

Zн: It's not worth writing denunciations any more. They only pay twenty kopecks a throw.

V: That's not to be sneezed at! Ten of them bring in two roubles. You can live for a week on that.

Zн: Vaska, did the girls of Ancient Greece go around in knickers or not?

V: Not. Knickers were invented in the nineteenth century. Who invented them? You ignoramus! James Watt invented shorts and Charles Darwin – knickers.

Zн: I thought it was Marx and Engels.

V: They invented underpants. Lenin moved from the abstract to the concrete. He taught that underpants would serve the proletariat and poorest peasantry during the transitional phase, but that they would wither away under full communism together with the state. That's enough, now! Let me get to sleep! There's an exam tomorrow on the history of the CPSU!

Zн: Vaska, sorry – one last question. Did Iron Felix wear underpants?

V: He went around without trousers altogether. In a greatcoat down to his heels. So as to be always on the alert. Z-z-z-z- . . .

SCENE 10

Night. A room in the hostel. There's not a f—— thing to be seen.

K: Tanya, hey, Tanya! Why are you so unapproachable? If I had your abilities, what wouldn't I have done with them!

T: I have been captivated by science. The first paragraph is already finished. Vladilen brought it. Zurab is writing the second. Shkurnikov – the third. Vaska has promised to do the fourth. So it looks like I'll get my project in on time. Consider me a post-graduate student already.

K: Tanya, lend me your knickers. I want to do post-graduate work as well.

T: You won't get into them, not with your behind. Tell me what happened at the eleventh congress of the CPSU.

K: I don't remember. Zurab dropped by. He's talking about organising a seminar on group sex. Shall we enrol? You only need to know two foreign languages.

T: We'll learn them.

K: Tanya, what are you reading?

T: The Ballad of the General Secretary. It was printed abroad in *tamizdat*.

K: Who's the author?

T: Most likely it's Zhenka. But it could have been Vaska. He's got contacts with foreigners.

SCENE 11

The KGB. The Colonel is talking to Zhenya.

C: Re-write these denunciations. They're not according to the format. Why the shoddy work, my lad? Why is there no mention here of the CIA? And here – not a word about anti-Soviet propaganda?

ZH: But they're members of the CPSU!

C: All the more reason. And bear in mind that we've got forty-three denunciations about you. Fifteen of them were written by Vasya, seven by Tanya, five by Zurab.

Zн: But I don't know him!

C: All the more reason. Another seven denunciations and we're going to have you. Bear that in mind for the future. Right now we need five American spies, nine ideological saboteurs, fifteen dissidents. We need to increase the percentage of teaching staff.

Zн: What have you got on me?

C: Dealings in hard currency. And verses.

Zн: What verses? I don't know how to write in verse.

C: And who wrote the 'Ballad of the General Secretary'? Vaska says it was you.

Zн: He's lying. He told me it was Pushkin.

C: Don't blame everything on Pushkin. We'll use machines to find out which one of you it was. You won't get away with it!

THE BALLAD OF THE GENERAL SECRETARY

Once upon a time, oh long long ago,
In a land near where rises the sun,
A Secretary ruled, so the story does go,
And not just any, mind you, but a General one.
He wanted to be the very wisest of all,
And to achieve this he thought it was best
To deliver long speeches with monotonous drawl
To his followers true without rest.
One day to his office he ordered be sent
The wisest of all his wise men.
'Write me a speech, I will brook no dissent,
Of such length as will ne'er be again.
That I may from angles a thousand and one
All the problems on this earth dissect,
So that for thousands of years after my labours are done,
To study it all will elect.'
For decades on end a large number of scribes
Write on parchment of many an ell
To produce for the Secretary the speech he prescribes,
And not just wise men, but lackeys as well.
At last an appropriate feast day drew nigh
That was for a speech just the job.

And the Secretary General gave his usual loud sigh
Through the mike and then opened his gob.
He talked with all main and he talked with all might
(So much so, his brains leaked through his nose)
All day long and eventually into the night,
But the problems and questions still rose.
A horrible boredom took hold of the place,
The snores rumbled from everyone's throat.
But the Secretary read on at his dignified pace,
Line by line, page by page, quote by quote.
Three days and three nights passed, his voice it grew hoarse,
His jaw scarcely moved from the pain.
Though all of his wisdom, his nous and resource
He struggled to show, 'twas in vain.
Musty cobwebs and mould gradually covered the hall,
The delegates were coated with dust.
And the Secretary at last from the platform did fall,
Having choked on a quote like a crust.
The whole country still sleeps and has yet to awake,
Overgrown by thorn bush and branch.
If ever you find yourself there by mistake,
Run away while you still have a chance.

NIGHT-TIME

'All the same, where are these friends of yours? At least describe
what they look like.'

'Very well. Marx is small, with short legs, a beard and lots of
hair. Lenin is small, bald, has a little wedge-shaped beard and
speaks with a burr. Stalin is small, with a pock-marked face,
moustache, smokes a pipe and speaks with a baboon accent . . .'

'You're having me on. Do you think I don't know what the
real Marx, Lenin and Stalin look like? I'm asking you about your
friends.'

'Oh, do you mean them? Marx has still got a beard and long
hair. But he's tall, taller than average. He's thin. Wears a worn-
out nylon anorak and very poor quality boots and trousers. But
they *are* foreign. He wears the same thing winter and summer.
Lenin has a beard and hair, is taller than average, thin, wears a

nylon anorak and low-quality foreign trousers and boots. Stalin
. . .'

'Are you joking?'

'Not at all.'

'So what is it – a uniform?'

'Not exactly a uniform. It's simply fashionable in these circles.'

'I see. How do they differ from each other, then?'

'It depends on the specific situation. Marx, for example, likes
to play the part of a pure, chaste young girl. Lenin is a dreamer
and loves music. Especially the "Appassionata" and "The International". Beria likes violating girls. Stalin is a pragmatist and
positivist.'

'I don't understand what that means. Is he a pederast, or
what?'

'Iron Felix is the pederast. But Stalin is thrifty, careful,
restrained.'

'Tight-fisted, in a word. Is he a Jew?'

'It's possible.'

'My son's fallen ill. What with? What do people usually get ill
with in kindergartens? Did you never go to one, yourself? So
what are you asking for? I'll have to get a medical certificate
again, so for the time it takes I'll be coming to you during the
day. Leave me the key, just in case. I don't want to have anything
to do with your neighbours. And do you know, I'm getting sick
of your pigsty here. It needs to be thoroughly tidied up.'

'Carry on. Only, don't throw anything out without my say-so.
Especially papers. I'm going to need them.'

'I won't throw them out, don't worry. Now, hurry up and
come to bed!'

SCENE 12

*A lecture theatre. Students are sitting about, doing their own thing. Petya
runs in.*

P: Comrades! Zhenya has hanged himself with Tanya's
knickers!!

T: What a nightmare! There's a scoundrel for you! Look how

he's landed us in it! Now we won't win the Red Banner Challenge Trophy for winning the socialist competition! How could he!

V: After lessons . . . No, instead of lessons, we'll immediately conduct a komsomol meeting *in camera*. The agenda will be a personal dossier.

K: I propose that we elect an Honorary Presidium (*names all the members of the Politburo*) and send a greetings telegram to Comrade Leonid Ilich, General Secretary of the Central Committee of the CPSU, Chairman of the Supreme Soviet of the USSR, (*names all his titles*) . . . Knight of the Order of Victory, ten times Hero of the Soviet Union and of Socialist Labour, Commander of the Order of the Garter and Knight of the Order of the Bath, (*lists all his awards*) . . . recipient of the Lenin Peace Prize and the Lenin Prize for Literature, recipient of the Karl Marx Gold Medal (*lists all his medals for his services to science*) . . . Brezhnev.

P: The student Zhenya in fact died as a hero, defending the honour of his chaste, beloved maiden.

V: Okay! In that case I propose the following text for the telegram. Dear and beloved Leonid Ilich! Standing over the corpse of our heroic comrade, we take an oath and promise to be, and if the Motherland and the Party demand, then . . . In honour of such a joyful occasion we take upon ourselves increased commitments in the socialist competition for the best marks in the history of the CPSU exam, namely that we shall all get five, twice.

Again stormy applause, turning into an ovation. Everyone bounces off the ceiling with rapture and love for . . . At this moment enter Zhenya. Tanya's knickers are flapping around his neck. Everyone rushes towards him with shouts of 'Zhenya is a brick!', 'Zhenya, the hero!' Zhenya goes up to Tanya.

Zн: Tanya, say, Tanya, let's go to my room. Vaska's not there. We'll put the light out. We'll lock ourselves in. I'll . . .

T: Let's go! Now I am yours for ever.

Holding hands, everyone sings a romantic song about love. Curtain.

DISCUSSION OF A SEXUAL TRAGEDY

'Well, now,' said Stalin, 'for a former member of the Central Committee and a stalinist lackey academician, that wasn't too bad.'

'A very original conception of how the world works,' said Marx.

'It would be terrifically successful in the West.'

'Success in the West is not a criterion,' interjected Beria. 'The question is, would it be successful here?'

'Under no circumstances,' said Lenin. 'The play is false from beginning to end. What does our young friend think?'

'Intelligent thoughts are only sparked off by something trivial,' said JRF. 'I have just this minute made an important aesthetic discovery and hasten to share it with you. In my opinion you have to distinguish between the veracity of a literary work and its adequacy as such. A truthful work is almost never adequate, and an adequate work is almost never truthful. What does this distinction consist in? When we talk about the veracity of a work, we juxtapose its content with the material it depicts, abstracting from the devices employed in the depiction. But when we speak of adequacy, we juxtapose the means of depiction with the mode of thought of contemporaries, with a type of linguistic expression, in short, we look upon this work as a participant in our own reflexions and conversations about whatever you like, life included. The worst situation arises when a work is partly true and partly adequate. Petin's play is exactly that: it contains a tiny element of truth and is a tiny bit adequate. You only get literary *chefs d'oeuvre* when they are either super-true or super-adequate. Never if they are both. Is that clear? Now get out of here! I need to finish that manuscript.'

CONFERENCE AT THE LUBYANKA

The conference was chaired by the head of the KGB himself. He said that a policy of détente inevitably leads to an intensification of the ideological struggle, that bourgeois ideology was flooding into the country by a variety of channels, that it was criminal to shut one's eyes to that fact, that the dissident movement got almost all of its inspiration from it, that not only many forms of outward behaviour were being assimilated from the West (fashions, hair-styles, songs, sexual relations), but also serious political actions. There had been an increase in cases of aeroplane hijacks, bomb explosions and arson. That explosion in the underground and the fires in the centrally located hotels had been in no way due to technical faults but had been the actions of terrorists whose tracks had yet to be uncovered. There was evidence of the possible existence of extremist groups similar to the 'Red Brigades'. We should not underestimate the seriousness of such groups. Experience showed that even one such group was capable of terrorising the country for a considerable period by taking hostages and organising attempts on the lives of leaders of the Party and government. It was necessary to take measures to prevent the very possibility of such groups coming into existence for if even one action by such a group had even limited success, it could give rise to a whole epidemic of such actions. Therefore . . .

'Therefore,' continued the Head of the KGB, 'we need to organise a well-planned assassination attempt, not by a chance individual, but by a group. JRF's Group seems to me to be the most suitable for this purpose. On the one hand it would seem to exist – and we can prove its existence and criminal designs explicitly. On the other hand, it would seem not to exist and, if the need arises, we can prove just as impeccably that all rumours about it are nonsensical. It will be easy to influence it to perform actions which could be classified as terrorist. It will be possible to attribute to it real terrorist actions committed by other people. At the same time it can be used to mask the real facts of terrorism and to present them in any light that suits us. In short, this group allows us to make any move we like and to control it completely from start to finish. All the unforeseen chance events which happened in the Ilin affair are in this case excluded. These degenerate intellectuals are incapable not only of acting unpredictably, but of acting at all. Compelling them to act is going to cost us a considerable effort.'

THE DREAM OF YOUR AVERAGE INTELLECTUAL

Your average intellectual, who has despaired of making an administrative or academic career, more often than not has one more way of making his life marginally tolerable: this is his 'library' day. Library days are days (one, two, or even three per week) when a member of staff can quite legitimately choose not to come into his institution but to do as he sees fit. Officially the member of staff is deemed to be working in the libraries. Unofficially everyone knows that the majority of staff members don't go to libraries. But it would be unjust to think that all members of staff idle away their time on their 'library' days, or get on with their own 'consultancy' work. For many people these are the only days when, by staying at home, they can get any work done, indeed work in connection with their official institutional duties, for it is practically impossible to fulfil these duties in the institution itself. This is one of the enigmatic paradoxes of our life.

By administrative fiat, JRF was also allocated a 'library' day. Just one, for the moment. But, after all, everyone started with just one. As she shook JRF's hand, Tvarzhinskaya said that she hoped that he would use this day, to . . . , that it had cost her a lot of effort . . . , but that she was confident that he . . . JRF listened to Tvarzhinskaya's impassioned speech, making timid attempts to extract his intellectual's hand from the tenacious grip of an old *chekist*, and burning with impatience for his drinking companions were waiting for him outside, round the corner. They were also burning with impatience and cursed JRF upside down, but they couldn't leave, for, by an unwritten law, it was JRF's treat as the lucky man. And here again the as yet unstudied laws of our new communist society come into play. Although the treat would not be up to much, a fact which was clear in advance, and although those being treated had more resources than the person treating them and would end up by spending twice as much, they were still looking forward to the treat, just as we are pleased by an unexpected inexpensive gift and are pleased from an excess of gratitude to pay for it, one way or another, twice over. Oh unfathomable (as usual) Russian soul!

THE WALL-NEWSPAPER, US AND THE WEST

A new issue of the wall-newspaper was put up on the board. On the first page there was a portrait of Brezhnev in marshal's uniform and full regalia. The artist (one of the director's lackeys from the department of the philosophy of natural science) had depicted him as a handsome man approaching forty. Beneath the portrait there was a quotation from a Brezhnev speech about intensifying the ideological struggle. The paper was, as usual, monotonous and devoid of interest. But two items attracted general attention. One was a veiled hint that certain people in certain sections of the department of dialectical materialism had adopted a conciliatory position with respect to certain philosophical trends in the West. Veiled though the hint was, everyone immediately understood what was what. A recent article in *Communist*, a specific selection of items in *Party Life*, and an abusive article in the 'Literaturka' directed at a well-known theatre producer, told experienced people that the intention of the authorities to lower the 'iron curtain' a little was completely serious. The second item was devoted to the progress of junior members of staff and had been written by Tvarzhinskaya herself. Among other departmental successes in relation to staff development, special mention was made of the fact that JRF had been literally re-born since joining the friendly collective in the Department, that he was now on the right road and that it wouldn't do the department of logic any harm to, etc. And again it was clear to everyone what was what.

These two items determined the topics of the drinking companions' conversation as they set off to the House of Journalists to celebrate JRF's 'library' day. There were two opinions about the item referring to JRF. Some congratulated him, saying that everything would be all right from now on. Others sympathised, since the item would arouse the logicians' anger and they would stop at nothing in the name of defending the achievements of world science. As regards the West, opinions were unanimous: They, of course, would try to eliminate contact with the West, but They would be unlikely to succeed since too many people in the most privileged strata had an interest in contacts with the West. In practice they were now consumers of the products of Western culture and felt, in a certain sense, foreigners in their own country. The children and grandchildren of the leaders were vitally interested in somehow arranging to live in the West. And if anyone was interested in restoring the 'iron curtain', then it was the grey Party bureaucracy, emanating from the loins of 'the people'. The people? The people were dreaming of a new Stalin? What for? What do you mean, what for?! Stalin lowered prices, whereas this lot puts them up. But chiefly because the Russian people has always put its hopes in strong, central, supreme power as its only defence against the arbitrary rule of those in power locally.

They were joined in the House of Journalists by Gleb Stepinsky, who had at one time held quite important posts in the Central Committee of the komsomol and then in the apparatus of the Central Committee of the Party. He had been expelled from the Party a few years before for attempting to set up an anti-Party group and sacked (after a series of gradual humiliations) from his post. The incident was not reported in the press and, although it was spoken of for a short time, it was soon forgotten. Gleb was without work for a long time. Then he managed to fix himself up somewhere as a bibliographer on a salary of seventy roubles a month. During that time he had thoroughly taken to the bottle. But he was, as ever, cheerful, talkative and witty. A chaotic, rumbustious conversation got going on every subject under the sun, with everyone trying to out-shout and out-mock everyone else.

THE KHRUSHCHEV BOYS

Gleb Stepinsky is a characteristic representative of the 'liberal' youth of the time, or the 'Khrushchev boys', who were aroused to activity by the Twentieth Party Congress and Khrushchev's secret speech. They grew up under Khrushchev in the most diverse places, chiefly in and around the upper echelons of power. Gleb, for instance, rapidly became a secretary of the Central Committee of the komsomol in charge of ideology (the First Secretary was Shelepin, future head of the KGB). Others made their way up the ladder via the editorial offices of newspapers and journals, the apparatus of the Central Committee of the Party, the Ministry of Home Affairs, institutes, etc. After the fall of Khrushchev, they managed to retain their distinctive quality for a little while. Gleb, for example, continued to show demonstrative respect for Khrushchev, even after the latter had been disgraced. When Brezhnev and the Brezhnevites came into their own, many of the 'Khrushchev boys' went over to their side, others faded and lapsed into obscurity, others suffered. Gleb, for instance, was demoted a few grades and shunted sideways into a position in which he would henceforth be unable to make a career. This circumstance intensified his critical attitude which had developed under Khrushchev. He began to develop rapidly as a critic of the defects (still only the defects and not the essence) of the existing regime. It is not impossible that he came under the influence of the growing dissident movement.

The 'Brezhnev boys' were merely 'Khrushchev boys' who had grown older and become sated, or, on the other hand, had become disenchanted and had fallen by the wayside. Gleb belonged in the second category. Together with a group of capable lads he decided to graduate from slogans and demagogy to a serious study of reality. In a couple of years he prepared a collection of articles which were supposed to lay the foundation of *dlyasebyaizdat* – publishing only for private consumption – and to serve as a means of enlightening the Party leadership and fuelling serious discussion of pressing problems by the thinking members among the Party workers. But the authorities neither understood nor accepted the good intentions of the *Dlyasebyaizdat* group, and dealt with them more harshly than they treated the dissidents. In so far as all the members of the group were conscientious Party members and remained in their hearts communists, despite their expulsion, the incident made no impact.

The 'Khrushchev boys' shared one illusion: that they could achieve a gradual liberalisation and rationalisation of society by infiltrating into the leaders' speeches all sorts of progressive little ideas and hints and by pushing the leadership in the desired direction without its noticing. While doing so, however, they did not neglect their own earthy interests. And it must be confessed that they were more successful in that sphere than they were in achieving the progress of society. Nor did any of this prevent them from carrying out their routine duties in exactly the same spirit as their predecessors and 'dyed-in-the-wool stalinists' had performed them.

> Hip, hip, O Comrades mine, hooray!
> Now soon will dawn the wished-for day,
> When common sense at last takes o'er,
> And we'll at last be given power.
> Although Their hands are steeped in blood,
> Through Them we're going to get things done.
> And ideas liberal, among the crud,
> We'll feed into Their heads. What fun!
> We'll shove a saucy quote in here,
> Who knows the good that it might do?
> And, there, will 'tween the lines appear,
> Disguised, the sign of fingers two.
> And after that we'll go abroad
> And with our freedom shake the earth.
> We'll cancel death by firing squad
> But still crush folk for all we're worth.
> And then upon a world scale,
> With missiles we will have a ball.
> We'll stuff the gobs of those that wail
> With corn-upon-the-cob, that's all.
> It's time now, Comrades, do you see?

What was before now will not be.
A verdict's one of History's chores,
And we'll get on with settling scores.

FEAR OF ASSOCIATIONS

'Our Party fears nothing more than any type of group formation,'
said Gleb. 'Why? Because it senses what it could lead to. After
all, the Party itself started as an opposition group. And even just
before the Revolution it was numerically still very small. Yet look
what it managed to achieve! Nowadays, of course, no group, or
even party, will be able to accomplish a new revolution. But even
a small group can sow disorder and thoroughly get on Their
nerves. You can't imagine the commotion we caused when we
first made our existence known – we had made ten copies of our
collection of articles and sent the first one to the Central
Committee. They put a whole operational team on to us, headed
by a general! Until they found all ten copies and the rough drafts,
they literally followed us into the toilet.'

'Why on earth did you send it to the Central Committee?'
asked JRF. 'You should have sent it to *samizdat* or *tamizdat*.'

'That's easy to say now. But at that time we were honest and
upright communists, we held positions and hoped to discuss the
most important issues within the Party. Even now I don't
consider myself a dissident, nor do I want to become one. And if
there were the slightest possibility of my working along the lines
I wanted to within the framework of the Party leadership, I
would immerse myself in it completely.'

'There won't be.'

'Of course there won't. But there's no other way. I am one
hundred per cent convinced that progress in our society is only
possible via progress in the government of society. Until the
higher leadership admits younger members (between forty and
fifty), people who are educated, capable and with initiative, we
will see no significant change for the better.'

'In that case, there won't be any.'

'It looks like it. But one doesn't want to think so.'

'Why did they, in fact, remove Khrushchev?'

'The fact that he was removed at the height of his power also speaks in his favour: people were not afraid of him. But just try removing "nice old" Brezhnev, who has been senile for the last five years! The people who removed Khrushchev justify themselves by the fact that he had worn them out with his idiotic and unexpected projects and his costly adventures. But just name even one risky project which they didn't use to buttress their own position! But that's not the point. Towards the end he was beginning to incline towards a decisive restructuring of the managerial apparatus and of the whole economy. They attacked our little group so savagely because it reminded them of Khrushchev's projects. The ones who wanted to get rid of Khrushchev were worried about saving their skins, their posts and their prospects. And when Khrushchev began to talk about restructuring the KGB, he signed his own death-warrant, figuratively speaking.'

'It's strange. He was such an experienced political intriguer and yet he got caught with his trousers down.'

'They weren't down. He was, of course, an arch intriguer. But he was also amazingly naive. And then, he was unable to impose the apparatus of his own personal power on that of the Party bureaucracy and make it subordinate to him. However, this couldn't have happened, anyway. Why not? Can you imagine me, let's say, as a secretary in the Central Committee of the CPSU? We (and I was in the apparatus of Khrushchev's personal power) were too intelligent and cut too much of a figure in society for that.'

DOBRONRAVOV'S DREAM

'If I were younger,' said Dobronravov, 'I would definitely knock together a little secret group. What for? Well, even if it were only to get on the nerves of our highly placed dregs. A couple of well-planned and successful assassination attempts and They'll even take a powerful bodyguard to the toilet with them. And They won't sleep at nights. It's a worthwhile enterprise. But what's needed are young, desperate lads. If I were in your position, I'd . . .'

FROM AN INFORMER'S REPORT TO THE KGB

JRF has established contact with Gleb Stepinsky. They made each other's acquaintance at the House of Journalists on such-and-such an occasion. Present were some members of staff of the Institute of Ideology and the editorial office of *Questions of Ideology*. JRF was interested in the anti-Party group which Stepinsky organised at one time. He asked about the aims of *dlyasyebyaizdat*, about the contents of the collection of articles prepared by the group and about the fate of the group's members. Stepinsky promised to bring them together. Afterwards JRF walked home with Stepinsky. The content of their conversation is unknown to me.

ON SOVIET IMPERIALISM

'Soviet imperialism is an extremely curious phenomenon,' said Gleb. 'We've got territory of our own in abundance which we are still unable to exploit. We don't need to seize territory as such.'

'Why then have we seized half of Europe, gone into Africa and are now getting into South America?'

'There are many reasons for that. Here are a few of them. We strive to make everything around us similar to ourselves, in order to destroy a basis for unwelcome comparisons, exclude harmful influences, criticism of the way we do things and support for the dissidents. We are very much afraid of being unmasked and criticised. And our whole ideological demagoguery would be more secure without the capitalist world. Then, we want to be considered as a model, to be admired. Our leaders are desperate to be leaders on a world scale. They sense that people are laughing at them somewhere, and that's a violation. Our imperialism is of a particular kind – it is ideological.'

'I don't think that our aims are limited to ideology.'

'Of course not. Of course ideological pretensions become transformed into the usual business of usurpation and coercion. But here, too, there is one particular feature. When we seize something, a large number of people are involved in seizing it. They like that kind of life. They have influence in our system of power and they themselves stimulate our imperialism.'

'And what's new in that? It's the same old striving on the part of the population of a colonial power to become a race of masters.'

'That's all still in prospect. I'm talking about the here and now and what's at the root of things.'

BACK AT THE FLAT

'Where did you get to? I got tired waiting for you.'

'I've been having a walk with a very interesting person. He was a big deal under Khrushchev and, for the first few years, under Brezhnev. Then he got the reforming bug and came tumbling down. A living example of how reform from above is doomed to failure in advance.'

'And what isn't doomed?'

'I don't know yet. But dissidence as such is also doomed. It's more than likely that everything has to happen at once for there to be any effect. Without some major catastrophe on a national level which will be noticeably felt by all strata of the population, nothing essentially will change.'

'May God preserve us from that.'

'That's precisely the whole point. We are panic-stricken about the one thing which could be conducive to improvement.'

'What do we need improvements for? Things aren't so bad as they are. Just don't let them get worse.'

'He's a very interesting bloke. He knows a lot about everything. And he can talk well. A pity that it's all wasted.'

'He should write it down.'

'He says that there's no incentive. And anyway, to do that

he'd need to lead a sober life and have at least some means of subsistence. But he's got to toss something off wherever he can. And he's so into the drink now that he won't be able to kick the habit.'

'You're all drunkards.'

'But I'm not quite there yet.'

'Just the same, you're heading in that direction.'

'It's funny!'

'What's funny?'

'I've just remembered. Gleb was talking about the dialectics of our life. He kept quoting funny examples. Take, for instance, the problem of crime. Let's consider two parameters: the crime-detection rate and the drop in crime. According to our ideological directives, the crime-rate is decreasing. But the police are supposed to be working better every year. This means that the crime-detection rate is going up. But if the crime-detection rate is going up, then the crime-rate can't be coming down. There's a paradox for you! Gleb says that it takes dozens and hundreds of conferences at all levels before the corresponding sets of figures can be made to match. I don't understand how They still manage to get themselves out of these difficulties.'

FROM AN INFORMER'S REPORT TO THE KGB

JRF has begun to meet Stepinsky more frequently. I do not know what they talked about. I tried to join them on one occasion, but Stepinsky rudely snubbed me and called me an informer in front of everyone. What does that mean? They loaf around the remote outskirts, go into the most inferior snack-bars, drink and associate with all sorts of riff-raff.

FROM THE INSTRUCTIONS OF THE KGB

Find out exactly where JRF and Stepinsky hang out, and the routes they take to get there. Infiltrate operatives into these places disguised as workers and drunkards and provide them with the appropriate apparatus. Put all the material on the Stepinsky group affair back on the agenda and go through it thoroughly again. Organise surveillance of all the former members of that group.

A CONVERSATION WITH TVARZHINSKAYA

Tvarzhinskaya had a confidential chat with JRF in her office. She said that she was finishing a new book and would like to include a special section on the role of contemporary logic in the struggle with anti-communism. Along the lines of that paper of his. She was counting on, etc. JRF said that it would be a pleasure, but that he would need a couple of weeks, and it was impossible to get any work done in the Institute. Tvarzhinskaya said that she understood and that she would make arrangements with the administration for JRF to work for that time 'in the library'.

EVERYTHING FLOWS

In Stalin's time there was a system of public denunciation which existed alongside a system of informing in secret. Ivanov, for instance, has the floor. He's talking about the wisdom of Stalin's agricultural policy. He says, of course, that Stalin is the greatest genius of all time and all peoples. He talks – and is pleased: everyone will notice what a dedicated lackey he is, ready to do anything. What he doesn't know is that, five minutes later, he will be trying to return to the platform in the preliminary stages of a heart-attack, and tearfully pleading . . . However, let's not get ahead of ourselves, but give the floor to Petrov. Petrov unhurriedly mounts the platform, pours himself a glass of tepid cloudy water from a jug, crumples up his notes and smiles maliciously. 'Just a few minutes ago citizen Ivanov (what?! there is a deathly hush in the auditorium) . . . eloquently and at length demonstrated to us how, apparently, he . . . (surely Ivanov hasn't had it, too?! O God, save us! . . .) But at the same time, this Ivanov, whoever he is (is that an allusion? But Petrov and Ivanov have been friends since they were children! Maybe Petrov, himself?!) . . . paid no attention whatsoever to Stalin's most wise policy in the matter of the industrialisation of the country. Is that a coincidence, comrades?' And just at that moment Ivanov can't restrain himself any longer and throws himself at the platform in tears, both hands clasped to his heart. At that time they still didn't know what a heart attack was and so it was encountered much less frequently. Party activists seize Ivanov and break his arms. Obliging lackeys run to telephone the Organs. But Petrov doesn't succeed in finishing his denunciatory speech before someone shouts out from the audience (this is Sidorov): and what about you, citizen Petrov!! You've forgotten something too!! But Petrov is lucky – he's still on the platform. Petrov quickly stoops, drinks the jug empty and immediately begins to admit that in his speech he failed to take sufficiently into account this, assumed that, underestimated the other . . .

A great achievement of stalinist times (and one of Stalin's qualities for which the people love him to this day) was the strict observation of the principle of adequacy with respect to the denunciation, both private and public, on the one hand, and punishment, on the other, namely: 1) an arrest was made for every denunciation; 2) you were arrested on the basis of what was said about you in the denunciation. For instance, if Petrov exposed Ivanov as a disguised Trotskyist, the latter was shot as a Trotskyist. If Ivanov wrote that Petrov was the personal adjutant of Denikin, Kolchak and Makhno simultaneously, Petrov was shot as such. They say that during the whole stalinist period there was only one mistake, and that was when a monarchist was shot as a kulak. And the whole leadership of the Provincial Cheka paid for it with their heads.

During the first years after Stalin's death, the system of denunciation and exposure which he had created continued to operate, but the principle of adequacy began to be infringed with regard to the first point: not everyone who was exposed or denounced was arrested. Many were left in freedom until further notice. After Khrushchev's secret speech, the principle of adequacy began to be infringed with regard to the second point, as well: cases began to occur when a person was denounced for one thing but arrested for something quite different. After that there was a short period of confusion, during which denunciations and exposures lost all significance altogether and people were arrested totally independently of them. The fact of the matter is that there was a crisis during this period in the denunciatory-expository activity of the citizens of our slightly underdeveloped socialist society, which had to do not so much with the exposure of the 'cult' and the rehabilitation of its victims as with the elimination of the actual content of denunciations and exposures. The world situation changed radically, and denunciations again referred to spies, Trotskyists, monarchists, Bukharinites, menshevik idealists, disguised kulaks . . .

After the period of confusion was over, the efficacy of the system began to be restored. But with two substantial amendments. Firstly, denunciatory activity as a form of spontaneous social behaviour on the part of the broad mass of the population became separate from the professional activity of the Organs of state security in the matter of collecting information about the criminal intentions and behaviour of citizens. As a result of this, things began to happen which earlier would have been absolutely impossible, when the above-mentioned Organs would suddenly remove someone from a collective who had been universally respected and had been regarded as a rank-and-file Soviet shyster like everyone else. Secondly, the principle of adequacy was lost entirely. Almost no one was arrested and arrest was replaced by other methods (a person would be dismissed from work, or declared ineligible for an increase in salary or a prize, or would be unable to improve his or her housing, or would have his or her career prospects drastically curtailed, etc.) And if anyone was arrested, the denunciations and exposures merely served as a formal excuse, or as a supplementary feature. For example, a Jew by the surname of Smirnov was arrested in the Institute of Ideology for apparent homosexuality (that was what the denunciation alleged). At the trial, the Institute representative said that Smirnov had made concessions to positivism, which intensified the man's guilt (could one imagine such a thing in Stalin's time: a homosexual positivist!!). But Smirnov was sentenced for the Crimean Tartar affair, even although all he had done was prepare to emigrate to Israel. Analysing this incident on the upper landing, Doctor of Philosophical Science Barabanov (who had been the Institute expert at the trial), the biggest cretin in the Institute, observed profoundly that this was precisely how the advanced socialism of today differed from the full socialism of yesterday. True, his listeners never did understand how, exactly, advanced socialism differed, but that didn't matter, for it was clear to everyone, anyway, how it differed: not by one iota.

In response to the expository hints in the wall-newspaper, in which paranoiac Smirnyashchev detected the hand of Tvarzhinskaya and her new favourite JRF, the activists in the Department of Logic (Zaitsev, Smirnyashchev and Sazonov) met in Smirnyashchev's flat. When they had drunk a couple of bottles of cognac and eaten a vast amount of *zakuski*, prepared by Smirnyashchev's mother-in-law, the guardians of the achievements of world science composed an open letter to the Party bureau of the Institute. In it they demonstrated the total absence of foundation for the reproaches addressed to them and expressed, on the contrary, apprehension about JRF's activity in the Department of Struggle against Anti-communism, since he was not sufficiently qualified for the assignment that he had taken on, etc. After Zaitsev had gone, Smirnyashchev and Sazonov drew up the rough draft of a secret report to the KGB on JRF, the Teacher, Dobronravov and many others. Sazonov promised to work it up at home and send it off or deliver it personally.

At the same time the most intelligent member of the department, Subbotin, wrote a circumstantial report on everyone. He was not at all bothered by the fact that denunciations had lost their former force. He wrote out of habit, just in case and from an instinctive urge to demonstrate his readiness.

THE NEW ARRIVAL

A new girl appeared in the Department of the Philosophy of the Eastern Countries. She was a junior research officer on the lowest point on the salary scale (about eighty roubles a month). Since the Institute was continually expanding, girls like her quite regularly appeared on the scene and no one paid any attention. These girls were usually unattractive and scatter-brained. After several scandals resulting in the opening of personal files, the Institute womanisers no longer found them attractive, even when they were drunk. But this time it was different. The new girl was very young, straight out of school (if you don't count her failure to get into university) and was extremely charming and attractive. The Institute's 'eligible bachelors' (womanisers who had long since been divorced or who were about to get divorced, and young, unmarried junior research fellows), under the most diverse pretexts, took to dropping into the room where the new girl was checking, cutting and sticking the manuscript of senior research fellows, who were famous far beyond the confines of the Institute for their dullness, inarticulacy and ability to cause trouble. JRF too, 'by chance' wandered into the room, having first cleaned his boots, changed his shirt and done something about his mind-boggling beard. He wandered in and . . . Imagine what it has come to with these scoundrels! . . . And spoke to her in an unintelligible foreign language. And she replied in the same language. French, decided the Head of the Section of the Philosophy of the Countries of the Near East. No, in her opinion it was Italian, remarked Doctor of Science Piskunova. Most likely it was English, since it was now fashionable for them (whom?) to speak English. Kirusik reported the fact like lightning to all the departments, sections, groups and services in the Institute. The Institute pricked up its ears, held its breath, clenched its jaw and curled its lip. 'What cheek!' said Tormoshilkina. 'On no account can that be permitted!'

Then JRF invited the new girl during the lunch hour to have a bite to eat with him in a pub. And this 'trollop' . . . This is what the young people have come to nowadays! . . . This 'trollop' agreed! And the Institute decided to put a stop to this outrage before matters got out of hand. The first person to have a talk to Trollop was the chief guardian of Institute morality – forty-year-old Ninochka, in charge of the research office, who had changed her 'fancy man' about fifty times and was currently living (according to rumour) with the homosexual (also according to rumour) Kachurin. Pressing the slender Trollop into a corner with her mighty bosom, she read her a long lecture about how she had come to a very important institution, how important it was that her moral behaviour be exemplary, how she should behave and that she should listen to what she, Ninochka, told her. Ninochka was replaced by the secretary of the komsomol organisation, who told Trollop the same thing, only pressed her, not into a corner in the corridor, but against his secretarial desk. The female staff of the sector who would drop into the room where Trollop was 'just for a minute', began a determined and systematic campaign to open her eyes to the 'real' JRF. In the first place, they would whisper to each other in such a way that she could not but hear what they were saying, he had no future at all as an academic. He was untalented. A loafer. Secondly, he was an inveterate drunkard. Thirdly, he had had more than a thousand women. He would sleep with one for a couple of nights, give her a child, then move on to the next one. Didn't pay alimony. And he was a miser. Didn't pay a kopeck towards an abortion. Finally, he kept doubtful company and was under observation by the KGB and a psychiatric clinic.

But these measures did not have the desired effect. On one occasion Kirusik reported that she had seen JRF and Trollop together one evening in the 'National' café. They were drinking wine and laughing happily! Tormoshilkina called Tvarzhinskaya down to the landing a floor below to talk to her as a young (?) communist to an old communist and to ask her to try to influence her subordinate. Tvarzhinskaya talked to JRF in her office for more than an hour, having double-locked the door.

'Of course,' she said, 'you are a young, unmarried man and she is of age. No one can say anything against you. But my advice to you is this: she's a nice girl. Marry her. You'll make a lovely couple. Only don't forget to invite me to your wedding.'

WARNINGS

'You shouldn't have got involved with that girl,' said the Teacher. 'What do you want with her? She's a silly little thing.'

'Actually, she's not all that silly. She's no sillier than these Institute smart-asses. And she's certainly no sillier than that cow Tormoshilkina.'

'Well, now, if these are your criteria!'

'She has an excellent command of English. She was at a special school. And her family taught her it as well. I get terrific practice in the language with her.'

'Stop trying to pull the wool! If you're all that keen, bang her a couple of times and finish it off.'

'Why are you so concerned, anyway?'

'I feel sorry for you. You'll end up in a mess. You couldn't set up a family with her type. You'll struggle along and after a year at most you'll get divorced. She doesn't need a husband like you. She needs a candidate, or even a doctor.'

'And supposing I become a candidate?'

'That's what she's counting on. And anyway, having a family in our times is a complete waste of time. And supposing the candidate thing falls through? She'll have your head. She'll need a self-contained flat. And your salary won't even keep her in boots.'

'And what makes you think that I'm going to get married? We simply spend time together. We're friends. Isn't that allowed? I like her company.'

'Of course it's allowed. But there are all sorts of rumours flying around. And, as they say, there's no smoke without fire. OK. Let's change the subject. How about sitting down somewhere and having a chat?'

'I can't today. I'm going to the Conservatoire.'

'With her? I never thought you'd sink so far. Next minute you'll be telling me that you're giving up drink. Come on, maybe we'll have a quick one, eh?'

'OK, but it really will have to be a quick one.'

'I don't know any more miserable institutions than our drinking establishments. And I don't know any more wretched phenomenon than our drunkenness. And yet we get into it up to our necks. We're ready to poeticise it and even raise it to the rank of a religion. Why is that? There are, as they say, many reasons. And yet, usually the main one is ignored. The fact is that your Ivan, when he's sober, is nothing but a vile social creature. When he's drunk, he turns into a more human kind of creature. When we drink heavily we are defending ourselves from ourselves and similar sober creatures. We simply don't have any other means of self-defence. Or, if we do, they don't last for long. Besides, drunkenness simplifies all our relations, short-circuits, for example, all the procedural preliminaries with women. Drunkenness slightly embellishes the monotony of our lives. It helps you to get out of the mess of family ties. It moderates careerist tendencies and administrative zeal. We engage in a bitter struggle with drunkenness in our country. But I don't believe that it is sincere. We all feel instinctively that getting rid of drunkenness would make our life even more of a nightmare. Drugs are now coming into fashion. But I don't think that they will replace hard drinking. They don't match the nature of our society, or your average Ivan. Look at that character over there. Can you imagine him injecting himself with a needle? Of course not. He'd not only break a needle, he'd break a beer-mug.'

JEALOUSY

'I hear you've picked up some beauty or other,' said Tatyana.

'How did you find that out?' asked JRF in surprise.

'That's a secret. You can't hide anything from a woman. I warn you, while you're with me I won't tolerate any other women.'

'In that case . . .'

'It won't work! You won't get rid of me as easily as that. I will put up a fight. To the last. Got it?'

'Got it.'

'Idiot! You won't find anyone better than me, anyway.'

'Why not?'

'Because they don't come any better than me. And, anyway, no one is going to love you more than I do.'

'Why not?'

'Because it's impossible.'

'How do you know?'

'From experience. I've seen a lot, after all. No one would believe it if I told them. If you only knew . . .'

'What?'

'Never mind. I was talking to myself. I feel like crying. I found out not long ago that my respectable husband has taken a mistress.'

'Well, so what? You yourself . . .'

'That's different. I'm allowed to. Do you know what hurt? It wasn't so much the mistress as the kind of mistress.'

'What kind was she?'

'An eighteen-year-old who fiddled her way into his department to get work experience.'

WARNINGS

'That new girl of yours isn't bad,' said Dobronravov. 'She's sexy. Got quite a nice figure.'

'How do you know she's sexy?' said JRF in surprise. 'She's still only a girl.'

'I know these "girls"! She's already had three lovers go through her.'

'Why are you talking like that? Lightning will strike you!'

'I'm only passing on what I heard. Ask Tormoshilkina. She knows her parents. She had an affair while she was still at school. It was hushed up.'

'Well, and what of it? What are you telling me for?'

'We're friends. It's my duty to warn you.'

'Thank you very much. Now let's change the subject.'

'As you like. Shall we have a quick one?'

'I'm busy today.'

'What time are you seeing her? About eight? Well, you'll still make it. There's masses of time. In here! What real man goes out on a date sober?! I'm loaded today. What'll it be? Vodka, of course? And a chaser. Look, chuck this Trollop! Surely you've got enough decent other women? You'll save yourself a lot of bother. Same again?'

'I've got to go.'

'You'll make it. Take a taxi. If it comes to the bit, she'll wait for you. She's still only a fledgling, when you think of it! Do you want a joke? Carter asks Brezhnev how the struggle against drink is going in the Soviet Union. "Very well," says Brezhnev, "we've banned *zakuski*."'

A CONVERSATION BETWEEN OP AND SUBBOTIN

OP: Tell me more about this conversation between JRF and the Terrorist.

SUB: They went into the Sub-department of the Philosophical Problems of Physics and went over to the window which looks out on to the Kremlin. They didn't shut the door. I was sitting in the next room behind a cupboard. I could hear their whole conversation. At first I was going to shut the door since it was getting on my nerves. But when I heard them talking about explosions I became interested.

OP: Who spoke, and what exactly was said?

SUB: The one who spoke most was the one you were pleased to call 'the Terrorist'. He said that the problem of getting explosives into the Kremlin by air was easily solved. It would also be easy to choose a time – a session of the Supreme Soviet or a Party congress or an anniversary occasion. According to him, They met nearly every week. The technical problem related to the remote control of the flying device by radio. That window would be the most suitable. JRF said that all the offices were checked and sealed before the Institute closed and that on important occasions there were people on duty. The Terrorist said that they could hide in a cupboard.

Op: What can you tell me about JRF's meetings with members of the 'Workers' group'?

Sub: I live on Gorky Street. In a writers' block of flats. My father, as you ought to know, was a very important writer. Recipient of a Stal . . . , sorry, a State Prize. I quite often walk to and from work. On one occasion, when I was walking past the reception area of the Presidium of the Supreme Soviet, I saw JRF in the company of some very strange-looking people. I can't, of course, categorically insist on the hypothesis that these people were members of the 'Workers' group'. But in the light of events . . . Well . . . E-e-er . . . I don't regard my hypothesis as being so improbable that it should be deemed to be totally, speaking in the popular idiom, unreliable.

Op: What can you say about JRF's contacts with foreigners?

Sub: Foreigners used to come to our Institute rather frequently, and to our section in particular. JRF usually acted as guide-interpreter. I won't take it upon myself to judge how conscientiously he interpreted. We don't have a good command of Western languages in their spoken form, and he could have been telling them God knows what under the guise of a translation.

Op: What did he talk about with these foreigners, apart from professional matters?

Sub: I told you already that I don't know foreign languages in their spoken form. Although I once heard him talking to some Poles. What about? The conversation was broadly speaking anti-Soviet. They were laughing and telling jokes. What kind? Well, this one, for instance. Terrorists have seized Gierek and present the government with an ultimatum: if they don't give them a million zloty, they'll let Gierek go.

Op: Ha-ha-ha! What else?

Sub: I don't see what there is to laugh at. It's strange to hear a reaction like that from you.

Op: I wasn't laughing at the joke. That's the tenth time I've heard it. It seems to be a password among them.

Sub: That is very likely. Oh, before I forget! I twice saw JRF in the 'National'. I was walking past and saw him through the window. On one occasion with someone who looked very like a foreigner.

AN ANONYMOUS LETTER

Trollop received an anonymous letter. An unknown woman wrote that she had loved JRF for a long time, that she was having an affair with him, that they were going to get married, that she (Trollop) was destroying their future married life together, that this was immoral on her part . . . that JRF was an alcoholic and mentally sick, that he and she would not make a good couple, that . . . that . . . that . . .

'Do you know,' said Trollop, showing JRF the letter, 'this is the first letter in my life I've ever got from a stranger. It's hurtful to have to start adult life with nastiness like that.'

'Don't pay any attention,' said JRF. 'Life is a journey through the mire. You are taking your first steps. Get used to it.'

'I understand,' she said. 'People tell me in this place from morning to night, in unison, what a depraved, hopeless and even dangerous person you are. But I want to do the opposite of what They say, just to spite Them.' And she tore the letter up. At the end of the day, she went into the research office where he was waiting for her, and in the presence of everyone took his arm and went with him along the corridor and then down the stairs. She looked for all the world like a blissful bride walking down the aisle towards the longed-for consummation.

WORK

The General said that it would be expedient to get JRF out of Moscow for a while under some pretext or other. And during that time . . . The Colonel ordered the Operative to remove JRF from Moscow by whatever means available. The Operative telephoned the Institute. The Academic Registrar said that it might be possible to organise a business trip. But none was planned for the near future. How would it be if he were to be given sabbatical leave for a while and sent to a rest home?!

Wonderful idea! It would never enter his head that . . . Especially since he was supposed to have been taken ill.

JRF'S ILLNESS

When academicians, professors and other people from the upper reaches fall ill, no one is surprised or indignant. They are permitted to by their rank. Their illnesses merely awaken a feeling of justified sympathy. For doctors and the community to believe that they are ill, a mere word or even a veiled hint is sufficient. Any one of their illnesses is interpreted by those around them as an event of major importance. Even the word 'haemorrhoids', when it is associated with one of them, sounds almost like 'cerebral haemorrhage', 'coronary thrombosis' or 'cancer'. When Petin, for example, simulated for the umpteenth time an inflammation of the prostate gland, all that was to be heard in the Institute for a whole week was the whisper of syllables like 'pros', 'infla', 'gla', 'tate', 'mation', 'nd'. Kirusik, who genuinely believed that the prostate gland regulated the opening and closing of the back passage, informed the whole Institute confidentially that Petin now did it all through his nose with the help of a super-modern Japanese electronic calculating machine.

Everything said up till now relates to the upper crust. But if you said, for example, that JRF was ill, no one would believe it. They would say that he was malingering. And they would be indignant about the lack of idealism on the part of the youth of today. And if you said that JRF had haemorrhoids, the Institute would be amused for a whole week. And if it became known that there was something wrong with his prostate gland, then even Kirusik would guess what was going on and the Institute would laugh till the tears came for at least two weeks. And JRF's name would immediately be struck off the waiting-list for getting on to the waiting-list for membership of the CPSU. Why should we let people into our Party with doubtful illnesses (he's bound to be a homo!) when there's no room for the healthy ones!

But in fact JRF *was* ill. They took his temperature twice at the clinic and unwillingly wrote out a medical certificate. One hundred degrees for a junior research fellow is a mere bagatelle and isn't worth his while going to bed for. 'Do you think he'll go to bed?' the doctor asked the nurse, when JRF had left the surgery. 'Not likely! He'll immediately go and drink himself senseless. And by evening he'll be as strong as an ox. They're all like that nowadays!'

When he got home, JRF flopped down on his ottoman and became feverish. Marx, Lenin, Stalin and company appeared, and leaned over him.

'Oho,' said Beria, feeling his forehead, 'that's bound to be nearly a hundred and three.'

'That's all right,' said JRF. 'A small effort of will, and I'll be well in a few hours. I know how to do that. And after that I can swan around for three days on the strength of the medical certificate. That'll be great! But since you're here, I'll read you a short lecture on medicine.

'I don't complain about my health. Not because I have no grounds to, but because I have grounds not to. Our doctors don't cure people, they simply take measures to avoid being accused of not curing people or having caused the death of a patient through negligence. For that reason they make patients undergo countless analyses, and acknowledge, just in case, that they have all sorts of illnesses, and they write it all down on medical cards for page after page. And if a patient requires a health certificate, the decision of the doctors depends on general directives from above, calculations about the safety of their own position and the intentions of the authorities with respect to the patient concerned. For instance, when Petin wanted to take me along as an interpreter to an international congress, they checked me over in a couple of hours in the clinic reserved for doctors of science and gave me a chit testifying that I was in good health, while in reality I could hardly stand after an excessive drinking bout. But when I wanted to visit the same country as a tourist, I spent two weeks in the clinic for all sorts of scientific nonsense. And although I was healthy and in good spirits, they managed to diagnose high and low blood-pressure simultaneously, stenocarditis, sclerosis, gastritis and much more besides. Even the head doctor, who had seen a thing or two in his time, although he refused to sign a chit to the effect that I was fit to undertake a trip abroad, admitted that they had gone a bit too far. And when he found out that the "abroad" in question was only Bulgaria, he became quite courageous and struck some of my "illnesses" off the list. But he still didn't sign the chit. When I later tried to dodge my military service, I brought up the subject of these illnesses. But the same head doctor refused to sign a chit saying that I was unfit for military service, even although military service takes more out of you than a trip abroad. And I had to spend three months kicking my heels in the political instruction unit of the infantry reserve.

'My late granny used to tell not so much me (I was a healthy lad) as herself (as an old woman she was always poorly) that the important thing was not to be ill. "Not ill" for her meant still having the use of her arms and legs. Anything to do with the internal organs she regarded not as an illness but an indisposition. She didn't recognise mental illness at all, regarding it as a whim of the bosses. They were too well off. From this point of view, Granny expressed the general attitude in the country and the general line of the Party on medicine. Recently there has been a slight shift in this line. Mental illness has begun to be recognised, but so far mainly in relation to dissidents. Indispositions are now fully recognised illnesses. There has been literally an avalanche of indispositions, mainly among healthy people. Hence the endless queues in hospitals, the reams of paper-work, the shoddy treatment. I assure you, the number of those ill has increased ten-fold as a result. Since these indispositions of the past have been officially declared to be illnesses, people really contract them. It's all whim and caprice. If I could eat a clove of garlic now and rub myself with another one, I'd get up in the morning as right as rain.'

At that moment the Teacher and Dobronravov entered the room without knocking. 'We'll have you on your feet in two shakes,' said the latter. 'A bit of garlic inside you, another bit to rub yourself with and you'll get up in the morning as right as rain.'

UNHEARD-OF GENEROSITY

'I've squared things with the management and the local trade-union committee,' said Tvarzhinskaya. 'You're being given sabbatical leave, all expenses paid, in a rest home. Get all your material together and off you go. Take my whole manuscript with you. Here it is. Read it! Perhaps you'll have some comments to make. If you need foreign sources, we'll order them. The messenger will bring them out. I've marked the places where it would be nice to have some quotations. And you'll have a rest. Just recently you've been looking tired.'

'Well, off you go and rest,' said Tatyana. 'I'm working the first shift as from next week. Then I'm going on a long trip, so we won't be seeing each other for a while.'

'You're going off to have a rest,' sighed the Teacher. 'Lucky lad. You'll be able to make up for lost sleep. You'll put on some weight. Get some fresh air into your lungs. Look in on Petin while you're there. He's got a dacha out there. Stalin gave it to him. If we're in the right mood we'll take a turn out to see you on our day off. There are some lovely spots around there. And the food, they say, isn't too bad.'

'We've had to cut your paper down by half,' said the Acquaintance. 'But it's improved as a result. It's being discussed at the next meeting of the board. You won't need to come along, we'll manage without you. I think it'll go through all right. You've got such powerful support these days.'

'Have a good rest,' said Herself. 'You can phone from there, you know. And write letters. Send me a letter. I want to get a nice letter.'

GETTING READY FOR THE ROAD

JRF shoved the pages of the shyster's manuscript under the ottoman. He got out a briefcase on its last legs and covered with dust from behind the cupboard, and threw into it a towel, toothbrush, a piece of soap, socks, a nearly clean shirt, a sweater which could still be worn, Tvarzhinskaya's manuscript and a bundle of grease-stained papers of Petin's containing what purported to be a historical tragedy. He sighed heavily. He checked to make sure that he had his passport and ticket. He counted his money. He sat down on the ottoman for a moment, as required by Russian custom, before setting off. He looked morosely at the torn wallpaper and the dirty grey, peeling plaster. He locked the door behind him and was about to take the key out of the lock when he thought better of it: anyone who needed to get in would get in, so they might as well have the key. A group of men were having a drinking session on the stair landing. One of them pushed JRF. JRF apologised and squeezed past sideways. 'Should we give that bearded guy a bottle in the back of the head?' he heard behind him. The others laughed. 'It's not worth getting your hands dirty,' said another, hoarsely. Outside it was slushy and miserable. There was a feeling of spring in the air.

PART THREE

In Defence of
Practical Unreason

THE BEGINNING OF THE ROAD

When we were doing (not studying – doing!) Ancient Rome at school, our teacher asked us by way of ideological training who we would have liked to be had we lived in those times. All the pupils in our class declared that, out of solidarity with those exploited, they would have liked to be slaves. But I said that I didn't want to be a slave, that I was ready to be anyone you liked, even a slave-owner, but not a slave. This caused a tremendous fuss. I was hauled over the coals at a class meeting, a Pioneer meeting, by the headmaster, at a pedagogical council and at a parents' meeting. My father gave me a good thrashing and ordered me to recant, otherwise he would send me to a children's reformatory. I held out for a whole week. But the sides were too unevenly matched and I capitulated. I acknowledged my guilt at a specially convened Pioneer meeting and solemnly swore that, just like all my friends, I wanted to be a slave. And to this day I have kept that oath. And I don't regret it in the least.

AND THE END OF THE ROAD

And yet there have been times in my life, right up to the present, when I can hear resound within me hymns of divine beauty. Were I to admit that to anyone, no one would believe me. This stalinist leftover has hymns resounding within him?! they would say. Rubbish! Nothing can resound within him except Party slogans! Well, I can partly agree with that. I am in fact a leftover. But I'm not a stalinist. I was never a stalinist. I can't say that I fought against stalinism. But, I repeat, I was never a stalinist. I lived through the best part of my life in that period and that's all. But is that sufficient to be considered an accomplice to a crime? And what was a crime then, and what not? And as far as membership of the Party is concerned, even avant-garde members of the intelligentsia and fighters for this and that were in it, and are now. Or are trying to get in. Not that everyone, mind you, succeeds. For instance, that profound bearded young man (JRF from our Institute) has been trying to join our ranks for five years now, but for some reason they won't admit him. Why is that? Perhaps it's because he too has divine music inside him but they've learned to detect it. You don't get into the Party if you hear divine music inside yourself. They let me in in my time because there was a war on and a different kind of noise was drowning out everything else. Besides, after that capitulation in my childhood I learned to 'control the volume' and the music became inaudible to those around me.

But I still hear those hymns, although rarely. And there are other things going on inside me. Horses gallop. Brigs and corvettes pass by under full sail. Beautiful women waltz in a luxurious palace. Swords flash. Fairy-tale cities and valleys and islands spring up. And again there are mysterious, unattainable women who slip past. What *don't* I have going on inside me! And when that happens, it's depressing. I look at the real people around me and I feel like a creature from some other world with fire in my soul but destined to live in a perpetually funereal atmosphere in an alien world. What is the reason for that? I was once listening to our Institute bright sparks on the lower landing. The conversation was about this very topic. And somebody said that inner loneliness is the inevitable consequence of an imposed external collectivism. That bright spark was possibly right. However, just to be contrary, I said at the time that that was rubbish. But these Institute bright sparks paid no attention. For them it was as if I didn't exist.

OUR LITTLE WAYS

They've put up a new bust of Lenin with legs in the courtyard of our Institute and a new bust of Lenin's head in the main lecture hall. These are not my words. I have not, alas, attained such heights of eloquence, nor am I likely to. These are the words of the director of our Institute, Academician Petin, one of the greatest marxist-leninists of our age. He pronounced these words during his report on the results of fulfilling the plan for the second quarter of the third year of the current (which one even the secretary of the Party bureau couldn't tell without doing his homework and consulting the district Party committee) five-year plan. To be more precise, he pronounced these words in the part of his report devoted to the increase in the well-being of the workers. And, in fact, he didn't pronounce them so much as declaim them, or, indeed, bawl them out. No, even these words don't convey the full sublimity of that particular moment. He stood on the tips of his toes, so that his broad red tie with a green stripe became visible from behind the lectern as well as his ugly mug, raised his right hand, opened wide his orthodox marxist gob, noisily sucked in air . . . It was as if he weren't standing at the lectern in the chief ideological institution of the country but in an armoured car. And from the deepest depths of his rectum he produced the following exultant fanfare. 'We don't,' he roared, 'need to go far to find an example. Take our own Institute! In the last two weeks alone they have built a marvellous new bronze bust of Lenin on legs' (there was a rustle in the hall and people began whispering) '. . . I mean, life-size' (there was laughter at that since Lenin, like Petin, was under five feet tall, the 'bust of Lenin on legs' was nearly fourteen feet high) '. . . And in the main lecture hall' – continued Petin exultantly, drowning out the laughter of the politically immature members of the Institute staff – 'they have erected a new bust of Lenin's head! Only in the last two weeks! What does that tell us, comrades?! It tells us a lot!'

He's right, this titan of marxist thought, pygmy Petin. It *does* tell us a lot. It's not coincidence that these were the first words to come into my head when I decided to jot down these notes out of boredom. It's not Lenin in an armoured car summoning people to revolution after it has already happened that symbolises our era, but Petin on the platform trumpeting all sorts of nonsense. Lenin was only an idea and Petin is its realisation. Lenin is a myth, whereas Petin is the reality.

MY CREED

My ancestors appeared on this earth with some *a priori* inclination to do their Duty and serve the Cause. And if their Duty was done and the Cause served, they left this world with a clear conscience, without fear, contented. Their lives, however, had one major drawback: there was always this Duty, this Cause, looming before them. I decided to eradicate this drawback – by removing Duty and Cause from the life-process altogether. And I can give a fully scientific justification for this. What is the most important element in the sensation that Duty has been done or that the Cause has been served? Is it positive or negative? Having studied the evidence of history and the confessions of my acquaintances who have passed on, I have established with absolute conviction that it is negative. What is most important, it turns out, is not the realisation that you've done something important, but the realisation that there is nothing on this earth which needs to be fulfilled, or where the fulfilment depends on you. And once that has been established, the problem of what to do with one's life has a trivially simple solution: live as if you had no Duty or Cause. This is extremely convenient. You're ready to leave this world at a moment's notice. And you won't be tormented by the realisation that you didn't manage to get your children into an institute, that you didn't manage to get a separate flat, that you didn't finish your research, that you didn't finish your novel, that you . . . In a word, you feel like a soldier who matches up to the formula of the ancient Greek sages: all that I have, I carry around with me. And if Fate issues the command 'On your feet! Attention! To the Next World – quick ma-a-arch!!', you stand to attention, pull in your stomach, raise your head and . . . And that's all! And you're no more. Somewhere in your subconscious, of course, there will be the thought that you'll be leaving behind you on This Earth your dirty socks and a dozen empty vodka bottles which you never got around to taking back. But you won't even have time to transfer it to the plane of the emotions (what a beautiful expression, don't you think?!) before it disappears, making way for that Great Peace which is the culmination of life.

So – no Duty, no Cause! My colleagues and superiors sense this approach to life of mine. And it would be laughable if they didn't sense it: a bloke spends decades under their noses trying not to do anything. But they can't find fault with me: I present my inactivity in such a way that I appear to be a model worker. And the strangest thing of all is that they don't want to find fault with me: I suit them just as I am. Some of them even feel sorry for me. These are the ones who are doing their Duty and serving the Cause. For them Duty and Cause contain the meaning of life. How can you live like that, they say. They don't ask, but rather express surprise and a little disgust. And, of course, a little sympathy. I expound the same theoretical justification I introduced above. But for some reason they don't understand it. They think it's some kind of joke. Then I ask them what their Duty and their Cause consist in. They begin to think about that. And they look quite pitiful when they discover how paltry these foundations of their existence really are. And then I begin to console them. Spit, as it were, on this lousy Duty and this rubbishy Cause! Let's go on a bender without a Cause. Just like that. We'll have a drink and a chat. Sometimes they listen to the voice of reason. And then, when they've had a few, they complain that it's already too late to spit on their lousy Duty, and that although their Cause is rubbishy, they've invested too much energy, thought and feeling and in it to abandon it now. Sometimes they smile sadly and go off about their Duty, slipping along the corridors in their crumpled grease-stained trousers or shapeless skirts. Watching them, I sigh and pronounce to myself something along the lines of the following. Oh, Homo sapiens! The acme of creation! Why, one asks oneself, do you study the binomial theorem and Ohm's Law, read Shakespeare and

Dostoevsky, listen to Mozart and Tchaikovsky, clean your teeth and change your socks?! Surely it's not just so that you can check idiotic quotations from the classical writers in some rubbishy article of a degenerate Party ideologue and help the beloved collective to win the Red Challenge Banner of the district committee of the Party in the socialist competition for the title of Model Enterprise of Communist Labour? Stop, you blockhead!! Look around you! And marvel at life! Chuck everything! Open your eyes, look and marvel!! And you will see that, foul and miserable as our life is, it is still worthy of your attention.

And surprise, of course. For instance, we've just had a section meeting. The meeting was hyper-important (as the bust of Lenin loved to express himself): the work we're supposed to have been doing for the plan has been rotting for three years, we're falling behind. What are we to do? If we admit it, there will be a scandal. Our institution can then say good-bye to the Red Challenge Banner. All my colleagues turned grey and blue with suffering, for this was their Duty and Cause. They clutch their hearts and stomachs, swallow pills, drip drops. And there's not a ghost of a thought. Then I proposed my own variant of the solution to this insoluble problem: re-title our *opus*, which has been lying in the publishing house for three years (this was our plan for the previous five-year plan) and will lie there for another year, write a new preface for it, taking account of the present situation, insert into the articles a dozen references to the latest decrees and speeches, and . . . I didn't even get a chance to finish my thought. And in half an hour the section was transformed. And I was surprised: why are these titled idiots incapable of solving a trivial little task like that when they take it upon themselves to solve problems of global, epoch-making or cosmic importance?! And later I was again surprised at the simplicity of the answer to my question: because they are in the grip of their Duty and their Cause.

After the section meeting, we went off to one of the senior staff's place to 'christen' this solution worthy of a genius. When we came out into the courtyard, someone said that birds had taken up residence in the empty head of 'Lenin's bust with legs'. They were flying in and out of the wide open mouth of the leader summoning people to revolution. We admired this stunning display for a while. The birds flew in and out of the leader's mouth like bullets. It was as if the leader was spitting, now that he had seen what had become of his venture in reality. The section Party organiser said that this could be nasty if foreign correspondents and dissidents got wind of it. And he went back inside the Institute to report the matter to the appropriate authority.

ON FOREIGNERS

Talking of foreigners incidentally, I was once summoned to the director's office. With the director was a man who looked very like an American but who turned out to be English.

'This comrade . . . or rather, gentleman,' said the director, 'will be spending some time with us. He's writing a dissertation on the Soviet Union. He's an Englishman, but a progressive one.'

'An Englishman?' I said with surprise. 'That's strange!'

'Why "strange"?' asked the Englishman in good Russian.

'Because you look more like an American,' I said.

'That's right,' said the director. 'I thought he was American, too, at first. Anyway, I want you to put yourself at his disposal.'

Afterwards the Englishman asked me why I had taken him for an American. After all, there were all kinds of Americans. I said that they all had something in common. What exactly? A kind of self-importance which is common in a person who has just eaten a thick steak made of fresh meat, and not mashed potatoes which have gone off. And a certain naiveté which is common in a person who imagines that because he has eaten a thick, juicy steak he understands everything in the world a lot better than someone who eats rotten mashed potato. The Englishman brought out a notebook and wrote down what I had just said.

'I like the way you think,' he said. 'I would like to know the truth about Soviet society. And I hope that you will help me.'

'With pleasure,' I said. 'What shall we start with?'

'With vodka, of course,' he said.

I wasted six months on that Englishman. I dragged him round

all the Moscow snack-bars and drying-out stations, showed him
the over-crowded flats and the endless queues, fed him with all
the rubbish in our canteens, acquainted him in detail with our
powerful system of propaganda . . . He swore to God that he
would write a book about our life which would shake the whole
world. But then he went away. A year passed. And again I was
summoned to the director. And the director handed me a thin
little brochure – the Englishman's promised book.

'You did well,' said the director. 'You did a good job on that
bourgeois, just like a real communist. On the next public holiday
you'll get a fifty rouble prize.'

I left the Institute after that and dumped the Englishman's
booklet in the first available litter-bin. 'The swine!' I said, not
sure whether I had the Englishman in mind, who had written
such a stinking pro-Soviet book on the basis of so rich a source of
anti-Soviet material, or the director who had only given me a
measly fifty roubles for re-educating the Englishman along Soviet
lines. And since then I have lost all confidence in the West.

ABOUT MY INTENTIONS

I'm not going to talk about the pollution of the environment. I'm
in the environment once a year, and even then I'm drunk, so I
don't care about it at all. The first thing I do when I hit the
'environment' is to get drunk and the second is to pollute it with
fragments of empty vodka-bottle. I know, you censure me on
that account. But if you yourself were to turn up in the
'environment' with an empty vodka-bottle in your hand, you
wouldn't find a more entertaining way of passing the time than
polluting it by smashing the bottle against the nearest tree. You'll
miss the first time, of course. And the second. But at the fifth or
sixth attempt you'll score a bull's eye. Smash, tinkle! And . . .
Nor am I going to talk about the threat of a nuclear catastrophe –
I care about that even less. I lived through the war. And whether
I am vaporised by an anti-personnel mine, an ordinary bomb, an
artillery shell or a hydrogen bomb is immaterial. And I am
totally unmoved by the fate of mankind. And I don't believe

those people who act as though they are worried at the size of the earth's population, and what people will look like in the future. Explain to me, if you please, why I should exult at the thought that there are going to be ten billion people living on this planet, seven billion of whom will be Chinese, that they will be two metres tall and live for five hundred years?! And why I should be despondent that there will only be one billion people left on this earth, nine hundred million of whom are again Chinese, that they will all be small and only live for fifty years?! I know from experience that concern about the welfare of mankind in the future is simply business for a particular category of people. Among them, of course, are sincere and well-meaning nutcases who are appalled at the very thought of damage to genes and chromosomes in people and animals. I know someone who doesn't sleep at nights because of the reduction in the population of some sub-species of Ryazan sparrow. There are all sorts of eccentrics. But things don't depend on them. Least of all the preservation of a disappearing sub-species of Ryazan sparrow and the refinement of the heredity mechanism.

I'm going to talk about something else – about things which are accessible and useful to every person who wonders about how best to get through what's left of his or her life without having to make a titanic effort, who doesn't have any outstanding talent for that, who is not making a breath-taking career, in short, who doesn't have any particular advantage over other ordinary mortals.

OUR LITTLE WAYS

That senior staff-member whose place we went back to turned out to have a one-room co-operative flat with combined lavatory, without, however, any form of acoustic insulation. And if anyone went to the toilet, no matter how hard he or she tried not to make any noise, even the slightest rustle was audible in the room. This became the central topic of our conversation.

'In the West,' said the head of section, 'the lavatories are now silent. They're fitted with special mufflers.'

265

'What's more important is that they eat well,' said a young doctor of sciences (not young in years, but in the sense that she had only recently defended her thesis). 'So they don't need any mufflers.'

'My wife,' said the deputy head, 'has made mufflers out of Terylene.'

'We're still all right in Moscow,' said the Party organiser. 'In China it's worse still. There the members of the collective monitor what you shit.'

'Don't exaggerate,' said the head. 'Where the situation is very good is in Africa. There are no toilets at all. Everyone does their business in the open, right in the jungle or the desert. Insects and lions eat the lot in seconds.'

'What happens if a cobra or tsetse-fly bites your behind?' asked the doctor of sciences. 'When the natives in Latin America excrete in the waters of the Amazon basin they get their arses, and something else besides, bitten by piranha fish.'

'As for the USA,' said the secretary, 'they've got no sewerage system at all. They compress everything into bricks and build skyscrapers with them.'

'The whole world,' said a candidate of sciences, 'has long since rejected toilet-paper. They wash themselves with some pressurised spray or other.'

'I have a wonderful solution to the problem,' said a junior research fellow without a higher degree (JRF), who had come to us not long before from the university. 'What is it? It's very simple: don't eat or drink. That way you kill three birds with one stone: the need for lavatories is removed, your health is preserved and we don't need to improve agriculture.'

MYSELF

The Programme of the CPSU talks about the task of 'educating a new man who harmoniously combines within himself abundant spiritual resources, moral purity and physical perfection'. As for me, I embody this ideal absolutely. I have more than enough spiritual resources, especially since having been compelled to read Brezhnev's *Little Land* and *Restoration* and to demonstrate at a specially convened readers' conference that we really had read these literary masterpieces of our leader. I wonder what he's going to do next. Sing in an opera or dance the Kamarinsky in the Red Banner Folksong and Dance Troupe? . . . Actually, between ourselves, I haven't read that turgid rubbish and when I had to speak at that conference, I simply spouted the sort of nonsense which, it seemed to me, the authors of his 'memoirs' would have attributed to that universally gifted leader of ours. From a moral point of view I am as pure as the driven snow: there is not a scrap of morality within me and never has been. For instance, if ever I was caught AWOL I would unhesitatingly give the name of the deputy platoon commander of our neighbouring company rather than my own. If I issued myself with a false pass I always used to make it out in his name – he was a real swine. When I was a junior research fellow (I was at one time, for my sins) I presented for discussion without batting an eyelid a plan for a three-year departmental project which I had copied out of some provincial publication which our intellectual aristocrats from the capital could be guaranteed not to have read. And I nearly got into a mess over that one. The stuff I had copied out went off to the printer and I only just managed to rescue it at the galley-proof stage for 'minor emendations'. Fortunately, my colleagues were pleased (they were afraid that the article might have been a success) and the whole affair passed off without any scandal. I was credited with the fulfilment of the plan in three years, but after that I was soon demoted back to senior technical assistant.

That leaves the third feature of the CPSU Programme's ideal man: Physical perfection. I have never been worried on that score. And after I had four rotten teeth pulled out on the left side of my mouth and stainless steel crowns inserted on the right, learned to comb my hair in a way which hides my bald patch and conceal my paunch under a loose-fitting, unpressed jacket, even lift operators and cleaning ladies noticed my physical perfection. I would like to know whom They Up There have in mind as an example of physical perfection. This question arose when we were being instructed as propagandists at the head-quarters of the district Party committee. We had a very interesting discussion. Someone suggested Yuri Gagarin as an example. Everyone agreed, although four feet eleven inches would seem to be a bit on the short side for a physically perfect citizen of communist society. Someone else suggested the weight-lifter Vasily Alekseev. And again everyone agreed, although the main purpose of future society is not deemed to be totally fulfilled by winning all the first places at international athletics meetings in the weight-lifting event. I then proposed the candidature of the Gen Sec. There was an ominous silence. I don't know how the story would have ended if it hadn't been for the secretary of the district committee himself. He said that the Gen Sec had been a very handsome man in his youth, and even now wasn't so bad. We had probably never had such a handsome man before as head of government and leader of the Party.

WHO AM I

I am a senior technical assistant, shortened to STA. Don't be put off by the word 'senior', for a senior TA differs from a junior one only to the extent of twenty roubles a month. If he is particularly cosy with the management he might differ by thirty roubles, even by fifty. But that is very rare. And the professional committee of the institution is hard at work to make sure it happens even more rarely.

An STA is an absolutely insignificant creature. Along with the JTAs they are the unskilled labour of science. Their functions consist in wiping up, cutting and sticking, fetching and carrying, again cutting and sticking, typing and re-typing, again fetching and carrying, and re-typing everything churned out in abundance by the powerful intellects of junior research fellows with a higher degree, senior research fellows with a higher degree and scientific title, candidates and doctors of science, lecturers and professors, associate members of the Academy of Science and academicians, heads of department, deputy directors and directors. And the above-mentioned intellects produce a horrific amount of shit. And it's only scissors and paste and the patience of the STA which can turn it into something palatable. But what is that worth?! Only junior research fellows without a higher degree or scientific title are more insignificant than STAs, and that's only because they make themselves out to be such a big deal. STAs don't make themselves out to be anything – they don't have time for that. And in general they are deprived of any imagination. And not just of imagination. They are simply deprived.

So, for many years I was an STA. But, just like an old soldier, with every year that passed I worked less and less and got more and more thanks – the only way for a nonentity to sort himself out an existence which is in any way tolerable. The upshot was that I ended up by doing no work at all and being counted among the best workers on the staff. When it became aware of that, the management began to rack its brains about what to do with such a model parasite. And it decided to promote me to the rank of junior research fellow, as an exception and *pour encourager les autres*. It was during that time that I came up with the solution to the work-plan which I mentioned earlier. After that I was demoted back to STA. But I don't regret that at all. When I was a JRF I acquired a scholar's vanity, I began to suffer from insomnia and heart-burn. As soon as I was demoted, composure and sleep returned and all trace of heart-burn disappeared. And I completely forgot again that I had anything material or spiritual inside me.

OUR LITTLE WAYS

The telephone call from the Party organiser to the district Party committee had an effect that time. A gang of all sorts of specialists and technicians appeared in the courtyard of the Institute. They laboured for two weeks. Finally they stopped up Lenin's mouth. However, the junior members on the staff espied the grating in Lenin's mouth and began to interpret it symbolically. They began to bring their friends along, as if it were an excursion. One female post-graduate student brought along some foreigners with large cameras. The militia dispersed them and exposed their films. One foreigner had his camera smashed and another lost a tooth. The post-graduate student was expelled from the komso-mol and the Institute. Lenin was completely boarded up – supposedly for extensive repairs.

MURMURINGS WITHIN

It sometimes happens like this. I'll be standing on the lower landing, having a smoke and listening to the intellectual conver-sations of the Institute bletherers. No one pays any attention to me until I smile maliciously or produce some venomous com-ment. Let's suppose they are discussing, for instance, the role of cybernetics in the management of society. Our closet queen Kachurin (in which capacity he is a secret informer) predicts a great future for cybernetics in the sense of embodying the ideals of social justice in real life, all the while scratching furiously at his hair which he has not washed for a long time. He even admitted it himself, finding a satisfactory explanation in the fact that the hot water in the building where he lives had been cut off about a month ago. That, more or less, is what started the discussion on cybernetics. Kachurin's position is supported by Doctor of Sciences Subbotin, who, while he is doing so, however, is smiling cynically and wiggling his bottom. He is not doing that to tempt Kachurin but because he is convinced that he has good legs and a sharp wit. The Teacher and Dobronravov polemicise with them, but not very insistently, merely from a habit of arguing about everything with everyone. At this point I mutter something to the effect that the first action to be performed in the cybernetic management of society should be the reconnection of the water supply to Kachurin's building so that he can wash his unimaginably dirty hair. After that I am noticed at once. Sazonov warns those assembled to be careful in my presence. Inwardly I remove my glove and throw it at the feet of le comte de Sazon, draw my sword and say contemptuously: 'Monsieur le comte, I am at your service!' But outwardly I say coldly and calmly that the Central Committee has taken a decision to publish a full list of informers in order to . . . All those assembled turn pale and gradually melt away. I make my horse rear up on its hind legs (inwardly, of course) and gallop off to the Emperor's tent, i.e. I wander lazily (outwardly, of course) along to my head of department who ordered me half an hour ago (via his secretary) to come immediately.

In the corridor I bump into Verochka, a clerk in the office, who is shuffling along (giving the impression that she is hurrying) to get tea for the deputy director of personnel. Verochka is not yet old, but she is shapeless and slovenly and therefore appears to be ancient. She is so stupid that even Barabanov allows himself to be ironical about her. But she is unusually wily and resourceful. In the Institute she is mainly involved in speculation. Sometimes she'll get me to stand in a queue for musquash hats in GUM or gold rings in the jewellery shop 'Topaz'. As soon as she sees me, Verochka grinds to a halt and begins to rabbit on incoherently about Polish trousers (she means jeans) which are going on sale in GUM tomorrow. Inwardly I arrest my steed in full gallop, kneel in a flash before a beautiful marchioness, kiss the hem of her magnificent dress and . . . 'Fuck off!' I say to her (outwardly, of course), 'you still haven't paid me for the hats.'

At last I gallop up on my foaming steed to the Emperor's tent, i.e. I go into the head of department's office. My steed falls dead. The Emperor is sitting on a folding stool (i.e. is sprawling in a ragged armchair) with one leg stretched out on a drum (i.e. on a waste-paper basket). 'Colonel,' says the Emperor . . . 'Forgive me, Sire,' I say, 'I am but a captain.' 'General – ' insists the Emperor . . . 'Forgive me, Sire,' I say, trying to remonstrate . . . 'Marshal,' says the Emperor, 'do you see the town on the other side of the river?' 'It shall be yours, Sire!' I cry, filled with jubilation. 'To horse!!!' Outwardly our meeting goes like this. 'Comrade Ivanov,' says the Head, picking his remaining yellow teeth with a match-stick, 'I have asked you more than once to check the quotations in the collective manuscript on the forms of contradictions in a socialist society. And you still haven't . . . I shall be obliged to request the administration to penalise you . . .' 'Forgive me, Pyotr Sidorovich,' I say softly but firmly, 'in order to check the quotations in a collective manuscript, I do have to see the actual manuscript. I know these quotations by heart, but I don't have the manuscript in which they are supposed to appear.' 'What's that!' howls the Head. 'I asked! . . .

271

I demanded! ... I! ... Get me Sergei Sidorovich! ... He's not in the Institute? Connect me' (this to his secretary) 'with ...' While the Head is fulminating I leap on a fresh steed and struggle at the head of the Imperial Guard to the river, on the opposite bank of which is visible the enemy town. 'Follow me, you eagles! Let us die for the glory of the Emperor! ... Hurra-a-a-ah! ...' In other words, I quietly steal out of the Head's office, find Verochka and discuss with her the plan of attack on the Polish jeans. On condition, of course, that she pays for past services rendered. I'm not counting on a diamond ring, but she should at least come up with a tenner.

After that I go to the personnel department and tell them that, on the instructions of my head of department, I have to go to Sergei Sidorovich's to get the manuscript of a collective project. The rather nice young assistant to the director of personnel, without even looking at me, writes something down indifferently in the signing-on-and-off book. This indifference doesn't bother me at all. I know that it has nothing to do with my appearance or my age (I'm still a tough old nut and could sort out any junior research fellow with one hand tied behind my back) but my position in society. Barabanov and Subbotin are older and uglier than I am but even they are successful with young female staff in so far as they have separate flats, higher degrees and a high salary. 'I know, Princess,' I say (inwardly, of course), 'that I am unworthy of your attention. But if I should die in battle, know that I did so with Your name upon my lips!' I leap on my horse ... and unhurriedly leave the Institute to go and stand in a queue in GUM for Polish jeans for speculator Verochka.

FINDING A WAY OUT

I'm sick and tired of the intellectualist whining about the blemishes of our society. As they say in learned circles, such whining is not constructive. It becomes all-consuming and leaves no room for optimistic ideas. And where aren't there blemishes? A society without blemishes doesn't exist. Americans are up to their eyes in blemishes. And the English. And the French. The

Italians are not even worth talking about: they've got nothing but blemishes, they've not got one healthy feature. There's a rumour that you even have to stand in a queue now for macaroni. Do you think that if we got rid of the defects which so alarm our intelligentsia and satisfied its freedom-loving aspirations, things would get better? Not a bit of it! It wouldn't be better. It would almost certainly be worse. Directors and principals wouldn't be able to come to their institutions – they would be spat at. Factories and plants would cease to function – instead of putting in an extra stint in honour of some forthcoming anniversary, the workers would be off on a demonstration to demand meat. And drink themselves silly, of course. Young lads would get religion in order to dodge military service. At border crossing-points there'd be long queues of folk wanting to scarper to the West. And what do you think would happen in the arts field? It doesn't bear thinking about! The little bit of tolerable literature we've got would be drowned in a flood of 'revelations'. The number of people repressed, according to them, would reach a billion. Even the Khanty-Mansi would have surrealism and in Chukhloma you wouldn't be able to move for abstractionists. And it would be like that with everything.

But what's the answer then, you ask. A legitimate question. An answer is necessary, for our intellectual . . . But if you are seeking a solution, then you must be an intellectual, for an intellectual by definition is one who seeks a way out of a situation, whether it exists, has ceased to exist or hasn't yet existed. Anyway, our intellectual, if I can pick up the thread again, can't live without a way out. Or rather, without looking for a way out, since if a way out is found or is there without its having to be looked for, our intellectual is not an intellectual at all. Our intellectual absolutely has to look for a way out. A way in is not obligatory but a way out is essential. Our intellectual is so constructed that he has hardly got into something before he is raising the question of how to get out. There's even a joke about it. 'Tell me,' says one intellectual to another, 'do you think you could get into that bottle?' (The bottle in question is a pint vodka bottle which they have just emptied.) 'Ah, but how would I get out again afterwards?' asks the other.

It doesn't follow from what has been said that the intellectual will make use of the way out he is searching for. It is more likely that he will not make use of it. That's not why he's looking for it in the first place. He's not a pragmatist. Utilitarian interests are foreign to him. For him a way out is important in principle. Why is that? An explanation of this phenomenon has yet to be found. All that is known is that these agonising searches for a way out are a distinctive feature of our intelligentsia which, from that point of view, is a direct descendant of the pre-revolutionary intelligentsia. They too spent a long time looking for a way out. But they made two mistakes, due to inexperience. Their first mistake was that they actually found a way out. And their second mistake was that they actually used it. What the result of that was, you know very well. Our intelligentsia has learned from their bitter experience and won't make mistakes like that. Ours doesn't so much look for a way out as demonstrate its moral superiority over the West which has lost all its spirituality in the pursuit of material goods.

But I find the way-out problem interesting in general. And I listen to what people have to say on the subject. For instance, one of my chance drinking-companions advanced the 'rhinoceros principle'. What is that? Rhinoceroses don't see well and react more to what they hear. How do you save yourself from a rhinoceros if it is charging towards you? You go off on tip-toe in one direction and stamp loudly somewhere else. We should take a lesson from that. Our authorities behave like a rhinoceros: they make a bee-line for where they hear a noise. But why make a noise? They'll only crush you anyway. 'That's a very good theory where the rhinoceros is charging straight at you,' I said. 'But what happens if he starts to stamp around in a rage, crushing everything that stands in his path?' 'All the more reason,' said my drinking-companion, 'not to meet it at all.' Why, indeed, should we meet it at all?!

CHATS ON THE STAIR LANDING

They're always chatting on the upper landing as well. But their conversations are beyond me. They speak unintelligibly and use lots of incomprehensible words even although they discuss the same trivia as they do on the lower landing. I understand almost everything that's said on the lower landing and sometimes I feel that I could chip in no worse than the others. On the upper landing they're always trying to 'explicate' and substantiate. But I know from experience that you kill a thought off if you have to explain it, that what is essential is understood instantly, without explanation. And accepted without back-up arguments. Argumentation is only permissible in so much as it is inadequate. When the argument is strong, the thesis always turns out to be doubtful. But on the lower landing they merely toss out ideas. And what is particularly good about the conversations is their lack of purpose and their chaotic nature. They are conversations for their own sake. This type of conversation is a particular form of life – possibly a higher form. When cretin Subbotin said on one occasion that a refined, high-class conversation is the highest product of civilisation he wasn't far from the truth.

On this occasion it was the youngest members of the staff who had gathered on the lower landing. They were talking about the purpose of life, about death and other gloomy subjects. 'The purpose of life is banal,' said a seventeen-year-old lad who is doing a stint in the Institute before going on to university. 'All it is is making sure that you have a peaceful, care-free old age, with everything provided. All your passions and desires fade away. All that is left is the desire to live for as long as possible, deriving satisfaction from the fact that some of your acquaintances have died, even although they were younger than you are, and others are vegetating in poverty, are ill and are about to snuff it. And that's it!'

'There's another aspect to this problem,' prattled a female post-graduate student from the university who has been taken on at the Institute on the lowest possible salary and after a great deal of string-pulling, 'and that's the social one. Billions of people live only so that a few million can live well and be happy. With scientific and technical progress these people become superfluous. The fortunate millions can already get by splendidly without the unfortunate billions. People sense this and that's what gives rise to all the madness that's going on in the world.'

'Death is the result of a mistake,' said a weedy chap in spectacles who had graduated from some natural science faculty of the university (biology, I think) and who had been assigned to the department of the philosophy of natural science by mistake. 'Moreover, a mistake which is insignificant but inevitable. Life opens up two possibilities at every step: 1) the possibility of a mistake and the possibility of its correction (compensation); 2) the possibility of avoiding a mistake. The second possibility ultimately leads into a blind alley, i.e. to death. In the case of the first possibility, a mistake is corrected at a high price: something gets lost. When we correct the mistakes of our organism, little by little we lose parts of our life. These losses accumulate and lead likewise to death. Logically, then, it is only possible to live for ever on condition that you lose everything. Helping people to live longer is good from one point of view, but bad from another. Moderation in everything! In this case, too.'

'Particularly in the case of our leaders,' said the seventeen-year-old.

After that remark they fell silent and turned to look at me. And dispersed to their work-places. Whereas I smiled. I know very well that that seventeen-year-old is an informer. I heard him talking to a KGB operative once with my own ears. He's a sharp lad and has an excellent memory. And he already understands perfectly who's worth what around here, whom you have to keep an eye on and things like that. At the same time he takes many of the staff (me included) to be KGB agents and is scared of them. But that fear will pass with time. He's not the first and he won't be the last.

ON ROMANTICISM

Many of the staff of our institution are sent twice a year to work on our sponsored farms (both state and collective) – once for the vegetable planting (for some reason they call this in our institution the sowing campaign), and once for the harvest (as our director once said, a great specialist on the problem of surmounting the contradictions between the town and the countryside – for the corn-making). In between these major expeditions, they are sent to work in the vegetable depots of Moscow itself, and also to the construction brigades in the country to help our sponsored farms to build some epoch-making building or other – a pigsty, a rabbit-hutch, an awning for lorries to park under or a vegetable store. They don't, of course, build anything. That's all talk, for there haven't been any pigs for a long time, the rabbits haven't arrived yet, and although there are vegetables from time to time, they rot perfectly well even without a vegetable store. They do, on the other hand, give a lot of help. They haven't once returned from such a trip without a vote of thanks or a prize. The prizes, of course, are nothing. But, then, they do have great value on the theoretical and moral-political plane: they inspire, challenge and for the umpteenth time confirm. And sometimes I go to the country, too. Absolutely voluntarily. You will, of course, be interested to know why, since these days it's rare to come across such an idiot. Because, I shall answer, I am a real communist, one of the few real communists who are by a miracle still alive. Don't laugh too soon – I'll explain myself and you'll see what I mean. And perhaps, instead of laughing, you'll shed a tear of sadness and commiseration.

I go to work in the village above all to devote my energies to carrying out the resolution of whatever plenum of the Central Committee it happens to be to raise our agriculture to an unattainable height. I asked the representative of the district Party committee who was instructing us before our departure for the village, how one was to interpret the phrase 'unattainable height' and for whom this height was supposed to be unattainable. The representative stared at me with bulging eyes, turned pale and went off to consult with the district Party secretary himself. An hour later I was invited into the secretary's office where I was advised, in the interests of avoiding any misunderstandings, to let the matter drop. 'I understand,' I said. 'After all, I'm an old communist. I understand that our difficulties are the hardest to overcome.' 'That's the spirit,' said the secretary, shaking my hand with feeling.

I foresee that you won't for a minute swallow this explanation, so I'll reveal to you the real reason for my behaviour: it's romanticism. Yes, that same romanticism which nearly everyone has forgotten about and to which those who haven't are ashamed to admit. And not just any romanticism, but a special, communist kind. And its essence is contained in two words: formation and attack.

The fact of the matter is that I am a born combat soldier. I loved marching. Even in winter I went into the attack without my greatcoat, just in my tunic. And the sweat was running off me.

I quickly made a career for myself at the front – I got as far as company commander. But not for long. Once my company was almost completely wiped out. But I survived. Afterwards the appropriate people asked me why I had survived. I told them where to go. And for that I began my military career afresh as a private. This was a typical incident in war. Unless my memory deceives me, something similar happened to a member of our brigade, Ivan Vasilievich. Afterwards I was asked more than once why I had survived. True, they were asking for different reasons. And I would sometimes give them a different answer. But I didn't survive, I would reply. I was killed. This is my soul which is living on and observing the consequences, that's all. I was one of the first to be demobbed after the war, although I was already a member of the Party and had made it back to company commander – the army was being purged of front-line soldiers. And of genuine communists, as well. They were needed throughout the starved, exhausted country. What happened after that? The same as with everyone else, i.e. nothing much. In fact, nothing at all. Afterwards life virtually ceased. My life came to an end with the last attack.

So I go to the country for a reason which you now fully understand: I feel a little bit as if I were back in the ranks and a little bit as if I were back at the front. There is the battle for the harvest. There is mud, slush, cold, semi-starvation. And there are casualties. Last year we lost a lad when the side of a lorry was ripped off. One was sentenced for nothing at all. About ten people were crippled by excessive drinking. And how many cases are there of colds, influenza, pneumonia, diarrhoea. Curiously, many people behave here as if they were at the front. The Commissar (one of our brigade) has an aggravated stomach ulcer, but he wouldn't dream of leaving us – he doesn't want to be a deserter.

There is one more reason why I go to the country voluntarily. You have to go in any case, there's no getting out of it. Well, you might duck out of it once, but not twice. If you start ducking out, you get a bad reputation and you then have to go twice as often. But if you agree voluntarily, you get recognition for that and don't have to go the next time (you volunteered, after all!), and you can get out of other social work for the whole year. So being a true communist is sometimes worthwhile, and profitable.

A GUIDING PRINCIPLE

Everything which people produce can be divided into three groups: products which are well made, products which are badly made and products which are neither one thing nor the other. Products of the third group are produced in abundance everywhere. They constitute the norm of human activity. And societies are not to be differentiated on the basis of that category but on the basis of the percentage of products in the first and second categories in a society's gross output. For example, you have found out that a given society this year has produced two hundred and fifty-five million pairs of sandals and two hundred and fifty-five million tons of potatoes. You have to define the type of society. In order to do this, you have to establish the percentage of well-made sandals (which will be worn by leadership) and the percentage of badly-made sandals (which no one will wear and which will lie rotting in warehouses at a cost of millions of roubles). Similarly you will have to work out the percentage of good potatoes (which will be eaten by the leadership) and the percentage of bad potatoes (which will be eaten by the workers and pigs). If you succeed in doing that you may consider that you have established the type of society. You say that there are five million pairs (tons) of good sandals (potatoes) and a hundred million bad ones? Right! You have a society of advanced socialism on the eve of its transition to full communism. Why, you ask, is it not yet full communism? The answer is very simple: the percentage of good production is still too high. Now, if your calculations had produced the following result: eleven pairs of good sandals (two pairs for the Gen Sec and a pair each for the chief members of the Politburo) and two hundred and fifty-four million nine hundred and ninety-nine thousand nine hundred and eighty-nine bad pairs, and similarly eleven tons of good potatoes (two tons for the Gen Sec and a ton each for the chief members of the Politburo) and two hundred and fifty-four million nine hundred and ninety-nine thousand nine hundred and eighty-nine tons of bad ones, then you could say with complete assurance that you are dealing with a society under full communism.

Our society belongs to the type in which very many people produce the widest possible range of badly-made products. Moreover, they don't just produce them any-old-how, but ahead of time, with overfulfilment of the plan per head of population. And in all spheres of life – including the spiritual. If I were to parade before you now all those who are active in our system of power and culture, you would immediately understand the essence of my method for defining a type of society. But, between ourselves, even the lower strata of society, in which so much hope has been invested by you-know-who, that Great Writer of the Russian Soil, and many of our dissidents, are very little better than those at the top.

MATRYONADURA

Take, for example, the mistress of the barn where they've housed us. After our normal (usually rather tiring) work in the field she makes us saw wood, clean out the cowshed, dig around in her private plot (vegetable garden) and drag hay pinched from five kilometres away to feed her chestnut mare. She does it with a squalid little chuckle expressing a fantastic combination of toadying request, cynical demand, boorish cordiality and other attributes of our luminiferous 'simple folk'. We hardly have time to collapse on to the straw covered in torn sackcloth and begin our intellectual conversations before she appears in the gateway: well, now, you weakling intellectuals, that's enough of sitting on your backsides, it's time to pump up your muscles, there's a saw over there . . . At first we tell her where to go, but she doesn't take offence, giggles, even jiggles her huge bum quasi-flirtatiously, but is stubbornly insistent. And in the end one of us unwillingly gets up and goes off to saw wood, dig the vegetable garden or fetch water.

Our mistress is called Matryona-Dura, or Matryonadura for short. Matryona is her own name and *dura* (fool) is the role she plays in society. And she plays it absolutely successfully. She has been playing it for so many years that she now really is an impenetrable *dura* and at the same time horribly wily and a painfully good-natured nasty piece of work. There are Matryonas by the dozen in the region. And naturally, they're all dumb-clucks. Therefore, whenever there's likely to be any confusion, the inhabitants say that our Matryona is that same Matryona who, when he observed her, inspired the Great Writer with the hope that it would be she who would save our Mother Russia. Save her from whom? Save her for what? What Russia? I can imagine the scene vividly. Matryona is fussing around the stove. The Writer is looking at her with rapture and beseeching her to save Russia. 'You know what you can do with your Russia,' she says in reply. 'Because of your chatter my milk's just boiled over.'

I wouldn't like to make any judgments about the future, but

for the moment this Matryona shed tears of rapturous emotion when the Great Writer was banished from Russia, and she told things about him to the representatives of the Security Authorities which he himself could not have imagined. She informed them in particular that he had misbehaved himself when he had visited her house (Matryona's house!) and had never admitted it. I will record in this connection the first attribute of the 'simple folk': it's readiness to render anyone a service who asks for it. If, of course, the person making the request is superior. If, however, Matryonadura feels even slightly superior to her interlocutor, she changes instantly. And then her whole appearance and her every word express the haughty, cosmic contempt of a celestial creature for an insignificant insect of this earth. We experienced this more than once when we dumped manure in the wrong place or bent the saw too much while sawing her firewood.

Matryonadura embodies all the finest attributes of the Soviet people, and above all its faithfulness to ideals and its unwavering sense of principle. The latter attribute in her case is encapsulated in the crisp marxist formulation: she shares the views of those she screws. When she sleeps with the Commissar she totally and unequivocally supports the general line of the Party, condemns the dissidents, the Jews and the Chinese, supports the communists of Chile and Ethiopia and believes that we have the highest standard of living on earth. When she sleeps with any of our young lads she immediately becomes an unbridled dissident herself, abuses the higher leadership, praises the American president and Israel, condemns the Arabs, the negroes and the Chinese (the Chinese she condemns under all circumstances). On the other nights she rests, i.e. she snores loudly enough for the whole village to hear, demonstrating profound indifference to everything on this earth, apart from her own tiny little smallholding. For that she is ready to sacrifice anything and everything – marxism, the Party and the government, the dissidents, the American president, the negroes, the Jews, the Arabs and the Chinese. She is quite ready to sacrifice the peoples mentioned irrespective of her smallholding, for no particular reason, just out of the goodness of her heart and a sense of justice.

And incidentally, she's not all that dumb. In addition to a cow, a pig, fleas, cockroaches and other livestock, she has a television, a motor-cycle and a transistor radio. The radio and motor-cycle have been left behind by her son who has been called up by the army and sent off, it seems, to some special training institution or other. She doesn't use the motor-cycle, of course. It stands in our barn. But she forbids us to touch it. It's a valuable object! On the other hand, she has the radio on non-stop. She listens to all the 'voices of the enemy' – everyone listens to them here since they are easy to tune in to (and they're not jammed at all). And it's interesting, of course. These so-and-so's, listen to that! And it's all absolutely true! Where on earth do they get it all from? Matryona has had nine years of schooling in her time, and even tried to study tannery at a technical college, but regards herself as barely literate.

'Here we are,' she likes to say, 'we're barely literate. Ten-year schooling? Don't make me laugh! This isn't Moscow! It's only in Moscow that you teach all these "abasractionists" and other zionists. Here all we've got is the land and manure.'

'You're exaggerating about the manure,' we object.

'Well, fertiliser,' she says, not giving in. 'What's the difference? The smell's the same. All you've got round here is that smell, and nothing more.'

'The harvest looks as if it's not too bad this year,' we object.

'So what!' she says, destroying our arguments. 'It'll go to waste, anyway. It'll rot. People will steal it. The Arabs and negroes'll have it, God rot every black-arsed one of them!'

I'll add just one more stroke to finish off this preliminary portrait of Matryonadura: she quite often goes around in jeans and a T-shirt with the words 'Heart of America' written on it. The jeans, it is true, were bought for six roubles at the local shop and the T-shirt is a fake, the work of Georgian rip-off merchants. Although Matryona has never been outside the district, let alone outside the country, she has a confident opinion about everything that happens and doesn't happen abroad.

MURMURINGS WITHIN

I prefer our Soviet way of life to any other. Why? Well, if for no other reason, it's the only one I know. And I call upon all foreigners to follow our example. Why? Well, if for no other reason, so that we don't need to feel so bad. And certainly because we could then say to them with a great feeling of satisfaction: well, you poor fools, now do you understand what real communism is?! It serves you right! We warned you, but you didn't believe us; now you can experience for yourself the real meaning of these radiant ideals, espoused by the most *avant-garde* fighters for the happiness and freedom of mankind!!! Honestly, life would be worth living for that moment alone. Can you imagine the self-satisfied roar of laughter which will reverberate in our country of advanced socialism when the West falls into the communist trap?! There will be a national holiday. People will be all smiles and congratulate each other that henceforth all the workers of the world will be living in the same pigsty as we have been living in for over six decades.

Not everyone, of course, will be living in the pigsty. Many will live well, some very well. Especially these nations who like to sing and dance, but not to work. They'll be the source of song and dance ensembles. And their leaders, who have no ear or voice, or movement in their joints, will still not be too badly off! And then the bosses. My, oh my! What a lot of bosses there are going to be in the world! In the USA alone there will be two million secretaries of party organisations (communist, naturally) and five million party activists (members of different bureaux, commissions, conferences, delegations), and that's a conservative estimate. There will not be fat juicy steaks made from fresh beef any more – except for a select few of the top members of society. On the other hand there will be abundant supplies of bluish-violet purée made from rotten potatoes. There will be no unemployment, that is certain. Everyone will be assigned to some institution, and compelled to work. Those who resist will be locked up as layabouts. They will lock up some who don't resist too. And anyone who is discontented will be sent to Siberia. At last we will be able to harness its inexhaustible natural resources. And justice will be re-established: why should it just be our countrymen who have to live in the taiga or beyond the Arctic circle? Let the representatives of other freedom-loving nations have a turn as well!

TOWN AND COUNTRY

Back in our student years we used to have animated discussions in our seminars on scientific communism about erasing the distinctions between town and country. We used to make fun of the utopian socialists who imagined the future like this: people would live in towns and from time to time would go to the country to work in the fields. We, of course, were a lot more intelligent than the utopian socialists. We understood the erasure of the distinctions to mean that town and country would be homogeneous in social terms, that there would be an improvement in the productivity of labour, the nature of work, culture, way of life, etc, to match the level of these things in the town. Now we can see with our own eyes that, in general, everyone was right. It's an amazing phenomenon! People are always wrong about the past, and in particular about the present. People never understand the present! But they are never mistaken when they predict the future. It's impossible to think up some piece of nonsense which doesn't turn out afterwards to exist in one form or another. What am I talking about? Take the case in point. The utopian socialists were obviously talking nonsense. And yet here we are, along with another twenty million town-dwellers sent out to work in the country, doing exactly what they predicted: digging the land. And yet life in the country now differs very little from life in the towns. The majority of those who live outside the towns receive a salary. Salaries are minimal. But in the towns they're not all that high either. And the private plots yield something. And the local inhabitants work like they do in the towns, i.e. haphazardly, desultorily, negligently, in fits and starts, etc. Don Juan (an engineer from an 'accommodation

285

address' who lives in our barn) asserts that that is precisely what the dialectics of social development consist in. It is precisely because the grand designs of these classical marxist geniuses have been embodied in real life that country people have fled to the towns and the ones who are left have become your typical, average, shoddy workers. It's precisely for that reason that we temporarily have to corroborate the predictions of the utopians. In material and cultural respects the country is also fast catching up with the town. Refrigerators, television sets, motor-cycles, jeans, tights have all become common, everyday objects. Don Juan is even somewhat displeased about that. He thinks that they could have waited with the tights. As it is, the local lasses wear them both in forty degrees of heat and forty degrees of frost. And since tights are so ridiculously expensive, the girls take very good care of them. And consequently, getting out of them what a healthy man needs is extremely difficult: the girls are scared of tearing these damned tights. I said that that particular problem surprised me: after all, they could go to a rendezvous without tights, you can't see them at night, anyway. Don Juan said that they hadn't reached that level of awareness in the country. And we were reminded of the joke about the negro whom a white colonial woman had ordered to put on a condom just in case and who asked his party leader after the liberation of his country if he could now take it off. Incidentally, our Matryonadura also has two pairs of tights. One pair is quite new, and Matryonadura wears them on public holidays. The other pair has been darned and darned again. She wears them on hot days when she walks around in a skirt, and not in jeans. How do we know all this? It's very simple. Matryonadura demonstratively washes all her smalls and hangs them up to dry in front of the entrance to our barn.

But not all the inhabitants of our barn are unanimous concerning the solution to the town-and-country problem. The Commissar (an economist from some patents office or other) asserts that the latest decrees of Party and government obliging the inhabitants of rural areas to breed cows, pigs, rabbits, hens and other edible livestock (and not only bugs, fleas and cockroaches) have seriously retarded the process of erasing the distinctions between the town and country. The Commissar uses specialist politico-economic jargon and therefore it's impossible to understand him at all. And we don't even try to get the hang of what he's talking about, because he's tedious as well as being the Party organiser for our brigade. A candidate of mathematical sciences from some computing centre or other, on the other hand, considers these decrees of the Party and government to be a valuable new contribution to the treasure-house of marxist-leninist doctrine on communism. 'Otherwise,' he said, 'we wouldn't have anything to eat at all. What would be better, to erase the distinctions and die of hunger, or leave the distinctions and be well-fed?' The Commissar said that the Candidate didn't understand the first thing about marxism, that according to marxism it was precisely the other way round, only a removal of the distinctions would allow ... But at this moment Matryonadura appeared and signalled to the Commissar. The Commissar is 'sleeping' with Matryonadura, and for that she supplements his diet.

OUR BRIGADE

Our brigade is in some sense experimental, at any rate it is certainly something of an innovation. The secretary of the district Party committee said so at the meeting held in honour of our arrival in the district and our dispersal among the collective and state farms: 'you (i.e. we) are destined to trail a new blaze ... no, trail ... along the highways of an unheard of new upsurge in our agriculture, and, like ... also along the other highways of our irrepressible movement towards victory,' etc, etc. While he was giving his inflammatory speech with the aim of inspiring us to selfless struggle (struggle, mark you) for a timely (why not ahead of time? This is something new!) potato harvest, sugar-beet harvest and some other kind of harvest ... we weren't listening. We had heard more than enough of that kind of rubbish in our lifetimes ... So, while he was rabbiting on about highways to this and highways to that, we were chipping in for our first (absolutely legitimate) booze-up in the open air. 'The swine,' grumbled the Candidate, whom the whining, pompous yelping of the secretary was preventing from working out complicated calculations with our crumpled rouble notes and small change. 'The battle for the harvest! Harvest headquarters! The struggle for carrots!! Attack on the sugar-beet!! How are we going to split the money between *zakuski* and booze? What should be the proportion of vodka to "red"? Mark my words, they'll be introducing military ranks next. Imagine, lance-corporal of carrots! Captain of potatoes! And the higher leadership – generals and marshals of the battle for the harvest!'

Don't imagine that 'red wine' stands for the red wine that is drunk in well bred urban circles with kebabs and roast veal. As soon as the train passes beyond the confines of the town, the word 'red' changes its meaning: now people call 'red' everything that isn't vodka, and 'white' refers to everything that isn't red (in the new sense). But that's not the point. The point is that our brigade constitutes an innovation. Previously every collective and state farm was affiliated to some urban enterprise or institution. Every year the urban enterprise or institution ear-marked *n* members of staff to be sent to their affiliated state or collective farm for whatever seasonal work was required, where they were employed as the local authorities saw fit. And it's still done like that in the majority of cases. This time however, in line with the decision of the Plenum of the Central Committee to raise agriculture to a new, higher level and create an abundance of foodstuffs in the towns, the decision was taken to conduct the struggle for the harvest in centralised fashion, on all fronts simultaneously, taking into account the professions of those working in the sponsoring organisations and the skills we had picked up in previous sojourns in the country. The result was that we spent two days kicking our heels in the district centre, finding a place to sleep as best we could, so that the district authorities could conduct their campaign re the battle for the harvest on the optimal demagogic-bureaucratic-idiotic level. With a corresponding hullabaloo in the press, on the radio and in newsreels and with other attributes of genuine struggle. We were dragged round various classrooms of the school which had been taken over as headquarters for the duration of the battle for the harvest, where we were asked questions about our personal circumstances, our professions, what kinds of social work we had carried out, what kind of work we'd done in the country in the past. Finally we were invited to have a 'heart to heart' chat. This is something similar to what happens in the Special Section of the KGB. It was drummed into us how important the task was which had been allotted to us and we were asked to nip any undesirable (demoralising) conversations in the bud and to help the Organs to expose those individuals, who ... We weren't required to sign anything. We were simply asked to help them in the name of and for ... This was something new. Don Juan said that on previous occasions they had been obliged to sign an undertaking to act as informers. Usually the lads refused. But who knows, perhaps one or two of them signed after all. There was, when all was said and done, a battle going on for the good of the people, the Motherland and the Party. For the sake of such a noble cause one could agree to serve, could one not. I listened in silence to what the comrades FROM THERE had to say, and nodded my head in answer to their request. What else could I do? Adopt some kind of pose? For the sake of whom and what? I knew that I would not help Them in the least. And that is sufficient.

Our brigade has been deployed (if it's a battle, let's use military language!) in locality N, the older women in houses (three or four together), the men and younger women in barns. People think this means that we sleep in a hayloft, breathing in the aroma of fresh hay, etc, etc. In reality Matryonadura doesn't let us anywhere near her hay, even though we've stolen more of it for her than she's scythed herself, and we sleep on straw and dust from rotted wood or hay which has accumulated over the years. And do battle with the rats. We've got mice as well. Compared to the rats we consider them to be near and dear and we don't do battle with them.

OUR BARN

We defend our positions or go into the attack in Matryonadura's barn on the very edge of locality N. There are nine of us altogether. Some of them I've already named: Don Juan (the biggest womaniser in the brigade), the Candidate (the best mathematician in the brigade), the Commissar (politically the most literate in the brigade), the Lathe Operator (the most hopeless drinker in the brigade). The remaining five are myself, Forehead (the strongest and laziest in the brigade), Ivan Vasilievich (the oldest in the brigade), Kostya (the youngest, weediest and hardest working member of the brigade) and JRF (the most colourless member of the brigade). So, as you see, the most outstanding individuals in the brigade have for some reason ended up in our barn. You will be asking, of course, why the Commissar is slumming in such company. As Party organiser he has the privilege of sharing a room with the brigadier in the club. But everything has been cunningly thought out. If he's a commissar, then he should be in the thick of things along with the ordinary people, among the front-line troops, in the trenches, as it were. And that the front passes right by our barn is self-evident. You only have to take a sniff to know that the pigsty is right beside us. There are hardly any pigs at all, but the smell from the sty is prodigious. Besides, the notion that the Commissar lives in our barn is pure demagogy. He is merely recorded as being one of us. In fact he sleeps with Matryonadura on a soft mattress filled with that sweet-smelling hay I was talking about earlier. And yet we don't envy the Commissar. In the first place, you would have to be desperate to sleep with such a slovenly, ugly old bag. And in the second place, the Commissar gets eaten by bed-bugs and fleas, and that's worse than having rats since the rats haven't started eating us yet but merely demoralise us. However, Kostya reckons that attacks on morale are worse than physical attacks, and he would happily change places with the Commissar since Matryonadura is not that old and ugly, but he is scared that everyone would laugh at him afterwards.

MATRYONADURA ON THE WEST

'In England,' says Matryonadura, 'there is tradition at every turn. You can't move without coming up against tradition.'

'That means there's no freedom there either.'

'They've got freedom enough. It's simply that they can't do anything without tradition.'

'What kind of traditions, for example?'

'All kinds. For example, they'll all get together and talk about the weather and laugh with their teeth clenched, although it's not funny at all: their weather's rubbish, even worse than ours.'

A FUNDAMENTAL POSTULATE

But if you're seriously interested in the question of a way out, I'll show you one: live in your sleep and not in reality – that's my basic premise on that score. Live in your sleep and use your life awake (i.e. in a state of vigilance) merely as a preparation for sleep, as a training for it, as a means of creating the essential, favourable conditions for sleep. If you adopt that approach, you'll find that your life when you're awake isn't all that bad either. You'll have the same attitude to it as you have at the moment towards nightmares – the relationship between sleep and vigilance will be reversed for you. And just as there are people who interpret dreams (charlatans every one of them, incidentally) you'll find that there are people who will interpret your life awake (also charlatans, naturally). As far as the dream-world is concerned, its advantages are obvious and beyond dispute. It is beyond the control of Party and government in principle. The latter will not be able to invade it with their maniacal plans, armed forces and Great Construction Projects of communism. And they won't be able to smuggle in arms and secret agents – it's not Africa. The dream-world is also beyond the control of the beloved collective. And in that world you don't have to go on *subbotniki*, these festivals of unpaid, voluntary labour. Nor to vegetable depots. You can forget about meetings, and you won't have any stool pigeons spying and reporting on you. Your friends won't be tormenting you with well-meant advice and critical remarks. In a word,

> When you're asleep no one will fall
> Upon you, take your glass away,

291

> Nor in a meeting will they all
> About your boozing have their say.

And just think what possibilities are opened up for the noble sentiments of our intelligentsia!

> You'll curse Them all at every turn,
> At Their expense you'll have a ball –
> They cannot force you to adjourn
> To camp or mental hospital.

Believe it or not, but last week sitting in my office I was able in half an hour or so to attack our aspirations in Africa, re-unite Germany, organise the secession of the Baltic republics, liberate the Poles and Czechs, inflict a massive defeat on our hockey team and a lot more besides. And I take a rather tolerant and peaceable view of our society and government. Just think what you could achieve if you've got a lot to get off your chest! I'll bet you could even knock out Muhammad Ali in the first round, as he deserves. This 'simple American sportsman' as he described himself (twice champion of the world, a millionaire and the leader of some black organisation) spent a few days in the Soviet Union, immediately 'discovered the truth about the Soviet Union', was hailed by Brezhnev as 'an outstanding fighter for peace' and was inordinately amazed at what he saw in our part of the world. It's worth knocking him out in the first round for things like that. And keeping him out. No, it would be better to give him an even rougher deal. Change him into an average Soviet citizen, make him kick his heels in queues, get jostled around on public transport and have to fight for an extra square metre of living-space. Make him have to live there for a few years.

Living in one's sleep is still something new. In our part of the world they treat it in the same way as they treat parapsychology and 'flying saucers', i.e. on the one hand they expose it and on the other try to put it to use. They say that a special secret institute has been set up. They seize those whom they suspect of living in their sleep, incarcerate them in these 'institutes' and make them reveal their secrets. What for? Why, in order that this aspect of the life of Soviet man can also be brought under Party-

Government control. People spend at least a third of their lives asleep. And what do they get up to when they're asleep? Of course, nothing will come of Their efforts in this respect. I can confirm that experimentally and prove it theoretically. But They make people's lives a misery. So if you decide to follow my advice, keep quiet about it. Act as if you dream about the same things as every other Soviet citizen, i.e. either about nothing or about something that isn't worth talking about. The same kind of shit: Great Construction Projects, Ethiopias, space junk, queues and Party meetings.

And if you blurt it out, you only have yourself to blame. In our part of the world they treat people who can dream what they want to and live in their dreams according to how they please in the same way as they treat ideological saboteurs and internal émigrés. If your friends, neighbours, colleagues and social organisations ferret out what you get up to in your dreams, they'll do everything in their power to make sure that either you get no sleep at all or that you sleep as unpleasantly as they do themselves. How will they do that? In the first place they'll report you and you'll be arrested as a slanderer, a spy, a currency speculator, or a nutcase. Secondly, they'll deal with you themselves. For example, they'll stamp around at night in the flat above you, there'll be a noise through the wall, a tape recorder'll be blaring in the house next door. They'll appear on your doorstep uninvited, eat everything you've got in the fridge and stay till dawn. Your wife will dig you in the ribs and tell you to stop snoring. Your mistress will waken you up in the most important part of your dream and tell you that it's time she went home, otherwise God knows what her husband will think, and can she have money for a taxi? After that, you're guaranteed not to get back to sleep, and if you do, you'll have the usual Soviet dream about queues and Great Construction Projects. And you won't be able to say a word in a dream like that. And there'll be no place for you to escape to.

And how many ways there are of stopping a Soviet person from sleeping peacefully and having the dreams he wants to! A friend of mine has been waging a titanic battle for ten years with his flat-mates. Every night they play the same record ten times in a row – it's the song 'Our beloved town may sleep and dream in peace'. They play it at fifteen-minute intervals. And not loudly enough for the police to intervene. But loudly enough for my friend to hear it. And the neighbours can sleep because one of them installed some automatic device in the record player to regulate the intervals. He invented it at his factory as an efficiency measure but it wasn't accepted. They told him that they had suggestions for improving efficiency up to here. And another friend of mine had been practising living in his dreams for about two years and had already made considerable progress – there are more or less advanced dreamers, just like yogis. And he chanced to blurt out his success to an old university friend. The latter proposed him as candidate for a position on the union committee at the very next trade-union meeting. And he was elected. After that he never had a decent night's sleep again. He kept dreaming of becoming chairman of the union committee, then president of the All-Union Central Trade Union Council, then a member of the Politburo, then the Gen Sec. And of at last getting the self-contained two-room flat with separate lavatory they had been promising him for ten years.

So once you have learned to live in your sleep, don't tell anyone about it. Keep it under your hat and live in bliss on your own. Remember, secret dreams, as opposed to human rights, are not even formally guaranteed by our legislation. That great Russian poet Lermontov, as you know, sought forgetfulness in sleep. But he came right out with it, and in verse, to boot. How it all ended you know as well: the tsarist government killed him in a duel. And that was only the tsarist government, not a Soviet one. The latter won't even let things get as far as a duel if it even suspects that you're intending to seek forgetfulness in sleep. You can sleep the cold sleep of the dead to your heart's content. But that you should feel the forces of life beating within you, well, there's no question of that.

OUR LITTLE WAYS

'It's a lie that the people in our prisons are badly fed,' said an old Party member, a pensioner attached to our organisation. 'In reality they get fed till they drop!'

THEIR LITTLE WAYS AND SOME GENERAL CONCLUSIONS

'The West has its defects too,' said the Candidate. 'We have a doctor of sciences who spent a year in the West. On one occasion he received a thick package of official-looking papers. They love official papers over there – you can't even go to the toilet without an official instruction and a receipt. Anyway, our doctor gets these papers and decides that he's got to read them. Although he knew the language well, he couldn't understand a thing. He struggled for two weeks with dictionaries and phrase-books. He had about ten sessions with various experts. All that, of course, cost a lot of money. At last he worked it out: he was being asked to contribute ten marks and ten pfennigs to some charity organisation or other. Since then, he doesn't want to hear about the West. What's the moral to be drawn? It's very simple. Societies differ only in terms of their idiocy. Don't over-estimate the intelligence of *homo sapiens*. The fact that he can play the violin and journey into space doesn't mean a thing. Man is by nature a cretin. And all these little accomplishments of his are the result, not of great intelligence, but of impenetrable stupidity. So – everything idiotic in the West is the result of their surplus of clothes, food and various kinds of freedom. In our part of the world it's a result of our shortage of these things. And there's no golden mean. Or rather, there is, but it's at the root of both.'

CHATS ON THE STAIR LANDING

They talk about the next world war on our landing more or less every other day. Usually these conversations are gloomy and boring: the leadership will be sheltered and survive, and we'll all die; the European nations will disappear and the Chinese will colonise the whole planet; there will be a process of complete degeneration; and so on and so forth in that general vein. But sometimes the conversation will take a very interesting turn.

'The next war has in practice already begun. Cambodia, Vietnam, Iran, Africa . . .'

'None of that matters. Little wars don't lead to big ones. Let's hope they continue. Let them kill each other, as long as we're at peace.'

'Who's going to win the next war?'

'More likely than not it will be us. I have a theory that the next war will be won by the side whose leaders adhere to the following principles. There is nothing more valuable in the country than they, the leaders. Therefore they have to make their own self-preservation their chief concern. The population can be sacrificed so long as sufficient are retained to perpetuate the species. Naturally these people will be the families of the leadership itself, plus a few members of the privileged circles closest to it. The basic weapon in the next war will not be the atomic bomb, bacteria, chemicals or other achievements of science and technology, but the ordinary foot soldier, provided with the protection needed for one operation. That protection should be enough to ensure that the operation is carried out. After that it doesn't matter. It's cheaper that way. And these people won't be needed afterwards, anyway.'

'But they're not fools in the West either.'

'It's not a question of intelligence, but of position. The West has been forced into a trap. It has only two possibilities left. Either it can take a leaf out of our book and try to catch up with us. But we win there, since that option requires sacrifice on the part of wide sections of the population in the West. Moreover, the ordinary people in Western countries are scarcely likely to let their leaders take that particular path. Or they can opt out of the game, capitulate and meet all our demands. I would point out that that would be most dangerous for us, since we would thereby be presented with an intolerable burden. But fortunately for us the West will be too scared to capitulate.'

MATRYONADURA ON THE WEST

'What are you always on at me about the West for,' grumbled Matryonadura, although none of us was even thinking of raising the subject. 'You think they don't have any fools of their own? They do, and no fewer than we have. You remember when Nikita went to America? The Americans laid out more than a million dollars getting a sample of his urine. What for? To analyse it, of course. A whole institute spent the next six months analysing that urine. And by using the most expensive, up-to-date methods they finally came up with the explanation that Nikita was a schizophrenic. Whereas we knew without the help of science that he was only half there. And even if he was, so what? Then Brezhnev went to Germany. The Germans went to even more trouble to obtain a sample of his . . . excuse the expression . . . shit. What for? Again, to analyse it, of course. They had decided to find out whether he was going to live for much longer or not. What's the point of that? In our part of the world every last shepherd knows that he's going to live with the shit he's got for just as long as the Party and Government needs him to, and with good shit he'd be got rid of all the sooner. Moreover, these Western idiots don't realise that the leaders of our Party and Government have got all sorts of assistants and advisers to do their shitting and peeing for them.'

THE BATTLE FOR THE HARVEST

We have a political information session every day. The Commissar takes it himself. Five minutes on world affairs and half an hour on the battle for the harvest. He tells us the contents of newspaper articles in fairly garbled fashion, although he tries to demonstrate intelligence and scientific awareness, and reads us out quotations from them. Here, for example, are a few excerpts from the 'Harvest chronicle' column together with the Commissar's commentary. Quote: 'The farmers of such-and-such a region have sold (!!!) the government more than a million tons of grain, over fifty thousand tons more than was envisaged by the national economic plan.' Commentary: 'Sold, notice, and not just handed over like it used to be, which goes to show that . . .' Question from Don Juan: 'How much did they sell it at?' Answer from the Commissar: 'Fifty kopecks a ton, i.e. twice as much as last year.' Quote: 'The rate at which rice is being harvested in the farms in such-and such a district is speeding up. State granaries have already received the first hundred thousand tons – twice as much as this time last year.' Commentary: 'This is a striking example of the realisation in practice of the decision by the Plenum of the Central Committee to pay particular attention to the production of high-yield grains like rice, soya, maize . . . Incidentally, I was in that area last year on a business trip and not only was there no rice, there wasn't even any grass growing, and now . . .' Rejoinder from the Candidate: 'If there was nothing growing there last year, according to the rules of mathematics two times nothing equals . . .' Quote: 'Combine-harvester operator, Hero of Socialist Labour I. Ivanov from Karl Marx collective farm mowed a hundred hectares of grain in five hours, thereby fulfilling fifteen norms.' Commentary: 'I think that this speed of harvesting exceeds the American.' Rejoinder from Ivan Vasilievich: 'What's he got on his combine-harvester, then? A jet engine?!'

An article entitled 'The force of example', taken from a newspaper column headed 'Experts set the pace' was read out in full – by a pushy twerp from the neighbouring brigade who was attached in some subsidiary capacity to the representative of the district Party committee. 'It is early morning,' began the Twerp, with a catch in his voice. 'The autumnal air is fresh and clear.' 'Autumn is wonderful,' says someone, interrupting the speaker, 'the frosty, invigorating air restores one's flagging energy.' 'Comrades,' shouted the brigadier in charge of the neighbouring brigade, 'don't interrupt while important material is being read out! Remember that the district committee of the Party has taken on the commitment to . . .' 'From afar is borne the muffled rumble of engines,' continued the Twerp in heart-rending tones. 'It becomes steadily louder. And now machines drive out from a little gully. In front are the assemblies for taking off the leafy tops of root vegetables, and behind them, the sugar-beet harvesting machines. And all around, humming like bees, are tractors with their little trailers . . . And in this seemingly chaotic movement . . .' 'Why "seemingly?"' asked a lad with a black eye who had been drunk since he got up. 'It only appears like that to you because you're drunk,' said a girl with blonde hair. Everyone laughed. The representative of the district committee called the assembly to order and gave the lad with the black eye a warning, threatening to report his behaviour to his place of work. 'Some of the tractors and trailers, laden with the leafy tops of root vegetables,' continued the Twerp after this interruption, 'hasten to a strip of woodland where a green mountain is rising alongside the ricks. Others, laden with beet, rush to drop their load at the side of the road. The beet-loading machine has already been switched on. The conveyor-belt works tirelessly and reliably, and one feels that everything has been well thought out and organised.'

After the political information session is over we slope off to work, by no means in a hurry to get started. And the picture of us at work has got absolutely nothing in common with the idyllic spectacle as read out to us by that fussy little toady. Half of our machines don't work at all or are constantly breaking down. And those that *are* working don't work well, or don't work as they should. We've long since grown tired of criticising this abysmal mess, and we discuss it lazily, merely from force of habit.

'Surely it must be like the papers say somewhere,' says someone.

'Only the odd exception,' says someone else.

'Hardly,' says a third. 'That's all a pack of lies – it's a mess everywhere.'

'And even if it is like the papers say somewhere, do you think that makes things any better?' says a fourth. 'If they were to try bringing order out of chaos here, we'd all be forced to get stuck in to the point where we'd even give up drinking, never mind women. Just thank your lucky stars, maties, that we don't have that kind of order, never have had and never will have.'

When we reached our patch at last, the machine to which we had been allocated (what the machine is called I have no idea, nor do I wish to know) had broken down. We found a suitable spot behind some bushes and flopped down to catch a bit of shut-eye. An hour passed before it dawned on the management to transfer us to another patch to drag away by hand those same leafy tops of root vegetables and by hand to load the machines.

AFTER WORK

We talk a lot about women and booze. But don't get the idea that all we do is drink and copulate. However badly we work, we still actually do work, and thoroughly knacker ourselves. It's a ten-hour day, after all. Even to stand for ten hours is difficult enough. So we're not all that tempted by the women. Our activist womanisers have to make an effort to meet these women. What for? It depends. Mainly for the sake of male pride. And so that you didn't live your life for nothing. So that there is something to look back on. A bloke'll spend a couple of nights rolling around on the wet ground with some ugly old bag or other, and later on, when he's recalling the incident, she'll have turned into a 'beautiful ripe young blonde'. And, curiously enough, he'll believe it himself. And others will believe him. And envy him.

In actual fact it is almost impossible to meet an attractive and interesting woman in the countryside – they all took off long ago and are not being replaced, and the few that you do come across are already spoken for, and more than once. And it's not so easy to find a decent one among the women who have come for the harvest from the towns, either. Only your second- and third-rate women come for the harvest. The first-rate women usually manage to arrange not to get sent.

As to the booze, well, it costs money. And we're a long way from being well-off. It's your penniless riff-raff who get picked in the towns to work in the country. Many come voluntarily, to get some fresh air and save a few kopecks (they keep their salary, get fed for nothing and even earn a little bit). What we basically do after work is sleep and chat. So we do a lot of talking, not because we are morally or intellectually superior to the West, as our dissidents and intellectuals would have it, but because it's our cheapest, most easily available form of relaxation.

JRF

Although JRF is the most colourless member of our brigade, he deserves special attention, if for no other reason than that he's from our institution. That's what they said to me in the Party bureau when they were unofficially putting me in charge of all the staff who had been assigned by the Institute for work in the country: keep an eye on that lad! I was told the same thing by a Comrade from the Organs at the district centre. But the reason I paid him any attention had nothing to do with the requests of the Party bureau and the Organs – I don't, in general, give a hoot for these requests – but because he's got long hair and a beard.

'You're a handsome young lad,' I said to him while we were still in the city, 'and yet you've let this hairy mess sprout all over you. Why?'

'In order', he said, 'to provide food for thought for sages like you.'

I laughed at that answer and suggested that we celebrate our forthcoming joint trip to the country. He agreed. While we were drinking I shared some of my thoughts with him.

'On one occasion,' I said, 'I suddenly realised that something very important had happened to me, as a result of which I had completely lost the fear of death and was ready for my life to end at any moment. The circumstances were these. My drinking mates had gone off somewhere. I had no money for drink left at all, and I didn't feel like borrowing any. And I simply drifted aimlessly around the streets of the city, thinking about anything and everything. I ended up wandering into the places where I had spent my youth. Our street had completely disappeared. The whole area had been re-built with high-rise blocks of flats. My school, which had always appeared to me to be huge, now looked rather insignificant. I began to think about the past. I remembered my dead parents, my brothers and class-mates who had been killed at the front, the girls I had fallen in love with . . . There's very little left from the past, I thought. And soon there won't be anything left at all. Did all that really happen? And where has it all gone to? Why? And I became not just melancholy but desperately depressed. I wanted to throw myself down on the pavement, beat at it with my fists and cry. Soon I won't be here either, I thought. A little more time will go by, and as far as the world is concerned it will be as if I, and everything that is part of me, had never existed. And then the centuries will rush past, and the millennia, eternity . . . Why on earth, in that case, did my parents and brothers exist, my school friends, my neighbours?! . . . Why am I here myself, and soon it will be: why was I here myself?! . . . It's a nonsense! . . . It's unjust! . . . It's a deception! And what have I done to deserve it? What crimes have I committed?

'I went on in that vein for two or three hours. And how many times I cursed Nature! And how many decisions I took! And suddenly my madness passed. I was at ease. And now I looked humorously at that little bit of the world I had been destined to inhabit for an instant and at everything that I had experienced. It's all correct, I said to myself. There's nothing unjust or cruel about it. Once you've had your lot, it's time to go. Time to make way for others. Are you ready for that? I'm ready! At any moment! Here and now, if necessary!

'After that a new period in my life began (probably, the last) – one in which I found myself ready to part with life. And then strange thoughts began to come to me. If you are ready to part with your life, then make an intelligent use of this state of affairs. How? For example, escape abroad and see the world. Or protest about the flouting of human rights. Even better – blow yourself up in the Mausoleum (they say that there have been such attempts), set yourself alight in Red Square as a sign of protest, bump off some higher official, the Gen Sec himself, if possible. At the very least, get involved in the underground, distribute "samizdat", collect material for the *Digest of Current Events*, help the families of imprisoned dissidents . . . There are lots of ways of using your life intelligently! I thought about these problems many times. And came to the conclusion that I wouldn't do any of these things, because I don't want to. I emphasise that: I won't do these things, not out of fear, but because I *don't want to*. That is what all these critics of our society and way of life cannot understand.

'Why don't I want to? The answer to that question is the key to all our problems. I have not exactly made a success of my life – I only made it to STA. At my age, and with my inclinations! It's laughable – STA! I've got no close friends, no family, no flat and no prospects of a decent pension. So what's the point? The point is that this society of ours is MY OWN SOCIETY. It is an integral part of my ego, with all its horrors, its difficulties and its tattiness. And the Mausoleum, and Red Square, and the stupid, vain Gen Sec, and the hounding of the dissidents, and the dissidents themselves, and the KGB and that dreg of a director of ours – all these things and everything else are not just circumstances in my life and the conditions in which I live my life – they *are* my life, they are the body and soul of my life, its tissue, content, nucleus, basis. I repeat, this society, with all its loathesomeness, is my society. Not that I accept it, or that I am satisfied with it. I don't accept it. I abuse it all the time. I despise it. I hate it. But that doesn't in any way alter the fact that it is mine. It is like the situation where we might know that our children are physical and moral freaks and not love them for that, or heap abuse on them, and at the same time not be in a position to do anything about the fact that they are our children. I am a product of this society. But it is also a product of me, it's my offspring, or rather, the collective offspring of millions of people like myself. And all those despicable actions which I have had to perform in my life (and will have to perform in the future) are the result of that very simple fact and not of cowardice, greed, cruelty, envy, or any other ordinary attribute of ordinary people. These attributes merely lend our despicable acts a particular form, but do not determine them as such. There's where you have to look for an explanation of everything that goes on around us, and of ourselves.'

'I haven't,' said JRF, 'lived long enough to reach a turning point like that. I haven't yet lost anyone, or anything. And I have not yet been visited by the fear of dying. But I understand you very well. I was born, and have lived all my life, in the neighbourhood of the Lubyanka. And not only in the territorial sense. I feel it in my bones. And if they were to destroy it, either literally or metaphorically, it would be the greatest loss imaginable for me. Perhaps I wouldn't get over it.'

'Aha,' I said. 'I'm sorry for you, my lad. You're going to have an even harder time than I had.'

OUR LITTLE WAYS

They say that the following slogans hang in the Central Committee: 'Our Party has entered the contest for the designation "Communist"', 'Long live the Soviet people – eternal builders of communism!' and 'Those of us who don't work, don't eat'.

THE WEST AND US

'They eat fruit in the West,' said Matryonadura. 'They hang about the Louvre or Versailles for days on end gawking at their "abasractionists". They have a look, go outside, drink coffee right there on the pavement, then back into the Louvre!'

'Nonsense!' objected Ivan Vasilievich. 'Do you think that all they do is go to impressionist art galleries and make pacifist speeches? They work over there. And think twice about every kopeck. And the philistine reigns supreme in the West as well.

Our philistine is a little better in as much as our lack of organisation compels him to be less than a total philistine. People are the same everywhere. The laws of human society are the same.'

'Well, what do you think about this stirring topic?' I asked JRF.

'I don't think about the West at all,' he replied.

'Does that mean that you only think about us?' I asked.

'No,' he said, 'I don't think about us either.'

'What do you think about, then?' I insisted.

'I don't think about anything,' he replied.

MATRYONADURA ON THE WEST

'That West of yours,' said Matryonadura, 'is about as much good to me as a pair of tights is to my cow. My cousin's nephew on her brother's side was over there. And from what he said, I wouldn't go there if you paid me, never mind pay myself. You even have to pay to go for a pee. And not just any old how – you have to have a specific coin. One of the members of their tourist group died because of that. He wanted to go for a pee, but he didn't have the right coin. They wouldn't let him in without paying, and, anyway, he wouldn't go in without paying – his Soviet pride wouldn't let him. He offered them a banknote (that was all they had been given) but they wouldn't take it. They're honest, the so-and-so's! His comrades told him just to pee round the corner and they would watch out. He was scared to do that. They had been instructed before their trip that there was to be no disgraceful behaviour, otherwise there might be all sorts of provocation from the other side. And his comrades would report him and he wouldn't be allowed to go the next time. And so he held on till he got back to the hotel. And collapsed at the entrance. They didn't call for a doctor. Doctors are too expensive. They'll rip you off for more than the Georgians at the Cheryomushki market in Moscow.'

'Why didn't his comrades give him a coin?' asked Kostya.

'Huh, listen to him!' laughed Matryonadura. 'They didn't

have a penny to spare, and every penny'll buy something over there. Her nephew brought back a whole trunk-load of stuff.'

THE BATTLE FOR THE HARVEST

'The battle for the harvest,' we were told at our routine political information session, 'is approaching the final stages. The front is being switched from sugar-beet, carrots and cabbages to potatoes. The unexpected deterioration in the weather which our experts already forecast two weeks ago (admittedly in the wrong area) has not prevented an intensification of the struggle. The team of cabbage-harvesting machine driver A. I. Grechko, Hero of Socialist Labour, working without pause for three shifts, has harvested fifty thousand clumps of potato tubers from an area of a hundred hectares, which is seventy per cent more than last year. Beet-growers in the Voroshilov district . . .'

The only thing that was true in the above communication was the bit about the weather: it really had deteriorated. We began to have cold, drizzly rain which threatened to be endless. We went around wet all the time, up to our knees in mud. Our barn began to leak. Or rather, we discovered that it did leak already. The reason that it hadn't leaked before was that it hadn't been raining. Not far from the barn we discovered a scrap-heap of building materials – boards, tarred paper, slates, plywood. We asked the local authorities for permission to use some of these materials to repair the roof of our barn. Naturally, it was refused: these materials had been allocated for a new pigsty and repairs to the school (how many years ago!). Matryonadura, who was very keen to get her barn repaired, egged us on to take what we needed without asking. We wouldn't need much, would we? No one would notice. And one night JRF and Kostya repaired the roof, covering up their work with some old, rotting boards. But somehow the management found out about our DIY repairs. No doubt someone shopped us. There was an amazing scandal. The police came and took statements. They threatened to charge JRF and Kostya with theft of state property. Then JRF and Kostya took all these lousy materials off the roof again (they weren't worth more than ten roubles) and took them back. With the exception of the Commissar, who slept on Matryonadura's mattress stuffed with the fresh hay, and Forehead, on whom, for some reason, it didn't leak, we declared that we wouldn't go to work until they fixed the roof. The Commissar accused us of being deserters. He said that during the war (and the battle for the harvest was being carried out on a war-footing) we would have been shot on the spot for tricks like that. Ivan Vasilievich asked the Commissar which front he had fought on. The Commissar regarded that question as provocative. Finally we did go to work and they gave us some stuff to stop up the cracks in the walls. But it was decided to report the behaviour of JRF and Kostya to their respective places of work and to print a note in the wall-newspaper. Yes, in the wall-newspaper. It's a kind of 'military broadsheet' a few copies of which are printed and hung up on stands in the brigades. The article was entitled 'Every family has its freak'. The brigades held special Party-komsomol meetings, which all non-Party people had to attend. There it was said that the battle for the harvest was entering a decisive phase, that, naturally, difficulties would arise, that we were obliged . . . that the Party and government . . . that the whole Soviet people . . . We denounced unhealthy behaviour and took on increased commitments.

JRF and Kostya didn't attend the meeting, claiming that they were ill (and, in fact, they had managed to get drunk somewhere, and to avoid any more trouble we hid them so that they could sleep it off). And that was also held against them. All the signs are that they will now be forced into the role of those 'freaks', without which the life of every healthy collective of ours is unthinkable. They will be used as an example to others and the leaders will demonstrate correspondingly how much society needs them and how quickly they can nip in the bud, root out, forewarn, react . . .

KOSTYA'S PHILOSOPHY

'One ought to give up work,' said Kostya, 'in the sense of a permanent job in an official institution.'

'Why?'

'To get away from the senseless and degrading dependence on the collective.'

'And what does one live on?'

'That's no problem. You can live on fifty roubles a month. I've tried it.'

'But you have to get those fifty roubles from somewhere.'

'That's easy. You can earn enough in two months in the summer to last the whole year.'

'You won't go very far on that kind of money.'

'Don't go very far, then. Give up smoking and drinking. Don't eat meat. Walk everywhere. Wear the same clothes in winter as you do in summer. Sleep . . .'

'What about women?'

'They're not essential. If they come along, take them. If not, don't go after them.'

'What's the use of being alive, then?'

'For the sake of your soul! For self-contemplation. For contemplation in general. The pleasures of the intellect are superior to the pleasures of the flesh.'

'So what's the problem, then?'

'They won't let you. They'll make you do hard labour in a collective which is a lot worse than the one you're working in at the moment. At least here you've got some little bit of freedom of choice. And they pay a little more.'

OUR WOMEN

It has to be admitted that our women are depressingly uniform and dull. There's a pair with fairly poisonous tongues, a couple with good figures, a couple with nice-looking faces and a couple with some dress sense. But all of them have more or less obvious defects. There's not a flawless one among them. I'm not talking about perfection, simply ordinary quality. It would be nice if they were all averagely pleasing. Like the vegetables we have to harvest. Under God's sky they look as if there was nothing wrong with them, but by the time they reach the consumer it's difficult to find even an unblemished potato or semi-decent cabbage, never mind an outstanding potato or terrific cabbage. However, why should that be surprising?! If we can't even grow potatoes and cabbages properly and keep them in good condition, what's the point of talking about such a delicate and sensitive creature as a woman? Delicacy and sensitivity are not catered for in principle.

'Food and clothes don't matter,' said Don. 'To hell with them! But the cult of woman – that's a real problem. We're not just fifty years behind the West in this respect. We're a million years behind them! This is what I can't forgive this advanced social order of ours. I'm serious, lads. Understand this: the cult of woman, her body, her dress, her home, her sex is the fundamental basis of any culture. If there's progress there, then we men begin to progress as well. Even if it's only to get our teeth filled, have a shave, trim our beards, develop our muscles, change our underwear. And many other things would change from that point on. Supply our women with safe, reliable contraceptives, decent lingerie and a basic education in the art of love-making, and our society would rush ahead on the road to progress immeasurably faster as a result than from space-flights and atomic energy!'

MATRYONADURA ON THE WEST

'In England,' said Matryonadura, 'cats don't eat mice.'

'What do they feed on, then?!' we remonstrated with one voice.

'Oh, listen to them! And they call themselves intellectuals! They eat pudding! Everyone eats pudding in England.'

AN OBSERVATION FROM IVAN VASILIEVICH

'It's no use blaming a snake for having no legs or wings,' said Ivan Vasilievich, when we were having a discussion about the people. And after that we were silent.

ON REVOLUTION

The Commissar is an interesting case. Perhaps no less interesting than Matryonadura. If she personifies our people, he personifies our leadership. Perhaps that's why she prefers to sleep with him rather than with anyone else, although he's less of a man than any of us, and feed him, even though the cook lets a bit extra come his way and he's always buying something to eat at the shop. I'll have more to say about the Commissar later on. For the moment I'll let him have the floor. Not that I need to let him have it – he takes it himself. Matryonadura gave him some of her hooch today. That made him drunk and he began to talk a lot of nonsense about the need for a new, 'real' communist party and a new revolution. At first we just laughed, but the point came when we couldn't take it as a joke any more and we rose up in arms.

'We've had enough revolutions,' we shouted. 'We've had them up to here! And we don't need any new parties. The one we've got is enough. And we don't need a multi-party system. That would only make things worse. We can't even harvest potatoes competently with one party. What would it be like if we had the representatives of several parties hovering about and giving instructions?! There wouldn't be a thing left standing!'

While the lads were demolishing the Commissar, from a purely marxist-leninist standpoint, I asked JRF what he thought about the possibility of forming a party of opposition. He said that that was nonsense and that it would be crushed, anyway. Besides, in our conditions any organisation would turn into a typical Soviet institution. And what that meant was familiar enough. We would organise an opposition just as badly as we harvest vegetables. Much more effective than a large organisation would be a certain number of people who thought, felt and acted the same. It would be difficult to crush them – it would be difficult to find fault with them. And the organisational effect wouldn't come into force. What was that? People uniting in a common cause weaken each other. The strength of an amalgamation of people is not the sum of the strengths of its members, but a magnitude which diminishes relative to that sum as the number of members increases and the organisation is consolidated. Notice that political parties always strive to increase their membership. That wasn't a coincidence. As its organisation intensifies, a party can only retain its strength at a given level if it expands. I said that I didn't understand that abstruse theory and cited by way of counter-argument the case of small, well-organised terrorist groups. He said that they were of short duration, abnormal, and relied for their existence on nervous energy.

YET ANOTHER IMPORTANT PERSON

In the municipal Party committee there is an agricultural section – a brilliant example of the marxist thesis on the disappearance of the distinction between town and country under communism. The person in charge of this section is a woman, or more accurately, a 'woman!'. In fact, more accurate would be, not 'woman!' but 'wo-man!'. 'He-woman' is what our womanisers call her. And they laugh knowingly. Boy, oh boy, they say, if I could only lay my hands on a he-woman like that! Cor, what wouldn't I do to her! This, of course, is mere self-delusion and self-importance, since before 'doing' to any 'he-woman' what she 'deserves', our womanisers would have to be fed for a year on meat and shown foreign magazines with dirty pictures. But where would you get them from? You might get hold of ten-year-old magazines, but what about the meat? The womanisers are right about one thing. This 'he-woman' has plenty you can hold on to. This was precisely why she got on to the municipal district committee of the Young Communist League, from where she was transferred to the agricultural section of the municipal Party committee (there was nowhere else to put her, given her outstanding stupidity), where she gradually made it to the post of head. Her name is Evdokia, and the people, who love her, call her Avdotya (saying at the same time that she's a real he-peasant) and the local intelligentsia (there's no escape from them here either!) call her Dun'ka. A few years ago some Moscow joker who had been in the neighbourhood for a time nicknamed her Mao-Tse-Dun'ka. The joker was put in a psychiatric hospital. And even the dissident campaign against punitive medicine could not save him. When dissidents were told about this case they laughed – but didn't do anything about it. Ha-ha-ha! – they laughed, – what normal person would make jokes like that?! The chap has obviously gone off his rocker! The nickname, however, did not catch on with the local people, although they abused both the Chinese and Mao-Tse-Dun'ka from top to bottom. We laugh at the Chinese, but secretly acknowledge that it was just as bad with us at one time. Nevertheless, we think that we are better than the Chinese.

Mao-Tse-Dun'ka acquired her nickname in the following circumstances. Evdokia Timofeevna had decided to talk with the Muscovites frankly, i.e. 'as man to man, and not as a Party leader'. During this conversation she enunciated the Principle 'Let all the flowers in our garden grow!' in a tone befitting our conditions (i.e. 'Just let them try to grow! . . .') Of course, she didn't enunciate it in such highly poetic terms, but more simply, more in our idiom. We don't forbid anyone anything, – she said. Let them say what they like . . . But she pronounced the word 'Let' in such a way that no doubt was left as to her meaning:

'Let them try! We'll show them a "thing or two" and "where to get off".'

I wasn't present when Mao-Tse-Dun'ka made that speech. I first saw her when she was blaming the weather for everything. 'The weather is to blame for everything,' she said. 'Our weather is good, not like the West's. But it's let us down a bit as far as the harvest is concerned. If it hadn't been for the weather, we'd really have shown them!' No one bothered to ask who 'they' were, since it was clear enough: imperialists, zionists, dissidents. It was also clear *what* we would have shown them: a 'thing or two' and 'where to get off'.

Mao-Tse-Dun'ka appears in our part of the world quite frequently, always accompanied by her new 'fancy man'. She loves to talk to the 'people' and the 'people' love her for this: being talked to means not having to work. And she knows how to drink. Every speech is bound to contain phrases like 'We won't be destitute!' 'We'll get by!' 'We'll win through!' 'We won't tolerate!' 'We've seen worse than this!' 'Well, now, you manly lot!' she will say to the women. 'We'll win through! We won't tolerate . . . ! We've seen worse than this!' 'Well, now, you effeminate bunch,' she will say to the men. 'We'll win through! We will not tolerate . . . We've seen worse than this!'

People make fun of her, but not maliciously. They like her rather than dislike her, since she's one of their own kind. She was born and bred here. She made a spectacular career for herself on local terms. She will die here, and the collective farm where she was born and where her relatives still live will be named after her. She is the flesh and blood of her people. On one of her visits the Commissar drew her attention to the fact that the sugar beet had been left in the fields, and that it would rot or be stolen. Sugar beets aren't carrots, she replied, you can't eat many of them. And she won thereby the applause of those assembled. But the next morning it turned out that the beets had been stolen anyway.

FROM THE SPEECHES OF MAO-TSE-DUN'KA

'What's the climate to us?! We've seen worse than that! We'll win through! Remember, my hearties,' (this to the women) 'how we dug the carrots out of the snow with our bare hands?'

'But the carrots were still ruined, anyway! . . .'

'Ach, you, and you call yourselves politically literate!' (this to us) 'There's intellectuals for you! Do you think that the carrots are the most important thing? Enthusiasm – that's what's important. Being prepared to surmount difficulties! And all you can say is – the carrots are ruined! . . .'

Mao-Tse-Dun'ka's speeches can be divided into those she gives as a Party leader and those from the heart which she delivers 'man to man'. The latter are particularly impressive. 'Our girls are not what they used to be,' she will say out of the blue, slapping her mighty hips with the palms of her hands. 'It was different in my time. Remember, my hearties,' (this is addressed, naturally, to the women) 'how many abortions we had? And who carried them out?! It was a joke. And you got no time off. You had your abortion and back to the ploughing. Look how it is now!'

This 'man to man' approach usually ends in vulgar boorishness. She lets her hair down, swears like a trooper, makes dirty remarks and more or less behaves like a general in a soldiers' latrine. Even we get embarrassed, and we've seen a thing or two in that respect, and are inclined that way ourselves.

'And don't worry about the West,' she will say on leaving. 'Sooner or later we're going to screw its arse!'

Mao-Tse-Dun'ka comes from the people, or, as she puts it, from the workers and peasants. She is not an exception. Attempts are still being made to recruit people like her into the Party apparatus, not out of fidelity to marxist dogma (i.e. our Party is above all a party of peasants and workers), but from a social instinct to recruit people into the apparatus who would be entirely dependent on it and intellectually adequate for it. Now, however, the ranks in the Party apparatus are being swollen by recruits from the privileged strata. And it has to be admitted that their cultural level is significantly higher than that of the recruits from 'the people'. That doesn't mean, of course, that they are any better.

KOSTYA'S COMPLAINT

The dissidents have it easy. If anything happens to them, the West immediately creates a fuss. It's some protection, at least. But what about our ordinary Ivan? They can do what they like to us, and no one is even interested. No one is interested in our affairs. No, my friends, we need something more than a feeble dissident movement full of wind and piss, only I don't know what. It's appalling to think what trivial matters govern our lives, and to what a dreadful extent we are at their mercy. For instance, they decided to change the voltage of our electricity. They posted an announcement to the effect that people should be in their flats on such and such a date, since someone was coming to change their meters. And we stayed at home for two weeks waiting for these experts – they didn't come. A lot of people were put to a lot of bother: they had to take time off work, postpone trips to rest homes. The 'experts' finally appeared – but without warning. Many people weren't at home. There was all sorts of fuss, mutual insults, etc. The 'experts' (drunk as lords, naturally) took advantage of the situation to get on their high horses. Eventually they got around to changing the meters. Then a new reign of terror began: we waited for the switch-over. We waited for months. We wrote complaints. Useless. Finally the switch-over took place – but without warning. Many people had their refrigerators, televisions and radios burned out. We set up a commission to prepare an indictment and sent in a claim for compensation to the courts. My God, you should have seen what happened then! We were accused of everything under the sun! Even of setting up a politically hostile group. Our barrister said that we might win the suit, but that it would take us at least a year.

MATRYONADURA ON THE WEST

That same nephew said that, over there, dogs choose who they want to live with. You'd never find a Great Dane, for instance, in a working class family. It needs a sitting-room all to itself. A poodle won't stoop lower than a lecturer. Whereas what goes on in our part of the world? It would make you spit! They've produced a special Moscow breed. Even bigger than these St Bernards and Newfoundlands. And what for? To guard the cows? There aren't any cows. To guard the farm shops? But there's nothing to steal. And, anyway, a burglar who knows his stuff won't be put off by a dog. They burgled the department store in town during the winter. There were three guard dogs, but they cleaned the place out. They say that they got one dog drunk on vodka. They shut another one up with a sausage. Where did they get the sausage from?! They must have brought it with them from Moscow. And the third dog went off with the burglars of its own free will.

LITTLE LOCAL ESCAPADES

The breeding bull is dead. It was healthy enough, but for some reason just died. Now if anyone becomes seriously ill around here, the locals say that he's as strong as an ox. And everyone laughs. Our life here is so grey and monotonous that the death of that bull was almost like a holiday.

Your Russian is clever and sharp-witted by nature. But in a topsy-turvy kind of way. I don't know of a single incidence of monumental stupidity in which this innate cleverness and wit did not come to light. For instance, they bring cabbages and carrots from the neighbouring farm and dump them on our fields. Then we load them on to lorries which take them to the station right across that same farm. What's going on? It turns out that the regional Party committee has decided that ours should be designated as a model farm and that we should over-fulfil the plan for carrots and cabbages. We, in turn, are supplying that farm with beets so that it can come top in the region for that. I said to the agronomist that it would be simpler to take the vegetables to the station in the first place, and doctor the books afterwards. The agronomist said that they hadn't yet gone completely off their rockers and didn't fancy being sent to jail for fraud. As it was, even ten commissions and expert criminologists couldn't do anything about it. People would talk? What don't people talk about? But just try proving it! And he explained the whole thing to me in detail. And I realised how wise our simple people are, and how stupid we intellectuals are.

I talked to Matryonadura afterwards about this topic. At the end of the conversation she said the following, word for word: we won't fulfil the five-year plan, that's certain, but we'll do it ahead of time, in four years. What is that? A joke? A serious statement of the essence of the situation? I didn't seen any sign of a smile while she was speaking.

Later on Don Juan, JRF, Kostya and I had to take vegetables and a calf (slaughtered, of course) to Mao-Tse-Dun'ka's in town. She has a detached house there, with an excellent cellar. Her husband is a totally brow-beaten nonentity, the head-master of some school. They have children, but they didn't deign to have anything to do with us. We were allowed to eat and drink a little something in the kitchen.

MAO-TSE-DUN'KA ON THE EXPECTED CHANGE OF LEADERSHIP

Don't hope for anything!!!

DON JUAN'S BEWILDERMENT

Our farm had an unexpected visit from one of the secretaries of the regional Party committee. My God, you should have seen the fuss that caused! But the funniest thing about it was that the visit was anything but unexpected. They had been waiting for the Secretary to visit them and had prepared for it. Even our behaviour had to be rehearsed. Moreover, they prepared for it dialectically; the arrival of the Secretary should appear to be totally unexpected, but he should find everything not in its usual mess, but in a state of 'newspaper readiness'. In order to achieve this, the farm managers and representatives from the district Party committee were dispersed among the brigades in the fields, so that the Secretary would find no one in the office but the accountant, but in such a fashion that all the managers could appear before the Secretary at his summons with the speed of lightning. We were shown what pose to adopt at our allotted work place so that the news photographers and film camera men wouldn't have to waste any time but yet would be able to take shots which would look absolutely natural. Everything went off as planned. All the actors in this grandiose event played their part impeccably. We were duly photographed. A couple of hours later the Secretary and his huge entourage went off to dine with our bosses – a magnificent spread had been prepared for them in the club. We listlessly got through to the end of the working day and dispersed to our huts, bath-houses and barns.

A tremendous amount of noise emanated from the club. The local inhabitants, in the old Russian tradition, looked out of their windows and tried to find out who had come and what was going on.

'Notice,' said Don Juan, 'the size of that regional louse's personal bodyguard. And he's not even from the top of the pile. The President of the USA has a captain in charge of his personal bodyguard, but this one's got a major. But that's nothing. I once had occasion to observe an official whose chief bodyguard held the rank of colonel at least. Moreover, that official was only third-rank on a national scale. Can you imagine! No one needs that official. Even dogs don't bark at him. And you can believe it or not, as you like, but I noticed that even flies wouldn't settle on him, he was such a nonentity. And yet he had a personal bodyguard of fifty people at least, under the command of a colonel! Well, now, you theoreticians, explain the meaning of that!'

MATRYONADURA ON THE WEST

'About these toilets, again. Latrines, we call them. I don't like them. I don't like them at all. Where we are, we've got wide open spaces. Shit where you want to. Whereas over there? That same nephew said that he hung on for a whole day on one occasion but couldn't find one. So he ended up by having to change his underwear. But what upset him most was that when he went into a toilet, he couldn't bring himself to perform. He said that the lavatory had no hole in it. My goodness, surely they haven't learned to do away with shitting over there?! Anything's possible. All they eat is vitamins, the swine.'

THE USUAL GUFF ON WESTERN TOPICS

Our prattle on Western topics and comparisons between ourselves and the West usually arise out of some innocent joke.

'There was a friend of mine,' said the Candidate, 'who only knew three sentences in English. But he knew them perfectly. He went on a trip to England. He was invited to some very posh house. He, of course, kept quiet. During the course of the whole evening he only spoke these three sentences. When he had gone the hosts said that he was a real gentleman: he had a marvellous command of English, but didn't overdo it.'

'A diplomat friend of mine,' said Don Juan, 'wandered into a brothel. The manager came up to him and began to tell him what a rich choice there was in his brothel. Now, for our Ivan who finds himself in the West, the problem of choice is most difficult, since he always has to choose from a great variety of good things. Naturally my friend was at a loss. At last he hit upon a solution. 'I'll rely on your taste,' he said to the manager. And the manager led him to a big hairy Armenian.'

'You're exaggerating about the Armenian, of course.'

'Not at all. That's the only true part, for the West has got more Armenians than we have.'

'But you're right about the problem of choice. My friend decided to buy a coat in Geneva. He wanted a good, cheap coat that he could wear all the year round. But he couldn't find anything like that in the whole of Geneva. He ended up having to buy three coats: a good one, a cheap one, and one that he could wear all the year round.'

'Nonsense! Where did he get the money for all that?'

'He sold out to foreign intelligence organisations.'

'Who needs him?'

'He offered them his services cut-price.'

'Is that so . . . One good thing about them over there is their attitude to the past. They look after it, the swine.'

'I wouldn't have said that. They've got too many monuments over there. It's very difficult and expensive to look after them all. We do that sort of thing better.'

'Are you feeling all right?'

'Never better. We've got nothing left from the past. And it's much cheaper and easier to keep NOTHING in good condition.'

Later on, the tenor of these conversations passes imperceptibly from the facetious to the serious. And then the main topic is whether the West will be able to escape our fate. It's strange, isn't it? We're less worried about our own fate, we're reconciled to it. And we're concerned for the West.

'The West has more than enough problems of its own. Can the capitalists solve them? Evidently not. What about the communists?'

'They can, of course.'

'But how? OK, let's suppose they solve them in the best possible fashion. Let's suppose there's no unemployment, you've got free medicine and education . . . But just as there's no evil without good, there's also no good without evil. Will they be able to avoid the horrors that we went through?'

'Western communists promise that they wouldn't let these things happen.'

'What wouldn't they promise? When I was trying to get my way with one particular girl, I promised to marry her. And when it comes to having power over a country, you can promise a bit more than that.'

'Well, did you persuade her?'

'No, the girl wasn't stupid. She didn't believe me. Do you know what she said to me? Promises are only made to be broken.'

'Surely they must know in the West by now what communism and communists are all about.'

'They're beginning to get an inkling. But they don't know how to deal with them properly. They argue with them, but on a serious level. And you know yourself that you can't deal with marxists seriously by arguing with them seriously. You need other means.'

'What other means?'

'Laughter.'

Finally we end up by getting on to military topics. The main one there is the question of how long it would take us to seize Western Europe and make it over in our image, and whether the USA would prevent us. The majority believe that we only need two days to seize Europe, and that's basically to destroy Yugoslavia and West Germany. The rest will shit themselves and give up without a fight. Perhaps the Swiss will have something to say for themselves, but there aren't enough of them to matter. We've got thousands of agents in the West and tens of thousands in our fifth column. There would be many millions of volunteers to help us. We could smash the structure of Western Europe in two days and impose our own. That's not a problem. The West is too surfeited and is therefore not capable of offering any resistance. Everything depends on America. China, of course, is a force to be reckoned with. But it's counting on the Americans starting a war with us over Europe and on us destroying each other, leaving China free to dictate to us as it likes.

When we have settled all these internal and global issues in that fashion, we fall asleep. We don't feel like going after the women, although it would be possible to do so: we simply don't have the strength, and we have to start work more or less at dawn. We don't even feel like drinking. Even boozing, it turns out, requires a standard of living beyond our means here: we have neither the freedom nor the money.

MATRYONADURA ON THE WEST AND US

I get a lot of pleasure from Matryonadura's opinions about the West. And I provoke her into giving them. I've already collected more than a hundred of her pronouncements. It wouldn't half cause a fuss if I published them in 'samizdat' or 'tamizdat'.

'What's so great about the West?' she'll say. 'No doubt they've got their old and infirm as well. That nephew was saying that the man who invited them to his house had his car stolen. And anyway, what would our Ivan do with Western civilisation? We'd only foul it up good and proper.'

'But, Matryona Ivanovna, what about space flights? We were the first!'

'That's a different matter. That's to do with prestige and doing things on a grandiose scale. And when it comes to grandiose scale, we're OK there.'

'Everyone says that it's more fun living in the West. It's supposed to be boring, the way we live. Do you never get bored?'

'What's there to get bored about? I'm not bored. I don't have time for that. Only fools and idlers get bored. There used to be a library assistant in our club. She used to walk around with her face tripping her. She said it was boring here. But I said, mark my words, there'll be a simple explanation. She doesn't want a child and it's too late for an abortion. And that's the way it turned out.'

DISAGREEMENTS

Although our barn is considered to be a model of harmony in the brigade (we have no outstanding drunkards or rowdies), we have had our disagreements right from the start. They first made their appearance in the form of jokes, then they began to be discussed more seriously, albeit in friendly fashion, finally we reached a kind of bedrock of principle. These differences centre on the practical and theoretical attitudes we adopt to the work which we are required to do here. If you really want to know a person, observe how he works. Even JRF doesn't refute that rule. Admittedly, he left a way out for himself by observing that it depended on what you meant by work.

It became clear on the very first day that Ivan Vasilievich and Kostya were model workers. The Commissar is a good worker and I am a conscientious worker. Ivan Vasilievich radiates experience, energy and love for any task, right down to chopping firewood or washing the saucepan when it's his turn to be in the kitchen. Kostya works himself enthusiastically into the ground. Our group, then, contains the sloggers. Ivan Vasilievich has formulated our ideological position, and I'll set out his views below. Forehead turned out to be an absolute loafer and parasite, thereby earning the contempt of everyone. Although he's the strongest in the brigade, he began to be given the lightest tasks. Finally Don Juan suggested that he be given the duty of swatting flies off the Commissar. Someone said that there didn't seem to be any flies. Don Juan said that was precisely why he had suggested Forehead for the job, and not Kostya. Forehead, for his part, returned our contempt with one hundred per cent interest, which solved the problem for him once and for all.

It was a bit more difficult with the other group which contained JRF, Don Juan, the Candidate and the Lathe Operator. You couldn't say that they were loafers, but they work with complete indifference to the job in hand. If it's possible to dodge work, they'll dodge it willingly. They will only work overtime after much persuasion and threats. And if they agree to work overtime, it's not so much because of these threats as from a desire to be left alone. Getting them to work at night (and we sometimes have to) is absolutely impossible. The theoretician of this group, by unspoken agreement, is JRF.

Folk usually call people like that skivers. And if you really want to know, it is in this respect that people differ most from each other in our society. Not in their conversations – anyone can learn to say anything you like – but precisely in their attitude to the job in hand.

Here are the principles to which that group adheres, as expressed by JRF in intelligent, albeit cynical form. If a person

323

is forced to engage in a particular activity against his will, the fact that he is forced relieves him of all moral obligations in regard to that activity and gives him a full moral right to act in the way most advantageous to himself, including the right to avoid work, pretend to work, or to pull the wool. He is fully justified in not binding himself by any commitments to other people engaged in the same common enterprise and in acting according to his own lights with respect to that enterprise, if the others are not of the same mind. Only when other people participating in the activity demonstrate an analogous attitude, can and must a person co-ordinate his behaviour with the behaviour of people who think like himself.

Ivan Vasilievich said to JRF that the latter had come voluntarily. The latter replied that he had been forced to come, like the majority, but that the coercion had not been apparent. Coercion incidentally (said JRF) is rarely apparent. Usually it takes the form of voluntary behaviour, in the same way as resistance to coercion isn't always open. More often than not it takes the form of submission. We have all submitted, but in such a way that we express our protest in accordance with the principles enunciated above. And generally speaking, everything in our society is a matter of compulsion. Even our favourite occupation, if it becomes our profession, turns into a form of compulsion.

Ivan Vasilievich told JRF to stop 'trying to bedazzle him', that he wouldn't be taken in by words, that he had seen a thing or two in his time, and that that wasn't what it was all about. There were more important and fundamental laws governing people's behaviour which were independent of parties, epochs, or social formations, laws which governed any concerted activity. 'It doesn't matter how you come to be in a particular human collective, or what your principles happen to be. But once that collective is given a job to do, every member of it is obliged to put in the effort regarded as adequate by that collective. In our time people like JRF were considered to be dodgers, and we dealt with them ourselves. And then they would begin to work properly.'

'In the first place,' objected JRF, 'just try and see where hitting people gets you. That might be the norm in the camps or in the army. But here you've got your normal, untalented, free society.

So you would do better to save your strength for heroic labour. In the second place, I don't work any worse than anyone else. I work according to the "same as everyone" principle, a principle which your collective approves of entirely. And if my heart isn't in it, that's also a common phenomenon, it's an attribute of any kind of forced labour. And I do not intend to demonstrate any "labour heroism". I am not obliged to. That is the prerogative of cretins and careerists, and I'm neither the one nor the other. Amen!'

'That means that I'm a cretin and careerist, does it?' asked Ivan Vasilievich. 'And Kostya, as well? If I were a cretin and careerist, I wouldn't be lying around in this barn. I'd be a minister or important general. And right now I'd be on holiday in some wonderful resort. Everything you've said is just words. I admit that the words are intelligent – you've learned more with your mother's milk than we have in our old age. But there are purely human qualities. Manly ones, at least.'

'When it comes to manly qualities,' said the Lathe Operator, 'our Don Juan is a past master. And the Commissar doesn't miss out, either.'

'Don't dodge the issue,' said Ivan Vasilievich. 'Do you think that people like me threw themselves under tanks and into embrasures just for the Motherland, Party and Stalin? They didn't, not exclusively. They also did it partly because they were real men. When they said to us "Volunteers, two steps forward march!", we took these steps without a thought. That was human nature at work. Do you think that Kostya here literally burns himself out at work for love of Party and government? Ask him, and he'll tell you where to go. And I understand him: he isn't bothered by any theoretical problems. Whereas for you, problems arise. Problems arise where there shouldn't be any, that's the curse of our situation. We've began to doubt fundamental types of behaviour which characterise us as human and swamp them – if you'll pardon the expression – in the shit of problems and conversations.'

'I respect your convictions,' said JRF. 'But you and Kostya are, sad to say, exceptions in our society. If it weren't for you, our group would consist only of one parasite and shirkers like me. And we would be typical. And solid with each other. And perhaps we would even win the "Red Challenge Banner". But because of you it is evident that our collective is divided and that we are shirkers. And so we won't win that banner.'

'To hell with it, then!' said Ivan Vasilievich.

Our profoundly principled argument finished peaceably at that point. We each contributed a rouble and bought a bottle of 'cognac drink', as Matryonadura put it, which had been lying around in the farm shop since Khrushchev's time. But genuine unanimity was not achieved. Although I belonged to the sloggers, I couldn't accept Ivan Vasilievich's outlook. Heroic and selfless labour without reward is nonsense, when all is said and done. But deep down I didn't like shirkers like JRF either, although I couldn't come up with any arguments against the way he sees things. Later on, a very simple thought occurred to me: Ivan Vasilievich is a stranger from a heroic past, whereas JRF is a product of our monotonous today. Who is to be preferred? Neither one. They are both products of their respective times, and yet both of them constitute departures from the norm for those times. They stand too naked. They are both individualists, although poles apart from each other. The man of our time is a collectivist. And a collectivist, well, that's something pretty tricky.

MATRYONADURA ON THE WEST

'That nephew said that they believe in marxism over there. Not like here. Here they laugh at it. What don't they laugh at here? They laugh at our leaders. They even laugh at Lenin, that's what things have come to! But they believe in it over there. And treat it with respect. You have to hand it to them. There's culture for you. They even respect marxism.'

'Why "even"?'

'What would you respect it for? If marxism gets power into its own hands over there, they'll take away property, put people in prison and create just as big a mess as we have. Why would you respect it? But they respect it. Not like us. We don't respect anything.'

'But not everyone over there believes in marxism and respects it, after all.'

'Of course not. They're not all idiots! You get intelligent people in the West as well. Not often, but you get them. And, anyway, what are you on about? Do you think that if they don't believe in it and don't respect it, they won't come up with anything like we've got? Of course they will. How can you get away from it?!'

THE INDIVIDUAL AND THE COLLECTIVE

The collectivist is a creature without any principles whatsoever, but who is ready to adopt any principles at all, depending on the circumstances – and sincerely to boot. And he is just as ready to renounce them if the circumstances change. And again, sincerely. He is a creature, as it were, of *external* rather than inherent principle. He is inherently capable of adopting any principles external to him as his own, if circumstances require it. I fear that I have not expressed myself sufficiently clearly. A collectivist is a creature devoid of any personal principles of behaviour within the collective, but who reflects the impersonal principles of collective behaviour and interprets them as his own, personal principles.

And so, although there is a certain amount of feuding within our group about attitudes to work (the sloggers graft and thereby bear the brunt of the work-load, the dodgers just pretend to work), there is a more serious division on a different plane, and that is the one between individualists (Ivan Vasilievich and JRF) and collectivists (everyone else). The one who discovered this fact during a routine squabble was none other than Forehead, someone to whom we usually paid no attention. 'Get off your high horses!' he said to Ivan Vasilievich and JRF. 'You two deserve each other. Both of you just want to demonstrate your individualism, and that's all there is to it.' And that really is all there is to it! When people in our part of the world say that someone wants to demonstrate his individualism, they thereby get to the heart of the matter. And the difference between Ivan

Vasilievich and JRF is to be found in the way they demonstrate their individualism. In the former it is an instinctive eagerness to devote himself to the good of society and earn personal recognition. In the latter it is conscious contempt for the collective and resistance to it.

I don't believe that Ivan Vasilievich and Kostya get stuck in as they do just for nothing. You don't get 'just for nothing', – it's not in the nature of things. They are unaware of the nature of their compulsion. Kostya is a beginner, and in his case it is a distorted form of instinctive reaction to his circumstances. After all, there can sometimes be pleasure in suffering, too. Ivan Vasilievich has elevated his ability into a principle and developed a whole outlook based on it. The possibility cannot be excluded that this quality, in the course of his long life, a life which in all probability has not been an easy one, has not once brought him to the attention of the bosses. We once had a colleague like that in our Institute. He admitted that he owed his life to that particular quality. He first came to the attention of his commanding officer when he was putting his back into digging a latrine for him and he was not included in the list of those who were sent to the front. All his comrades were killed, but he survived. On another occasion in the camp, as a model worker he was given the job of burying the corpses of all the inmates who were shot (practically everyone in his camp was shot on the eve of rehabilitation) and afterwards they either forgot, or didn't have time, to shoot him as well.

These two types of individualist differ in the subjective terms of strength (Ivan Vasilievich) and weakness (JRF). I very much suspect that my attitude to JRF is similar to Ivan Vasilievich's attitude to Kostya, only, as far as work is concerned, I have ended up in a different camp, and this confuses the general picture. And the fact that I often recognise myself in JRF annoys me. Up till now, I had inwardly regarded myself as a unique phenomenon, from which I derived a great deal of pleasure. Now I see that I am not alone. And I see that my successor is by far superior to me. It would be interesting to know how Ivan Vasilievich reacts to Kostya. In principle, people like that don't like it when their exclusivity is violated. But he is a good-natured, strong individual, with the power within him to control his feelings. Whereas I am not good-natured, nor strong. Nor do I want to control my feelings. There, incidentally, is a problem for the theoreticians of harmonious communism. What do you do if the mere fact of a person's existence becomes a vitally important problem for someone else, fills his life with torment and excludes any possibility of a positive solution?

THE AGITATION BRIGADE

The townspeople who go to the countryside to engage in the most primitive forms of physical labour are accompanied by voluntary brigades which give concerts and conduct agitation. For the members of these brigades trips into the villages are part assignment (by Party or komsomol), part relaxation and entertainment, part substitute for physical labour, part opportunity for creative activity. In the majority of cases these brigades are voluntary and many people participate in them with pleasure and return from these trips with a great many pleasant impressions. Whenever a brigade comes back from a trip, all our Institute does for a while is listen to, and discuss, the adventures it's had. These brigades don't just go into the villages during the harvest campaign, but during the winter as well. This is a very interesting phenomenon which has yet to be described in the belletristic, technical and descriptive literature. It deserves the attention, in my view, of everyone who is interested in the reasons for the success of communism.

These brigades are constituted for a period which is long enough for the participants to get to know each other and show themselves at their best, but not long enough for them to show themselves at their worst and fall out with each other. Besides, whether by design or accident, people tend to be selected for them who are psychologically more compatible than the people one finds in normal social groups. And you get people of talent among them, people who can tell a joke or who will get up to some prank or other – or who like drinking (but not pathological drunkards, who are never selected). Therefore, the period during which the brigade is in operation is a bright spot in the cheerless lives of those who take part, a holiday, a period of creative uplift and little happenings. The leader of the brigade is usually an authoritative member of the Party (often a member of the Party bureau). But there is no sense of Party control, for it is quite unnecessary in this context. And, as a rule, members of a brigade never do anything reprehensible. There has never been a single incident in our Institute connected with these brigades. Usually it is the other way round: the trips usually generate expressions of gratitude, complimentary articles in the wall-newspaper and bonuses. These brigades are a form of national creativity in the best sense of the term. And yet, strangely, almost nothing is said or written about their importance from this point of view on the level of society as a whole. There has been a noticeable decline in recent years. The brigades are becoming less colourful and more dismal with every year that passes. The reasons are said to be radio and television. But I categorically disagree. Whenever an *agitbrigade* concert is announced, people fill the club to bursting point. A concert takes precedence even over detective films on the television. I know of cases where people were even prepared to forgo a televised hockey or football match for these concerts. And that's saying something!

The population likes *agitbrigade* concerts for many reasons. The main ones are these. Firstly, it's an opportunity for people to get together and have a chat. There is usually a dance for the young folk afterwards. Secondly, the propaganda lecture which precedes the concert is usually meaty and interesting. Lecturers take liberties which would be unacceptable in other circumstances. They improvise as they go along and sometimes answer tricky questions in a way which makes you wonder how they manage to stay out of prison. Often people working in the district and regional Party apparatus come to these lectures and listen open-mouthed. But the lecturer is from the capital, he must have been given permission. Incidentally, sometimes permission *is* given to allow a little steam to be let off. The same thing happens in the cities at 'private' lectures. Thirdly, when brigade members arrive in the country, they begin to collect all sorts of things to criticise, and this, too, is permissible. Moreover, the locals help them. What they dig up is then played around with in the wall-newspaper, which is posted in the club just before the concert, and forms the content of the compère's humorous ditties and jokes. Finally, the concert programme itself is interesting and is performed with great enthusiasm and inspiration. There is not a single item which does not attract applause. Often an encore is requested. Although it is clear to everyone that the standard of performance is far below the professional, it is still a whole order higher than the locals can produce and is appreciated as such.

I have written this panegyric of the *agitbrigade* and I am horrified at myself: why did I write it? After all, if the phenomenon is examined a little more closely, even someone of undemanding intelligence is going to notice how impoverished it is! I wrote it because what is around is even more impoverished. Just think about it. For instance, the members of the brigade collect things to criticise. Criticise whom? Who gives them their material? Answer the question honestly and you will realise it all comes from public denunciations, sanctioned by the local leadership and the population, who thirst for at least some scapegoat that can be dealt with. The lecturer feeds them some intriguing information 'in secret'. What information? Information which the authorities think it would be desirable for the people to know. For instance, that the Chinese are getting ready to attack (and will attack!), that Jews are spies, that we have to feed Africa, that our armaments are stronger than the Americans'. And as for jokes and laughs . . . Take it all down word for word and read it the next day with a clear head! I assure you that you won't find anything apart from hoary old jokes and vulgarity in good old-fashioned village style.

THE TRUE STORY OF THE GOOD COLLECTIVE FARM CHAIRMAN

I heard many different accounts of this story from the local inhabitants. Here I shall give only the gist of those versions I heard which were more or less reliable.

It was soon after the death of Stalin. The Party and the government had decided to improve radically the life of the workers in the countryside. They sent out enthusiastic volunteers

331

from Moscow and other large cities as collective farm chairmen and state farm directors. Most of these Party Envoys quickly established what was what, adapted themselves to the circumstances they found, and made a profit not only for the nation but for themselves as well. Or rather, not so much for the nation as for themselves. They kept their town apartments, and earned themselves decorations. Some of them set themselves up in the countryside very well indeed. Many went back to the city afterwards and made a career for themselves on the basis of what they had done in the country. Not, of course, a very significant career in as much as these Envoys were not high flying careerists or valued specialists when they were in the cities. Still, they managed to hive off something for themselves.

There was, however, among these Envoys of the Party the occasional idealist who did believe in the approach of a new, radiant era for the workers and who put all his heart and soul into the effort to improve the situation outside the towns. Or rather, tried to. The person whom this story concerns was one of them. Since he firmly believed in his role of Envoy of the Party, I shall simply call him that – the Envoy.

The Envoy had graduated from some technical institute or other just before the war. When war began he was given the status of an important specialist, but he refused it and obtained a transfer to the front, and went through the ranks from commander of a platoon to commander of a regiment. He was wounded three times, and decorated more than ten times. He finished the war in Berlin. He had the opportunity to stay in the army (they wanted to send him to a military academy), but he turned it down. He decided to obtain a demobilisation from the army and to devote his energies to the reconstruction of industry. He worked as an engineer in factories in Siberia and the Urals. To his war medals he added a few civilian ones for his unselfish, unstinting toil. Ultimately he was recalled to Moscow as an expert in an important sector of industry and given quite a decent post in the appropriate ministry. It was not a very high post by Moscow standards, but high enough for a provincial. He obtained a good flat in Moscow (good, at least, in those days) and began to live the ordinary life of an official in the capital, i.e. a life entailing floods of paper, meetings, conferences, reports, accounts. Occasionally these paper-shuffling and conference activities entailed a business trip out of town, which in its turn naturally entailed booze-ups, women, and mutual favours. His hair began to go grey and his teeth began to rot. A paunch appeared, and nostalgia began to eat into his soul. What after all, had all the effort been for?

At this moment of psychological crisis the Party issued the call: 'office workers to the villages!' And he was the first to respond to the challenge. Although he counted as a highly valued worker where he was, he was released. There were reasons enough for this. In the first place there were colleagues who had wanted his post for a long time. Secondly there were colleagues competing for the post he would next occupy. Thirdly he had gone a little beyond the General Line of the Party and had spoken unnecessarily sharply at a Party meeting. His wife categorically refused to go with him to the country. Since by this time they were heading for a divorce anyway, this provided a suitable excuse and they did in fact go through with it. He relinquished his Moscow residence permit (and therewith his flat), since he genuinely believed that the Party intended to raise the rural living standard to an unassailable(!) level, and decided to link his fate with that of the countryside. He asked to be sent to the poorest village. There he refused a separate house and took up residence in a squalid little box-room in a semi-dilapidated hovel. He refused remuneration – Party Envoys continued to be paid their monthly salary as municipal officials (as opposed to the collective farm workers who received – or rather, were supposed to receive – the means of existence in the form of goods in exchange for labour days*). When he was 'elected' as chairman of the collective farm, he swore that his own living conditions would improve exactly in line with those of everyone in the village.

Then harsh reality set in. Investment credits were practically non-existent, and his power was illusory. All of the Envoy's attempts to increase labour productivity and establish a highly productive farm foundered upon the total indifference of the

* This was a system which amounted to labour being paid for in kind. A 'labour day' was a (very) flexible unit of account. (*Translator's note*)

population and the concealed opposition of the authorities. The farm workers openly mocked him and abused his indulgence by evading work, concentrating on their own private plots or going to the market in town. The authorities, while they encouraged his initiative verbally, and made use of it for newspaper propaganda, in practice cancelled it out completely. Finally the secretary of the district Party committee had a serious talk with him, the substance of which boiled down to the secretary's concluding sentence: 'We, that is, the Party, will not permit the dismantling of Soviet power in your collective farm!' And as a good communist he kept his initiative within the limits of general Party directives. They began to write about him in the newspapers, and when he had become a model chairman, he was decorated, once, and then twice. There even began to be talk of his nomination for the award of Hero of Socialist Labour. Since not a single question could be settled without a drinking session, he gradually began to drink again. On one drunken occasion he married the widow of a front line soldier and moved in with her. His wife turned out to be resourceful and within a few months the chairman's house was like Aladdin's cave. She also took firm control of those aspects of collective farm life which went on behind the scenes, and certain things began to happen to such an extent that there was a stream of anonymous letters to various organs of the government and of the press. And at the next routine chairmanship elections, they passed a vote of no confidence in the Envoy (as the newspapers later reported). At the meeting they said that he had done all sorts of things which would never have entered his head; for example, that he plundered the collective farm, that he encouraged loafers and thieves, and that he smothered initiative. And they quoted as examples instances of his own initiative which had been undermined by these very people and the district authorities. The representative of the district Party committee said in conclusion that the Party always listened to the voice of the people, and that the people present were their own masters and free to elect any chairman they liked (although without the consent of the district committee no one would have dared to say one word against the Envoy).

After the meeting people drank and had lots of fun. The new chairman, an inveterate drunkard and with a reputation as a scoundrel, promised them the earth. The Envoy went home, put on his best suit, appended all his decorations, had a shave and – hanged himself at the club entrance. His Party ticket lay torn up in pieces on the ground beneath him.

If I were a writer I could write a stupendous novel on that subject. And it would be considerably more horrifying than those describing the horrors of the repressions under Stalin.

In spite of everything, the collective farm during the Envoy's stewardship had been put on a much better footing and life had become noticeably better. The new chairman succeeded in undoing everything in two years and the local inhabitants began to remember the Envoy's term of office as the best time in the history of the village. Someone even had the idea of raising a monument in memory of the Envoy, but the oblast committee forbade it. It was not long before they had to liquidate the collective farm and transfer its assets and population to a newly created state farm. The odd inhabitant of the village retains to this day some faded, yellow photographs of the Envoy. Then came a directive from higher up to stop the rumours about the Envoy's suicide and the business about his Party ticket. The rumour began to spread that certain enemies had arranged all that on purpose. Moreover, these 'certain enemies' were very similar to contemporary dissidents. And there is also the rumour that the Envoy fought in the War alongside the General Secretary himself. So it is possible that the Envoy might be awarded posthumously the title of Hero of Socialist Labour and have his monument. The Party and the people remember their faithful sons.

The case of the Envoy was far from being exceptional. I know dozens of cases like that. A factor common to them all is the attempt on the part of genuine communists and, on a personal level, very good people to inspire those around them to engage in selfless and honourable toil for the general good. And they all failed and were punished one way or another, either by the Party authorities, or the people themselves. The worst of it is that their unhappy end is absolutely predictable, since it is impossible in principle to improve the quality of life by the idealistic methods forced on others by people like the Envoy. What it is most important to realise is that, with their honesty and self-denial, they upset the applecart for those who had already done quite well for themselves and had acquired some real power. The swindlers against whom the Envoy had begun his campaign were well in with the district, and even the regional authorities, and set him up to such an extent that he would normally have been jailed for ten years. What saved him at the time was that it was the beginning of a big campaign, and his trial could have compromised the outstanding initiative of the Party regarding the improvement of the agricultural sector of the economy.

. . . IN THE RAIN . . .

The rain got heavier. Our supposedly waterproof capes were soaked through. It became practically impossible to move in the mud. A girl from our Institute lost a shoe in it. We carried her over to a relatively dry spot under a make-shift awning. We never did find her shoe. The old woman scolded the girl. There's your young folk of today for you! They even flounder around in dung on high heels with their hands manicured! The younger woman took the girl under their wing. What was wrong with that? They had to spend their whole life slopping around in mud. Did that mean it always had to be in rags with chapped hands? Somebody promised the girl a spare pair of rubber boots. 'Let's stop this madness!' said the Commissar. 'Lorries aren't going to be able to move in this mud, anyway. Time for a smoke!'

We crowded under the awning. There were so many of us that there was no room to sit down. We had to stand crowded up against each other. As is customary in such situations, things started off with the usual witticisms and banter between the sexes. But as people tired of standing, our conversations grew more serious. The direction of our thoughts was radically altered when Matryonadura ploughed past us with a basket full of mushrooms and a patched sack covering her head from the rain. She slipped past our lascivious gaze without saying anything. And we remained silent. We didn't even greet her.

'Here we are, decadent intellectuals, rooting around in the

mud while the people are off mushroom-picking!' exploded the Candidate.

'She's not the people,' said Ivan Vasilievich. 'We are the people. The people are those who create material and spiritual wealth, the people who feed and dress society. Who make the cars, houses, things? Who plants the seed and gathers in the harvest? You call her the people? She's what's left over from a previous people which has long since ceased to be a people. We, I repeat, are the people.'

'What kind of a people are we?!' objected a female voice. 'We're an unpaid work-force, not a people. We are slaves, only twentieth-century slaves who imagine themselves to be the freest creatures in history.'

'What can you do?'

'Nothing. Our situation is like that knight's in the old Russian fairy-tale who arrived at a cross-roads and read on a stone . . . (Read, notice! That means he, too, was one of the intelligentsia of his time.) And he read this: if you carry straight on, you will lose your head. If you go right, you will be eaten by wild animals. If you go left, you will be consumed by fire. If you go back, you and your horse will be drowned.'

'It's enough to send you off your head! It's more than sixty years since the revolution. More than thirty years of peace. And we still live as badly as it is possible to imagine.'

'Don't despair! The dissidents will save us.'

'Don't give me those fairy-tales for Western idiots. They aren't going to save anyone except themselves. I've seen enough of them to last me a lifetime.'

When it became clear, towards evening, that bad weather had set in in earnest, we dragged ourselves home, wet, hungry and bad-tempered. Back 'home' we had another unpleasant surprise – our barn was awash, and even the local management conceded that it was impossible to sleep there. We were dispersed to other houses for the duration of the rain. The Commissar, Kostya and Ivan Vasilievich stayed at Matryonadura's. The Commissar stayed in the heated part of the house, the others in the store room. JRF, the Candidate, Don Juan and myself shacked down under canopies in a neighbouring house. After supper there was a general meeting of the brigade. A representative from the district committee told us that the weather forecast was bad and called on us all to be seriously concerned, demonstrate and be imbued with . . . He promised to supply us with special clothing – heavy-duty canvas jackets with sleeves and hoods, and rubber boots. They would be coming very soon. Meanwhile could we get by over the next couple of days with what we'd got? 'In a word,' he said, 'the battle for the harvest is entering a decisive stage.'

MATRYONADURA ON THE WEST

Over there they even sell newspapers by weight. You come along and ask: bitte-dritte, give me three kilos of time, five kilos of frankfurtyalgemeiny, seven kilos of carriera-delasera. And what do they print?! It would make you laugh! Nothing but adverts about how much things cost. And naked women. Have they never seen naked women over there, or what?! It's ridiculous!

CONVERSATIONS OVERHEARD

JRF was sitting with Katyusha on a bench near the barn. All the other inhabitants of the barn had gone off to the club. I had stayed behind, since I wasn't feeling well. No doubt it was 'flu'. JRF and Katya didn't know that I was in the barn and I didn't want to let on that I was there and thereby interrupt their conversation.

'You'll be going away soon,' said Katyusha. 'It'll be boring without you.'

'Why will it be boring?' said JRF with surprise. 'You've got a decent club. You sometimes get good films. You have dances. There are lectures. You've got a library. There's television and the radio.'

'It's still boring. The films are rubbish. There's a good film perhaps once a year. The books are even worse. There's a month-long queue for every decent book. The local lads drink, use foul language and fight. None of them knows how to dance. All they want to do is grope you. It's foul.'

'Get married, have children.'

'Children are nothing but trouble nowadays. And who am I going to marry?'

'You've got enough suitors.'

'I know, but I don't want to marry any of them. You see yourself how they live here. But I want to live decently. I want everything to be honourable and pure. I want someone I can respect and who would respect me. Someone I could talk to openly. I'd marry you, for instance.'

'That would be even worse. I'm selfish. And quite depraved. I drink worse than the locals here.'

'You'd change if we got married. I'd be a good wife to you. I would never be unfaithful. I would look after you. And I'd read all the books I had to. I did well at school, you know.'

'Thank you for the kind words. But you don't have an inkling of the environment in which I circulate. It's not one whit better than here. I would suck you dry inside a year and you would forget all your good intentions.'

'I wouldn't forget. I'm strong. I know what's what. Try, you'll see for yourself. If you don't like me, you can throw me out. I'll go. I won't be a hanger-on. If you try, you won't regret it.'

They got up from the bench and went off somewhere . . .

Then some local lads made their appearance, sat down on the same bench, lit up and began to talk. And what a conversation! Nothing but cynicism, vulgarity and foul language. And yet they've had eight, and some of them ten years at school. They said that they would have to keep an eye on that bearded bloke (JRF) and Katya, 'sort' Katya 'out', cut off a certain something belonging to JRF and throw it to the dogs. This doesn't mean that they will necessarily carry out their intentions. It's merely a form of words in which they make sense of the world. Mind you, sometimes these 'innocent' conversations get turned into reality during drunken behaviour. I understand Katyusha. If I were in her place, I wouldn't want to marry any of these local lads, either, although no doubt there are handsome, intelligent and decent ones among them. But what can you do?! She'll hang on for another couple of years waiting for her non-existent 'Prince' and then she'll get married to the first passing 'Van'ka'. And she'll forget her dreams of everything being pure and above board and open. And you can't get away from it. It will always be like that. Surely not always? What a nightmare!

Later on the lads returned from the club. They sat on the same bench and talked about the vices and virtues of 'broads', and in more or less the same terms as their predecessors had used. And yet these are people with higher education and even higher degrees. The last to return were the Candidate and JRF. They, too, sat down on the bench for a few minutes. The Candidate talked to JRF about his exploits on the 'woman front' and was interested to hear about JRF's. The latter didn't respond.

'If I were you . . .' began the Candidate.

'She's not bright enough,' said JRF, interrupting him. 'Whereas I'm used to "intelligent" conversations and can't do without them. And apart from anything else, she's absolutely not sexy.'

These words of JRF's shocked me somewhat. I got up, went outside and sat on that damned bench till dawn.

'Why?' I wondered. But no answer came to me. It was only as dawn was breaking that a simple explanation came to me, while I was looking at the sorry apple-trees in Matryonadura's garden. Just as, for some reason, the apples in her garden grow with worms in them from the very beginning, we appear on this earth with similar worms in our souls. And it is just as hopeless trying to find someone among us with a wholesome and healthy nature as it is trying to find an unspoiled apple in Matryonadura's garden.

CRIMES AND PUNISHMENTS

While we were working in the fields our barn was done over. Although what was stolen did not amount to much (a razor, shoes, a pair of trousers), their loss was tangible. Worst off was Matryonadura – they took her motorbike! I think actually that the thieves were after her motorbike in the first place and simply grabbed our stuff while they were at it. What really made us angry was the fact that they fouled our beds. We created a real fuss, and one of the local police was sent round. The first thing he did was to accuse us of having flogged the bike ourselves, drunk the proceeds and then made up a story about the burglary. At this the whole brigade got up on its hind legs. It was obvious that the thieves were locals and that it would have been easy enough to find them. But the police for some reason did not do this. Mao-Tse-Dun'ka appeared and talked to us 'man to man'. At such a crucial moment, she said, it would be a grave mistake to unmask thieves and hooligans and thereby drive a wedge between workers and peasants. We – she said – will find these scoundrels and show them what we're made of. But we will not allow our dirty linen to be washed in public! The policeman in charge of the investigation spent a couple of days drinking at Matryonadura's expense and then simply went away, promising on his departure to show Matryonadura and us 'what was what' if we didn't 'shut our traps' (he meant, if we didn't stop talking about the burglary). We naturally 'shut our traps'. What else could we do? We weren't about to find out 'what was what' on account of old boots and trousers!

Don Juan, whose razor had been stolen, decided to grow a moustache and beard. A few days later he began to look like the handsome prince in Russian fairy-tales. The women became markedly more interested in him. Every cloud has its silver lining, he admitted. If it hadn't been for that stupid burglary, I'd never have taken the plunge. Just you wait (he said to JRF)! It won't be long before I've beaten you into second place around here. 'Don't jump to conclusions,' said JRF. 'When I began to grow a moustache and beard I too thought that life for me was starting afresh. But soon everything was the same as before. A beard doesn't solve any problems. It just produces new ones.'

'But just between ourselves, I believe in communism,' said Don Juan and looked at us suspiciously, expecting to see expressions of derision on our faces. But we met his declaration with complete indifference. 'And the basis of my conviction,' he went on, 'is technological progress. The creation of abundance is not really the difficult problem it appears to be at first glance. They've already begun to produce indestructible footwear and clothing, and various domestic items . . .' 'And also uncookable food,' added JRF, thereby cutting off short Don Juan's spirited rehash of a popular brochure before it got under way. 'You tell me, what is communism? The slogan "To everyone according to his needs" isn't a definition of communism. If communism means a time when everyone receives according to his needs, then the West is immeasurably closer to that time than we are. Communism is first and foremost the socialisation of the means of production at all levels of society, and the organisation of all social life along more or less the same lines as we have it here (if we leave out the shortages). And now pose the problem this way: what are you more likely to believe – the words of a man who lived more than a hundred years ago and who had not the slightest conception of what his ideas would look like in real life, or the experience of a huge country accumulated in the course of sixty years, and the experience of many other countries which followed its example? The dreams of vainglorious word merchants or the inexorable facts of reality? You talk about technological progress and human nature. Certainly we have nuclear energy, space flights, the discovery of chromosomes, higher education, better teaching methods . . . But what do we actually have? Here we are, you and I, with our higher education, digging and loading badly grown potatoes a long way behind schedule ("ahead of time" according to the newspapers!), using the most antediluvian methods. We were promised special clothing. How long ago? Where is it? And the people? Look how they "work"! Just take these local and regional parasites, for example! And all the eye-wash! And drunkenness! . . .' 'I'm not a child,' said Don Juan, 'I can see and understand all that for myself. But we don't have communism yet. When we do . . .' 'When we do,' interrupted JRF, 'they won't be chasing us out here voluntarily for a couple of months; they'll nail us down here for good, put us in communal barracks, post guards and surround the place with barbed wire. And, speaking generally, full communism is definitely coming. After nuclear war all the people will perish and rats will take over, as Ivan Vasilievich has already predicted. They will insinuate themselves in the pores of the remnants of human society and carry on the cause of progress. And the people that are left will be bred by the rats for food.'

The scene is a strange one, seen from the sidelines. A cold rain

342

is drizzling down. We stand in mud up to our knees and drag vegetables as best we can nearer the 'firm' road, along which lorries crawl with great difficulty. We're dressed in a way which, if it weren't for the soaking wet conditions, would provoke howls of laughter. The promised clothing has not materialised, nor will it. A girl with pneumonia has been taken to the town. Many are lying ill at home, many are very nearly ill or are struggling along on their last legs (like Kostya). And meanwhile we frenziedly stand up for these 'radiant ideals'. Why?! What for?! As some sort of psychological compensation for the real poverty of our lives? Perhaps. But then why do we need this compensation? As a means of self-preservation!

And there is another problem which bothers me: why are we here? Why don't we tell them all to piss off, and go home? After all, probably nothing much would happen. They wouldn't imprison us. They wouldn't even sack us. But nevertheless, here we are. Why? Is it enthusiasm like there was in the years just after the revolution? And what if that enthusiasm had been of the same order as our work now? That bitch Mao-Tse-Dun'ka didn't call us latter-day Pavel Korchagins* for nothing. She called the women Pavel Korchagins too. At first she was going to call them Joans of Arc, but then changed her mind for some reason. Joan of Arc was burned at the stake, whereas we're drowning in muck and slush, so the image of Pavel Korchagin is more appropriate.

'You're touching on one of the most complex problems of our life,' said JRF. 'What we're talking about is a specific form of coercion. Our situation here is an instance of coercion masquerading as free will. Let us take a crude example. You hear a sentry or an enemy say "Hands up!" You are at liberty to raise your hands or not, as you choose. But you know what the consequences will be if you do not raise your hands, and so you do raise them. Is this an instance of free will or not? Obviously not. I'm sure you know how people are coerced into coming to the police station or presenting themselves for interrogation. They don't break your arms. They give you an appointment, and you

* Pavel Korchagin was the enthusiastic revolutionary hero of an early socialist-realist classic. (*Translator's note*)

go. But the summons counts as coercive. It's the same in our case here. We all know very well that a refusal to come on this trip would sooner or later have had negative consequences for us, and we do not wish these more or less long-term consequences. We've decided that we'd rather suffer in the short term here than ... anyway, you know exactly what I mean. Now, what I'm saying is that forms of coercion differ in terms of the extent to which coercion takes the form of free will. Under communism that extent is maximal. People here take account not only of the real consequences of their actions, but also of the potential consequences. Furthermore, they do this throughout the course of their lives, including their potential future. That is why people here almost always act apparently of their own free will, although all their actions are the result of coercion. That is why the concepts of free will and coercion are meaningless when applied to our way of life. And you will never solve this problem which agitates you so much, because of the meaninglessness of its formulation in words. The question as to why we are here has purely sociological significance and no psychological significance whatsoever. And the answer is trivially simple: because this society needs a multi-million strong army of slaves.'

PLANS AND OUTCOMES

Although the harvest this year is pretty lousy ('bigger than usual', as the papers put it), vegetable delivery points at the station were soon overwhelmed, the railway system was clearly unable to cope and, naturally, vegetables began to be dumped any old where, any old how. A potato-carrot-cabbage catastrophe was clearly in the making. And an instruction came down from on high to get by on our own resources and construct vegetable storage facilities on the state and collective farms themselves. Since it was a question of temporary difficulties, it was recommended that the storage facilities be in the form of pits. This was exactly what was needed, since it was still raining and it was absolutely impossible to dig a hole more than a metre deep which didn't fill up with water. Especially since people knew from experience that these so-called temporary storage facilities would be here to stay, i.e. that they would load vegetables into them which would rot away entirely, having first polluted the atmosphere with an abominable smell. So people didn't exactly put their heart and soul into digging these storage facilities, but did just enough to indicate a readiness to carry out the sage designs of the powers that be. You would have thought that it would be simpler to stop the harvest, leave everything in the ground and let people gather it for their own use. I'm convinced that the local inhabitants would work day and night and harvest the whole lot, down to the last potato. Even if they were allowed to harvest it for themselves on the understanding that they then gave up a proportion to the state (even half), they would still harvest it and look after it. But God forbid that there should even be a squeak about that! We're supposed to exhaust ourselves in the mud and rain in order to convert what we gather into a mass of unusable putrescence. And if the locals were to take even a single potato, they would be prosecuted. That is the real dialectics of our life.

Our farm is prosperous and advanced and consequently it was allowed to build a permanent vegetable store – of bricks, concrete, wood, iron. Although winter was staring us in the face and although our time here was nearly up, after which you wouldn't be able to find the local workmen in daylight with a torch, they began to deliver building materials (although materials for a projected pig-farm had been lying around being pilfered for years), and organise a construction brigade. Our Commissar immediately saw which way the land was lying and signed up our whole group (with the exception of Forehead) for inclusion in the construction brigade. And by the next morning we could already sense our privileged position: we had a lie-in, didn't go out to the fields in the rain, made ourselves familiar at a leisurely pace with the building site and repaired to the club for a smoke and a chat. Later on, a foreman arrived with a gang of workmen and proposed that we have a drink to celebrate the beginning of the project.

FROM THE IDEAS OF MAO-TSE-DUN'KA

Mao-Tse-Dun'ka was sitting on a pile of logs, smoking. She smokes and drinks in the interests of unity between the Party and the People. Moreover, she likes drinking but detests smoking, so that even she is a complex and contradictory phenomenon. On this occasion she was talking to the local youth about sex. She was speaking 'heart to heart' as 'man to man' and not as a 'major Party figure'.

'You've let your hair down a bit too far, I'll tell you that for nothing. You've had it too good. You're a bit too educated now. You let the West set you a bad example. But just you wait. Everything in its own good time. Once we get agriculture in a bit better shape, we'll see to this matter, as well. We'll sort you out, you can be sure of that! We won't castrate you. We're not your Hindus or your Chinese! We'll give you all sedatives. Or injections. Injections can do a lot now! And, of course, we'll carry out a programme of education.'

'What about children, then?' asked a timid voice from the back row.

'What have children got to do with it?! We have a sacred duty and obligation to our children. They will come after us. You won't build a new communist society without children. And who's going to defend the Motherland?! Pushkin, do you think?! I'm talking about sex, I'm not talking about children. We won't allow anyone to damage our healthy socialist family!'

I listened to Mao-Tse-Dun'ka and laughed, but in the depths of my soul I heard the faint rustlings of horror. They will, in fact, give everyone these sedative powders and injections. And not with any evil intent, but out of the goodness of their hearts and concern for our welfare. And they'll do it somehow in passing. 'Here, what about? . . .' some Mao-Tse-Dun'ka will say somewhere and give a knowing wink. And other Mao-Tse-Dun'kas will wink knowingly back and nod their managerial skulls. And that will be that! And everything will be done and dusted! They'll leave a little bit of sex around for the purposes of producing builders of communism and defenders of the Motherland. But no more than that. None of your over-indulgence! And entertainment, and all that, They'll keep that for Themselves. And why not! It's Their due, for They are toiling for the welfare of the whole of progressive mankind!

'What do you think?' said Mao-Tse-Dun'ka, continuing her lecture. 'If it's from Nature, then help yourself? Sleep with anyone who comes along? Oh, no, my dears! You have to earn that! You have to stand up and be counted! You have to show yourself in a good light. And then we'll see who merits it. Sex is a serious affair! An affair of the State. Even a Party affair, you might say.'

CHOOSING THE PEREDOVIKI

It's a funny word, *peredovik*, isn't it? It means a model worker. It's related to the word *peredovitsa*, or leader, as in leading article in the newspaper. And just as a *peredovitsa* in our newspaper is devoid of content, yet at the same time full of deep meaning and significance, a *peredovik* in the production sphere is an individual jointly selected by the collective and management to play the role of model worker. Choosing a peredovik is a highly serious and responsible business. A peredovik has to meet many different criteria. He has to be a model of behaviour (for that read: he must at least not be a chronic alcoholic), politically active and literate (read: he must at least blather something at the odd meeting, pay his Party and komsomol dues promptly, carry out certain assignments, visit a propaganda circle from time to time and not snore too loudly), reliable (read: will not do anything unexpected) and a good worker (read: is not the most obvious loafer). He must be selected in the spirit of the campaign which is being conducted in accordance with local circumstances and be to the taste of the local authorities. And their choice should be a cause for laughter, but not too much laughter, for a peredovik is at least no worse than anyone else. And the educative aspect should be borne in mind as well. A peredovik, in short, must embody the results of everything which the Party has already

347

decided, confirm by his appearance that they were the right decisions, and act as a beacon for everyone else (our newspapers have a special column entitled 'Our Beacons'), and to show by his example what is possible.

The process for selecting peredoviks began in our brigade as well. The names of the best workers were read out at a general meeting of the brigade from which would later be selected those whose photographs would appear on the board of honour, about whom articles would appear in the newspapers, and who would receive awards, medals and even decorations. From our barn, the names which were read out were Ivan Vasilievich, Kostya and the Commissar. Although it is generally recognised that Kostya is the best worker in the whole district, activists made themselves heard to remind everyone about the roof incident. The first person to speak against Kostya was a rather nice-looking, intelligent woman. And she emptied such a pail of slops over Kostya that even the representative of the district committee of the komsomol called upon her not to exaggerate that trivial incident. But no one spoke up in Kostya's defence. His candidacy was rejected by a majority of votes.

I voted for Kostya. But I didn't speak in his defence since I don't consider that it is worth paying any attention to this whole procedure. And yet I felt rather rotten: I knew how important this meeting was for Kostya himself. Kostya said afterwards that if we had spoken in his defence and if his name had been left on the list, he would have withdrawn his candidacy himself. He was shocked that no one had stuck up for him.

'But we voted for you!' said Ivan Vasilievich.

'That isn't the same thing,' said Kostya. 'You would have done better to vote against. That would have been more honest.'

'Let that be a lesson to you,' said JRF. 'Now you know what value to place on the moral worth of our positive characters. As for me, I am against including people like you in the peredovik lists in principle: you're too good for that.'

At the next stage of the selection process (at the level of the whole farm) Ivan Vasilievich's candidacy was excluded. There was a rumour that the representative of the district Party committee had made some remark about Ivan Vasilievich. Ivan Vasilievich himself took the news calmly.

'I've never got beyond the second stage yet,' he said. 'There's always a question mark against my name which prevents my getting any further. Even when I die, that question mark will prevent me getting buried in a cemetery in Moscow or its environs.'

That only left the Commissar for selection at the all-district level. He is approved of: last year he even figured among the peredoviks at regional level. But this year he won't make it beyond district level. I think that his goings-on with Matryona-dura will prevent him.

TRANSFER

When the news got around that a permanent vegetable store incorporating the latest in science and technology was to be built ahead of time, there was great excitement in the village. Everyone had accumulated their own building problems. One needed a roof re-covering, another needed the foundations put in for an extension to his house, someone else needed a new barn. Matryonadura was taken with the idea of having a permanent cellar. Secret meetings and talks began to take place in the village, accompanied by awe-inspiring booze-ups. As a result the lorries carrying the building materials would first drive round the houses of the local inhabitants and arrive at our building-site half empty. This suited us fine: the work was reduced by half. The foreman and the brigadier taught us how to stack the materials to give the impression that they hadn't been 'taking a walk' and later on how to construct a building 'in full accordance with requirements' with only half the materials. And the mind-boggling drunkenness which developed around us reached a level of intensity which even I had rarely encountered before. People wandered around like shadows, green and puffed-up, their breath stinking. We had a touch of it, too. But our time in clover soon came to an end. Matryonadura entertained the right people and JRF, the Candidate, Ivan Vasilievich and I were put at her disposal – to build her cellar for her. And we rapidly experienced for ourselves what was meant by the 'private sector'.

Matryonadura watched our every movement and demanded conscientious work – we weren't working for the state now. By evening we were at the end of our tethers, but it didn't enter Matryonadura's head to feed us. We rebelled. We summoned Matryonadura and issued an ultimatum: if we worked an eight-hour day, she would have to feed us more. If not, we would go and work in the fields. Although it was wet, you could at least swing the lead. And it was more fun. At first Matryonadura tried to object and threatened to set the management on us. She even threatened to report our little conversations. We called her a shit, as she deserved, and threatened to report her machinations with the building materials. She capitulated and immediately became kind and generous. And we began to work conscientiously.

MATRYONADURA'S PHILOSOPHY

This is the most difficult part in the description of Matryonadura. It would be possible, of course, to divest oneself of the problem in a single sentence: Matryonadura's world outlook, like that of other Soviet citizens, is dialectical materialism. That would be true, but not absolutely honest, since she herself doesn't know it. As she puts it herself, she's 'seen that diliktitski materilize in a coffin with white slippers'. What perplexed us in her pronouncement was not the reference to the coffin for the highest product of world culture – we had nothing against that, ourselves – but the reference to the white slippers. Why in white slippers, we asked her. What else would it be in, she asked, surprised in turn. JRF has defined Matryonadura's philosophical position as diabolical matryonalism, placing it between marxism and the doctrines of the Russian revolutionary democrats, who came closest to marxism, although they arrived on the scene a little later than it did. 'They went smack up against marxism,' objected Don Juan. 'That means that you can't place anything between them and marxism.'

'That is not a problem for diabolical matryonalism,' said JRF. 'There are no insoluble problems, as far as it is concerned. Ask Matryonadura any question you like and you will immediately receive an exhaustive and murderously compelling answer. "Matryonadura," we'll ask, for instance, "who's going to win the next war?" "We will!" she'll say categorically. "Why will it be us?" we object. "Because there's no one else," she'll reply in a flash. And she's right – there is no one else.'

Russians, like the ancient Greeks, are all born dialecticians and materialists. Even more so than the Greeks in fact, since we can't live without materialism and dialectics. All the Greeks have left are a few miserable fragments along the lines of 'Everything flows' or 'Achilles won't catch the tortoise'. Whereas the Russians would leave tomes of sage pronouncements and insoluble paradoxes if anyone could be bothered to write them down for posterity. And you wouldn't have to go all over Russia to find them. You'd just need to go to a harvest operation. Here are some examples. Matryona's neighbour's son asks if he can go swimming with his mates in a lake five kilometres outside the village. 'Off you go, then,' says the neighbour. 'But if you get drowned, don't bother coming home, 'cos I'll belt you!' How could she say a thing like that without being a born dialectician?! It became known (and in the Russian village not only is everything knowable in principle, it is known straight away in practice) that the accountant's daughter had been impregnated by someone from the district Party committee. 'You get less as a virgin and more as a woman,' says Matryonadura in response to this, not realising that she is thereby rediscovering the philosophical law of conservation and conversion of matter.

On one occasion the lads had somehow got on to the fashionable topic of telepathy and parapsychology. Matryona would nod in agreement and narrate her own heart-rending incidents. Naturally they were all at second and third hand, like our own 'scientific' facts: a friend had told her . . . Her sister-in-law had seen with her own eyes . . . Her cousin had once . . . And just when we had begun to give some credence to our own nonsense, Matryonadura suddenly declared that it was all 'for the birds', that we had talked enough nonsense, and that it was time for her to milk her cow.

I remember Matryonadura's conversation with the local militiaman who had discovered bricks in her hay

'Where did you get them?' he asked her severely, although he knew perfectly well, since he had taken bricks from exactly the same source for the stove in his bath-house.

'Where I got them, they aren't there any more!'

'If they were there, they wouldn't be here.'

'Just you prove it!'

'I'll prove it, all right! And you'll rot in jail!'

'You'll be a fool, then. Do you think the bosses are going to thank you for not keeping a good enough look-out? And what did you make the stove in your bath-house out of, eh? There you are! All you'll prove is that you won't be able to prove anything.'

After the militiaman had gone (having drunk his half-litre nevertheless) Matryonadura rattled off a speech, in comparison with which the chrestomathic models of dialectical thought from the classics of marxism are but impoverished metaphysical babblings. 'Oh, Lord,' she said in conclusion, 'what a lot of know-alls have appeared on this earth! And all they do with their brains is find ways of showing how stupid they are.'

Matryonadura loves to talk 'about life', and on a level the height of which you rarely meet in intellectual circles in Moscow, never mind the West.

'What's this life of ours worth?! It's enough to make you spit. What it is and what it isn't, it's all the same. Here I've lived my life. And what have I got to show for it? I didn't even have time to fart properly and already it's time to think about pushing up the daisies.'

'Matryona Ivanovna, suppose there is a next world. And God. And Hell. Aren't you scared?'

'What's there to be scared about? After what I've seen, my lad, that Hell of yours'll be like a steam bath. Pure pleasure. And I'm not scared of God. What is he to me – a chief of police, or what?! Let him summon me! I'll tell him straight to his face: here you are chattering idly on a cloud with your little angels while I've spent my life floundering up to my knees in mud! You should have been working with me in a collective farm in those days and you'd have found out the price of carrots! And do you know how old I was when I had to start ploughing the fields and cutting timber? There you are, then!'

'Well, how do you reckon your life today, then?'

'What's the point? You can see yourself whether there's much

352

good about it. But it's much better now than it used to be. There's enough bread. And potatoes. The shops have always got sugar, sweets, biscuits, soap. Sometimes they've even got herring. What more do you want?! We're pleased with our life as it is now. Just don't let there be a war.'

THE SIGNAL

No matter what we do in our part of the world, it is always accompanied by disorder and confusion. To put it more precisely, we first of all create the disorder and confusion and in the middle of all that something by a miracle (and by no means always) will get done. And you will always find righteous people (usually old, 'real', communists) who write letters to all sorts of organs about that disorder and confusion. These letters are called signals and are of great sociological and psychological interest. They contain an element of truth, an element of invention, an element of trouble-making, an element of genuine concern for the interests of the cause in question and an element of denunciation. Throughout the country hundreds of thousands of such letters are written every day. They find their way into all sectors of the Party-State apparatus and special departments exist for processing these workers' letters. In the vast majority of cases nothing happens as a result of these letters. But sometimes they are taken up so that concern about the workers can be expressed in line with special decisions taken by the Central Committee about how such letters should be treated. While we've been here in the country, letters like that have been written about the disorders in our sector of the front in the battle for the harvest. This time someone's letter scored a bull's eye. There had been a disclosure not long before of a major embezzlement in some Great Communist Construction project in the Volga region. Even the newspapers had written about it. A confidential letter on the subject went out from the Central Committee to Party organisations. And the effect of that letter had not yet died down – local Party organisations had not yet managed to give an account of what they had done to carry out the letter's instructions. And so, when ours got a letter about the misappropriation of building materials it decided to set up a commission to investigate the affair. Rumours of this hit the village at dawn. How did they get on to it? I think that someone from the regional Party committee, which was setting up the commission, dropped a hint about it to the district Party committee, from which a hint was dropped to our management. And that meant that within ten minutes, even schoolkids in the primary classes were whispering about a commission FROM UP THERE.

Then Mao-Tse-Dun'ka appeared, half drunk, her eyes round with panic. She tore around the village like a mad thing, swore at anyone who crossed her path and threatened to get the lot of us put behind bars.

The village then began to engage in feverish activity to cover up all traces of the crime. Lorries rushed here and there at insane speed returning the building materials to where they belonged. New planks were ripped off roofs and replaced by the old rotten ones. We hastily filled in Matryonadura's cellar and dumped a load of logs on top of it. We did a month's work on the vegetable store in a couple of hours. Nothing solid, mind you, all of it just for the sake of appearances. If they go on building it like that to the end (and they'll have to, since there's no other way), it'll fall down by the spring or else be flooded.

Although that was not the first time I had witnessed situations like that, I was still shaken by what went on. How much energy, invention, talent, selflessness people demonstrated! And for what? Not at all for the cause, but in order to pull the wool and conceal disorder and crime!! A paradox? No. It was in fact only natural, for people were working for themselves, in their own personal interest, and not for the sake of abstract ideals of communism which people had long ridiculed. It's surprising but it is a fact. People in our society tackle any actual business in a slipshod fashion and as if it were something alien to them. They only put their hearts and souls into something fictitious or illegal, for it is only fictitious and illegal activity which affects them personally.

The commission from the region arrived after lunch – already tipsy. They had no doubt been very well looked after at the district committee headquarters. And it was immediately clear to everyone that the commission wouldn't have been able to spot the disorders which had so bothered the righteous communists even without our heroic efforts to conceal them. And we regretted all that wasted effort. If only we had known!! . . .

CONSEQUENCES

The members of the commission let our local management know who the authors of the letter were, and how the letter had reached Moscow. It wouldn't have gone by normal post, since there were people in the post-offices who read our letters. Doubtful letters would be withdrawn and sent to the Special Department at the district centre. Mindful of this, the authors had prepared three copies of the critical letter and sent them direct to Moscow: one with a propagandist from the capital, a second with the leader of the *agitbrigade* and the third with . . . operatives of the KGB. One copy reached its destination and there is every reason to believe that it was the third. Five people signed the letter. All of them had been members of the Party for many years. And among the signatories was – our Commissar. That was a surprise!! And he had already been selected as a peredovik and had his photograph taken for the newspaper!!

Although nothing had come of the letter, its authors publicly declared (they didn't really have any choice) that they wouldn't let the matter rest there and that when they got back to Moscow, they would raise the matter in higher Party circles. This threat alarmed the local leadership. And it decided (naturally, with the support of the higher leadership) to take prophylactic measures. In charge of this noble mission was Mao-Tse-Dun'ka herself.

The first measure to be considered was the approved collective rape variant. But on mature reflection, it was discarded. In the first place, it had been used several times before, and the last occasion had been the year before. And it had come unstuck. Not in the sense that it hadn't succeeded. It had – and the lads who had been talking about things they shouldn't have been were convicted of multiple rape. But the militiamen, who had in fact raped the girl on the instructions of the organisers of the affair, had a fight among themselves afterwards when they were drunk and gave the game away. And now the whole region knows that it was a put-up job. And there might even have been a suggestion of reviewing the judge's decision. In the second place, the authors of the letter were all elderly people, Party members, they had acted with the best of intentions and they hadn't expressed their condemnation aloud. In the third place, and no doubt this was the main argument against adopting the variant under discussion, it would be difficult to find a girl in the whole district who would fit the role of rape victim. All of them were either so ugly that they would flatter no one's self-esteem or so well-versed in matters of love that no one would believe that they hadn't voluntarily agreed to be 'raped'.

And in the end Mao-Tse-Dun'ka took the only correct Party decision in such a situation.

'We have to take a dialectical approach to the problem,' she said at a meeting of the commission set up to investigate the slanderous letter. 'You have to approach every slanderer from a concrete-historical angle. Every one of them is bound to have a skeleton in the cupboard. We have to find that skeleton and . . . well, you can work it out for yourselves!'

And they decided to discredit our Commissar on account of his shenanigans with Matryonadura.

> I'm afraid it is a poor to-do,
> They'll blab how you the whole night through
> With 'n old bag weighing half a ton
> Crush fleas and fart in unison.

MATRYONADURA GETS THE TREATMENT

At first Matryonadura denied that she was 'sleeping' with the Commissar. But the Comrade from the district committee of the Party threatened to begin digging around that business with the cellar if she didn't 'come clean'. And Matryonadura agreed to testify against the Commissar. But only on condition that he was deemed to have taken her 'by force'. The Comrade from the district committee said that that would sound far-fetched, si. Matryonadura could sort out three weedy types like the Commissar with one hand and scatter the whole brigade with one kick. Then Mao-Tse-Dun'ka suggested a milder variant: the Commissar had seduced Matryonadura by promising to get a divorce and set up a new, healthy socialist family with her. Matryonadura liked the idea very much. She quickly convinced herself that it was true and a couple of hours later had phoned round the whole village to tell people that the Commissar had turned out to be a scoundrel, that he had only persuaded her to 'sleep' with him by promising to marry her and now that he had had his way with her he had forgotten all his promises.

The inhabitants of the village believed Matryonadura in so far as Russian women agree to 'sleep' with their seducers only if the latter promise to marry them, and Russian males don't have any means of seduction other than the promise of marriage. But no one believed that the Commissar had really intended to marry Matryonadura, for they knew perfectly well that a promise of marriage is a purely verbal element of Russian sex. The commission which was collecting material showing the Commissar in his 'true, immoral colours' did not go into these linguistic niceties: it was establishing the 'naked facts'. 1) The Commissar had been unfaithful to his wife, thereby undermining marxist-leninist doctrine on the healthy socialist family; 2) The Commissar had seduced Matryonadura 'by way of a cynical deception', having promised to marry her, thereby destroying that same healthy socialist family.

The Candidate proposed a solution of genius to the Commissar's problem: he should admit to having cohabited with Matryonadura, but declare that she had been palmed off on him by local opponents of criticism. When news of this idea reached Matryonadura, she promised the Commissar that she would rip off the very thingummy he had used to damage marxist-leninist doctrine on the healthy socialist family if he alleged any such thing.

Matryonadura demonstrated her high moral standards from the very outset of this incident and even went to bed in her fake foreign jeans with the genuine American leather label.

PROCESSING THE WITNESSES

Since the Commissar rejected Matryonadura's allegations as 'tendentious' (what can he have meant?), the commission decided to lean on us as witnesses to the Commissar's immoral behaviour. And it has to be admitted that, in the beginning, the tactic was quite successful. Forehead said exactly what was wanted. Kostya was caught out by his immature capacity to deceive (by his 'unhealthy truthfulness', as he put it himself). They bought the Lathe Operator with a free booze-up. The Candidate confirmed their testimony 'to keep them company'. Ivan Vasilievich and I refused to discuss the subject, which suited the commission just as well, all things considered. The flies in the ointment were Don Juan and JRF. Don Juan declared that he, too, had 'slept' with Matryonadura. Perhaps not as often as the Commissar, but he had slept with her nevertheless. This confession of Don Juan's somewhat dimmed Matryonadura's moral image and consequently enhanced the Commissar's a little. But that was still bearable in so far as the Commissar had in fact, according to Don Juan's testimony, still 'slept' with Matryonadura. JRF, however, declared that the Commissar hadn't slept with Matryonadura, but that chiefly it had been himself, JRF, who had slept with her. Sometimes Don Juan and the Lathe Operator had stood in for him. Moreover, Matryonadura had seduced him, JRF, by 'a cynical deception': she had promised him a jug of warm milk, but after she had had her way with him she had broken her promise. At that point the Lathe Operator sobered up. Since the Comrade from the district committee refused to finance a second free booze-up, the Lathe Operator joined forces with JRF. 'Why not admit it,' he said. 'The whole barn had her.' These confessions drove Matryonadura to the other extreme. She went around the whole village in her old darned tights and roared that no one had 'had' her, that these rumours about her and the Commissar were all lies, and that she was a 'good girl'. It was all very embarrassing for the commission. The second charge against the Commissar had to be dropped and the first had to be watered down to the following: the Commissar had committed immoral acts on several occasions which disgraced the name of communist and undermined marx-ist-leninist doctrine on the healthy socialist family and marriage by entering into extra-marital relations with certain of the local inhabitants.

THE DEAL

The Commissar drowned his sorrows in drink.

'They'll give me an unofficial reprimand,' he said, with a catch in his voice. 'And the wife'll go on at me for a week or so. None of that matters. It wouldn't be the first time. What gets me is something else. Now no one will believe me if I tell them what goes on here.'

'Well, don't tell them,' said the Lathe Operator. 'It wouldn't change anything, anyway.'

'If I were you,' said Don Juan, 'I'd get a divorce and marry Matryonadura. And live in clover.'

'I'd get divorced with pleasure,' said the Commissar, 'but I wouldn't get married again, God help me. Especially to a bitch like Matryonadura. She's already seen off two husbands.'

'That's good,' said Don Juan. 'God likes a trinity.'

The incident involving the Commissar was closed when Ivan Vasilievich and I took Mao-Tse-Dun'ka to one side and promised her that the Commissar wouldn't make a fuss. An analogous undertaking was given by the other 'signatories'. Mao-Tse-Dun'ka promised in turn to keep the 'dirt' on the Commissar 'up her sleeve'. But if 'that nit' ever created a 'stink', she would send it immediately to his Party organisation.

Afterwards we organised a drinking-session and invited Mao-Tse-Dun'ka. She drank herself into a state of utter swinishness and almost all of us in the barn 'banged' her till morning. But we still couldn't satisfy her.

'I wouldn't have thought that our Party had such a passionate temperament!' said Don Juan.

'It's got nothing to do with temperament,' said JRF. 'She's

simply fulfilled and over-fulfilled the month's sex plan ahead of time. Our Party is insatiable, not because of its large appetite but from a complete absence of appetite. It is sexless.'

In the morning Kostya found Mao-Tse-Dun'ka's underpants, which she had left behind. The Lathe Operator examined this article of Party underwear and said that it could be used as a sweep-net for catching fish. We wanted to make Matryonadura a present of them but she categorically refused to accept them. 'If that bitch sees me wearing her underpants,' she said, 'she'll do away with me.'

And then the Candidate had the bright idea of sending them to the district Party committee with an expression of gratitude from the collective of our barn. They would be bound to recognise them immediately and . . . In short, we cheered up and had a good laugh. The Candidate swore that he would carry out his idea: we had to cause Them some unpleasantness, too! Ivan Vasilievich, who hadn't taken part in our orgy, said something about male honour where women were concerned, and our mood reverted to normal. Don Juan, fastidiously holding the trophy in two fingers, carried it off to the rubbish dump. When we got back from work, the neighbour's puppy was dragging it through the village, to the great amusement of the locals. It gave them enough to talk about for a whole year: Mao-Tse-Dun'ka lost her underpants when she was drunk again! There's a he-woman for you! Not like these town trollops.

> And never more will serenade
> A damsel young awake or hence-
> forth will a fleeting gesture made
> Be a sufficient recompense.

END OF THE BATTLE

We organised a booze-up to mark the end of our sojourn in the country. Matryonadura wept buckets. She was sorry to part with us, had become 'attached to us with all her heart'. The Commissar was in an exhilarated mood since they were going to drop that business with Matryonadura, and drank himself senseless. Matryonadura took him under the armpits and dragged him off to her mattress. A real feather mattress, this time, which she had been taking good care of since her maidenhood, and only used on special occasions. JRF and I left the company and took a walk in the fields. We got talking about the Commissar's 'group'.

'It's curious,' I said. 'Dissidents undermine the very foundations of society and are allowed to get away with it for years. The Commissar's group wanted to strengthen society and it was immediately crushed. What's it all about?'

'It's very simple,' said JRF. 'The dissidents don't threaten the individual well-being of members of society, whereas the Commissar's group touched on the interests of the whole regional leadership.'

Later on Katyusha looked for us and called JRF. They went off somewhere together. The local youths were about to go after them like dark shadows, but Don Juan provided them with 'protection' by getting a group of Moscow lads to start a fight with the locals. Aware of the superiority of the forces against them, the local heroes slunk off, their tails between their legs. I saw the Commissar outside Matryonadura's house. He was retching in such sepulchral tones that all the dogs in the village had hidden themselves and fallen silent. Matryonadura's choicest language could be heard issuing forth from the house, from which it was possible to deduce that the Commissar had thrown up all over her virginal feather mattress.

I felt sad and alone. The sooner we left the better!

THE SEND-OFF

A meeting was arranged in the district centre. Many leaders and representatives gave speeches. The Red Challenge Banner was awarded to our neighbouring brigade. The names of the peredoviks were read out. The Commissar, naturally, was not among them. Mao-Tse-Dun'ka rattled off an inflammatory speech.

'Brother front-line soldiers!' she howled, to the friendly laughter of those present. 'Yes, front-line soldiers!!! For the battle for world-wide communism has been waged these last days here, on our soil. And we have won that battle!! (*Stormy applause, shouts of 'Hurrah!'*) Yes, *we* brothers, for we have spent these days with you in the same trenches! (*More laughter*) And eaten out of the same mess-tin! (*Laughter, turning into stormy ovations*). Now you know the price of potatoes! Tell them back there behind the lines!' (*again laughter, but of a positive kind*).

Then we sang the anthem of the brigades of communist labour. Instead of the words 'Lenin is up here with us' many sang clearly the words 'Len'ka is up here with us'. But they were not called to order, since it was interpreted as a manifestation of love for the Gen Sec, rather in the way that Khrushchev in his time was lovingly or mockingly (which for us is the same thing) referred to as Nikita.

BACK HOME

We returned to Moscow thinner, sun-tanned and exhilarated. We told everyone what a good time we had had, how well we had worked, what good fun we had had on our time off and how living conditions in the country were improving before one's very eyes. And it would be difficult to determine what was true in what we said and what was false. Having survived our difficulties and left them behind us, we already remembered them only as something very significant and sublime. We felt superior and worthier than those who had not experienced these difficulties. When we were taking our leave of each other, we exchanged addresses and telephone numbers, promising definitely to meet up sometime. A week later we threw those addresses and telephone numbers away. And, of course, we didn't meet. The ordinary routine of life swallowed us up. An anonymous denunciation about me arrived in the Party bureau. According to it, I was a secret dissident and internal émigré. I called the author everything under the sun. The secretary agreed with me but asked me to watch what I said a bit more carefully in future. And he also said that my case was a simple one, whereas JRF ... Such a 'cartload' had arrived about him that there would have to be a special investigation. One couldn't ignore a signal of that magnitude.

Many of the workers in the village were decorated (and our Matryonadura among them) and some of them were awarded the title of Hero of Socialist Labour (our Mao-Tse-Dun'ka among *them*). The level of agriculture predictably reached an unassailable height and some food products rapidly began to disappear from the shops and others just as rapidly began to increase in price. Officially this was known as a regulation of the pricing mechanism to reflect an improvement in quality. JRF was again removed from the waiting-list of people waiting to get on to the waiting-list for Party membership. My attempts to cement the friendly relations which we had formed in the country were not successful. I did not take offence. When I was young, I too always withdrew within my shell whenever anyone tried to become intimate with me.

PART FOUR

Eternal Peace

BACK TO NATURE

When summer holidays draw near
I remember with nostalgic frown
That Nature primary is here
On every side around the town;
That fields there are, and streams as well,
Deep forests, like in fairy tales,
That folk in thatched hamlets dwell
And that the cock each new morn hails;
That I'm a part of Nature, too,
That life in Nature is more free
And that the wasted years I rue
Because I was too blind to see.
Enough! From here on I'll exchange
My nasty noisy urbanism
For Nature's wide and open range
And end my former cretinism.
I'll sing the praise of babbling brook,
The nightingale that trills at dawn,
At hamlets thatched I'll have a look,
Fresh milk and eggs I'll feed upon.
With senses keen I'll apprehend,
In short, the wealth of Nature's store
And then my life I'll start to spend. . .
Exactly as I did before.

THE MAGNETIC FORCE OF THE CITY

The suburban electric train, moving at great speed, tried to transport JRF out of Moscow. But Moscow refused to come to an end and release him. Houses, factories, chimneys, cranes, houses, buildings under construction . . . And portraits everywhere of Lenin and the Gen Sec. Again the Gen Sec. And again the Gen Sec. And slogans: 'Glory to the Communist Party of the Soviet Union!' 'Long live Communism – the bright future of all mankind!' 'Long live . . .', 'Glory . . .', 'Onward . . .', 'We will fulfil . . .', 'We will transform . . .', You would think, laughed JRF to himself, that we build the slogans first and then attach the buildings to them. What a wonderfully progressive way of building!

The passengers sitting next to him began a game of cards and invited him to take part. He said that he did not know how to play, provoking thereby surprise and general derision. 'What can you expect of these dissidents!' said a fat woman. He was asked to move to another seat. The people next to whom he sat down already had a drinking session underway. Now *that's* something I know how to do, thought JRF to himself, but they're unlikely to ask me to join them. Meanwhile trees had begun to appear. A little stream flashed by. And once more it was houses, houses, houses . . . They crossed the motorway ring-road, the official city limit. But the city continued as if nothing had happened. How many decisions and decrees have there been about limiting the city, thought JRF. How many town plans have there been! But it just keeps on growing and doesn't give a hoot for plans, decisions or decrees.

At last the train tore itself away from the city and JRF observed an indefinable change in himself and in the people around him. It was as if they had torn themselves free of some magnetic field and relieved themselves of a heavy, invisible burden.

'Mama, mama!' cried a little girl in the next compartment. 'Look, a cow! A real, live cow!'

A HYMN TO THE CAREER

I will assert categorically that people find nothing more wonderful or seductive on this earth than a career. Any career. It is immaterial whether the career is distinguished or undistinguished, whether it is made with ease or with difficulty, whether it is meteoric or depressingly slow, conventional or unconventional, blemished or unblemished, deserved or undeserved. As long as it is a career. As long as you can look back at the end of your journey through life and exclaim with exultation: is that really me? What was I and what am I now?!! Where did I start and where did I get to??!!?! It doesn't matter, I repeat, who you were and what you've become. What is important is that there be a difference. One person might exclaim that he was only a simple, hard-working man, and not very bright, and yet had become . . . it's awesome to actually say it . . . a member of the Politburo. Oh, if only my poor dead Mum could see me now! Oh, if only my class-mates at school and university could see me now!! There's your sneak for you! There's your mediocre student for you! There's your secret informer for you!! A second person might exclaim that he was only a simple peasant lad and not very bright, yet had become . . . Oh, awesome even to pronounce the word . . . an Academician! Oh, if only my poor dead mother! . . . Oh, if only my class-mates! . . . There's your absence of talent for you! There's your scoundrel for you! A third might exclaim that he was a loafer and a chancer, yet had become . . . he still couldn't believe it . . . a chief of police. Oh, if only Mum! . . . Oh, if only my class-mates! . . . Oh! . . . Oh! . . .

It is the dream of being able to exult like that about his career which keeps the citizen of our society going. A Soviet citizen, if you really want to know, differs from the ape not by virtue of the fact that he began to work (in this respect he's nearer to the ape, rather than further away from it), but because he dreamed up a career and began to make it to the extent of his possibilities. And these possibilities are truly immense. In practice every citizen in our society can make a career, whether he becomes a janitor, senior janitor, policeman, senior accountant, instructor, inspector, assistant, deputy, head of department, director, sergeant-major, marshal, minister, senior technical assistant or even doctor of philosophical science. And if a citizen of our society doesn't make a career, this is explicable totally in terms of innate defects, the rudimentary remains of a capitalist consciousness and ideological sabotage by foreign intelligence services. For if a citizen doesn't succeed in becoming a senior accountant, a sergeant-major or the manager of a beer kiosk (by no means so simple!), then in the absence of the afore-mentioned defects and machinations of foreign intelligence services, not to become a candidate or doctor of philosophical science is impossible, both in theory and in practice.

Such dreams of exulting about a career visit our JRF as well. Look, for example, at his noble and inspired countenance at this very moment as the speedy suburban train transports him from the hustle and bustle of Moscow to commune with eternal and peaceful Nature. What is he thinking about, in your opinion? I'll write an article, he thinks, looking with one eye at eternal Nature through the window and with the other at the legs of the young personage sitting opposite who knows that she has seductive legs and is intent on showing as much of them as she can to all and sundry. What will the article be about? God, who cares? Her legs are nice, you have to admit. And, generally speaking, her figure's not too bad. But her face . . . Oh, no! That's not for us! Too vulgar. Anyway, this article . . . Let's say it's about the contradictions in our society. I'll express original views in it. Which ones? Who cares?! Her face, incidentally, is bearable. In the dark, at any rate. As far as culture is concerned, we're not in a seminar! I wonder where she's going. It would be quite good if . . . Yes, these views . . . Let's say the following. For instance, the general opinion that antagonistic contradictions disappear in a socialist society is erroneous. They are retained, but they too are subjected to control by the Party and government, are noticed by them and are overcome under their supervision and leadership. They are gradually and skilfully made to be non-antagonistic. They don't change of their own accord, but are transformed by a process of management. Yes, this creature is not at all bad and she's got rather a nice face. She looks reasonably fresh. Got a sense of humour, by the look of it. How do I approach her? . . .

The article by a fluke gets printed, JRF continued to day-dream. The editorial board didn't look at it carefully enough. The article is a sensation. Everyone is talking about it. The secretary in charge of ideology himself gives it his attention. He is jealous, of course, that it is not he, the top Party Theoretician, who has made this astounding discovery, but an insignificant JRF. But now it's too late. He has no option but to praise the author. A month later they give me a doctorate and the title of professor. In a year I am elected an associate member of the Academy of Sciences. I am quickly admitted to the Party, moreover to full membership, by-passing the stage of associate membership. I am elected as a delegate to the regional Party conference, then to a Party Congress. Before I know where I am, the daughter of some high-up is available. In a couple of years' time I'll be an Academician. Then a member of the Central

Committee. Vice-President of the Academy of Sciences. In a couple of years there's a house with ten rooms and a swimming pool. A car, no, two cars. A dacha. Access to the secret food shops, moreover to the top category ones. Use of the Kremlin hospital . . .

In reality a career is not made as brilliantly or romantically as it appeared in JRF's imagination. In reality one has to demean oneself, behave despicably, deceive, be hypocritical, tremble, shiver with revulsion, go grey with disappointment and suffer all sorts of other trials on the road through the cesspit of life. But believe me, the game is worth the candle, the end justifies the means. Once you have reached those cherished heights and cleansed your soul of all the dirt that got attached to it on your way up, you will experience that same exultation and produce the same exclamations of 'Oh, if only Mum . . . !', 'Oh, if only my class-mates . . . !', 'Oh, if only . . . !' It is worth living for the sake of that moment alone! It is no coincidence that Mitrofan Lukich Poluportyantsev himself, in a private conversation with his henchmen, after his eighteenth vodka (they were celebrating the award to Mitrofan Lukich of the order of the 'October Revolution' for his services to agriculture) literally said the following: 'If I had had to crawl for fifty years on all fours, eating what fell out of dustbins in order to get this post of mine, I would have done so, just so long as I got it.'

Once more JRF immersed himself in his wonderful dreams: but what if that degenerate Secretary for Ideology acts differently, pinches my discovery and accuses me of a non-existent error?! And then they'll let me rot in the Mordvinian camps as a homosexual, black-marketeer and dissident. Or, even worse, they'll put me in the Sychovka for the rest of my life. And is it really worth living for that moment of exultation? No, it's not. But what else is there to life? Only one thing: helping others to achieve their career aspirations. Which is better? They're both worse. What, then, is to be done? Blow the whole world to kingdom come. It looks like it's going that way, anyway. But what happens after that? Start the whole of evolution from the beginning again? But would the result be any better next time around? No, it'd be the same. Or else there would be nothing at all. What's the solution, then? Disappear and take all one's problems with one. But you can disappear as an Academician or

371

as JRF. You can disappear in the Novodevich'e cemetery or in an unnamed cemetery a hundred miles from Moscow. That's not very pleasant and it's a bit far away. But what does that matter to you? You won't be exactly wanting to go to Moscow, will you? No, of course not. But it's unpleasant, nevertheless. It's still better to disappear as an Academician. So sit down and write your article. What about? Who cares?! I'll slip it into some impoverished journal. Foreigners will take note of it. They'll reprint it. They'll say that not all marxists are fools, that some progress in marxism is to be seen. They'll give me a doctorate at once and elect me to the Academy of Sciences. If only my parents make it till then. Let the old folk be pleased that they didn't put their hopes in me in vain. And my class-mates from school and university! They'll die of envy. And what about Smirnyashchev and Subbotin! Ho, ho, then I'll show these dregs where to get off!!

THE REST HOME

In our part of the world facilities for recreation and rest, like everything else, are allocated according to rank, starting with those used by the lowest-ranking citizens at a reduced rate or free of charge and finishing with those used by the highest ranking figures in the state, also free of charge. Describing the difference between them in ordinary words is quite impossible. If you were to see the first type and then the second type, even if you never use indecent language, you wouldn't be able to use any other kind.

And yet even the most impoverished rest homes have their own incontestable charm. Very many citizens picture a future communist society as a rest home taking up the whole planet and lasting a whole life-time. The average worker of our advanced socialist society, on entering a rest home which conforms to his position in society (and sometimes it is even a little better), feels himself almost in paradise. He has torn himself away from the crippling medium of his place of employment and the tensions of domestic life. He communes with nature, breathes fresh air and doesn't hear the rumble of motor cars. He is ready for anything.

There is no need to rush off anywhere. He can sleep in. Chat as much as he likes. Flirt a little. Drink. There are no feuds or intrigues like there are at work. There is no need to make a career or do the dirty on anyone. Here you can be noble and generous. It doesn't matter whether you're a member of the Party or not, whether you're married or single, whether you live in a self-contained flat or a communal one. Everyone is equal. Everyone is kind and attentive to each other. And above all, there is Nature. When people see the striking beauty of their native countryside, they stand stock still in amazement. Oh, God, they cry with one voice. Why do we flounder around in our bad-tempered, suffocating, over-crowded conditions back in the town when everything is so beautiful here! What do we give up all this beauty for! How insignificant all our apprehensions and troubles appear compared with this beauty!

A special bus met the rest home guests at the station. And twenty minutes later they were driving under an arch which for some reason had been built at the entrance to the rest home territory. An excerpt from a speech by the Gen Sec was written on the arch in golden letters: 'We shall achieve the point without fail where rest will not only be a right, but the sacred duty of every worker!' The bus stopped in front of a building with maniacal columns dating back to the time of Stalin. The new arrivals clambered out, laughing and joking and bumping each other with suitcases. A fantastic looking pack of mongrels met them with yelps of joy and much wagging of tails. 'Well, here we are in the countryside at last!' said a middle-aged woman with a tense and emaciated face. 'It's really very nice, isn't it?'

JRF was about to agree that, indeed, it was very nice, but he didn't have time: something very heavy crashed before his very nose on to the step of the main entrance and exploded into pieces. 'Watch out!!' somebody shouted, somewhat tardily. Looking upwards apprehensively, the new arrivals hurried into the vestibule of the main building where they would be registered and assigned to dormitories.

THE MAIN BUILDING

The main building of the rest home was famous throughout the region for its sculptural ensemble entitled 'The Socialist Family' which consisted of a naked woman and a naked man holding high a naked infant. The sculptor and the authorities had had the honourable intention of protecting the guests from depravity by reminding them of the healthy socialist family, temporarily abandoned for the sake of health-giving rest. But since each member of the socialist family had been endowed with prodigious sexual organs, the ensemble clearly promoted the spread of depravity. Even the infant had been endowed with a member which was the envy of the most inveterate womanisers among the guests. The composition was not set in durable materials such as marble or bronze, but in a short-lived mix of clay, cement, boards, wire and broken brick. And after the very first fall of rain the sculpture had begun to fall apart. Bits of it fell on the heads of guests and staff. The first thing to fall off was the left breast belonging to the mother of the socialist family which shattered with the noise of a fragmentation bomb. A fragment removed the eye of a vice-president of the Academy of Sciences of some far-off national area with a very long name. The next thing to go was the infant's member, after which he looked like a Renaissance angel. This time there were no casualties if we don't count one of the cleaners who had an obvious piece of luck: her invalid's pension turned out to be more than her old-age pension. The member belonging to the head of the family lasted longest, but it, too, fell off, got caught on some iron rods sticking out of the pediment and was now poised above the entrance. It had lodged firmly but looked as if it were going fall off at any moment. So guests didn't enter the building and exit from it, but rushed headlong in and out, thanking their lucky stars for their escape from mortal danger.

The sculpture had to be restored at least once a year. The sculptor who restored it was paid by weight, not for aesthetic quality – about a hundred roubles per kilogram of sculpture. Every year, therefore, he increased the dimensions and individual weight of the pieces he restored. At the moment when JRF arrived the mother of the family group lost the rear part of her body weighing about . . . fifty thousand roubles. 'I wasn't half lucky,' thought JRF. 'If I had been killed, they'd have choked with laughter at the Institute when they found out.'

THE REST HOME

The rest home in which JRF found himself did not rank very highly but it was by no means the worst. It had dormitories for six guests, four guests, two guests and even single guests. The administrative staff who allocated guests to dormitories unerringly established their social status and placed them exactly where they belonged. If there were any misunderstandings, they were quickly resolved. For instance, on one occasion a female candidate of science was allocated to a dormitory for six. She created a fuss that could be heard two villages away. So as compensation for the damage done to her morale, she was allocated to a dormitory for one, normally the exclusive preserve of doctors of science and institute administrators. A quick glance at JRF's beard and worn trousers was enough for the administrator to allocate him to the worst dormitory for six, nicknamed the 'young people's dorm'. The words 'young people's' were pronounced with a low-minded little chuckle: 'the hee-hee-hee-so-to-speak-young-people's-hee-hee-hee'.

Sharing the 'young-people's-hee-hee' dormitory with JRF were a sixty-year-old employee in the editorial office of an academic journal, a bald engineer from an institute of economics who was clearly approaching fifty, a worker of indeterminate age from a technical institute and two young lads who were significantly quiet about their profession and where they worked. The worker straight off told everything about himself that he knew. He was an all-round craftsman who carried out the most varied functions in his institute, from the preparation of weird and wonderful 'concoctions' for extremely refined instruments to the performance of delicate personal services for the management. He preferred the latter, since they were always preceded, accompanied and terminated by a free drinking session. This 'All-

Rounder' arrived in the rest home drunk and didn't dry out before he left. In addition to everything else, he very much enjoyed talking about politics. When he referred to leaders of the Party and government, 'fool' was the least offensive word in his vocabulary. The young lads (the Students) had a limitless stock of dirty stories and political jokes. From the very first moment they used the informal mode of address with everyone in the dormitory.

After they had chosen their bunks and introduced themselves, the All-Rounder suggested that they celebrate the beginning of their sojourn together and placed on the table a half-litre of spirit which had been given to him at work for technical purposes. The Students produced a couple of bottles of 'red'. The others hadn't come empty-handed either.

A HYMN TO THE RUSSIAN COUNTRYSIDE

Still, there is nothing more wonderful than the Russian countryside! I have never been to the Niagara Falls, nor Bermuda, nor the Canary Islands, nor the Riviera, nor Dubrovnik, nor California, nor Tahiti, nor Ceylon . . . And yet I am prepared to bet that they are all as nothing, compared with our miraculous Russian countryside. If, of course, the sun is shining. Usually we have rain or wet snow, slush, mud under our feet, a cold wind, a grey and gloomy sky . . . In short, it is deeply depressing. But if the sun shines, then there's no argument. Of course, you have to watch where you put your feet. There are empty tins, broken bottles . . . Not long ago one of our colleagues went flying and spent the next six months in an intensive care unit. I told you to watch where you put your feet! What are you staring at the sky for?! Have you never seen the sun, or what?! You've landed in someone's shit? Oh, dearie me! I warned you, after all!

After a 'dance' JRF got hold of that same lady who had been in such rapture over the beauties of the Russian countryside on their arrival and moved off with her in the direction of that same countryside. A foul rain was drizzling down and they could still feel the remains of late spring under their feet. When they had gone a sufficient distance from the rest home, they silently spread one mackintosh on the wet ground, covered themselves with the other and devoted themselves to that most wonderful miracle of nature. And . . . 'The swine!' she suddenly exclaimed. 'They've fouled the whole environment, the pigs!' And they were brought from the heavens of innocent love back to an earth both sinful and covered in shit.

. . . Oh, Russian Nature, where are you?!!

CLIQUES

Rest home guests very soon divide into more or less permanent groups, or cliques. The members of such groups usually go for walks together, drink together and go as a group to the cinema or to a dance. These groups are numerically surprisingly uniform (usually from six to ten people). JRF found himself in one such group, along with the Old Man, the Engineer, the All-Rounder, JRF's new female acquaintance (the Little Lady), a doctor of sciences trying to look younger than his age, the women with whom the Engineer and the All-Rounder 'passed the time' and a couple of unattached 'girls' who knew the whole of samizdat and tamizdat literature by heart.

The Little Lady went out of her way to draw attention to her liaison with JRF. He found that most oppressive. He would have preferred one of the Girls, but it was already too late. Ah, well he thought, I'll bear it somehow. But just till we get back to Moscow. And it wouldn't be a bad idea to keep away from these old bags altogether. Presumably it is no coincidence that guys who know the score go for the young birds. They hope to teach them their favourite tricks. Only I don't know of a single instance when these hopes were realised.

The live wire in the group was at first the Engineer. Then a young candidate of science from the first block joined the group and took over the initiative. The Engineer didn't like that. He tried in all sorts of ways to maintain the leadership. And, naturally, achieved the opposite. A society without conflict, thought JRF *à propos*, is impossible even in the most ideal circumstances, even when people unite in groups absolutely voluntarily. People, incidentally, get married voluntarily nowadays, apparently because they love each other, but do we have all that many happy families? Non-antagonistic contradictions are fairy-tales for the weak-minded. Take, for example, that toothless female doctor of sciences and that monkey-faced associate member of the Academy from the first block. They hate each other just as much as capitalists and workers, or landowners and serfs. And yet they spend whole days at a time in the same group.

Although the leader was the Candidate, or sometimes the Engineer, the heart and soul of the group was nevertheless the All-Rounder. He devoted himself entirely to the group, asking for nothing in return. Not even attention. The Candidate was listened to with interest and respect. Every one made fun of the All-Rounder. But they liked him. No single group event was complete without him. As for JRF, people somehow didn't notice him. That suited him perfectly, since he didn't like attracting attention to himself. If he had any bright ideas he 'sold' them to the Engineer or the Candidate. And only then did they become the 'property of the masses'. This would infuriate the Little Lady. She was prone to vanity.

A CONFLICT OF MOTIVES

JRF took two files out of his suitcase – a thick one and a thin one. The thick one contained a 'scientific monograph' by the bitch Tvarzhinskaya, her wits dulled by vanity and devotion to the Party. The thin file contained a 'work of art' by the senile Petin, his wits sharpened by vanity and a readiness to sell any party down the river. It was even written on the file in red pencil: 'Stalin. A Work of Art'. Which rubbish should he start 'editing' first? Petin was the director of the Institute and an Academician, whereas Tvarzhinskaya was merely his head of department and a candidate for associate membership of the Academy. Clearly he should start with Petin. But in terms of the damage she could do, Tvarzhinskaya was now ahead of Petin, and every page of her 'scientific monograph' contained a reference to comrade Brezhnev. So doubtless he should start with her. What was the answer? 'Begin both at once,' sniggered an inner voice. 'Mix all the pages up and add nonsensical commentaries. Then you'd have a book and a half!' 'It's tempting,' thought JRF in reply. 'But what would happen to me afterwards? If they join forces to punish me, what do you think will be left of me?'

STALIN

JRF looked at Petin's papers and threw them in the waste-paper basket. 'And that cretin wants to reconstruct a psychological portrait of Stalin!' he thought. 'How many "writers" like that have there been just recently! And yet there's no particular problem about Stalin. There's only a problem about stalinism. And a so-called psychological portrait of Stalin can only be a more or less successful literary device in a description of stalinism. And from that point of view, there can only be one correct solution: it has to be shown that people like Stalin are in fact not the creators of history, but merely its creatures. So, why don't we try doing that?' And JRF began to write.

A LETTER TO HERSELF

The country around here is absolute bliss,
But I am bored out of my mind.
I have to read crap without taking the piss
And find quotes for that bitch – it's a grind!
What a beautiful sky! What a wonderful scene!
The sunsets are great every day.
What a pity it is, it's almost obscene,
That our life just gets frittered away.

STALIN

Period of the action: before the first world war. Scene of the action: abroad. Lenin and Krupskaya's room. Stalin is with them. Stalin is sitting at a table in his boots, smoking a pipe. Lenin is running up and down the room, gesticulating and cursing. Krupskaya frowns each time and says: 'Volodya, you mustn't be so coarse!' *Stalin takes his pipe out of his mouth each time and says:* 'Our cause can't do without coarseness.' *Lenin freezes on the spot each time and says:* 'That's right, dear comrade! You don't make a revolution using kid gloves. I'm absolutely in agreement with you, my dear . . . Forgive me, what is your name and patronymic? . . .' *Krupskaya looks out of the window at the well-dressed passers-by, at the richly stocked shop windows and other delights of the Western way of life.*

KRUPSKAYA: It's amazing! I've been looking out of the window for a whole hour, and I haven't seen a single drunk, or any coarse behaviour, or anything indecent. Everything is as it should be. No, Volodya, you're wrong. They'll never have a revolution here. They don't need it. They're living here like lords without revolution. It's Russia that needs a revolution and that's where it will start.

LENIN: Nadyusha, how many times have I asked you to stay out of politics. It's not a thing for a woman's mentality. Until the proletariat of Western Europe rises up and carries through a socialist revolution, your Russian peasant won't lift a finger. Note the word 'peasant'! We don't have all that many workers, do we? And, anyway, they're peasants too, or half-peasants, still partly tied to their village. And we don't have all that many revolutionaries, either, do we? You can count them on the fingers of one hand. And they're basically gasbags.

STALIN: You are right, Teacher! What do all these Trotskies, Kamenevs and Bukharins and the others get up to? They chatter, scribble articles, lounge around pubs.

LENIN: We need an organisation of professional revolutionaries and not professional gasbags. Give us an organisation of revolutionaries and we will turn Russia upside down! And we need money. You'll never achieve a revolution without money. Even less will you hold on to power. Money! Money, above all else! And again, money! Lots of money!

STALIN: My dear Teacher! We'll have an organisation of people for the Cause. In fact, it exists already. There'll be money, weapons and so forth. But . . . There are conditions.

LENIN: Excellent, dear . . . Joseph Vissarionovich! I agree to all your conditions in advance.

STALIN: I must have a party post, and one that is sufficiently senior and authoritative. Membership of the Central Committee. Articles in the Party journal.

LENIN: Consider yourself co-opted on to the Central Committee and on to the editorial board of the newspaper. What are you doing at the moment? Concocting a pamphlet on the nationality question? Ha! ha! ha! Drop that nonsense – our women'll do it for you in a week. Act! Let us confine our discussion to purely technical details.

Lenin sits down at the table. Stalin unfolds the street-map of some town or other. They bend over the map, conversing quietly between themselves. Krupskaya looks out of the window and exclaims from time to time: 'It's amazing! Not a single drunk! What do they want with a revolution?!' Two hours later Stalin leaves, having declined the offer of tea and without taking his leave of Krupskaya.

KRUPSKAYA: Volodya, he's a typical highway robber! How can you consort with objects like him?! And besides, rumour has it that he's an Okhranka spy!*

LENIN (*thoughtfully*): And who do they not claim is an Okhranka agent? They spread the same rumours about me. So what? And even if it is true, what significance does it have?! For the sake of the revolution I'm ready to deal with the head of the Okhranka himself. At least this is a real cause. I think that the Okhranka is probably not against collaborating with us a little. These cretins still think that the enemies who threaten their system most are not us but the socialist-revolutionaries. Let them think so – it does us no harm at all.

KRUPSKAYA: But this . . . Armenian is thinking of robbery and murder!

LENIN: That's good! You don't have revolutions without that. Let these bandits serve the cause of the liberation of mankind. When the revolution has been accomplished, we'll scrape our heels clean of scum like that and wash the blood from our hands. And we'll enter the hallowed portals of communism without these abominations. But at the moment we cannot do without them. We need fighting units, weapons, channels of communication, safe houses . . . We need to bribe some people here, discredit some people there, remove yet other people from the scene . . .

* *Okhranka:* the Tsarist secret service. (*Translator's note*)

And money. Lots of money! We need to begin with money. Do me a favour, play me some Beethoven!

AUTHOR: Stalin told me about this conversation himself. He also took the opportunity to inform me of the expressions Lenin used during that conversation. But I decided not to quote them. It would be unseemly. Anyway, no one would have believed the authenticity of the description. Time is an amazing thing. It passes, and an exact description of an event begins to be interpreted as lies, and the most grotesque lies begin to look most like the truth.

STALIN (*in the street outside says to himself*): They regard us as a necessary, but temporary, evil. Oh you naive dreamers! It's you who are a necessary, but temporary . . . let's say, good, I don't mind. Life, however, is based not on good, but on evil, because the good is ephemeral, but evil is solid and unshakable. If the revolution triumphs, we shall decide who shall enter the radiant portals of communism and who shall not.

BETRAYAL

The process of becoming a Soviet citizen begins with betrayal. When Herself got JRF's letter, she boasted about it to her closest girl friend. Naturally, in the strictest confidence. Her friend, after swearing to keep it a secret, promptly told two other people and they all had a good giggle about Herself and JRF. In a couple of days the whole Institute knew about the letter. Herself was summoned to the komsomol bureau and instructed to produce it. She was told not to forget where she worked and that she would need a reference for the university. She cried for a little while, but she handed the letter over.

She never received any more of his letters after that even although he wrote to her practically every day. He didn't know that she wasn't getting his letters and carried on writing to her.

A SECOND LETTER TO HERSELF

The cock awakes us every morn at dawn.
Inquisitive dogs are at our heels all day.
The local lasses give us the 'come on'.
The local lads would have us put away.
With vodka breath they ask us: 'Want a fight?!'
The sun-flower seeds lie strewn on the ground.
And I have this sensation of delight:
I feel that Mother Russia's still around.

ON HAPPINESS

'Our great writers could spout a lot of trivial nonsense,' grumbled
the Old Man *à propos* a remark of the Little Lady's to the effect
that 'a person is born for happiness just as a bird is born to fly'.
'Happiness is a very relative thing. Shall I tell you what was the
happiest moment in my life? When we had drill in the army, or
were rehearsing for a parade or a march, they would give us time
off every so often in order to answer the call of Nature. As soon
as we heard the command: "Dismiss! To the loo!" we would start
a game. One of us would "draw the others' fire", i.e. shout out:
"Company, piss on me!" And we would all chase after him,
trying to piss on him. Naturally he would try to dodge us and
more often than not we would piss on each other. It was great
fun. On one occasion I managed to piss right on the new forage
cap of one of our goody-goodies who got top marks in his military
and political training tests. To say that I was happy is not saying
much. I was boiling over with happiness. I'll never forget that
moment as long as I live. We talked about that event more than
we talked about the victory or defeat at the front. And you talk
about happiness! Does that mean I was only born in order to
piss on the head of the best soldier in the company?!'

STALIN

St Petersburg. A luxurious hotel. A gendarme colonel is looking at himself in a mirror. Enter a beautiful young woman. She whispers that 'that man has come'. The colonel asks the lady – no doubt the owner of the establishment – to ask 'that man' to come in. Enter Stalin. He has a beard and moustache and is dressed as a worker. But his bearing is dignified.

COLONEL: Well, now, Mr Alexandrov, what news have you got to tell us about Mr Ulyanov and his gang?

STALIN: You mean Lenin and his party? Yes, well, I have something to report on that. But first offer me a seat. And address me by my name and patronymic.

COLONEL: Are you drunk?

STALIN: No. The fact is that I am a member of the Central Committee of Lenin's party and in charge of his expropriator and terrorist squads.

COLONEL: Oh, I do apologise! That changes everything. You mentioned those expropriator-terrorist squads. Surely Lenin doesn't have such things? As far as we know, he seems to be in principle against . . .

STALIN: Lenin hasn't got such squads yet. But he will have, soon. With your permission, of course.

COLONEL: You have my complete attention, dear Joseph Vissarionovich! First tell me about how Mr Lenin intends to plan a revolution!

STALIN: Lenin is not planning a revolution. He's waiting for a revolution. He thinks that we should be ready for the revolution and make use of it for our own purposes.

AUTHOR: Afterwards this thesis of leninism was distorted in such a way as to suggest that Lenin and his party prepared the revolution, that the endless blather at party gatherings and all the writings were a genuine preparation for revolution. Revolutions are not prepared. They happen of their own accord, unexpectedly for everyone, including those people who claim to be its active creators. Our revolution came as a complete surprise to Lenin himself, and his comrades. But that is totally irrelevant to an assessment of individuals and parties. I was the first to falsify that aspect of leninism, and with Stalin's knowledge too. 'If we have the possibility of convincing people that it was us who prepared and carried out the revolution,' he said to me on that occasion, 'that means that we really did plan the revolution and carry it out.'

COLONEL: He's no fool, your Lenin. Maybe it would be a good idea to nab him now?

STALIN: It's a bit too soon. When the time comes I'll do it myself.

COLONEL: How, then, is Lenin preparing for revolution? Incidentally, do you believe that there will be a revolution?

STALIN: That is unimportant. Anyone who wants to be prepared for revolution must live as though it might happen at any moment. As for preparation . . . Lenin understands that the ideas of a revolution and their embodiment in reality have nothing in common with each other. What is important is not summoning people to revolution nor blathering on the subject, but being the first to recognise it when it comes and not hesitating to use all the means discovered in past revolutions as well as inventing new ones which have never been heard of before.

COLONEL: Be a bit more specific.

STALIN: Lenin is convinced that there is no one more capable than he and his party of being ready for revolution and making use of it. Therefore Lenin's main enemies on a personal level are those in the party who compete with him. Therefore, argues Lenin, now is the time to direct the behaviour of his comrades who are competing with him in such a way that afterwards none of them will have any claim to the leadership of the revolution. Therefore the main enemies of Lenin's party are other revolutionary parties. And they have to be treated as deadly dangerous opponents.

COLONEL: And what do you yourself think of this claim of Lenin's?

STALIN: Lenin's party is the only one in which I can have a post among the leadership, and Lenin is the only person I can call Teacher. I have put my money on Lenin.

COLONEL: What means does Lenin recognise in practice?

STALIN: Any. Forgery, blackmail, extortion, slander, demagogy, robbery, theft, murder . . . In short, anything which will strengthen the position of the party and his own personal position.

COLONEL: And what's the most important thing in all this?

STALIN: Money.

COLONEL: But . . .

STALIN: We are not intending to burden His Majesty's treasury with our requests.

COLONEL: In that case . . .

STALIN: A bank, for instance.

COLONEL: That's risky.

STALIN: You can't have a revolution without risks.

COLONEL: I see. But how much can you get in a bank? Perhaps a lot for one person, but enough for a party? Large sums are rarely . . .

STALIN: We shall be relying on your assistance.

COLONEL (*thoughtfully*): Yes . . . But . . . You see . . .

STALIN: Of course.

COLONEL: There are two major transfers of capital in the offing. One not far from your homeland. The other one is far away . . .

STALIN: One more bout of exile won't hurt the reputation of a revolutionary.

COLONEL: Right! It's a bargain! Is there anything I can do for you personally?

STALIN: There is. Forget about our previous relations. I would ask you to destroy all the documents. From now on everything will be on a basis of mutual trust. Otherwise . . .

COLONEL: You have my word as an officer!

STALIN: You have my word as a revolutionary.

AUTHOR: The colonel did not keep his word. His deception was discovered when a special commission was examining the Okhranka archives. What was to be done? I took a risk and reported the documents to Stalin. And he got rid of all the members of the commission except me. Why did he spare me? I suspect that he kept me as a living witness to the fact that his genius was superior to that of his Teacher. Then he gave orders to find the Colonel dead or alive. He was located in Paris and died soon afterwards of a heart attack, although he had been in the best of health. A rumour sprang up in the West to the effect that some documents existed showing that Stalin had collaborated with the Okhranka. But if any documents did appear over there, they were false. Stalin and I had burned all the genuine documents. We burned them and ate the ashes. Why the theatricality? Stalin was an actor. Of all the operations that were carried out only very few became a part of history, and even then in a highly distorted version on the basis of rumours, gossip and piece-meal information. Only one of these operations is associated with Stalin's name, and then only because it took place in his native land and because there was a known link between Stalin and some of the people who carried it out.

AN EXCURSION TO PETIN'S DACHA

One of the compulsory group activities for rest home guests is a sight-seeing tour of the village, particularly that part of it containing the dachas of many bigwigs of the recent past, including the dachas of Academicians. The dachas had been given to these bigwigs free of charge on the personal orders of Stalin. Petin's dacha made the biggest impression on the guests. There was a high fence with barbed wire along the top of it. Behind it was a huge two-storey house. There was a conservatory. There was a host of smaller buildings of no obvious designation. Someone said that one of them was a sauna and another was for the watchman and his dog.

'That Petin', said someone to JRF, 'was one of the vilest creatures of the Stalin era. At one time it looked like he'd had it. But he got off scot-free. He's still holding down posts although he's nearly eighty. Here's a characteristic example from his biography. Someone called Stanis wrote an article for the Large Soviet Encyclopaedia. The article, of course, was the usual load of old cobblers. Nothing but toadying to Stalin. But that's not the point. Soon afterwards Stanis was arrested and shot on the strength of a denunciation by Petin. This was established afterwards (thirty years later!). The article appeared in the Encyclopaedia almost unchanged, but this time as an article by Petin. The only insertion he made was a sentence to the effect that 'menshevistic idealists' had misinterpreted and distorted everything, and in brackets he indicated the name of the representative of that idealism, i.e. Stanis, the real author of the article which was supposed to be giving the correct interpretation. By a miracle all the documents pertaining to this incident were preserved. They say that they even opened some kind of personal file on Petin. But – with no results. And now we are brought on this curious excursion and are shown that dreg's dacha.'

'Petin's nothing,' said the Engineer. 'Much more important figures escaped unpunished. Who? Molotov. Voroshilov. Kaganovich. Malenkov. Mikoyan . . . And thousands of others.'

'Many people think,' said JRF, 'that it was the same Stanis who wrote Stalin's *On Dialectical and Historical Materialism*. That was why he was shot, although he was accused for the sake of appearances of "menshevistic idealism". But I have my doubts about that. We had a madman coming to our Institute for a while claiming that he wrote it. He also said that he wrote the article that Petin stole from Stanis. The story of Stanis's article is a detail. Petin has published five books. Someone wrote them for him. Where are these people? He's got another book coming out soon. His colleagues at the Institute knocked that one off for him. But that's legitimate. As director he has every right to use his subordinates as "technical assistants". And he expresses his gratitude to them in the foreword.'

'Why don't they kick up a fuss?'

'What for? They've got something out of it, too. As regards their contribution to the book, it's a horrific load of shit, if seen as the product of average scientific staff. That shit only acquires significance if its author is an Academician or somebody higher. If the same shit had been signed by Brezhnev it would be regarded as a phenomenon of epoch-making significance.'

REST HOME NOSH

The staple food in the rest home, as in the rest of our society, is kasha. In a context of fresh air and inactivity it produces a startling effect: rest home guests rapidly begin to put on weight. They are weighed on the first day of their holiday and on the last, and the difference in weight counts as an index of the degree of rest achieved. In the last few years, it is true, it has become fashionable to lose weight. And here too kasha has turned out to be a remarkable food product: people wishing to lose weight avoid eating kasha and consequently drag out a half-starved existence, which is very good for the health.

When JRF stood on the scales, the doctor was somewhat surprised. 'You're a bit under weight for your height, young man,' he said. 'But don't worry, we'll feed you up.' The Little Lady had the same idea. 'You're very thin,' she said. 'We'll have to feed you up. I'll see to that. I have to lose ten kilograms, so I'll give you some of mine. And no arguing! Kasha . . .'

'I can't eat the shit!' said JRF. 'I can't bear the word "kasha".'

'There's a word worse than that,' she said, ' – "groats". Groats – listen to the sound of it. There's something mousey and dusty about it. Our whole miserable history is concentrated in it. What a feeling of immense boredom wells up whenever the word is pronounced. I'm telling you, the grain problem as far as our people is concerned is synonymous with the food problem in general. Gr-r-r-o-o-a-a-ts!! When they appear in the little local shop, they're quickly sold out. What a nightmare! I'll tell you what! I'll get us fresh eggs and milk from the village!'

'Don't be naive,' he said. 'The locals have to go to Moscow for their butter and eggs.'

IDIOT LOGIC

The 'Students' had a transistor radio and were always listening to the 'Voices' from the West. Every broadcast contained some fact or other about the terrorism which was the scourge of the West.

'Thank God,' said the All-Rounder. 'At least we don't have terrorism like that over here.'

'In our part of the world terror is a privilege of the State,' said the Old Man.

'Did you know that these "Red Brigades" are pro-communist? It's still not known who finances them.'

'Whereas we have corruption, protection, privileges, careerism, all of them flourishing.'

389

'Do you think they don't have that over there? They've got it as much as we have.'

'So what? It's amazing! All you have to do is mention some defect of ours and immediately you'll find some bright spark who will declare that you'll find it in the West, too. And once you've got it in the West, then, according to idiot logic, we don't have it here. Suppose you say, for example, that in our part of the world people get locked up for what they say. That's a thesis. Now we have the antithesis: they lock people up over there, as well. From which you get the synthesis: here people don't get locked up. Hey, you with the beard! I'm giving a true picture from a philosophical point of view, am I not?'

'Absolutely. You're a born dialectician.'

'I've always been interested in the logic of people's thought processes, but I have yet to understand it. For instance, during a seminar at the Academy I expressed the view that any weapon developed after a war becomes obsolete before a new war. And that therefore one should not so much manufacture arms as create the potential for manufacturing arms which will be adequate for a new war, which, although always expected, will be unexpected at the time when it breaks out. An investigator charged me with undermining the defence capability of the country. And yet I was only thinking of how to improve the defence capability of our country.'

STALIN

A train is speeding through beautiful Georgia. Mountains, rivers, little villages, ruined castles flash by. Stalin is sitting lost in thought. His travelling companion urges him to look out of the window. It's Georgia, after all! How many years has it been since they were last at home!

TC: Look, Koba! It'll be Gori any minute now! How lucky you are! You'll see your mother, father, wife, son! Your friends . . . Here, let me carry your bags!

STALIN: Leave them alone! This is not the time. We'll get around to that later on somehow. Right now we can't afford to lose a minute. You know yourself, there's the Cause!

TC: I know! But I wouldn't have minded living for a few days like we used to when we were children, free of care. What are you thinking about all the time?

STALIN: You wouldn't understand. You see, history is a pretty tricky thing. Anything that depends on the intelligence and initiative of a single individual is not taken seriously. Tell me, who in the Party thinks the Cause for which we shall be risking our lives is worth mentioning? No one. When history takes its great step forward, will they devote even a line to this Cause? No. What do our party leaders great and small talk about day after day, year after year? What do they write their endless stream of books and articles about? About the objective course of history, about the movement of the masses and other things that don't depend on the initiative or intelligence of any individual. And another thing – the historical importance of a person's actions does not coincide with how these actions are evaluated in the conditions and at the time they were carried out. Do you understand?

TC: No. Dialectics are not for me. But it's interesting to listen to. Carry on!

STALIN: Don't worry about not understanding. Our leading theoreticians don't understand this either. Lenin included. And Marx. And history's got another nasty trick up its sleeve and that's its laws of historical focus and illusion. I'll explain what I mean. Sometimes people's interest focuses on one spot (like rays of light). It sometimes happens that such spots are individual people. Moreover, a complete nonentity might become the focus of mass interest. Of course, it might be a significant individual. But more often it is a nonentity. Now, because outstanding individuals sometimes become the focus of mass interest and because, with the passage of time, the scale of events transfers itself to those people who were in the focus, nonentities too begin to look like great men. As a result it is afterwards impossible to distinguish between the great and the insignificant. And sometimes everything is stood on its head: great people appear as nonentities and nonentities as great people. And it's impossible to establish the truth. Just look at who is the centre of attention in Russian social life at the moment! If you survive, remember our conversation in twenty or thirty years' time. And you will be amazed how the view of our time will have changed.

TC: What do you think about our Cause, then?

STALIN: I don't think about it. I get on with it.

A TALE OF JUSTICE

'Why is it such an unjust world?' She asked. 'Good, kind people suffer, and bad people do very well for themselves.'

'What can you do?' replied JRF. 'The world is so constructed that the strongest survive and get ahead.'

'How are they the strongest? They're all untalented, lazy cowards.'

'In our society they are the strongest. They adapt themselves more successfully.'

'You can't get at them! At least there used to be robbers who would rob and murder the rich and give to the poor. But nowadays . . .'

'They still exist. Do you want to hear a story about a contemporary robber with a sense of justice? No one knows any more who he was. Some say he was an Academician. Others say that he was a general. Or a high-up Party functionary. But I don't believe them. He is more likely to have been a school-teacher, a pediatrician or a junior research fellow without a higher degree. In any event, one day he saw the injustices that there were in the world and was shocked by them. But being shocked by them – that's not given to everyone. That's a divine gift. And having been shocked by them, he decided to wage war against these injustices. But how was he to do that? Nowadays it's not so easy to rob the rich. Just try taking the rank of Academician away from that plagiarist and denouncer Petin, or the Doctor's degree from paranoiac Smirnyashchev, or the title of professor from that female side-kick of Beria's! Try stealing a marshal's private house, or the special shop for the functionaries in the Central Committee apparatus, or the car, chauffeur and bodyguard of the regional Party secretary! Try stealing free access to the best sanatoria, trips abroad, ridiculously inflated honours, things like that! The robber thought things over and decided to start with something small. He discovered that there was a family of five in their building living in one little room. He went to see them and said: "I'll help you." "It won't work," they said. "We've been trying for four years ourselves, but it's like banging your head against a stone wall, for we are entitled to exactly four square metres per person and they've stopped all house building because of the forthcoming Olympics. We don't want to be shown up, after all, in front of the whole world!"

'Then the robber got a measuring tape and measured the room. And discovered that it was not twenty square metres, but only 19·6. And then he began to write to all the various authorities. And to go and see them in the district executive committee, the municipal executive committee, and higher. It took two years of visits and writing letters to get what he wanted: a commission was sent to measure the room again and change all the documents accordingly. The commission came to measure the room five times. And every single time they got a different result. A year later, however, they admitted that the room was only 19·8 square metres. And again he began to write letters and wear out shoe leather, trying to get better accommodation for that poor family. He spent another two years on that. And again he got his way: they were offered a room of twenty-one (!) square metres in an old house on the outskirts of the city. But they didn't want to go there. And the higher authorities said: "You do what you can for people, and what do they do?! ... " And the matter was closed. "There are others," said the authorities, "who are worse off but don't make a fuss." And then the robber went to a pub. And got drunk. But not drunk enough for his liking. He went outside, stole a passer-by's hat, sold it to someone else and drank the proceeds. The police hunted him for two months, using every man at their disposal, including members of the Voluntary People's Patrol. And they caught him. And put him in a strict-regime camp for three years. End of story.'

STALIN

Tbilisi. A little house on the outskirts. A room is full to bursting point with bearded men. They are smoking. And drinking wine. Enter Stalin, followed by two men with large, and to judge by looking at them, heavy bags. They greet the others and sit down at the table. They drink wine.

RINGLEADER: Well, Koba, what's it to be this time? Spit it out!

STALIN: A bank!

(Shouts): Try pulling the other one!

RINGLEADER: Quiet! Let the man speak!

Stalin signals to the people who came in with him and they distribute pistols, bombs and masks. Stalin takes a sheet of paper from his pocket and unfolds it. It is a plan of a bank and the surrounding buildings and streets. They all bend over it. Without wasting words, Stalin explains his plan.

RINGLEADER: Well thought out! It looks like a sure thing. There might be casualties . . . But the game's worth the candle. How much? . . .

STALIN: Half.

RINGLEADER: Done!

Stalin and the Ringleader shake hands. The gathering breaks up. The Ringleader leaves. Only the owner of the house, Stalin and his two companions are left.

OWNER: What are your instructions, Koba?

STALIN: Half is not enough for the Party. The Party needs the lot! Do you understand me?

OWNER: Perfectly!

STALIN: Disguise your men as policemen. Arrest every one of the burglars as soon as the operation has been carried out.

OWNER: And the ringleader?

STALIN: Make sure he's the first to be arrested!

OWNER: And, er? . . .

STALIN: Ten per cent.

OWNER: Done!

Stalin and his companions leave the house and walk slowly through the town. It is night. Shadowy figures emerge from the dark and shine torches on them.

MAN WITH TORCH: Is that you, Koba?

STALIN: Yes.

MAN WITH TORCH: Are we in business, then?

STALIN: We are. Come closer. Take a dozen reliable lads and wait for my people . . .

ONE OF THE COMPANIONS (*after the people who stopped them have gone*): Koba, do you want . . .

STALIN: Yes! The interests of the revolution demand it. And, as Lenin says, you don't make revolution wearing white gloves. Get on with it! I want to see every last kopeck of that money . . .

BOREDOM

There was a foul drizzle. In the club there were the same old wearisome games and dances. And amateur activities totally devoid of any talent whatsoever. People waited impatiently for the film about the restoration of agriculture in the first years after the war. Everyone had seen it about ten times before. But still they waited. According to the film, thanks to an emissary of the Party, a one-armed invalid from the war and a gang of emaciated widows, our agriculture, which had been destroyed during the war, is restored, indeed raised to a level which later would not be achieved by healthy, multi-armed graduates from higher Party schools, agricultural and economics institutes and military academies, plus millions of labourers sent out 'systemackilly' (as our leader puts it) to do harvesting and other work on the farms. The inhabitants of low-density dormitories had brought in women (or men), after asking their neighbour to get lost for a couple of hours, locked themselves in or put a stool against the door, drank a bottle each of some foul rubbish from Rossglavvino and devoted themselves to a bout of galloping love-making. Those who were less fortunate formed cliques in the more densely populated dormitories, collected tumblers from the other dormitories and drank the same rubbish, sang romantic songs of a hundred years ago in dreadful voices, told stupid jokes and talked about how good it was there and how much they didn't want to go back home to the daily, nerve-racking grind. The older folk watched television, all the programmes in a row, even the 'Time' programme. JRF edited Tvarzhinskaya's manuscript. His roommates talked about the usual things. Through the slightly open door could be heard the voice of the announcer expressing rapture at some new batch of routine success stories.

'Shut the door,' grunted the Old Man. 'When you think about it! Great minds have applied their genius and invented this wonderful machine so that we get a constant flood of propaganda effluent. It's absurd!! Just think about it! They invent powerful flying machines so that parasites can be transported in them! Potent medicines are invented to prolong their senile lives! What for?! and we patiently put up with everything for the sake of a few crumbs or the transparent hope of ending up as an item in the bibliography appended to some lousy article.'

'What do you suggest then? A new revolution?'

'If it were up to me, I'd cancel the old one.'

'It says here in your boss's manuscript that there were occasional mistakes during the Stalin period. Is she being serious?'

'If it were up to her, there wouldn't be a word about mistakes at all.'

'That's rich, "occasional mistakes"! These occasional mistakes went on for almost forty years.'

'They're still going on. And they will for ever.'

'You're exaggerating there. There have been some improvements, after all. And not insignificant ones! Here we are, talking pretty frankly and telling jokes. And we're not afraid of being suddenly arrested. Was that possible earlier? Of course not. So there has been some improvement. And more will come. And there aren't too many bitches like the author of that book left.'

'Compared with Stalin's time, their number has grown by a factor of ten. And when it comes to doctors of philosophistry, there's a hundred times more of them!'

'Yes, but not the same types!'

'They're better educated, of course. They're more cunning and adaptable. Many of them know foreign languages. But essentially they're still the same dregs.'

'I wish this holiday would end! It's horrifically boring. The first few days it seemed like paradise here. How long did that feeling last? and the people . . . My God, where do they get them from? Imagine if we had to stay here for ever! At least at home, "in freedom", there is some sort of choice. Sorry, I wasn't talking about you. We've been lucky. We've ended up in an intelligent dormitory. At least you can talk to someone. But what about the food?'

'It's specially for losing weight. That's the current fashion. It's laughable. They used to measure rest by the amount you put on. As soon as you arrived, you had to stand on the scales. And again, just before you left. The doctor would write that the patient had got three kilograms better. And he would smile. And you'd be very happy. The swine fiddled the amount you'd put on, of course. They needed to for their records, their accounts, their socialist competition. But still. But why was it like that? They fed us very badly and we looked like emaciated goats. And what happens now? Somehow we all put on weight.'

'Because of an excess of bad food.'

'If I'm honest about it, the scenery here isn't all that fantastic. It's only nice to look at. But it's boring being here all the time. It's very monotonous. I don't know why we boast so much about our scenery. Look at your "Cine-tourist club" on television! You wouldn't get bored at some of the scenery they show there. But in our part of the world? Endless steppe? Endless ice-fields? Geysers in Kamchatka? Our Black Sea full of shit and spit? It would make you spit, in fact. Come on, anyone for the cinema?'

FLYING SAUCERS

One of the guests had brought a lecture belonging to some staff member at some institute in Moscow on 'flying saucers'. And the whole rest home went mad about it. There was a whole queue of people waiting to read it. People read it at night. They read it out in groups. And they talked about nothing else. They talked about how creatures of another planet had brought people to Earth for experimental purposes, how we were under observation by them, how they lived for more than a thousand years, as if these were indisputable facts. The 'young' doctor declared that there was little in that 'authentic' information that was true. For example, he doubted that they flew at a speed ten thousand times faster than the speed of light. If they were in a vacuum, the vacuum would have to move as well. And it was simply foolish to reject the theory that man was descended from the animal world. Some of the information concerning the 'saucers' however was no doubt authentic. He would simply prefer to research each fact individually before reaching general conclusions. The All-Rounder rubbed his hands with delight.

'I should think so! Here we are, imagining ourselves to be the only rational creatures in existence, proud of our scientific and technical achievements, and there they are, flying faster than the speed of light (how is that possible?), living to be a thousand, never quarrelling. Our leaders probably lie awake at night with envy. Although, knowing them, the swine will probably soon do a deal with these aliens and get something out of it for themselves. There's one problem, though. They say that these humanoids are teetotal. Civilisation without booze-ups isn't for me. If I had to choose between a thousand years of no booze and seventy years of pubs, I'd choose the latter. And I wonder what they do for women. Maybe they're all the same sex?'

JRF said that he wouldn't change his civilisation for any other, no matter what.

'What do we need to live for a thousand years for when we can't even properly sort out our own six or seven decades? What's the point of flying faster than the speed of light if an ordinary suburban train can transport us to scenery which I guarantee is no worse than on the planet where these flying saucers come from? And if they come to us, it can't be all that wonderful where they come from. And your level of civilisation is not just determined by the level of technology – other factors count as well, such as culture and morality. And if they are thinking, sensate creatures, then they probably live in the same sort of mess as we do, for social laws are universal. Tell me, do you think that much of a judgment could be made about the character of our civilisations from an examination of the crew of one of our space-ships? These crews are composed of privileged people selected according to certain rules, rules which do not coincide with the rules which operate in our rest-home.'

The Old Man said that he personally was delighted by these 'saucers'. Perhaps they would instil a little fear into our leaders, cool their ardour a little bit, reduce their independence. Perhaps They would become a little less harsh, a little less greedy. The All-Rounder had his doubts. Perhaps if these aliens 'bumped off' two or three of our top leaders as an example to others, then they might soften a little. But for some reason these flying saucers weren't all that much in evidence in the vicinity of the Kremlin and the Lubyanka. And they weren't exactly entering the lists on the side of those struggling for human rights. Why was that, he wondered. The Engineer said that living for a thousand years was too long anyway: 'Imagine if Brezhnev lived for a thousand years! Even now he can hardly move his tongue and yet people are forced to bow down before him as if he were God. What will it be like if he lives for another ten years? We'll have to kneel for days on end, extolling his praises. And take the scientific field! You might get to defend your candidate's thesis after three hundred years, and your doctor's thesis three hundred years after that. And would junior research fellows without a higher degree like to spend two hundred years checking references?!?! Imagine the battle that would begin for degrees, positions, flats, dachas! It would be worth committing any crime to make it to Academician and spend the next eight hundred years in blissful idleness. No, I think that even seventy years is a touch too long.'

THE REGIME

The regime in the rest home is strict. And the management tries hard to keep it that way. But as history shows, the stricter a regime, the more often, and the more skifully, it is undermined. As a result a strictly regulated regime in practice metamorphoses into something which has only the appearance of being strict. Formally, everything seems to operate in strict conformity with the rules (i.e. for accounting purposes, or hoodwinking the management, or pulling the wool), whereas in practice not a single one of these rules is observed except for those which cannot be broken or which people don't wish to break. According to the rules, for instance, guests are supposed to go to sleep after 'lights out'. But for over half the guests, their 'real holiday' only begins after lights out.

> We have not yet lost our heads,
> We drink together on our beds
> And man to man's a brother.
> And oft we'll maybe have a lark,
> Or have a sing-song in the dark,
> Or e'en a touch of t'other.

The charm of such activities lies in the fact that they are illicit. Besides, a 'touch of t'other' in the dark isn't so shameful – the partner's defects are not to be seen. And the poverty of life is concealed under a veil of mystery. And even of romanticism. The Engineer observed in this regard that it was only thanks to difficulties and prohibitions that life in our part of the world acquired any meaning: 'Just imagine what it would be like if everything we get with difficulty and illegally could be acquired effortlessly and completely legally?! What pleasure, for instance, would you get out of a filling which they did for you at once and made a good job of and you didn't have to rush around for two weeks, sit in queues and keep changing your arrangements?! Would we be eating this synthetic sausage if it were freely available at every street corner?! But if you get it after standing in a queue for two hours, and in a shop which you just happened to chance upon and which just still happened to sell it, you're ready to have a bite at it right away with your badly filled tooth and to swallow it without chewing. After three years I'm still beside myself with joy at having moved into a twenty-two square metre flat for four people. Suppose they had given me it right away?! There you are, you see! No, I tell you, our classical writers did a good job of dreaming up our new society. The main thing is to make sure that the regime is strict. And then people will be happy when even little infringements take place. We, for example, are deliriously happy that we don't get arrested, since we silently recognise that repressions are the norm of this regime and that their absence is a blessed form of infringement.'

STALIN

Time – after the October events. Place – Stalin's office in Petrograd. There are a few tables. Officials are writing documents. Various people come in, some bringing papers, others taking papers away. Telephones ring. Typewriters chatter. The officials give laconic answers to questions, receive information, issue instructions. One of the people who have come in (a young man in a leather jacket, wearing an officer's peaked cap and carrying a revolver) has perched himself on a desk.

OFFICIAL: Citizen, you are disturbing me at my work!

VISITOR: Shut up, you pen-pushing, bureaucratic ratbag! Do you call that work?! There's a Revolution going on outside! People are at meetings! On platforms! Among the masses! They're fighting against enemies! They are dying, staining the ground with their crimson blood for which . . .

OFFICIAL: This is not a meeting but an institution. And all you've stained so far is our floor with the ink you've just knocked over.

VISITOR (*leaping up, reaching for his revolver*): What?!! Who do you think you're talking to, you counter-revolutionary git?! I'll have you! . . .

STALIN (*appearing at the door and addressing the official*): Arrange for this citizen to be taken to the Cheka on a charge of breaking revolutionary law.

VISITOR: Wait a minute! Let's just get clear who's speaking here in the name of the revolution! I am a personal representative of Trotsky!! Here are my credentials! . . .

Stalin goes over to his table without a word. Armed men enter and take the perplexed Visitor away. The officials once more immerse themselves in their papers and telephone conversations. Stalin works like everyone else, signs documents, issues instructions. It grows dark.

OFFICIALS: Comrade Stalin, the working day came to an end a long time ago.

STALIN: I won't detain you, comrades, you are free to go. (*Turns to the official who mentioned the working day*) Have you got these materials on the Volga basin ready?

OFFICIAL: No, not yet, Comrade Stalin. They'll be ready by lunchtime tomorrow.

STALIN: We need them by morning.

OFFICIAL: Very good, Comrade Stalin.

Some of the officials leave. Some stay. Stalin continues to work on his papers, only stopping from time to time to light his pipe. A clock strikes midnight. Stalin gets up and begins to walk up and down between the tables in his office. His colleagues devour him with their eyes.

STALIN: The historical process is a complex and tricky affair. There is the froth on top and deep currents which are concealed. It has its fatal whirlpools and its quiet, idyllic backwaters. The revolution . . . Where does the revolution take place? On the streets? At meetings? At mass-meetings? Of course. But that is only the froth of the revolution. Its deep current is flowing here: it is you and I and our monotonous routine work. The revolution-ary froth has carried off almost all the notable figures of the revolution and turned their heads. Where are they? They're on the platforms. In their mass they believed that the word is the demagogic weapon of the revolution. But after all, people have to eat and sleep. Clothe themselves. Move around. They need to be fed and armed. They have to be assembled and distributed in groups. Somebody has to appoint them to posts, keep track of things, issue instructions. The revolution is first and foremost a new way of organising the mass millions of the population. But our leaders only know one thing: the masses and us. Or to put it more accurately, the masses and I. Here's a very simple task for the revolution. There's an S.R. uprising boiling up in Yaroslavl. We have to send an armed detachment to suppress it, let's say a thousand men. That's a regiment. Two battalions. Four companies. Twenty machine guns, five other pieces of ordnance. Commanders and commissars have to be appointed, the troops trained, educational work carried out. We have to supply food, transport, opportunities for rest. It's the easiest thing in the world to produce a fiery speech at a meeting of the Central Committee and spit out a slogan such as: 'No mercy for the rebels!' How do you carry it out? Without us and without our boring work which goes unnoticed, not a single one of the slogans produced by our leaders on the platforms would get carried out. The real revolution doesn't get done during the day, but in the dark. At night. But just be patient, comrades! A little time will pass and the real creators of the revolution will make themselves known. But for now – it's back to work. The materials for the Central Committee have to be ready by morning. We have to make it clear to these bletherers what the true state of the country is. Let's get on with it!

AUTHOR: Stalin's habit of working at night was not a personal whim but a matter of principle. At night things appear in a different guise (I nearly said – in a different light) than by day. I myself was a witness to the fact that on more than one occasion decisions to kill people which were postponed until the morning were never, in fact, taken. Night is a time for tragedy, whereas the morning and the daytime are times for comedy or sentimental drama. But that's a detail. What is important is how one perceives the essence of revolution in principle. Lenin was only beginning to get over his romantic conceptions of revolution, whereas Stalin had been free of them from the start. Lenin sensed this advantage of Stalin's and at the same time was afraid of it. He sensed that there was going to be a changing of the revolutionary guard, and that there was a new type of revolutionary coming along, without whom it would be impossible to preserve the gains of the revolution and build a new society. But he did not want to admit it, even to himself. Lenin's 'Guards' put a lot of effort into preventing Stalin's approaching 'army' from taking over by distributing it in bureaux, offices and staff headquarters, thereby strengthening it and hastening their own destruction.

A LETTER TO HERSELF

Okay, I've had the fresh air up to here,
The stomping in the club, the whoring 'round.
Our next meal fills us all with dread and fear,
And friendship round a bottle's hardly sound.
The birds' incessant chirping leaves me cold,
I've had my fill of Nature's beauteous fare.
My restlessness can scarcely be controlled.
The boredom makes me want to tear my hair.

A NEW FRIEND

People get to know each other quickly in a rest home and JRF became friendly with the Candidate. The latter lived in a two-bed dormitory in the first block. For some reason the second bed was unoccupied and the Candidate persuaded the director to let JRF have it. There was a desk and reading lamp in the ward which the Candidate put entirely at JRF's disposal. If JRF worked late into the night, the Candidate would not get angry or demand that JRF put out the light. But more important was the fact that he turned out to be an interesting and tireless conversationalist.

'Who was really the author of Stalin's theoretical works?'

'What difference does it make? It's a pseudo-problem arising out of the modern practice of composing speeches, articles and books for the leadership.'

'It's interesting, nonetheless. I've had a look at what Petin wrote during that period, and Stanis and many others who were connected with Stalin's works one way or another and yet I never solved the riddle of the latter. There's a break in the pattern, a shift. I have the feeling that there's someone entirely unknown at the back of it. It would be interesting to carry out a linguistic analysis by computer.'

'Don't overestimate the power of machines. There's always some sort of historical enigma in such cases. There's an analogous situation with the authors of the New Testament. But I'm inclined to think that Stalin wrote his works himself. In the main at any rate. It's possible that somebody did the editing or provided the basis. But the main work was his. After all, he studied in a seminary. That's where he gets his style from. Even before the revolution he used to write to the newspapers and was inclined to theorise. And after the revolution almost everyone became a theorist. It was in the spirit of the times. There were word merchants of every description. And Stalin didn't have any success. His stuff looked pretty impoverished against that background. But the situation began to change rapidly. Important theoreticians and orators were removed and liquidated. Naturally Stalin's works began to become prominent and become thrust on people by an army of toadies. And they began to suit the huge mass of the population which was involved in ideological indoctrination. Stalin was the main author of *On Dialectical and Historical Materialism*. That was the effect of an epoch and not the product of an individual.'

'And yet I still can't accept that the problem is unimportant. Take Brezhnev, for example. You would think that he had everything: the rank of marshal, the Order of Victory, his Constitution, full power, a biography, his collected works ... But there's something missing which would allow comparison with Stalin. What is it? I think that it is the most important thing: an ideological revolution. You won't get very far on "developed socialism".'

'Well, that's impossible for him; he's not destined to be a classical writer on marxism.'

'Why not? All he needs are a few pronouncements to start with. Then a passage in a speech. Then a few little articles. Then a special Plenum and a special speech. Then a book. Then the gigantic political enlightenment and propaganda network and its tens of thousands of ideologists, writers and journalists. Technically that's not a problem. That's not the point.'

'What is the point, then?'

'There isn't anyone at the moment who could do for our times what the unknown "Stalin" did for his.'

'Do you think that there will be such a person?'

'It's possible.'

'I won't argue. But I have a piece of friendly advice for you: don't talk to anyone else about this. As far as I am concerned, consider that this conversation never took place. Tell me frankly, you surely don't consider him to be a genius, do you?'

'That's not the point. In the animal world things that crawl produce things that crawl and things that fly produce things that fly. We humans all derive from the same source but we go on to produce different types of both crawlers and flyers. And each type has its outstanding examples. From the point of view of some, outstanding examples of others are regarded as degenerate if the former came first. From the point of view of the highest achievements of culture, Stalin and his band are a bunch of dregs and cretins. According to the criteria which apply to the measurement of cultural achievement. But from our point of view, even the greatest cretin doesn't reach the level of normal mediocrity. They say that the Koreans consider Kim Il-Sung to be the apotheosis of creation. The Chinese thought it was Mao Tse-Tung. But we laugh at them. Stalin's not a joke, since he belongs to our ant-heap.'

'Do you know what is most irritating and seductive about stalinist history? It's that you can become the genius of geniuses with a primitive intellect and banal blather. Every untalented individual knows that he is brighter than this "genius of geniuses". This flatters him and gives him hope. Stalin, who excites us so much, isn't a real person but a general characteristic of the "new man" and his aspirations.'

FLYING SAUCERS

The room was suddenly drenched in a pleasant blue light and JRF saw Them. There were six of Them. Three of Them were unusually tall – over four metres, or so it seemed to JRF. 'That's strange,' thought JRF. 'How do They fit in to this room which is only three metres high?' They were of athletic build and very similar to Greek statues. Their faces were reminiscent of Michelangelo's David, a replica of which JRF had seen more than once in the Museum of Fine Arts. However, unlike the statues or David, They had no sexual organs. 'We don't need them,' said the one in the middle, who was evidently the chief of these humanoids. 'We live for a thousand years and produce a new generation when necessary in our laboratories.' The other three creatures were not more than a metre tall and looked rather ugly. They stood behind the giants. 'These are our servants,' said the Chief (JRF thought that it was the Chief although the latter was standing absolutely motionless.) 'They are bio-robots, artificial creatures.'

'Why have you come to me?' asked JRF (or rather thought.) 'And what do you propose to do with me?'

'To tell you that you are wrong,' answered the Chief. 'And to show you the real future that awaits your fellow planet dwellers. Come with us!' It was enough for JRF to think of getting up and moving and he was transported at lightning speed with the aliens into a ... for some reason he knew right away ... spaceship standing outside in a flowerbed.

'It's one paradox after another,' thought JRF. 'The spaceship is about two kilometres in diameter, not less, yet can be deposited on a flowerbed small enough to make even a cat feel cramped.'

'There's nothing paradoxical about it,' said the Chief. 'When we need to, we can make space expand and contract. Time as well, incidentally. By making time expand we have increased our life-span to a thousand years.'

'That's nonsense,' thought JRF. 'It's logically impossible, and I'm prepared to prove it.'

'That's one of the reasons why we chose precisely you,' said the Chief, 'for all our achievements have been obtained contrary to logic.'

'Surely not thanks to the dialectic?' laughed JRF.

'Precisely,' said the Chief.

'In that case, you should have chosen one of our marxist-leninists,' thought JRF.

'We have chosen you because you are right and therefore dangerous,' said the Chief. 'You are right and wrong at the same time. Who are we? From your earthly point of view we are gods, for we exist contrary to common sense and your science. For example, you maintain that it is impossible to move faster than the speed of light. But we do. How? There are different means. For instance, we contract space and expand time. Where are our homes? We don't need them, and therefore we can imagine any homes we like and they can be instantly realised. But we prefer to hover in an energy field which is most suitable for us. We derive all our sustenance from it without having to think about it. We don't have any sexes and therefore we can conceive of any number of different sexes and sexual relations. And that's enough for them to exist. Education and upbringing? We don't need them, for we acquire everything we need along with our physical size, which is practically instantaneous. We immediately appear as we are and remain in that state for ever. Our thousand year life-span is determined by the programme which is implanted in us at the embryonic stage. We merely cognise and derive intellectual pleasure. We have conquered the Universe to an unimaginable, virtually limitless extent. And we have created civilisations of rational beings on all the planets (all of them, mark you!) which are suitable for the existence of biological creatures. We have carried out a theoretical study of all the logically conceivable variants of civilisation and tested them in practice with the aim of selecting the most viable and promising ones. And do you know what conclusion we came to? The best of all conceivable civilisations is your communist one. Both Marx and Lenin, even Stalin, were created by us. Not Khrushchev and Brezhnev. They are your own product. We simply decided to let you see what you were capable of yourselves, without our intervention.'

'But on what criteria are you judging?' thought JRF. 'Why have you decided that the communist way of life is better than the Western?'

'Because it is more natural, stable and promising from the point of view of our planned ideal,' said the Chief. 'It is the only path which can lead to our ideal. All the rest are dead-ends.'

'But why your ideal?' thought JRF. 'We might have our own.'

'You can't have anything of your own,' said the Chief.

THE ENGINEER'S IDEA

Given the general excitement about 'flying saucers', the Engineer put forward the idea for a science fiction novel in pure Soviet style. For instance, some cosmonauts have been flying for a long, long time and want to land on a planet, let's say they need to spend a penny. They approach one planet and there's a huge queue of space-ships waiting to land. They approach another one and it's shut for repairs. They fly to a third one but it's out of space-rocket fuel. They want to turn back but all traffic has been stopped: the General Secretary of the Communist Party of our galaxy is meeting the Chairman of the Supreme Soviet of the neighbouring galaxy. It would make you despair, wouldn't it?

NIGHT-TIME CONVERSATIONS

'Take, for example, the key functionaries on the rest-home staff. The Director represents the General Secretary, the Chairman of the Presidium and the Supreme Head of Command, the Senior Medical Officer represents the President of the Council of Ministers and the Minister of Health. And the activities organiser epitomises in his idiot persona the Ideologist-in-Chief and the Minister of Culture. It is as difficult to explain how one gets to be an activities organiser in a rest home as it to explain how Suslov comes to be the Ideologist-in-Chief and Furtseva or Demichev Ministers of Culture. The culturo-educative aspect of the rest home (notice: not just cultural but also educative – with the accent on the latter) is unusually wide-ranging. It encompasses television, the showing of films, specially selected with an eye to the concrete situation in the country and the category of resident (and for that reason it is always the same films which are chosen – on Lenin, on improving agriculture, on Brezhnev); the organisation of lectures on the international situation, on the decisions of the latest Plenums of the Central Committee and the latest Brezhnev speeches, conducting excursions to model enterprises, and to places associated with military glory or with Lenin; the organisation of do-it-yourself activities, i.e. mainly singing old songs ('Katyusha', etc) or dancing Russian folk dances; the organisation of quizzes and mass-participation games in the club or in the country; the organisation of days of voluntary unpaid work, meetings and assemblies. And a lot more, depending on what is going on at any particular moment (e.g. public holidays) or on local conditions (for instance billiards). The activities organiser is also responsible for organising the music for dances, reasoning with drunkards and calling the police – if things get out of hand. From this point of view the activities organiser fulfils the functions of the Head of the KGB and the Minister of Home Afffairs. Finally, he has to organise sports activities – select volley-ball teams in the various blocks and organises a league championship, select a rest-home team and organise a match with the Ministry of the Coal Industry's rest home. The duties of the Director, the Senior Medical Officer and the other members of the staff are just as varied. So there is nothing surprising in the fact that there is an attempt to distribute these roles, functions and duties among different people. How is that to be done? By fighting for more staff. What could justify that? An increase in the number of guests. And what does that lead to? An increase in the number of beds. Add to that the concern of the Party for the workers' rest and recreation and an increased allocation of resources. That increase might be insignificant but it is still an increase in principle: self-financing beds might be squeezed out of it, and more staff. Generally speaking, there is a complex process of social development going on and it is moving in the only direction open to it – towards communism. If the rest home is large enough, the Director and Senior Medical Officer will have their deputies, instead of one activities organiser there will be several, there will be someone in charge of PT, someone else in charge of the club, there'll be a specialist in do-it-yourself activities. And the Party-State functions mentioned above will be distributed among different people. It goes without saying that the accounts department will grow, as will the canteen ... Perhaps we'll leave the canteen out of it, just so as not to spoil our mood absolutely. There are two conflicting trends as regards the inter-relationship of guest numbers and staff numbers. In so far as the rest-home budget depends on the number of guests, there is a tendency to increase the number of guests that can be catered for on a fixed unit basis. Moreover, this tendency chimes in with general decrees about concern for the well-being of the workers and the extent of their recreation. But with the increase in the number of guests there is an inevitable increase in the number of staff catering for them, moreover the rate of growth in the latter is greater. This chimes in with official decrees about improving workers' conditions in the field of recreation and about improving management. These conflicting tendencies produce a more or less stable correlation of magnitudes which coincide surprisingly well with analogous magnitudes in the sphere of labour. In theory, in our part of the world not every type of recreation is recognised as legitimate, but only the active type, as a result of which it becomes a serious affair. Work, on the other hand, given our general tendency to sloppiness and idleness, gradually becomes a means of recreation and a respite from menial housework. For that reason the boundaries between rest and work are erased for us – there's another source of development for you of marxist-leninist theory. How do you like the picture, eh? So you can imagine the situation in society as a whole. And of course, you have to keep an eye on this great crowd of staff and guests, otherwise they'd nick everything in a flash. So that means a system of checks, supervision and control. And that's again people, people and more people. Are you not asleep yet?'

'No. But I've been interpreting everything you've been saying to suit my point of view. If such a parasitical chain-reaction is generated, that means that the fundamental principles of social organisation themselves are defective. Tell me why it is that an analogous rest home in the West would be served by at most ten staff, instead of a hundred, and much more efficiently to boot.'

'Self-interest. A different type of guest. If we sent our Ivan to their boarding houses, we would instantly impose our own style on them, despite their self-interest.'

'But "our Ivan" is a product of our society.'

'Just as our society is a product of "our Ivan".'

STALIN

AUTHOR: I will take that last point further. When people say that Stalin was Lenin's faithful disciple and that stalinism is leninism in practice, they are talking nonsense. They are qualitatively different phenomena, arising out of different origins. Lenin is a historical figure, whereas Stalin is a sociological figure. To understand Lenin and leninism one has to study the concrete historical conditions and circumstances of Russia and Europe at the end of the last century and the beginning of this one, i.e. before the revolution. Lenin is to be explained in terms of the past. To understand Stalin, one has to examine what happened in the Soviet Union as a direct result of his activity and after it, i.e. after the revolution. Stalin is to be explained in terms of the future. Lenin signalled a changing of the times, whereas Stalin is something durable, regenerative, constant. History took its course. People climbed into armoured cars, delivered speeches, seized caches of weapons, telephone exchanges, stood people against a wall and shot them, galloped around with unsheathed sabres shouting 'Hurrah'. And during this time, unnoticed, invisible, something was maturing which I call sociology. After all, for Chapaev to be able to gallop around with his sabre unsheathed and his cloak fluttering behind him, there had to be an office in the division and desks had to be set up in it and people put behind these desks. Documents had to be signed, seals had to be affixed, stamps of various kinds were needed . . . And when the historical drama was played out and the smoke had cleared, it became clear just what the result was, what, in fact, had remained from history. History had galloped off into the past and the office with its papers and seals, boredom, titles, hierarchy, red tape, eye-wash and other delights remained. I repeat and emphasise the point that one has to take a society in its contemporary mould and as it operates before our very eyes. And then it will be clear why Chapaev galloped around with his unsheathed sabre: not at all in order to save suffering mankind but so that, in particular, officials from the apparatus of all sorts of authorities can travel in the cars put at their disposal to the

411

secret shops for goods which are not on sale at ordinary shops, acquire luxurious flats and dachas, use the best resorts, benefit from the latest achievements in medicine . . . Stalin understood this, or, more accurately, sensed it. And even more accurately, he simply acted in this sociological tranche of existence. And when history had played her part, she became a hindrance to sociology. History never has roots. Sociology is nothing but roots. And therefore the historical froth was carried away by the current, whereas the roots of sociology put forth shoots and then bore fruit. Lenin acted in accordance with the laws of history, Stalin according to the laws of sociology. And that is why Stalin won.

PREPARING FOR THE VISIT OF A VIP

The guests had been told on the very day of their arrival that comrade Suslikov himself, head of the rest-home-and-spa division, was going to pay a visit and they were asked accordingly to demonstrate a sense of acute responsibility. The VIP had been expected to pay a visit before, but had postponed it, firstly because of bad weather and then allegedly because of his health. But everyone knew what was meant by the 'bad weather' (the weather had been excellent, much better than it was now) and by his 'health' (comrade Suslikov always arrived in a state of playful drunkenness, scarcely able to move his tongue or any of his extremities). The fact of the matter was that the Presidium of the Academy was experiencing some temporary difficulty in connection with an investigation being carried out into the fraudulent machinations of the head of the housing department, and comrade Suslikov was afraid this investigation might spill over into his department.

Two days later it was confirmed that the VIP would arrive on Friday morning. He would be accompanied by his senior inspector of cut-rate rest-home holidays, comrade Kuktychapagirova, the vice-president's secretary Lenochka (who had taken the Friday and the following Monday off specially) and a colleague from the first department Yuri, the blue veins on whose face from too many booze-ups made him look as if he had been specially tattooed with the letters KGB. Everyone in the Academy knew Yuri, since there was never a banquet to celebrate the successful defence of a dissertation at which he wasn't present.

The rest home engaged in feverish preparations for the visit of the VIP and his suite. The guests were compelled to clean their dormitories from top to bottom. Great care was taken to ensure that there were no spirits on the bedside tables. Comrade Suslikov was very particular about that. After that the guests had to tidy up the grounds, especially the area around the bungalow in which the VIP and his suite would be staying, and the path between the bungalow and the dining room. The director himself instructed the guests in the club about their behaviour. During the visit women were forbidden to wear trousers – comrade Suslikov did not approve of these new fashions which had come to us from the decadent West. Besides, comrade Suslikov was used to putting his hand up women's skirts, and even the long, grasping paw of comrade Suslikov wouldn't get very far up a pair of trousers.

A four-bed dormitory in the house was assigned to Comrade Suslikov as his private quarters. They installed a double bed, covered with a crimson silk bedspread. Members of his suite were given single rooms on the first floor of the same house. The food prepared consisted of black and red caviar, sturgeon, cooked sausage, fresh chicken. There was a wide range of wines, including 'Crimean champagne', the existence of which had hitherto been unsuspected, and even fresh strawberries – comrade Suslikov adored fresh strawberries with whipped cream. A twenty-four hour duty roster was set up to forestall any possible provocative acts – you know yourself the kind of times we live in nowadays!

The next thing was to prepare the residents. All those who were inclined to complain were assembled in the director's office where he listened to what was bothering them. He gave instructions that part of their complaints should be rectified for the duration of the visit. They got round the more obstinate whiners by deception: a free excursion to a dairy farm was arranged for that Friday with a promise that they would be given milk fresh from the cow.

That only left the problem of the dogs, in particular Dissident. As far as the ordinary dogs were concerned, the solution was brilliantly simple. The cook collected a heap of bones in a sack and carried them off, followed by the fawning pack, to the rest home belonging to the Ministry for coal-mining ten kilometres away. And all the dogs stayed there for a while. In the case of Dissident, a bit more effort was required. The guests spent a whole day combing the grounds, but to no avail. Meanwhile Dissident was lying under the porch of the house in which the VIP was going to stay. The police were called in. They brought a tracker dog who found Dissident. The latter was put in a sack and taken off to the local police station.

THE FIRST BLOCK

The first block, to which JRF transferred, carried certain privileges. On the one hand it was situated two steps from the dining room and the club and on the other, two steps from the wood and a little stream. And he could see from his windows all the beauties of nature. Not to mention the fact that all the dormitories were for one or two beds (and some of the dormitories even had two rooms – for especially important people). These dormitories were for serious people who persistently demanded peace and quiet and consequently the arrival of JRF was met with a certain amount of suspicion, even hostility. But the New Friend circulated a rumour to the effect that JRF was an especially talented young scholar, that he would soon get his doctorate, bypassing the candidate stage, that he was working on X himself (ssh! that's just between ourselves of course!), and JRF was admitted to the intellectual élite of Soviet society almost as an equal.

In the dormitory to the right of the one occupied by JRF and the New Friend, was a professor of sixty or more (rumour had it that this was his third stay in a row), who was a fervent devotee of Academician Nikolkin. Academician Nikolkin had occupied major posts under Stalin and was responsible for the production of aircraft engines, but after Stalin's death he devoted his extraordinary talent and unshakable will, for which Stalin had liked him, totally and utterly to the business of self-preservation. To this end he invented his own particular system, which brought him immeasurably greater fame than his obsolescent aircraft engines. The key element in Nikolkin's system was jogging, taking large steps, and jumping up and down without bending the knees. The idea behind that was that the organism would be shaken up and everything that was harmful or dead would gradually be shaken out from the cells to the surface. The Professor used Nikolkin's system and every day, whatever the weather, he would jog for ten kilometres, taking large steps, and jump up and down for an hour without bending his knees, thereby making life miserable for the doctor who lived below him who was an aficionado of the gentle walk around the neighbourhood during which one could reflect on the meaning of life and enjoy the unique beauty of nature. And although the Professor lost a dozen or so of his last remaining grey hairs and his false teeth fell out at every jump, there was no power left on earth that could prevent him jogging himself into the crematorium.

The neighbour on the other side, on the contrary, was a fervent devotee of Academician Amukhin, who also developed his own system. The kernel of Amukhin's system was contained in the following principle: eat as little as possible and work yourself into the ground. Moreover, work was not interpreted by Amukhin in any marxist sense, i.e. as planned activity for the creation of material and spiritual wealth, but as a means of using up calories. In particular he recommended doing up to five thousand squats a day. But he was categorically against jogging at full stride and jumping up and down since he imagined that something useful and vital might get shaken out of the cells on to the surface. And the neighbour on the left, having first guzzled everything on offer in the dining room (it had been paid for, after all!), including seconds, would then expel with maniacal persistence superfluous calories from the organism, increasing the number of squats to thousands per twenty-four hour period. And nothing could stop him either, not even rapidly swelling veins in one leg and incipient embolism in the other.

The neighbours conducted endless discussions on the merits and demerits of each system, quoting from the specialist literature in four foreign languages, involving in these discussions almost every inhabitant in the block. The women's half of the block, occupied by obese and horribly ugly female doctors, professors and candidates, was going mad trying to solve the problem of losing weight by fasting. Ten times a day they remembered how much they weighed and what a figure they had when they were twenty, and, swearing by what they had read in Polish magazines, also swore to return to that mythical state. This, however, did not stop them eating everything they were given to the last crumb, including bread, semolina and porridge, macaroni and butter. 'The idea of self-preservation forms the basis of the life of our creative intelligentsia,' remarked the New Friend in this connection. 'This is what awaits you and me when we make it to doctor and professor.'

A two-bed dormitory on the first floor was occupied by a female associate member of some southern republican Academy of Sciences. She was obese, stupid, self-satisfied and haughty, festooned with ear-rings, cluttered with stones and chains and wore two rings on each one of her ten fat hairy fingers. Next door, in a single bed dormitory, resided a toothless female doctor, eaten up with jealousy and contempt for the associate member. The Female Doctor was a head taller than the Associate Member but felt ten times her superior intellectually. She constantly carried around with her a detective novel in English and gave the impression that she could read it and understand it without using a dictionary. To draw attention to this remarkable fact she would invite everyone to discuss the meaning of English words which crop up in the elementary stages of a primary school English-language course. Sensing that JRF knew the language she began to flirt with him, using that as a pretext.

'Watch out,' said the New Friend. 'Creatures like her tend to go in for primitive sexual perversions. Why doesn't she have any teeth? She's not short of money. She's most likely tight-fisted and is waiting to get her false teeth done for nothing.'

The Toothless Doctor was counting on being admitted as an associate member to the Academy of Sciences of the USSR, which is a whole order of magnitude greater than being an associate member of a republican Academy of Sciences. Although the Associate Member was convinced that the Doctor would not be proposed for membership, or that if she were, she would fail to be admitted for sure, the prospect disturbed her nonetheless. And therefore she demonstrated her friendly feelings for the Doctor in every possible way. The latter reciprocated in full. The Associate Member was a non-paying guest of the rest home – as a result of a phone-call from on high. The Doctor, for her part, had been offered a reduced rate and had not had to pay more than ten roubles. She regarded that nonetheless as daylight robbery, since she considered that she deserved better. Especially since an Associate Member of some republican Academy or other could stay for free.

NIGHT-TIME CONVERSATIONS

'I have never been to the West, but I've read and heard something about it. And I don't have any illusions about it at all. The very fact that, despite the nightmarish lessons they can learn from us, they are rushing headlong towards the same kind of mess that we find ourselves in, is enough to tell us that life in the West is by no means a piece of cake for everyone. And yet I still can't understand why it is being attracted into this abyss.'

'Because the abyss is too deep. The deeper the abyss, the greater the illusion of freedom and the longer it lasts.'

'But the less chance there is of escaping from it.'

'From what – the illusion or the abyss?'

'Obviously the illusion, for there's no escape from such an abyss.'

'Everything in the world is relative. If the fall lasts for long enough it's entirely possible to regard it as flight.'

'I've just had an amusing thought. Why did these idiots decide that the principle "to everyone according to their needs" was such a good one? Imagine the situation. You work worse than I do, yet get more according to your needs than I do, or just as much. Why should I regard that as fair? I assure you, even if this stupid principle were to be realised in practice, the best people of the future would oppose it with all their might. And anyway, why should we take the conjectures of our predecessors at their face value? We've got heads on our shoulders. We can think things through quite well for ourselves. And there's not such a wealth of wisdom invested in these slogans of the past. Rather the reverse.'

'The trial of the "Workers' group" keeps getting postponed. Even the authorities don't know how to deal with them – whether to treat them as mentally ill or try them as criminals for crimes they didn't manage to carry out. They would like to have it both ways, i.e. establish as ideological dogma the idea that only insane people could be dissatisfied with the way things are and want to criticise, but at the same time make such insanity punishable as a premeditated crime.'

'That "group" is the invention of a madman.'

'In this world everything is the invention of a madman. We're talking here of a second order of madness. And even of a third. This is an absolutely new phenomenon in psychiatry. I'm selling the discovery for a half-litre!'

ON THE FUTURE

For some, it seems to be the case,
The future from now on will be
The laser beam or flight in space,
Or synthesis of man-made pee.
For others it's the tone uncouth
Of leaders' demagogic swill
And camps for those who speak the truth,
Informers 'singing' with a will.
How can we solve the problem, pray?
I reconcile both points of view:
I see these same space ships, but they
Have labour camps aboard them, too.

STALIN

The year is 1922. There is about to be a Plenary session of the Central Committee of the Party. Party leaders have assembled in Lenin's office in the Kremlin. Among them are Trotsky, Zinoviev, Bukharin and others. Stalin isn't there – he is not yet one of the leading figures of Party or State. They discuss the agenda for the forthcoming session, nominate their candidates for elective positions, sketch out resolutions, in short rehearse the forthcoming show. The last question to be discussed concerns the secretariat of the Central Committee. This question is considered to be of tenth-rate importance since up to now the functions of secretary of the Central

Committee have been carried out by women, and a relatively small number of women at that. And for that reason it is discussed in a humorous fashion, rather than any other. Lenin tries to be serious, but even he can't conceal his off-hand attitude to this question.

LENIN: It's purely women's work, of course, no offence to the ladies present. But what can you do, now that our Party has become a party of government and the bureaucracy has mushroomed. Of course, we're going to get rid of all sorts bureaucratic nonsense in time, including inside the Party, but for the moment we have to face facts. We shall have to extend and strengthen the secretariat. As far as the post of first secretary is concerned, I . . .

TROTSKY (*interrupting Lenin*): It's demeaning for Party leaders to have to fiddle around with paper-shuffling. I consider that we should nominate for this post someone who is known in the Party, but who does not play a primary role in it. I should have thought that Koba would be suitable.

LENIN: Who? I don't remember . . .

BUKHARIN: Dzhugashvili. Recently he's begun to sign his articles on the nationality question with the pseudonym 'Stalin'.

TROTSKY: Stalin, of course, is barely literate. His pretension to the role of theoretician is laughable. But he is pedantically detail-minded, persistent and a through-and-through formalist. The bureaucratic aspect of our Party activity would be entirely to his taste.

LENIN: I have no objections. We'll propose Stalin. But how is he, himself, going to react to such an insignificant post?

ZINOVIEV: From his point of view it's a major promotion. Right now he's in charge of the People's Commissariat for Nationalities. It's a fictitious body, and any minor bureaucrat like Mikoyan or Molotov could handle it.

KAMENEV (*to general laughter*): Even Budenny or Voroshilov could handle it.

LENIN: I think we'd better invite . . . what's his name? . . . Stalin in for a chat.

Half of the assembled body rush off to look for Stalin. Lenin becomes immersed in thought, gets a piece of paper and begins feverishly to write down the main points of his speech. The others split up into little groups, chat, tell jokes about Lenin, Budenny and Chapaev.

TROTSKY: On the eve of the coup Lenin phones up Podvoisky and asks him to tell the Petrograd proletariat that they can go out for a drink that night by all means, but not to forget that there's to be a revolution on the following day. Ha-ha-ha-ha-ha-!!

ZINOVIEV: Budenny's orderly rushes into staff headquarters and yells that the Whites have attacked from the rear. Budenny leaps on his horse and yells: 'For-ward!' Ha-ha-ha!!

BUKHARIN: Did you hear the one about Chapaev, after he had been a month in the military academy explaining to Petka why you hear train wheels rattle on the rails? The area of a circle is Pi-r-squared, and it's the square that does the rattling. Ha-ha-ha!

Gradually the people who have been looking for Stalin come back. About ten minutes later Stalin makes an unhurried entrance wearing a paramilitary jacket and boots and smoking his pipe. He speaks good Russian without an accent.

LENIN: There's a proposal to transfer you to work in the secretariat of the Central Committee. As First Secretary.

STALIN: I don't object. But on one condition. The secretariat of the Central Committee is becoming more and more important in relation to the Party's work of governing the state. Therefore, instead of instituting a post of First Secretary, there should be a General Secretary, who should be in charge of the whole technical apparatus of the Central Committee.

LENIN: I think that comrade Dzhu ... Stalin's proposal is entirely reasonable. Are there any objections? Agreed, Comrade Stalin! We shall propose you for the post of General Secretary of the Central Committee. You are free to go, comrade.

TROTSKY (*after Stalin has gone, with a laugh*): General Head Clerk of the Central Committee!! Ha-ha-ha! I can just imagine what that bureaucratic clod will get up to in his red-tape machine! ... Anyway, it's time we went, isn't it?

THE VIP ARRIVES

At breakfast time on Friday everyone got a few grains of black caviar and a few grains of red caviar. This induced a festive mood and after breakfast everyone tripped off, suitably dressed for the occasion and singing patriotic songs, to the gate at the entrance to the rest-home grounds. They roared out in chorus the famous 'Katyusha' five times in a row. While they waited for the guest to arrive they played a variety of silly games. The Associate Member flirted vigorously with the All-Rounder. The admirer of Academician Nikolkin seized the Little Lady by her outstanding curves and tried in every way to discredit the 'youth of today'. A girl known as the 'Goodly Maiden' clung to JRF. The Little Lady was jealous and threw poisonous looks in his direction. The All-Rounder went off from time to time to throw up in the bushes – he had had a skinful the night before at the police station, drinking with the policemen he had accompanied when they were removing Dissident. In a word, everyone was very merry.

At last a mud-spattered Volga appeared, bearing the VIP and his suite. The guests clustered together at the edge of the road and waved in greeting. The car stopped. Comrade Suslikov got out, looked at those assembled through lack-lustre eyes, raised his hat and said 'Greetings, comrades'. The director himself rushed up to him, followed by a cringing head-cook and matron carrying bread and salt and a key to the house on a red cushion. Comrade Suslikov shook the director's hand, ordered the bread and salt and the cushion with the key to be dumped in the boot and got back into the car. And everyone moved off in the direction of the rest home. In front was the mud-spattered Volga, alongside, holding on to the open window minced the director, giggling with the passengers. Behind them came the guests, in order of their academic qualifications, titles and official positions. At the back trailed the All-Rounder, green from the previous night's booze-up and with bitten hands. He had tried to stroke Dissident the night before, but the latter had neither understood nor accepted his good intentions.

'Listen, mates,' said the Old Man. 'Who do they take us for? What's going on here?'

'They take us for what we are,' said the Engineer. 'Idiots and toadies.'

'This is merely a typical, completely normal, spectacle in our communist way of life,' said the Candidate. 'Don't pay any attention. Let these dregs amuse themselves. The main thing is that while he's here, we'll be well fed.'

HOMO SOVIETICUS

After the All-Rounder had expressed his opinion of the leaders of the Party and government in his usual terms, the Toothless Doctor said that he was not 'one of us'. The All-Rounder took offence and called her some nasty names. She in turn took offence and threatened to take the All-Rounder to court for 'insulting the dignity of a Soviet scholar'. The collective then took a hand and the opposing parties 'kissed and made up'. But a problem arose: how do you recognise 'one of us'? JRF came out with an unofficial lecture on the topic.

Homo sapiens is a complex creature, but *homo sovieticus* is super-complex. That is understandable: in him the development of all matter (living or dead, half-alive or half-dead) reaches its peak. Homo sovieticus is capable of having mutually exclusive opinions about one and the same question, and opposite emotional responses to one and the same stimulus. Imagine: he can be bitterly happy or cheerfully melancholy, protestingly agree or approvingly object, he can denounce while defending, take the mickey while praising . . . Can you imagine anything like it in the animal world or in Western people, i.e. creatures lower down the evolutionary chain?! Of course, you can find something similar in the West, and, what's more, lots of it. But that means only one thing: homo sovieticus is an international phenomenon. Moreover, he can do all these things not at different times and in different circumstances, as formal logicians erroneously suppose, but at the same time and in the same circumstances, as our dialectical logicians correctly suppose. I will remind you of the fundamental postulate of dialectical logic: truth lies (why doesn't it 'stand' or 'sit'?) not in 'yes' or 'no' but in 'yes-no' and 'no-yes'. Do you remember Lenin's argument with Bukharin about the tumbler? Bukharin asserted that in one respect a tumbler is a vessel for drinking out of, but in another it is an instrument for belting your drinking companion in the face . . . I beg your pardon, hammering in a nail. No, objected Lenin, arguing from the standpoint of dialectical logic, a tumbler is simultaneously, and in the same respect both a vessel for drinking out of and an instrument for bashing your drinking companion in the mouth . . . I beg your pardon, hammering in a nail. Why? Because, (and here's what that dogmatist Bukharin couldn't understand) a tumbler is in all respects a school of communism!

There's your homo sovieticus for you, your 'one of us'! And just try to predict how he will behave! For instance, he's just sworn to you that your conversation with him will remain a secret. And next day he has told the whole town about it. No sooner has he promised to help you than he starts to undermine you. He takes up the struggle for disarmament and doubles the rate of arms production. Having undertaken to liberate the proletariat he not only ends up by oppressing it but also its closest ally – the poorest peasantry. And as for the substratum of the intelligentsia – you might as well save your breath. Or take another example. Homo sovieticus goes off to get some potatoes and says he'll be back in half an hour. You wait for an hour or two and he's not come back. You wait for a third hour and he's still not back. There's no point in waiting. He might come back fifteen days later with a shaven head after a spell in prison for 'minor hooliganism' (he tried something on, for instance, with the drunken potato man for selling rotten potatoes). But he might come back after three hours. He might be happy. He might be cursing with rage. It might be that they were selling bananas round the corner and he managed to get hold of a kilogram. Green ones, of course. But that doesn't matter – they'll ripen instantly in the stomach of homo sovieticus. In short, formal logic has got absolutely no place here. What is required, and I quote our classical writers and Doctor of Philosophical Science Barabanov, is 'dialexical' logic. And the classical writers never lie, although they are constantly in error. Or, rather, they never err, but are constantly lying. They too, after all, are homines sovietici.

'If homo sovieticus is like that, and he seems to be like that, *why* is he like that?' asked the Old Man.

'We'll talk about that another time,' said JRF.

TABLE-TALK

'All this intellectual ferment we're getting these days is the result of two things. The first is connected with the denunciation of stalinism. It's simply a delayed reaction to the past. The second is Western influence – books, films, music, pictures, fashions, tourists coming here, our tourists going there, regular broadcasts from the West aimed at us, unpunished contacts with foreigners, telephone conversations, written correspondence. This factor should not be underestimated.'

'Stalinism is forgotten. The younger generation knows almost nothing about it. And it doesn't mean the same to them when they do find out something about it.'

'It's a bit more complicated than that. There's a kind of historical inertia involved here. It has to do with the transmission of certain attitudes from the older generations to the new. For example, lack of faith in the ideals, disbelief, contempt for the higher leadership. And then, I don't agree that the youth of today doesn't know about stalinism. It knows, all right. Perhaps more than we did. And we found out more than our fathers.'

'And the influence from the West is not all that significant. It's limited to Moscow and a few of the larger cities.'

'Wrong again. Have you done much travelling around the country? I've had to. People listen to the radio everywhere. And everywhere you get people with long hair. And beards are just as common. And they can paint pictures just as well as your Moscow non-conformists. And the jokes are the same.'

'But internal factors play *some* role, surely?'

'Of course. Dissatisfaction at the way things are badly organised. Price rises. Privileges. The occasional arbitrary rule of the leaders. All this is generally known. But take a look at what our dissatisfied and critical minds latch on to and at what causes this internal dissatisfaction. Do they coincide? Here's a surprising example for you. You are familiar with the school "reform" (or what amounts, more accurately, to a new policy for the schools). Do you think people like it? Of course not. But how do people react to it? They regard it as absolutely just. All they do is try and get round it (via string-pulling or bribes). The dissatisfaction itself becomes part of a general mainstream of dissatisfaction, part of that intellectual ferment I mentioned earlier. That's natural, after all. Incidentally, the hatred of the Czechs for us after we crushed them in 1968 manifested itself in part in the fact that the Czech ice-hockey team gave ours a good thrashing.'

'Ours is a country of unlimited possibilities.'

'Impossibilities, more like.'

'One of the regions reported to the Central Committee and to comrade Brezhnev personally that it had completed the harvest operation fifteen minutes ahead of schedule. It was a lie, of course. The General Secretary decided to celebrate this with a visit to the region in question. The local leadership got wind of it and mobilised all their forces. And managed to get the job done in a couple of days.'

'Get the harvest in?!'

'No, of course not! Plough in what they *hadn't* harvested.'

'Have you seen the notice downstairs? Brace yourselves. There's going to be a discussion soon in the club on the second part of Brezhnev's memoirs. The names will be taken of all those who don't show up, and sent to their place of work.'

STALIN

The year is 1924. Stalin and his personal bodyguard and Dzerzhinsky with two lorry-loads of Chekists approach Gorki, where Lenin is convalescing. Stopping short of the palace, the Chekists pile out of the lorries and surround the estate. Some of them with machine-guns are deployed along the road. Dzerzhinsky himself is in charge. 'If one living soul gets in or out of there, I'll shoot you on the spot,' says Dzerzhinsky to his next in command and joins Stalin's convoy. Stalin's motorcade drives up to the palace. Nobody comes out to meet them. Only a few dogs yelp. Stalin enters the building with his suite. Lenin's bodyguard salutes him. Dzerzhinsky says something to him. He answers 'Yessir!' and goes outside. His place is taken by one of Stalin's guards. Krupskaya appears and a frightened cook looks out from behind the door of the dining-room.

KRUPSKAYA (*without greeting them*): Ilich is tired after the hunt and needs to rest. And moreover, he gave categorical instructions that you were not to be received. He is upset by your behaviour and intends to raise the question at the next session of the Central Committee . . .

STALIN (*pushing Krupskaya aside*): Felix, talk to her while I have a chat with Ilich.

LENIN (*at his desk, not turning round*): Nadya, what's all that noise?! I asked not to be disturbed.

STALIN: It is I, Teacher!

LENIN (*spinning round and leaping up from his desk*): I have repeatedly asked you not to call me 'Teacher'. I do not recognise you as my disciple.

STALIN: Who *do* you recognise as your disciple, then? Tricky question, eh? That's the whole point. I'm your only disciple, and a faithful and consistent one. Trotsky, Bukharin and the other bletherers think that they're as good as Lenin. Even when they are talking about you, it's only an excuse to talk about themselves. Only I . . .

LENIN: That's enough! I know what your compliments are worth. What have you come for? I would ask you to make it snappy since today I have to finish an article on reorganising . . .

STALIN: That won't be necessary. We'll do everything that's necessary ourselves.

LENIN: What's that supposed to mean?

STALIN: I have brought you the decision of the Politburo of the Central Committee agreeing to your request about the poison.

LENIN (*confused*): But that request is out of date. I feel marvellous and am ready to take up my duties in the next few days.

STALIN: We know that. But that doesn't matter. The decision of the Politburo of the Central Committee was taken unanimously and has to be enacted to the letter. The interests of the revolution demand it.

LENIN (*alarmed*): You mean . . .

STALIN: Exactly! My dear Teacher, let us speak frankly. Your role in the revolution and in the history of mankind in general is a huge one, and I bow down before you as I would before God. And I swear to you that I shall compel everyone to treat you as God. But for that you have to die.

LENIN (*in shock*): Are you out of your mind?! Do you realise that . . .

STALIN: Absolutely. Lenin dead is more important for the

revolution than Lenin alive. Lenin alive is just another demagogue who has lost a sense of reality and who doesn't understand
that the revolution has finished and that it is time for the high-
flown phrase to be replaced by prosaic, routine work. Lenin dead
is unique, rising up above everyone, eternally wise, omniscient,
prescient. My dear Teacher, a new era has long ago begun in our
country. The people are sick to death of revolution. Your role is
played out. It was, I repeat, a magnificent role. But it's played
out. It is time to leave the stage and make way for other actors.
These last years, you've been behaving like an actor in a bad
provincial theatre who, having played his role, imagines that he
is irreplaceable, doesn't want to leave the stage, teaches other
actors how to act and even instructs the audience on how they're
supposed to watch the idiotic play. And therefore . . .

LENIN (*running to the door and trying to open it*): This is a counter-
revolutionary *coup d'état*! Take me to the Kremlin immediately!
Assemble all the members of the Central Committee! . . .

STALIN: It's too late! Farewell, dear Teacher! I swear that your
name will shine brightly for ever.

*Stalin leaves Lenin's study. Lenin tries to follow but two Chekists push
him back inside. The door closes.*

STALIN (*to Dzerzhinsky*): Get rid of these two immediately and
the rest later. Replace the hired staff in its entirety. And tell this
old bag that if she so much as squeaks I'll boil her alive. And I'll
dirty his name so much that they won't be able to clean it in a
hundred years. She is, when all is said and done, a communist.
She should understand. Get on with it!

BROAD HINTS FROM A DOCTOR

During breakfast the female doctor on duty came up to their
table, cracked a joke and invited JRF to look in at her office: she
wanted to give him a check-up.

'We know these "check-ups",' said the Engineer after she had
gone. 'You're not the first and you'll not be the last. But you're
not half lucky, my lad. Satisfy her heightened sexual needs a
couple of times and you'll get extra, high-grade nosh. Absolutely
legally and above board.'

'This is already enough for me,' said JRF.

'Well, you're a fool,' said the Engineer. 'With principles like that you're never going to make a career. If a bit of good luck lands in your lap – grab it. If you suit her, you'll be able to come here any time you like, without paying, and get a separate dormitory. If I were you . . .'

After breakfast JRF had a shower, changed his underwear, put on a clean shirt and went to the doctor's office. She received him in a short smock which kept coming unbuttoned, either at the top or the bottom, revealing something rather tempting. While she examined JRF she kept touching him with one or other of her protuberances (which was all she seemed to consist of). She pronounced herself satisfied with the results of the check-up.

'You're a little skinny,' she said thoughtfully, placing her hand in an area of interest to urologists. 'But if we feed you up, we'll make quite a man of you. Who looks after you at home? Your mother? Your wife? No one? Ah, well, that explains it.'

At that moment there was a knock on the door. The doctor swore and went out into the corridor. 'Listen,' he heard her say coarsely, 'it's written in Russian in black and white that surgery is from *then* to *then*. Is that clear?' Then she locked the door and sat back down beside JRF. And there was only one possibility of getting out of there. And he took it. 'Just don't prescribe any extra food,' he said as he got dressed.

'Why not?' she asked in surprise.

'It feels uncomfortable to be in a privileged position,' he said.

'Well, you're a fool,' she said. 'You'll never survive with attitudes like that. You're not a dissident, by any chance? No, well, that's good. And I'm going to prescribe a supplementary diet. And you'll spoon it down like a good boy. Otherwise we'll report you to your work! You'll come for check-ups on the following days . . . I'll write the times in for you here.'

He cancelled his walk with the Little Lady that day, claiming that he had a headache.

'And how often are you going to have a headache from now on?' she asked, giving a knowing laugh. 'Not every day, I hope. But it's good that you're being put on a supplementary diet. And don't think of refusing. Take what you can get.'

HOMO SOVIETICUS

You ask why homo sovieticus is like that. For the simple reason that his opinions about things play absolutely no role whatsoever, and, as they say, his emotions wouldn't be enough to make you a pair of underpants. He exists in a situation where opinions, emotions and intentions are merely remnants of the past, with which it is impossible to survive in communist, near-communist, pro-communist and other forms of modern society. The advantage that homo sovieticus has over everyone else, let me emphasise, is not that he has particular opinions, particular emotions, particular aims and goals, but that he has nothing of the sort at all. Homo sovieticus's strength derives, not from the presence of something, but from the absence of that presence. You can lose presence. Presence can be damaged. You can't lose or damage absence. That's the strength of homo sovieticus.

I'll explain what I mean in terms of the following model. Take any piece of matter and begin gradually to remove everything that it contains. But do it in such a way that the absence of every piece of matter can be designated in some way. So that anyone looking at the space occupied by that piece of matter can unerringly determine what was situated where before you removed it. A tricky task, huh? Well, what can you do? We live in a time of insoluble problems. That's just the way it is with homo sovieticus. Take homo sapiens, or his remains which by a miracle have survived in the West, and start to remove all these qualities acquired over the centuries, but in such a way that the empty spaces are clearly labelled to show what was there before. If, for example, you have removed courage, reliability, honour, dignity, morality, conscientiousness, goodness, leave markers in the denuded soul to indicate that here and there are supposed to be courage, reliability, honour, dignity, morality, etc, but that they have disappeared somewhere.

What, you might ask, would be left in a person after such an operation? Nothing, do you think? You're greatly mistaken! The intellect has remained. Do you hear? The in-tell-ect! The ability to think, speak, pose problems, discuss problems, exchange views, and again speak, speak without thinking, discuss without problems. The intellect will remain. And that is more important than that historical lumber which you have cleared out of his soul. And God help you if you make a bad job of cleaning out his soul. If any little bits of the qualities you've removed remain, they will begin to rot in that badly cleaned out soul and give off a foul smell, rather in the way that remains of food in the mouth attack the teeth with all the known consequences. The over-whelming majority of our people have had their souls well cleansed of all the nasty qualities of the past, have been disin-fected and have good steel fillings, some of them even have gold crowns. It is only in a few individual cases that the cleansing process has been carried out negligently. And then you have spiritual complications. But in fact they are a kind of caries of the soul, a bad smell, nothing fragrant.

THE VISIT

As the Candidate had predicted, they were fed excellently over the next few days. They had rassolnik, boiled chicken and rice, and mousse (!!) for dinner. The All-Rounder, who hated anything jelly-like and wobbly, at first squeamishly pushed the mousse away, but later on he pulled it back again and swallowed it with his eyes shut without chewing. 'They might have given us something stronger for the occasion,' he said. 'They're keeping that for this evening,' said the doctor on duty, her opulent curves contained with difficulty inside a snow-white smock.

The VIP and his entourage were served a specially prepared meal in their bungalow. The guest ate a lot but drank even more. After half an hour he was totally incoherent. The glass of 'Crimean champagne' fell from his hand, wine spilled all over the table-cloth and he fell asleep. The director and the senior medical officer carefully carried him off to the bedroom and left him alone with Lenochka, the vice-president's secretary. Yuri sought out the All-Rounder. When they had drunk everything that remained on the table they set off to hunt up some 'girls'.

'I'm fed up with big blondes,' said Yuri. 'Trim brunettes are more the fashion at the moment.'

'Jewish birds, do you mean?' asked the All-Rounder. 'They're even broader in the beam than our women. Well, so be it. Let's have your trim brunette. Only, as regards age . . .'

'That doesn't matter,' said Yuri.

That evening, instead of suppper, there was a sort of banquet laid on in honour of the VIP's arrival. There was a bottle of cheap wine per every four guests. The tables were pushed together. The VIP made a speech. He outlined the prospects for the rest-home/spa construction industry in the current five-year plan and for the next fifty years. When he said that the Party and Government would achieve a thirty per cent increase in the number of rest-home beds, the guests rose to their feet and gave him a standing ovation. The Associate Member made a speech in reply. She talked at boring length about the Party's wise nationalities policy. 'Before the revolution,' she said, 'my people was absolutely illiterate. And now it has its own Academy of Sciences in which there are already five hundred full Academicians and a thousand associate members. The republic has already overtaken England in terms of the number of Doctors of Science . . .' She didn't manage to finish her speech, since the VIP began to feel sick and he was hastily removed to the bungalow. Yuri began to harass the Students' girls. They told him to leave off or they would sort him out. Then Yuri produced his identification. The Students responded by telling him to go to f— and said that they didn't give a hoot in hell for the organisation he represented. This made a favourable impression on Yuri. He invited the Students and their girls and the All-Rounder and his women back to his room, where they could continue their pleasant conversation.

STALIN

Stalin's waiting-room in the Kremlin. The walls are lined with people standing to attention waiting to be received. Among them are Voroshilov, Molotov, Kalinin, Kamenev, Bukharin and many other famous people. Enter Stalin.

STALIN: Comrades! Ilich's condition is hopeless. We must be prepared for the worst. We must prepare the Party and people to accept this heavy loss without panic and with courage. We must convince everyone that there is a united and monolithic Leninist Central Committee. Let Lenin's death itself be a powerful factor in strengthening the Party and uniting the whole population of the country around it. It is necessary for all the important leaders of the Party and the state to be in Moscow these next days. Has Trotsky been told? . . .

BUKHARIN: Yes, comrade Stalin. But he replied that he was tired and couldn't interrupt his holiday.

Exclamations of disgust from those assembled: 'The scoundrel!' 'That's just like Trotsky', 'He must have gone mad!', 'He thinks the party is going to come crawling on its knees to ask him!' *Stalin raises his hand. Everyone falls silent and looks at him with servility.*

STALIN: I propose that we set up a special commission to oversee in a competent manner the culmination of Lenin's illness. After that, however much it saddens us to have to pronounce the words, we shall have to set up a commission to organise and conduct comrade Lenin's funeral. I shall ask you, comrades, to consider these matters in my absence.

Everyone goes out quietly. Stalin and his secretary remain. Stalin looks steadily at the secretary, who holds Stalin's gaze. Stalin laughs. The secretary smiles rapturously. They understand each other.

STALIN: So, comrade Trotsky is on holiday. Well, may comrade Trotsky regain his health and strength. For our part, we'll get on with the work. We'll have a rest later on, after the funeral.

The telephone rings. The secretary lifts the receiver. He listens and goes pale. The receiver falls from his hand.

SECRETARY: It's happened! Ilich is no more!

STALIN: Write this down! Taking his leave of us, comrade Lenin has bequeathed to us the sacred task of preserving the unity of our Party. I swear to you, comrade Lenin, that we will carry out this, your last will and testament. Taking your leave of us . . .

MORE ABOUT THE VISIT

On the next day the VIP was taken on a tour of local beauty spots and dachas belonging to academicians. The director shlepped a folding stool around with him, on which the VIP would perch from time to time, and Yuri had a bottle of Armenian brandy from which the VIP would slurp from time to time. They met some of the rest-home guests on a hillock overlooking a stream, and the VIP engaged them in friendly conversation. They talked about 'flying saucers'. 'We consider,' said the VIP on taking his leave, 'that this question requires much further examination. There's a lot in it which we would find unsuitable from our point of view, but it's not totally devoid of interest.' After the VIP left (moving off in the direction of his residence), the guests carried on talking about 'flying saucers'. The All-Rounder said that he had one principal objection about these flying saucers: out of all the eighty thousand eye-witness accounts there was not one from a drunkard. Well, if no one had seen these saucers when they were drunk, they would be impossible to see when you were sober. Ergo, they didn't exist at all. The Engineer said that he was bothered by something else – these humanoids were usually similar to local inhabitants and spoke the local dialect. The Old Man said that what bothered him were the assertions of the scientists suggesting that these humanoids had already built full communism in their neck of the galaxy. If that were really the case they would long before have polluted our planet with pictures of their leaders, installed their watchdogs everywhere, smashed capitalism and foisted their supermarxist doctrine on us. JRF said that if they had full communism, then in the first place there would be no need for them to fly to us, since they would have everything they wanted, and in the second place there would be nothing to fly *on* to reach us, since . . . well, they knew themselves why not.

There was another banquet that evening in honour of the VIP. This time it cost the guests five roubles each for the wine, a price designed to recoup the cost of the previous night's wine as well. The director delivered a weighty speech at the banquet in which he reported to the VIP about how they were putting into practice in the rest home the decisions of the February meeting of the rest-home-and-spa department and carrying out the instructions of comrade Suslikov himself. The latter fell off his chair at the end of the director's speech. He was carried off to his bedchamber. It was announced to the guests that comrade Suslikov was over-tired as a result of his journey. Yuri shoved his KGB document in people's faces so often that he ended up by losing it. The All-Rounder helped Lenochka to undress the VIP and put him . . . in the toilet, and then the pair of them gave themselves up to love on the luxurious double bed with the red silk bedspread.

TABLE-TALK

The Russian people doesn't have any notion of taking its bearings and is capable of wandering all over the place. Take, for instance, the following conversation.

'The Jews are leaving. Now the Germans have started griping. Before you know it, brother Ivan will be wanting to leave. If that happens, everyone will be wanting to leave.'

'And on what grounds would we be obliged to let them go?'

'Who's "we"?'

'The state. After all, a person has some value for the state. People can be put to work. They've got brains. And they can be used for defence.'

'But they are *people*. They have their own desires.'

'Anyone can have desires. We get on with it without bleating. How are they any better than we are?!'

A few minutes later the same people come out with the following.

'Why do these folk over there in the West put themselves out for our leaders? It's revolting to watch.'

'They're afraid.'

'And they don't know yet what real communism's all about. Wait till the General Secretary of their communist party becomes the head of state and comes on a visit to us, bringing along a few wagon loads of high-grade nosh and venerable old wine and, of course, a gang of their toadies, while they, the ordinary citizens, have to drag themselves round the shops hunting down rotten potatoes and gangrenous meat, then they'll know all right.'

'Or sojourn in our camps in Siberia.'

'They've got out of hand, the swine. Stalin would never have allowed things to deteriorate to this extent. You have to give him that.'

'Want to hear a joke? At the eighteenth congress of the komsomol, Brezhnev finishes his speech, takes his eyebrows off, puts them where his moustache should be and says: "That's it. The fun's over now."'

A few minutes later still the same people produce this:

'And what more did they want, these Sakharovs, Grigorenkos and co.? They had positions of rank, titles, flats, dachas. They had everything.'

'They went mad.'

'They wanted world fame.'

'They had no sense of responsibility towards their country.'

'They showed a complete lack of understanding of the laws of social development and of the international situation.'

'Speaking objectively, Solzhenitsyn's "Archipelago" gives a false picture in many ways.'

'Of course, he was tendentious in his choice of facts. And he interpreted everything in a biased fashion.'

'And this idea of his of writing a complete history of the Russian revolution is simply daft.'

'His method is rotten to the core. He wants to prove the unprovable all the time: you know, if so-and-so (the tsar, Kerensky, or whoever) had done such-and-such, there wouldn't have been any revolution.'

'God,' thought JRF, 'what a bunch of dregs you are. If you want a system made up of reliable elements like us to be stable, you need a cumbersome apparatus of power. There is no other way for us in principle. And there's no need to think about it any more. Everything's crystal clear. I'll finish that bitch's book. I'll defend my dissertation. I'll make it to candidate. I'll join the Party, of course. I'll buy a flat in a co-operative. I'll get married. I'll have children. A couple, no more. What more do I need?!'

'He doesn't want much!' giggled an inner voice.

A candidate you will not be,
Nor doze at Party meets all day,
At anniversaries you won't see
Awards and medals come your way.
A feather-quilt forget about,
Your chances there are close to nil,
And home-made cabbage soup is out –
You'll have to eat the usual swill.
You won't have kids and therefore grind
Your health down and end up in bed
Felled by a stroke while trying to find
A place for them in higher ed.
Although you're fashioned from the clay
Of fighters, writers, finks and narks,
Whene'er a slot comes free they play
The game and end up with the perks.
And furthermore an unsound brew
Flows in your genes from when a pup.
Although you look a toady too,
Deep down you want to stir things up.

NIGHT-TIME CONVERSATIONS

'I've thought about everything there is to think of on this earth,'
said the New Friend. 'Don't take this as a sign of conformism,
but I've come to the conclusion that our social order is the best.
And it's ours. And that's why we're miserable. Deep down we
don't want anything else, but there's a lot about our life which is
loathsome. And we can't rid ourselves of these loathsome aspects,
for they are an inevitable part of our life. Take, for instance, our
attitude to authority. To the head of section, or head of department. To the director. We can argue with them, after all. And
shout at them. Even slam the door. Threaten them. And we can
talk to them heart-to-heart. And drink with them. Is anything
like it conceivable in the West? We get away with shoddy work.
We pull the wool. Compared to the worker in the West we live
the life of Riley over here. That's true, isn't it? We earn less? Of
course. But we do get a minimum. The food is bad but it's cheap.
Accommodation is bad but practically rent-free. Here we are,
you and I, sunning ourselves.'

'What are you trying to say?'

'Before the revolution we lagged behind the West. And whatever our bright lads were saying at the time, they were secretly dreaming of catching up with the West. And now? Are we really thinking of having anything like the West in our part of the world? Under no circumstances. We merely want to import a few pluses from the West while maintaining our own order, keeping all our own pluses. We want to avoid their minuses. We want the impossible, for Western pluses are impossible without Western minuses, and our pluses are impossible without our minuses. And Western pluses are incompatible with our minuses.'

'What follows from that?'

'We have to look for internal sources of improvement which correspond to our own nature and history. Why do you think we talk about the West so much, compare ourselves with the West, refer to the West? What do we know about the West? What have we experienced there? In practice, nothing. In our life the West is not at all a model for imitation or a realistic model for the development of our society. It is merely a device to help us develop self-awareness and self-knowledge. To know and recognise ourselves, we must contrast ourselves with something which is the opposite of us. Therefore we concoct a picture of some "West" or other.'

THE END OF THE VISIT

On Sunday there was a banquet to mark the departure of the VIP. This time they charged the guests three roubles, which thoroughly annoyed the teetotallers. On this occasion the VIP was in good form, i.e. appeared without any lateral support, joked with the ladies and the Associate Member, and managed to walk to the bed-chamber, supported by Yuri and the All-Rounder, who, for the duration of the visit, had been the VIP's chief drinking-companion-cum-adjutant.

The farewell proceedings took place after breakfast on Monday. The VIP said that he had enjoyed his visit, that he considered that everything in the rest home was in order, that he would raise the possibility of its being awarded the Red Challenge Banner at the pre-anniversary socialist competition for the title of best convalescent institution in the sub-Moscow region, that . . . The car moved off. The guests accompanied it in serried ranks to the front gate. For dinner they were given potato soup without any meat in it, kasha and a compote made from dried fruit. The boiler man carted dozens of empty bottles out of the bungalow, got drunk on what he got back on them and spent the whole night singing revolutionary and prison songs in turn, repeating especially often the lines 'Here behind the bars I sit' and 'While but a lad I had my legs in irons'.

On Tuesday morning the Toothless Doctor rushed around the dormitories collecting signatures for a letter from the workers to the Presidium of the Academy of Sciences of the USSR requesting the removal of the boiler man from the rest home as a drunkard, hooligan and anti-Soviet agitator. The rumour began to go around that the boiler man was the personal agent of Academician Sakharov. The Candidate said that there would have to be an end to these dissident conversations, otherwise the director would order in the tanks.

Just before lunch, it was noticed that someone had stubbed their cigarette out on Brezhnev's eye in a photograph in an old *Pravda* flapping around in a breeze on the newspaper-stand in front of the dining-room. The effect was both horrible and funny at the same time. 'Get rid of this disgrace,' said the Toothless Doctor. 'There'll be trouble,' said the Associate Member. 'The real horror,' said the Old Man, 'consists in the fact that all our horrors in the end look ridiculous. If you like, I'll tell you about a funny thing that happened . . .' 'Wait till after lunch,' said JRF.

THE 'YOUNG' DOCTOR SEDUCES THE WAITRESS

The doctor who was trying to look younger than his age spent a whole week making himself out to be a highly moral individual and criticising the 'youth of today' for their depravity. But he couldn't keep it up and began a seduction operation on the young and rather attractive little waitress. As a first step he began to shave very carefully, cover his bald patch with strands of hair from the back of his head, dress up in all his finery, drench himself nauseatingly in eau-de-cologne and give the Waitress completely unambiguous ambiguous looks, attentively examine her legs and the exciting way she moved, and insolently look down her bra when she was putting the plates of soup down on the table. And he began to crack all sorts of stupid jokes and drop all sorts of hints. The Toothless Doctor, who sat at the same table, remarked with a flirtatious smile that Pushkin had been absolutely right when he had said in his deathless, etc, verse, that love, one could say, reigned over all the ages. The Associate Member, who sat at that same table opposite the Doctor, said that the girl was nothing much to look at, that she was an uneducated dumbcluck and an obvious trollop.

Next the Doctor concentrated on the dancing. And danced, of course, only with her, throwing back his balding head and quoting Dante, Shakespeare, Camus, and all the rest of them. After the dances he would walk the Waitress home and sit with her till midnight on a bench telling her about what a major scholar he was, how difficult it was these days for a man of talent to force a path through the hordes of untalented, conservative people who surrounded him, how little time and energy he had devoted to his personal life, having dedicated himself utterly to science, and what a lousy, unfaithful wife he had.

And on this particular night the Doctor couldn't sleep for excitement. 'She's not bad,' he thought. 'A bit silly, of course. A bit simple. But that's good. It'll be easier to talk her round. And then we'll see what happens. They'll write to the Party bureau, of course. And they might dump a reprimand on me. Who cares! The game's worth the candle. I'm not thinking of going abroad anyway. And they won't dismiss me for a silly thing like that. As for the wife . . . It's long since time to finish with her. The kids are grown up. A wife like her is no good to me in my position. The Waitress, of course, is no good either, as a wife. She's silly. And uneducated. I'd be better choosing one of the post-graduate students. Although the postgrads are no good, either. They all know too much what's what.'

The Doctor was right in his assumption that the Waitress was silly. But he was wrong to think that she was simple. She was shrewd and calculating. And what was more important, she had set herself a firm goal. She already had one example to go on.

Her friend had got round an elderly professor in the same fashion. He had fixed her up with a job in Moscow and paid the rent for a room for her. He had dressed her up like a doll. And she was doing very nicely, thank you. She had found a fiancé, a nice lad with a flat. Lucky thing! No, she would have to get out of this hole any way she could. With her beauty (as she put it herself) it would be stupid to get stuck in this lousy job which only paid sixty roubles.

The next day the Doctor presented her with some cheap perfume and a scarf which he had bought in the local kiosk. She said that these were the first presents she had ever received in her life. Growing bolder, the Doctor invited her to his dormitory after supper to share a 'good bottle of wine'. She drank the wine with pleasure but kept her wits about her. She let the Doctor do a lot of things to her except the main thing, bringing him thereby to a state of incandescence. He swore that he would love her for ever, got down on his knees, wept, promised her everything under the sun, beseeched her to let him do this main thing. He guaranteed that there would be no undesirable consequences. He even tried to take her by force, but was unsuccessful: she twisted his flabby, chubby little hands without any apparent effort and categorically declared that she was not like all the others.

Everyone in the rest home had already noticed that the Waitress had hooked the Doctor. There was a little bit of malicious gossip but people took it largely as a matter of course. This was by no means the first case of its kind. And when it came down to it, the Doctor wasn't a child any more, and she was of age. A couple of days later she stayed the night with the Doctor. But he didn't make it that time either. She, for her part, told him about her friend who had become 'friendly' with an elderly professor who had found work for her in Moscow and who had rented a room for her. And was even going to marry her. When all is said and done, thought the Doctor, why not? She's not all that stupid. At least she's honest, and, as far as one can judge, reliable. And he didn't need an intelligent wife. He had enough intelligence himself. He had already had an intelligent wife (he was already thinking in the past tense) and she had ruined his whole life. And the Doctor, despairing of having his way with her by means of male charm alone, promised to extricate her out of there to Moscow, find her a job and divorce his wife. Towards morning he fell asleep, tormented by his failure and worn out by his fruitless attempts. He didn't know that he wasn't the first, that, with every new batch of guests that came, she would find an elderly doctor or professor, or at the very least a candidate or lecturer, who promised her exactly the same – to take her to Moscow – bought her cheap perfume and shared a bottle of 'sweet' wine with her. But she still hoped that one day she would find an old sugar-daddy who would be able to change her life entirely. And she retained her virtue for the advent of that wonderful bright future.

THE TOOTHLESS DOCTOR WRITES A DENUNCIATION

The 'Young' Doctor, drunk with passion, lost sight of one not unimportant circumstance: although he was living in a rest home, that rest home was situated on the territory of a country which had constructed advanced socialism. And that means that among any ten wonderful Soviet people around him there will be at least one who privately disapproves of his behaviour and who will take appropriate measures. In this case it was the Toothless Doctor who sat at the same table. As soon as the 'Young' Doctor laid a flabby paw on the slender figure of the Waitress, the Toothless Doctor immediately saw what was what, took his immoral behaviour as a personal insult and, with anger in her soul, left the club and sat down to write a series of anonymous letters. Letters in the plural, for she decided to send one to the Party organisation where the 'Young' Doctor worked, another to the rest-home-and-spa department of the Presidium and a third to the Doctor's wife. In the first letter she wrote that the 'Young' Doctor was a disgrace to the profession of a Soviet scholar and communist, secondly that he was introducing an element of moral decay into a Soviet convalescent institution and thirdly that he was destroying a healthy socialist family. She found out the Doctor's home address from his passport in the office – the first ground for suspecting that she was the author of the anonymous letters. The second ground was her demonstrative refusal to submit a sample of her handwriting for expert evaluation. When the affair reached the proportions of a scandal, the Doctor had decided to expose the anonymous author and collect samples of the handwriting of everyone he suspected. The Toothless Doctor was the only one to refuse, declaring that she didn't live in some sort of United States of America were racism flourished, but in the country of victorious socialism. After that, any doubts about the authorship of the anonymous letters evaporated. But before that happened something else happened: the Doctor's wife appeared on the scene, followed by an inspector from the rest-home-and-spa department. The Doctor's wife did not divulge the real reason for her being there, spent the day at the rest home, visited the dining-room, gave the Waitress the once-over and realised immediately that nothing serious was in the offing. Then she showed the anonymous letter to the director and the party secretary, said that she would be taking proceedings against the anonymous author and calmly went back home. An inspector arrived with the aim of clarifying the issue, but when he established what was what at first hand, he replaced that aim with its opposite: he decided to hush the thing up. It was only after a chat with the Inspector that the 'Young' Doctor found out about the anonymous letters and guessed the reason for his wife's unexpected arrival. At first it looked as though he were going to make difficulties and alleged that he wanted a handwriting check carried out, but in the end he was persuaded by the Inspector not to make a fuss.

STALIN

Stalin is walking up and down in his office at a leisurely pace, smoking his pipe and talking out loud to himself.

STALIN: And they call this lot the Lenin Guard! They're nothing but a bunch of bletherers on the make. They've got no sense of reality. The country is on the verge of collapse, yet they're ready to spend days arguing about a comma in *Das Kapital*, which none of them has read. You won't save the country with speeches and slogans. You have to act, and act sharply and decisively. Slogans are supposed to complement the cause, not replace it. But what's to be done? Lenin was right: you have to find the basic link in a chain of events which, when you've found it, allows you to untangle the whole chain. Where is this basic link? It is power. Strong and reliable power. Strict power. Merciless power. Power which will stop at nothing for the sake of a great goal – the embodiment in real life of the glorious ideals of the revolution. But power resides in the Party and the Party is subordinate to an apparatus of management and that apparatus is ME. The basic link is the absolute authority of the Party leader. And not Trotsky, Zinoviev, Bukharin or any of the other twaddle-merchants, but Stalin! Stalin sounds just like Lenin, only stronger. And you've got a good chance. Moreover, the Russian people forms the heart of this country and is used to having a tsar lord it over them – and they are longing for a new tsar. And not another russkie, but a foreigner. Not a Jew, however. Nor a German. A Georgian – now *there*'s someone a Russian can get on with and yet he's more or less foreign. That circumstance has to be brought to the fore. I'll have to speak with an accent, otherwise I'll be taken for a Jew. From this moment on I will have to get everyone used to the fact that Stalin speaks with a Georgian accent.

There is a knock on the door. Enter Poskryebyshev, Stalin's personal secretary. He waits deferentially for Stalin's attention. Stalin stops, looks angrily at Poskryebyshev and says with a Georgian accent: 'What do you want?' *Poskryebyshev starts, raises his eyebrows in surprise, but immediately catches on and regains his previous composure.*

POSKRYEBYSHEV: Molotov and Voroshilov request an audience on a most important matter.

STALIN: Have them come in.

Enter the people named by Poskryebyshev. They stand silently to attention. They watch Stalin pace up and down the office. Finally Stalin stops in front of them, looks at them as if in surprise, takes the dead pipe out of his mouth, scrapes the dottle on to the carpet and puts the pipe in the pocket of his tunic.

STALIN: What do you want?

MOLOTOV: There is growing dissatisfaction among the workers, Comrade Stalin. There are strikes everywhere. The food situation is catastrophic. The party organisations *in situ* are incapable of combatting dangerous moods. There are more and more speeches about betrayal of the ideals of the revolution and about counter-revolution.

VOROSHILOV: There are rebellions in the villages. In N district the whole population has risen up. Communists and representatives of Soviet power have all been killed. Extraordinary measures are necessary.

STALIN (*after a long pause for thought, says with an accent*): These gasbags and posturers, led by Trotsky, are only interested in discussing purely theoretical questions while the one who is supposed to do all the dirty work is Stalin. Well, so be it. They don't understand the fundamental law of historical reality: the one who wins is the one who gets on with the job, no matter how dirty it might appear. Let these orators make their speeches. Try and get Trotsky to concentrate in his speeches and newspaper writings on the need to strengthen labour discipline, on the need to 'tighten the screws', so to speak. As for Bukharin . . . Let him think about the peasantry. As for us . . . The first thing to do is to renew rapidly the membership of the Party. We have to cast the net wider and make it easier for new members to join, and achieve a predominance in the Party organisations of level-headed people over the revolutionary idealists. Let anyone who wants to join at the moment sign on. We'll have a purge later on. Now about the grain situation. How serious is the uprising in N province?

VOROSHILOV: One corps of cavalry would have it crushed in two weeks.

STALIN: And is there much grain in that region?

MOLOTOV: There's some but not very much. And it's difficult to get hold of it. The peasants have hidden it all and won't give it up for anything. M district next door is much better off. But it's quiet there at the moment.

STALIN: The revolution demands sacrifices. For the sake of the salvation of the country we shall have to sacrifice the local population of a region. I think that we have to seize the grain in M region. What's more, the lot – down to the last stalk. Do you understand me?

MOLOTOV *and* VOROSHILOV (*in unison*): Of course, comrade Stalin!

STALIN: Who's in command of M military district? Tukhachevsky? Right, well, instruct him to carry out a merciless campaign to suppress a counter-revolutionary uprising in M.

WALK-TALK

'All you need to carry out a revolution,' said the Candidate, 'is one schizophrenic, a few dozen scoundrels and a few million cretins.'

'So what's holding it up?' said the Old Man.

'We've got enough cretins,' said the Candidate. 'We have more than enough scoundrels. Schizophrenics are the problem: our contemporary schizophrenics don't want to carry out a revolution! It's unprecedented in history. Our schizos want human rights and the freedom to travel abroad, but they don't want to take power into their own hands.'

'The so-and-so's!' exclaimed a girl known as the Spiteful Maiden. 'What kind of position do they place our leaders in! They're supposed to govern a people like ours and at the same time take account of some human rights or other? That's both a logical contradiction and a practical impossibility.'

'Surely there must be *some* people who would like to make a new revolution?' said the Goodly Maiden.

'As many as you like,' replied the Candidate. 'Only they're not schizos but cretins.'

'This is all empty chit-chat,' said the Engineer. 'Revolution, evolution, reforms, construction . . . We're stuck in this shit, whatever happens, and there's no getting out of it, for it is impossible according to the laws of nature. Our shit is the product of freedom and equality.'

'And fraternity?'

'No, *mat*-ernity*, more like. But seriously, judge for yourselves. People have been placed in an identical relationship to society in the sense that any possibility of an individual being able to exist independently of the collective or outside society in general has been reduced effectively to zero.'

'Sometimes a person . . .'

'Don't quibble, you know precisely what I mean. Personal initiative is excluded in our part of the world, everything is under

---

* *mat:* foul language; abuse. (*Translator's note*)

the control of the state. And in these conditions the only thing that can maintain order and keep society in an integrated state is a powerful system of authority. Authoritative power, moreover, which is not subject to chance or the idiosyncrasies of individuals. That is why our "elective" system of power is only for show and the people who are "elected" are selected by the organs of power themselves. Our system of power and control as it exists in practice is maintained on a daily basis by filling vacancies which occur by individuals selected by the huge apparatus. Am I getting through to you? This system is indestructible because every time an individual achieves a position of power he is confronted by the whole power system which has already been established. And it is never the case that our system of power is in any sense dependent on some "people" or other.'

'And yet unshakable systems don't exist.'

'But am I really saying that ours is unshakable? It is unshakable in the time-span of an individual life. It will, of course, collapse. But for how many centuries did Ancient Egypt exist? And China? And Byzantium? Even the Romanov dynasty lasted for three hundred years. Three hundred!!'

'You don't need to frighten us with periods of time like that,' said the Spiteful Maiden. 'In three hundred years I, personally, won't be wanting any kind of freedom.'

'What's the problem, anyway?' said the Engineer. 'Hands up all those who need human rights and civic freedoms. No one. Who wants more than one party, the freedom to demonstrate or to emigrate? Again, no one. And who wants to improve their living conditions, increase their salary, improve the supply of consumer goods? Everyone! Now you have to choose: improvements but a return to capitalism, or socialism without improvements? Who's for the first option? No one. And the second? Everyone. Well, there you are – we've solved all our problems!'

THE ALL-ROUNDER'S PROJECT

Under the wholesome influence of the creative surroundings, the All-Rounder decided to make his contribution to science and write a guide to Moscow watering-holes and places where you could sober up afterwards. The Candidate said that enterprise would not be at all creative since the central canteen administration kept a list of snack-bars and the police kept a list of sobering-up stations. The All-Rounder replied that, after that remark of the Candidate's, he was all the more convinced of the need for his guide. The point was that the concept 'watering-hole' did not coincide with the places where you could have a drink officially, nor did a place where you could sober up coincide with the official 'sobering-up station'. He, the All-Rounder, knew of at least a hundred watering-holes, about the existence of which your Moscow Canteens and Hotel Administration had not the slightest idea, and he knew of at least five hundred places where you could sleep it off which were totally unknown to the police. Incidentally, if the dissidents knew where they were, they could operate ten times more effectively and the KGB would be powerless against them. If ever a real opposition party were to be formed in Russia it could only occur inside this system of unofficial dives and doss houses. The Candidate said that if such a progressive role in Russian history had been envisaged for these places that was all the more reason not to write a guide: it would fall into the hands of the authorities and they would shut down all the places described in it. The All-Rounder again accused the Candidate of ignorance. These places were never permanent – they were constantly changing. Here, above all, one had to be genuinely dialectical about it. His guide wasn't supposed to provide a list of these places (like a telephone book) but a method of discovering them in any district of Moscow at any time of the day at any time of the year.

'Supposing,' he said, 'you've ended up in the Dzerzhinsky region on Marshal Pugovkin Street, in winter, at ten o'clock at night, with a mate, and ten roubles in your pocket. You've already been on the sauce but you want to carry on. What do you do? You open my guide. Dzerzhinsky region is third class, Pugovkin Street tenth class. You look up the section entitled "Winter" and the subsection "Evening". You read the following: turn left, walk straight ahead for two hundred metres, enter the "Sirius" café which is just about to close and tell the cleaner that you want to speak to Dusya. "You're having me on," she'll say. "There aren't any Dusyas here. There's a Klavka, but no Dusyas." "I beg your pardon," you say. "In fact it's Klavka we want to speak to." "You should have said that in the first place," the cleaner will grumble, "instead of asking for some Dusya or other. Anyway, it'll only take you five minutes to find Klavka. Do you see that green house over there? Well, behind it . . . " Five minutes later you're ringing the bell of a flat you don't know, saying "Hullo" to a woman you don't know with a swollen lip and a bruise under her eye, producing the cash and pronouncing the magic formula: "Booze and a bed". And after that everything takes care of itself. You get something strong enough to turn you inside out, nothing to eat, a basin to throw up in and a smelly lumber room to sleep it off in. All in all, a rare treat, and no cold dousings and no police. Has the penny dropped now?'

'That's marvellous!' exclaimed the Candidate. 'When we get back to Moscow I'll get hold of a tape-recorder, we'll record your guide and then make copies of it. It'll be the first really useful book to come out of samizdat.'

NIGHT-TIME CONVERSATIONS

'We're an amazing country all the same,' said the New Friend. 'I've seen a lot of things and yet I never cease to be amazed. You can believe it or not, as you like, but I'm telling you the truth: we now have a new branch of industry geared to the production of decorative materials for festivals – slogans, portraits of the leaders, etc, and the equipment for hanging them up. It used to be the local authorities which dealt with such matters but now the system has been centralised nationally. Because of its special importance, this new branch is under the supervision of the ministry of culture, the propaganda section of the Central

Committee and the local soviets. Can you imagine, commissions work for years. There are scientific research institutes working on it! Arts councils. I once had to attend such a council. More than twenty people spent ten hours discussing the configuration of coloured light bulbs for the streets of Moscow. Moreover, not your main streets like Gorky Street or Lenin Avenue or Marx Avenue. For that they must have been in session for weeks with the Minister of Culture and heads of department in the Central Committee. Our council was chaired by the first deputy of the chairman of the Moscow soviet. You should have heard the high-falutin' terms they used to solve the most banal of problems. For instance, what should the order be in which the lights are switched on and off – from the centre to the suburbs or vice-versa? The view that prevailed was that of a group who insisted that the lamps should be switched on from the centre to the suburbs since that conformed to the principles of democratic centralism.'

'It's an absolute waste of resources,' said JRF. 'No one reacts any more, anyway.'

'They do react! And how! They say that Americans have grown sick of advertisements. But advertising still goes on, still has an effect. It's the same here. You leave your building and the first thing you see is "The CPSU – guiding and directing . . .". You're on the bus and you see "Communism is the inevitable future of all mankind". You're bowling along in a commuter train: "Glory to the CPSU!", "Long live . . . ". Somewhere else there'll be a row of portraits of our rosy-cheeked leaders. You think that has no effect? It has an effect, all right! You see enough of that and you'll think ten times before so much as uttering a squeak. This whole massive clutter of slogans, challenges, portraits, posters and banners is just as intimidating as the activities of the KGB and the MVD.'

'Perhaps you're right. I somehow didn't think of it like that. It all seemed to me to be simply empty formalism.'

'Remember, nothing in our part of the world is done without a reason. All our nonsense only seems so on the surface. In reality everything is expedient to the nth degree. It might be formalistic, but it's not senseless.'

STALIN

It is early one sunny morning. The birds are singing. Leaves rustle in the trees. An army commander is sitting in a prosperous peasant's hut in the 'holy' corner underneath the icons. He is young, strong, handsome, clean-shaven and smells of eau-de-cologne. In front of him is a jug of milk straight from the cow and a crust of fresh bread. He breaks off a piece, eats it with obvious enjoyment and washes it down with milk straight from the jug. Division and brigade commanders festooned with belts, spurs, sabres, binoculars, mapcases, mausers, stand to attention before him. They have all, of course, been decorated with the 'Red Banner'. The army commander signals to the adjutant to remove the peasant, his wife and children from the hut – he is about to issue a secret order.

ARMY COMMANDER (AC): Comrade commanders! A high honour has been bestowed upon us – to save the republic from death by starvation. You are all graduates of the school of revolution and civil war and I don't have to teach you the rudiments of political literacy. Therefore we'll get straight down to business. Commissar – you have the floor!

COMMISSAR: Comrade commanders! The Party and comrade Stalin in person have assigned us a most crucial task. You will have to demonstrate the maximum of political maturity and consciousness. The population of the region is well disposed towards Soviet power. Our units will be met with bread and salt, songs and hospitality. But as real communists, your hearts will not tremble nor your arms waver. In the situation as it is you should firmly remember one thing only: before you stand the sworn enemies of the revolution and proletarian power, for on them depends the fate of world revolution and our own. And with an enemy one must act with complete proletarian revolutionary ruthlessness.

A COMMANDER: I'm not quite sure I know what we're supposed to do. Do we use the machine guns, or what?

AC: No, comrades! We shall need the machine guns to annihilate the world bourgeoisie. And it would make too much noise. You'll use your sabres – it's quicker and more reliable. Staff Commander, explain to our comrade commanders our tactics in the fight against counter-revolution in its current phase!

A COMMANDER (*another one*): If I understand you correctly, we're about to chop down an unarmed population with sabres. Women, old folk and children, too? But that's a crime! Surely . . .

AC (*to the adjutant*): Arrest that traitor to the cause of world revolution! And have him shot immediately! Let him serve as a lesson to anyone else who might dare to raise a hand against the gains of October.

The adjutant and the army commander's personal bodyguard disarm the recalcitrant commander and take him outside. A shot is heard, followed by a cry. The commanders inside the hut stand to attention, jangle their spurs and demonstrate readiness to do anything at all in the interests of world revolution.

AC (*continuing to eat bread and drink milk*): Staff Commander, read out the order to the troops.

STAFF COMMANDER: Political workers in the units should arrive ahead of the troops in the designated villages and explain to the inhabitants that everyone of them should turn out to meet a unit of the Red Army in the village square. Every last one of them! Is that clear?! Later on, the unit in question is to surround the inhabitants and kill every one of them. Without exception. If anyone survives, the commanders of the unit will answer for it with their heads. The corpses are to be thrown down the wells and the wells levelled off with the ground. There must be no traces left. Two hours later each village is to be in the control of the soldiers. Political workers should make sure that booty and food is shared out among the men equally. Don't forget that we are fighting for a radiant communist society in which there will be general equality. After the operation, units are to leave the villages quickly and regroup at a prescribed location for a new operation. They should be replaced by food squads whose objective is to collect up the grain, vegetables and farmyard animals.

ONE OF THE COMMANDERS: We've got natives from these parts in our ranks. What are we to do with them?

COMMISSAR: Give them all a day's leave today and shoot them tomorrow as deserters.

The commanders disperse. Through the window can be heard the noise of commands being shouted, bugles, the clatter of hooves, songs. The army commander gets up from behind the table, loosens his belt a couple of notches, calls his adjutant and orders him to bring in the peasant's elder daughter, so that she 'doesn't go to waste' (as he says to the adjutant). While he is waiting he hums a song which was popular at the time of the civil war:

> So let the Red Army
> Fight passionately . . .

LENIN'S BIRTHDAY

In connection with the forthcoming anniversary of Lenin's birthday the club was showing nothing but revolutionary films – *Lenin in October, Lenin in 1918, The Ulyanov Family, A Mother's Heart.* Two days before the anniversary, a lecturer arrived from the Moscow Municipal Committee and all the guests were herded in to hear a lecture entitled 'Leninism Today' in which the lecturer yelped out abuse aimed at right and left deviationists, right and left revisionists, Eurocommunists, sovietologists, and, of course, dissidents.

'That same aim of discrediting socialism and undermining its position is being pursued by the campaign unleashed as a result of enemy propaganda, engaged in the falsification of socialist democracy under the guise of "concern" for the so-called "denial of human rights" in socialist countries,' howled the lecturer hysterically. 'It is highly organised ideological sabotage which is designed by its authors to defame our socialist society and to conceal the truth about it and also to promote the myth that there exists inside it opposition to the socialist order. Malicious anti-Soviet propaganda portrays a group of renegades, alien to Soviet society and the whole socialist world and existing at all only thanks to financial help from the West, in the martyr's aureole of "freedom fighters" and "fighters for human rights" and tries to present them as expressing the alleged "real feelings" of the Soviet people. These people of so-called heterodox opinions operate on a platform which is inimical to the socialist order, engage in anti-Soviet activity, break the law and, getting no support within the country, turn to our ideological and class enemies. These people of so-called heterodox opinion often include people who are psychically ill and those whose aims are purely mercenary. Soviet people correctly regard these "dissidents" as enemies of socialism, people who are acting against the interests of their own motherland, as accomplices and even the agents of imperialism!!!'

JRF had wanted to skip the lecture but the New Friend had advised him against it. 'It's not worth the hassle,' he said. 'They'll report your absence to your work and you know yourself how that will be interpreted.'

On the following evening there was a ceremonial gathering of the guests and rest-home personnel at which (in addition to a speech by the secretary of the Party organisation) certificates of honour were distributed and gratitude expressed to the best workers. Then there was a concert, put on by those same guests and personnel. In conclusion the director announced that the next day would be a communist *subbotnik** in honour of . . . Afterwards there was a film about Brezhnev as the most faithful and outstanding marxist-leninist alive. It was impossible to get near the television – everyone was watching the ceremonial anniversary session in the Kremlin. JRF, the Old Man, the Engineer, the All-Rounder and the New Friend locked themselves in their dormitory, drank bottle after bottle, smoked and conducted gloomy conversations.

'How can we ever talk about reforms,' said the Old Man sadly. 'The "people" won't change this idiot life of theirs for any other. And anyway, the question of change doesn't even enter their heads. They claw their way into this life as it is, adapt themselves to it and try to rip off as much as they can for themselves by whatever means are available. And that's that! Finish! Doomsville!'

Next day at dawn, loudspeakers which had appeared from God knows where exploded into action and thundered out for the rest of the day exultant hymns about the builders of communism. At the same time the residents were clearing the grounds of broken bottles, tin cans, last year's leaves and other litter. Towards evening, the results of the socialist competition for the

* *subbotnik:* a day of voluntary, unpaid work; originally a Saturday. (*Translator's note*)

title of best block and best dormitory were decided. The most outstanding participants in the *subbotnik* received expressions of thanks, a report of which would be communicated to their place of work. The shop sold ten times more bottles of spirits that day than usual. The women made a special effort for the *subbotnik*. They decked themselves out in tracksuits, presenting thereby their delightful contours for all to see. And their undelightful ones.

'If you want my opinion,' said the New Friend, 'your "old lady" here seems to have the best figure. You've not grown tired of her by any chance? Otherwise I might step in.'

'I have grown tired of her,' said JRF, 'but I can't quite bring myself to drop her. Besides, we're not here for much longer. I might as well hang on to the end. But when we're back in Moscow, be my guest.'

'In Moscow,' said the Friend, 'I don't know what to do with the ones I've got.'

The All-Rounder slept through the whole *subbotnik* in a tangled embrace with Dissident on a heap of last year's leaves. They missed him at supper.

SCIENTIFIC PROBLEMS

'Our intake here is a bit strange,' said the Engineer. 'Riff-raff rubbish, most of it.'

'A bit like a Moscow rubbish dump,' said the All-Rounder.

'You end up with a paradox,' said the Old Man. 'The presence of every one of us here can be fully explained. But there is no causal explanation for the fact that we have this particular combination. How come you're here, for instance, at such an unlikely time?'

'They drew up a holiday roster,' said the All-Rounder, 'and I was shoved in this slot. They said that I would be needed in the summer in the Institute. And what goes on in the summer in an institute?! Almost certainly they want me to do up the director's flat for him.'

'For my part, I prefer to take my leave in separate chunks at times which are inconvenient to others,' said the Candidate.

'Our Institute is empty in the summer and there's nothing to do, so it's like having an extra long holiday.'

'The Associate Member hinted that she'd hidden herself away in Moscow in connection with some sort of unpleasantness back home,' said the Goodly Maiden. 'She's here on a research trip and prefers to spend it in the country.'

'Of course,' said the Engineer, 'once we're all here that means that there were some reasons or other which brought us here. But just try to characterise this group as a whole! Try coming up with even a working classification.'

'Nothing to it,' said the Spiteful Maiden. 'I can offer the following classification completely in the spirit of dialectical materialism and the achievements of modern science which confirm it. The residents in the current intake can be divided into the following groups: 1) those who people think are informers but who aren't; 2) those who people don't think are informers but who are; 3) those who are or are not informers, irrespective of what people think of them and whether people think of them at all; 4) the rest. What does contemporary logic have to say about that?'

'Contemporary logic,' said JRF, 'has advanced to such a point that it is no longer capable of handling such primitive tasks. Incidentally, the Old Man's idea is correct. Let's look at our whole society in the light of that. Every single event and every single act is explicable in causal terms. But take the whole aggregate of events and people's actions together and try and approach it from the same point of view. You won't get anywhere.'

'What's to be done in a situation like that?' asked the Little Lady.

'It's very simple,' answered the All-Rounder. 'While the shop is still open have a three-rouble whip-round . . . Well, a rouble . . . Women'll get a reduction of fifty per cent . . .'

LENIN AND WINNIE-THE-POOH

But, once they had started to drink, they couldn't stop. First of all the Engineer became maudlin, then confidential.

'I took my daughter along to the school to have her entered on the register,' he said. 'It's a special kind of school, even although it's in our district: not everyone gets into it. They organised a kind of entry examination. And they asked my seven-year-old Tanya to recite a poem about Lenin. She said that she didn't know any poems about Lenin, but she could recite them one about Winnie-the-Pooh. My God, you should have seen how that went down with our honourable pedagogues! "What!" they roared, foaming at the mouth. "She doesn't know a poem about Lenin but knows one about some Winnie-the-Pooh or other!!" Naturally that school didn't take Tanya. What's more, they wrote to my work, the swine, and told them that I was bringing my daughter up badly. A campaign had just started at the time about educating children in the spirit of . . . I was the subject of a special meeting of the Party at my work. They made an example of me. And after that I learned the whole of children's literature on Lenin off by heart, and I even interpreted for Tanya the fundamental tenets of *Materialism and Empiriocriticism*. Do you want me to quote some for you?'

'No!' shouted everyone. 'Recite something about Winnie-the-Pooh!!'

'We've forgotten everything we knew about Winnie-the-Pooh,' said the Engineer.

'I can't get over it,' said the Old Man. 'Here you all are, talking about some Winnie-the-Pooh or other. Do you know what would have happened in my time for that? There has been some progress after all.'

JRF ended up by being dragged back to his dormitory by the Little Lady and the New Friend, undressed and put to bed. As he dozed off he muttered that unfortunately he wasn't a Lenin but only a Winnie-the-Pooh.

'Who is this Winnie-the-Pooh?' asked the New Friend.

'Don't tell me you don't know?!' she exclaimed in surprise. 'You're supposed to be an intellectual!'

'To hell with Winnie-the-Pooh, whoever he is,' said the New Friend and had a go at getting the Little Lady on to his bed. She resisted at first, murmuring something about honour, dignity, fidelity, decency and other moral values. In the end she said that he, too, was no angel (she meant JRF) and capitulated.

OUT IN THE SUN

It was a sunny day. The residents were transformed. The men shaved carefully, drenched themselves in eau-de-cologne and wore their Sunday best. The women . . . Well, we don't need to say anything about them, it's obvious without words. Even the Associate Member squeezed her flabby hulk into a knitted trouser suit without making anyone laugh. The Toothless Doctor said with complete sincerity how much the outfit suited her (although, afterwards, when she was telling her friends about the incident, she giggled with pleasure at how she had allegedly taken a rise out of the obese fool). The All-Rounder exuded compliments and kissed the hands of all the ladies one after the other. He told the Associate Member that it would be dangerous for her to go around unescorted looking like she did and she nearly had a stroke from such a refined compliment. Dogs smiled, their tongues hanging out. Pregnant cats, paying no attention to the dogs, lay around in the baking sun in the most obscene positions.

'Hey, you people! What a day!' exclaimed the Engineer. 'Why don't we organise something?!'

The Engineer's suggestion was adopted unanimously without hesitation. They had a whip-round, some contributing three roubles (mainly the women), some five (mainly their bibulous escorts). They went to the shop but it was shut for stock-taking. The festive mood palled a little. But the Engineer said not to worry and that the All-Rounder, JRF and he would 'nip down' to the station and get all they needed there. It wouldn't take more than an hour or an hour and a half. In the meantime the ladies could get on with the preparations. And they should go and bag that little hill dotted with pine-trees above the stream. It was dry there, but more importantly it was a beautiful spot.

And that is what they did. While the Engineer and JRF 'nipped down' for the drink and *zakuski*, the others wandered along the bank of the stream, sang songs, said nice things and were unusually attentive to each other. The Little Lady sang gypsy songs, which she did quite well, and she was asked to sing them again and the others joined in. The Associate Member spoke about her marriages, particularly about her first one when she was literally abducted by her future (first) husband. She was only fifteen at the time and her abductor had to offer colossal bribes to the relevant authorities. The Spiteful Maiden remarked that she didn't know why women bothered to get married now that there was central heating.

They found the little hillock. Plastic macs, coats and jackets were spread out on the ground. The ladies took charge of the eats and the men set about opening bottles. As always happens in such cases, they had forgotten to bring a corkscrew. And the men proposed the most fantastic ways of uncorking the bottles, making themselves out to be experienced boozers. Some of them hit the bottom of the bottle with their palms, others banged it on a stump. Finally they resorted to the most banal solution of all – they pushed the cork into the bottle with a twig.

The sun began to beat down. The men smoked and talked about Vance's visit, Brezhnev's forthcoming trip, Moro's assassination at the hands of the 'Red Brigades'. Someone observed that these bandits were communists. Someone else objected, saying that they were pro-Chinese communists. At last the women announced that 'lunch' was 'served'. A leisurely conversation got under way in the midst of nature in all its beauty (ah, what a day it is today!). Everyone was overflowing with kindness and affection. After the first snort there is a moment when it begins to appear that man to man really is a friend and brother and that it is only idiotic urban life that distorts these wonderful natural relations. And such a moment is engraved on the memory for a whole year, until the next such unforgettable moment. Life is wonderful, my friends! Fill them up again!

In the middle of this spiritual harmony the Old Man suggested that there should be a two-hour break for people to take a walk, etc, and then to come back and carry on. Various couples wandered off into the bushes. Some people fell asleep right there in the sunshine. The All-Rounder assembled a group of unattached ladies and talked to them about yoga. 'The main thing,' he said to the unattached ladies who listened amazed, 'is to concentrate and detach yourself from everything around you. Watch this! . . .' After supper, however, he grabbed the first one he saw of his enraptured female audience and dragged her off to the nearest dry spot to engage in pursuits of a quite different order, more in keeping with the spirit and traditions of the Russian people than the gymnastics of the yogis. And God grant them a moment of simple, earthly joy!

THE END OF STALIN

One evening at supper JRF was handed a note from Petin. Petin had arrived at his dacha and demanded the speedy return of his 'documents'. JRF went cold with fright: he had thrown out these papers of Petin's! Without waiting for his kasha, JRF tore back to his dormitory and threw himself on the waste-paper basket. The papers were still there!! Tears of joy sprang from his eyes and irrigated the contents of the basket. When he had collected Petin's 'documents' and his own notes together, JRF went off to Petin's dacha, having forgotten about the kasha, the weak tea with the two lumps of sugar and 'Welcome' biscuit. Petin hurriedly leafed through his notes and having convinced himself that they were all there and having obtained JRF's word that the latter had not taken a copy of them, threw them in the fire that was burning in the hearth. Then he began to read JRF's notes. He read them unhurriedly, rereading certain parts from time to time. JRF stood immobile and watched unblinkingly his huge skull covered with sparse bunches of grey hair.

'Very good,' said Petin at length. 'You understood my sketchy ideas exactly. But, alas . . .' And Petin, without finishing his utterance, threw JRF's notes into the fire as well.

'And now,' he said, with obvious relief, 'we'll have a glass of tea. You, of course, are full up. They feed you to bursting point in that rest home.' Then an elderly, ugly and slovenly woman resembling Petin brought in weak tea with two lumps of sugar and a 'Welcome' biscuit. 'Meet my grand-daughter,' said Petin. The grand-daughter said something unintelligible and disappeared. JRF drank the tepid tea with revulsion out of a dirty glass. 'And now go back to your holiday,' said Petin, 'but remember, not a word to anyone!'

THE TRUE STORY OF THE NEW TESTAMENT OF MARXISM

Although life in the company of other people seemed to be good fun and interesting, loneliness and a sense of devastation made themselves felt in JRF's dreams. He dreamed that he was in a devastated city. He wandered the empty streets in search of a living soul. He sensed the presence of people but he could not see them. They kept disappearing before they had time to appear.

'Death,' he thought to himself, 'is eternal loneliness.' In one of these dreams he heard Petin's voice.

'If you like, I'll tell you who wrote the New Testament of marxism – the opus *On Dialectical and Historical Materialism*, attributed to Stalin. Listen! Only, not a word to anyone – they wouldn't believe you, anyway.

'So, my boy . . . I can call you that, can't I. Whatever may have happened, it turns out that you, after all, are my spiritual heir and successor. I sense that you, too, are nostalgic for the times I lived in. Well, my boy, I'll begin by telling you a very simple, but very important truth: some people are destroyed because they know too much, others because they understand too much. Sometimes the former survive, but the latter never, for they are more dangerous. You understand too much and your friends and colleagues have begun to notice that. Watch out! I know a lot but I don't understand anything. That's why I'm still alive. But there was a time when I, too, understood something although I knew nothing.

'I was always top of the class at my grammar school. I was all set for the gold medal. All the teachers were unanimous that there had never been such a pupil-genius in the history of the town. Already at the age of thirteen I was beginning to publish poetry and short stories. And they were by no means bad. I re-

read them not long ago and I was not ashamed of them. The governors and teachers at the grammar school were rather liberal. As a matter of fact everyone was at that time, including the police and the gendarmerie. I think that it was that liberalism and not the burdens of the tsarist regime that led to the revolution. It is when regimes become less harsh that revolutions happen, not when regimes tighten the screws. And so, our grammar school announced a competition for the best tract on a socio-political theme. And I decided to write a tract on marxism. We had marxist literature at home (my father and uncle were socialists) and I began to read it when I was very young. I worked day and night for two months on that tract. I submitted it – and failed spectacularly: it didn't even make the first ten. Something snapped inside me after that and I only managed to leave the grammar school with a silver medal.

'The years passed, dreadful, incomprehensible, hurricane years. We were preparing for Stalin one of "his" routine works of genius. Stalin hinted that he would not be averse to this work's having a philosophical section. And at that point I remembered my grammar school tract, dug it out of our domestic archive, edited it slightly ("refreshed" it a little) and brought it to Stalin. He read it there and then. His face turned grey, and his eyes took on a look which God preserve me from ever seeing again. "Where did you get that?" he whispered. "I wrote it myself," I whispered in turn. "You're lying, you hound," he hissed. "You stole it! Who did you steal it from? If you confess, I'll have mercy on you, if not, I'll have you executed!" And in terror I gave him the first name that came into my head: Stanis. That very night Stanis was arrested and shot. I also gave Stalin the names of the judges of that ill-starred grammar school essay competition, saying that they were acquainted with Stanis's manuscript. After that I finally lost any ability to understand anything. And that's the story. And do you know why I told it to you? And to you alone?'

'No,' said JRF. 'Why?'

'Guess,' said Petin.

'I can't,' said JRF.

'In that case,' said Petin, 'you'll never solve the riddle of Stalin.'

'Why not?' asked JRF.

'Because it resides in you and not in him,' replied Petin.

461

AN UNUSUAL INCIDENT

The Associate Member had her foreign fur coat stolen.

'What did she want to drag her fur coat along with her at this time of the year for?' asked JRF in surprise.

'What do you mean "what for?"' said the New Friend, surprised at JRF's surprise. 'The fur coat is foreign and she has to show it to everyone. Otherwise why does she need it? It doesn't keep you warm, it's only for decoration and prestige. Aristocrats in the West wear fur coats like that in summer. They drape them around their beautiful, bare shoulders.'

'What kind of shoulders is a monster like her going to have?' said JRF, continuing to be surprised.

'She's an associate member, after all,' remonstrated the Friend. 'She compensates for the shoulders by having an unusually highly developed intellect. If associate members are like that where she comes from, can you imagine what idiots full academicians must be!'

The theft of the fur coat disturbed the normal, peaceful routine of rest-home life. The police arrived. They brought a dog with them, but it failed to pick up the scent.

'I told you that it'd be a waste of time,' said the dog-handler. 'It's bound to have been nicked by one of the residents and they all smell alike of kasha.'

The Associate Member insisted that it had been stolen by 'that fellow with the beard', meaning JRF. The logic of her case was irrefutable: when he hadn't been in the block, the fur coat was there, and when he appeared, the fur coat disappeared. It was explained to her that JRF could not have stolen it since at the time of the crime he had been on an excursion with everyone else – including the Associate Member – to a former nobleman's estate ten kilometres away. She said that it had been stolen by his (i.e. JRF's) accomplices. The police captain said that that was logical.

They began a search. They started, of course, with JRF's dormitory. Then they searched the dormitory in which JRF had been before. Then they searched the remaining dormitories.

Without result. The captain said that it could have been stolen by outsiders. They could have got in the window which the Associate Member had carelessly left open.

But the fur coat turned up in the evening. It turned out that the Associate Member had hidden it herself. She had put it under her mattress so that it wouldn't get stolen while she went on the excursion and had forgotten about it. Everyone was pleased. But just in case, surveillance in the blocks and the surrounding grounds was increased. The New Friend said that now was the best time to 'nick' the coat in earnest. Nobody would believe that female ape any more. JRF said that it was a good idea and that it would be worth teaching the swine a lesson but that he didn't see any way of turning the coat into cash, since they'd be bound to find it. The Friend said that he didn't need to turn it into cash. He simply had to bury it somewhere deep in the woods and let it rot away in peace.

PROBLEM NUMBER ONE

'Here's a problem for you,' said the Old Man. 'You might call it problem number one. However bad as it is here, we live here as if it were under conditions of communism. We have enough to eat, we have clothes, we have enough folk to screw around with, we go for walks, sing songs. How long have we been here and yet we're already getting tired of all that. We're already straining to get back to our trials and tribulations which we left behind us in Moscow, i.e. in the period of advanced socialism. Why should that be, eh? Why, for instance, does that Toothless Doctor want to become an associate member if she already has everything, and why should the associate member want to be a full academician? What's waiting for me back at work? Here I am a thinker, on a par with doctors of science, there I am a total scientific-technical nonentity. And yet I, too, want to go back to advanced socialism and not prolong my sojourn here under communism. I assure you, the communist paradise will never be built, not because people aren't capable of it, but because they won't want to. But why it turns out like that, I just don't understand.'

'You have to reject the question "why" as having no meaning,' said JRF, 'and then you'll immediately understand everything. There are certain rules that govern the behaviour of people in society. We are formed in such a way that we observe these rules. The observation of these rules is what is quintessential about man as a social animal. We can never say that it is the ultimate cause of everything that happens to people. A fish, if it is to survive, has to live in water and not flap around on the sand or in a frying-pan. It's like that with us. When we arrived here we were torn out of our normal conditions of existence, in which, and only in which, what we essentially are comes to the fore. Extend our sojourn here to, say, a year, and we shall very soon reproduce in this place our normal social milieu in which we will carry out our normal social functions in conformity with the aforementioned rules. Communism as it is portrayed to us in our ideology is something like the rest home of history, i.e. an empty abstraction from real history.'

'I get it,' said the Old Man. 'But, still, it would be nice to find a reassuring explanation somewhere in the gut, or the liver or the genes. Maybe it's simply a question of habit?'

'Habit,' said JRF, 'is a false explanation. From that point of view death is also a kind of habit. The habit of not living.'

NIGHT-TIME CONVERSATIONS

'The attraction of stalinism', said the New Friend, 'can be detected even in the amount of attention that is paid to the person of Stalin in the literature. Moreover, the critical literature elevates him more than the literature of the apologists. What are we supposed to make of that? It's very simple. Who our leaders were or are (whether they are intelligent or fools, wicked or humane) doesn't matter. On the personal level they should be ignored. What is important are the results of their activities. That is what has to be revealed Moreover, calmly, dispassionately, systematically, in detail, demonstrably, scientifically. In themselves, our leaders are creatures with a defective "feed-back system", i.e. they are objectively semi-intelligent, not complete personalities. We have to show how incomplete the social milieu also is which generates them. When we get back to Moscow come and visit me. I'll give you something to read on the subject. But in general, the attraction of the past signifies one thing only: a lack of faith in the future and a fear of it.'

AND DREAMS

The New Friend carried on talking, but JRF drifted off into a dream. And at once Petin appeared.

'You're never going to get rid of me now,' said Petin. 'Do you think that I repent of my actions? Not at all. I am filled with nostalgia. What for? Well, for when I was waiting to be arrested for one thing. Do you think that was dreadful? No, not only dreadful. I would not exchange these thirty years of waiting for thirty years of untroubled sleep. Why not? Because I was waiting for grandiose history to burst into my flat instead of the grey monotony of today. Mark my words, time will pass and everything bad will be forgotten. And in people's memories will come alive wise marshals, courageous generals, audacious scientists, romantic youths . . .'

'Marshals who lost battles,' said JRF, 'generals who lost millions of soldiers for no good reason, scientists who broke the back of science, youths who wrote secret denunciations . . .'

'Yes,' said Petin, 'who wrote denunciations and blocked enemy embrasures with their chests. I wrote denunciations, too. A lot of denunciations. And I gave permission for people to be shot. And what of it? I'm proud of it. I wanted the number of my victims to be carved in golden letters on my tombstone. But, alas, immediately after Stalin died, our frightened leaders were in a hurry to destroy the evidence of our deeds.'

'Crimes,' corrected JRF.

'Well, all right,' said Petin. 'But monstrous crimes. Know, my boy, that only great crimes give rise to genuine good. Great crimes cease to be crimes. If I had been in our leaders' place, I would have exposed the whole picture of our deeds. Can you imagine what the numbers would have been! The whole world would have frozen in horror. And with respect for us. When a thousand are killed, that is cruelty. But when the figure is fifty million it is a mighty epoch. A thousand denunciations is banal. But when there are thousands of millions of them they signify a great ideology.'

'It can't be the case that no evidence of your deeds remains,' said JRF.

'It appears unlikely but it is a fact,' said Petin. 'In the first place, the most fundamental decisions were taken in a form so general that it would be impossible now to detect in them the traces of any crime. They made sense to us, who had to carry them out. But they meant little to anyone else, never mind to our descendants. In the second place, all the basic instructions from above concerning repressions were given orally. It is only by chance that a few documants bearing the signatures of Stalin, Molotov, Voroshilov and others have remained, and they're of secondary importance. So Khrushchev wasn't able to document his accusations. In the third place, people in the lower echelons went to a lot of trouble to conceal the traces of their crimes. And finally there was a special decision of the Politburo to destroy all the documentation, including the evidence about the activities of secret denouncers and informers. Party officials were worried about their reputations.'

'And live witnesses?' said JRF.

'They're people,' said Petin, 'and people aren't documents. Moreover, the majority of them participated in the crimes themselves. What's more, they understood nothing of what was going on and learned nothing. There is no such thing as an intelligent victim. Wisdom is the prerogative of the executioners.'

A HYMN TO RUBBISHING

Every natural and social phenomenon possesses qualities which, once we've discovered them, give us the unarguable moral right to declare that that phenomenon is just as insignificant as anything else on this earth. A conversation, for instance, has got underway about Pushkin. Who, you might think, could be more perfect than that. But you snigger and chuckle, as if by the way, that this genius of yours had skinny bow legs. And that's it! No more genius. There's just another little deformed gnome like yourself. And if you go on to suggest that he may have plagiarised on occasion, that makes him exactly like you, or even a little inferior. At this point you can afford to be a little magnanimous and say that some of his poetry wasn't bad. There's no risk in that for you. That won't be enough to change Pushkin from a gnome like yourself back into a great writer and human being.

I know, you're going to tell me that this truth was well-known long before the socialist era and you'll prove it with some pronouncement or other about sun-spots. But I'm not arguing. Moreover, I'm ready to agree that the socialist era hasn't discovered anything new at all. As far as that goes, it's more a case of its having buried the old rather than discovering the new. But one thing is indisputable: it has opened up unheard-of vistas for the old abominations, raised them to an inconceivable height and placed them at the service of the progress of mankind – it has radically changed their role in society. I'll explain what I mean with examples.

Let's suppose that a certain N has engaged in a heroic struggle with the authorities on behalf of some unjustly treated people. The punitive organs know the afore-mentioned fundamental law of rubbishing very well and quickly begin to hunt out the defects in N which will allow them to reduce him to the level of a madman or a scoundrel. It can be done in the old-fashioned way, empirically, by a process of collecting crumbs of information which discredit N. That takes time and effort. But at this point science lends a hand. If someone is fighting for the interests of a whole people – says science – it means that he's a homosexual who dreams of buggering an honoured party secretary or a shock-worker in a brigade of Communist Labour. And there and then it produces a quotation from Freud. This last point is very important: nowadays even orthodox marxists are more inclined to believe the reactionary ideologues of the bourgeoisie than they are the classical marxist writers. Or take another example. It has become known that a certain N in his mature years has been baptised and, with his head screwed on, has adopted the Orthodox faith. What does science have to say about that? It says that N was obviously a secret informer. This law, of course, is not all that useful to the punitive organs. But science is not part of the superstructure, even Stalin understood that. It can also serve progressive forces. There is another law from that same science which is very useful to these forces: if a person becomes a Catholic in his old age, it means that he wrote a denunciation voluntarily, without being an official secret informer. And these progressive forces should know the even more important law of rubbishing, according to which people who are morally pure as the driven snow practice onanism or are impotent.

What I like most of all about the scientific approach to rubbishing is the following: it is by no means required to discover these laws in empirical reality, one has to institute them as *a priori* laws in relation to reality and achieve their acceptance by members of society. After that, I assure you, you will never find a single exception to them. Here is a classical example for you. A few days before the end of his stay, the Engineer unexpectedly returned to Moscow, followed immediately afterwards by a dyed blonde female post-graduate student from the institute of micro-biology. What could that mean? The Toothless Doctor, without a moment's hesitation, declared that, judging by everything, the Engineer had contracted syphilis from her, or, on the contrary, had given her (the Blonde) a dose. The Doctor's assertion seemed to be nonsense on two counts. Firstly, no one had seen the Engineer and the Blonde together. Secondly, there had been nothing like enough time for syphilis to manifest itself. The Doctor surveyed her opponents with disdain.

'Huh,' she said, 'and you call yourselves scientists! You're no doubt for ever referring to the law of relativity! You harp on about cybernetics! But you don't know the fundamental laws of life!'

'Probably she's right, you know,' said the New Friend later. 'The Engineer, when all is said and done, could have caught it before he came here. Or the Blonde, for that matter. That's the crux of the matter. And the fact that no one has seen them together confirms that hypothesis more than anything else!'

CANDOUR

In connection with the departure of the Engineer and the Blonde, a conversation developed on the theme of sexual relations. The Goodly Maiden declared that she didn't see any problem there. Wherever else it had yet to happen, at least in this sphere the communist principle of 'to each according to their needs' had already been realised in practice. The Toothless Doctor, who always found something to object to, declared that they had still only achieved advanced socialism in this sphere as well, not full communism. Our needs were not yet satisfied in full. The Spiteful Maiden agreed with the Doctor.

'And elements of inequality in distribution have remained,' she said. 'Some don't get their needs fulfilled and others get them overfulfilled.' The Old Man said that that was precisely where the process of perfecting society should begin. Those who were getting more than enough should share with those who were getting less than enough. A habit of sharing a surplus would be established which would gradually transfer to other spheres of life. The Goodly Maiden asked how he imagined that would work in practice. Was she supposed to send a proportion of her admirers, for instance, to the Associate Member or the Doctor? And supposing they not only wouldn't sleep with them, they wouldn't even sit beside them in the toilet?! The Doctor declared that she personally would not sit beside the Goodly Maiden's suitors in the toilet, that she could find her own, that education and intellect completely made up for the absence of dimples in the cheeks or foreign bras and panties.

'Hang on!' exclaimed the Candidate. 'What's all the racket about?!' 'Personally,' said the Spiteful Maiden, 'to be absolutely frank, I am against egalitarianism in this matter. I am even in favour of communism being postponed as long as possible, or even indefinitely. I am in favour of men fighting duels over women, doing battle in tournaments, letting them go first, kissing their hands, giving them flowers and jewellery, singing serenades.'

'You're asking a bit too much, my dear!' said the Associate

Member. 'But I too would preserve something from the past. For instance, I am against the voluntary principle in these matters. I am for men taking us by force. A man should be strong, a woman weak. Marx himself recognised that, if I'm not mistaken. Did you ever take a woman by force? (this to the men) And were you ever taken by force (this to the women)? There you are then! Deep down, men are all violators and women the violated. That is nature's way and one shouldn't violate nature.'

'You're being inconsistent,' said the Old Man. 'Why is it possible to violate women, which is supposed to be natural, and yet not nature itself?'

'You may be old,' said the Associate Member placatingly, 'but you're a fool. You can't take a hint.'

'Well, I don't see any inconsistency,' said the Goodly Maiden. 'When I was young I was terribly attractive. Lads in the street and grown men wouldn't let me pass. And what didn't they do to me! They dragged me up to attics and down into basements. Singly and in groups. At first I struggled, but then I got used to it. I realised that it was good. And then I began to drag them into attics or closets or behind fences. And that was good, too. Willingly or by force, what's the difference? If they just leave us that, all the rest will come.'

'You're right,' said JRF. 'When they deprive us of that little bit of sexual freedom that we have now, that will be the day that they announce the arrival of full communism.'

'Do you think that'll happen?' asked the Old Man.

'Things are going that way,' said JRF. 'If it were possible to measure the level of sexuality in the rest home since we've been here (the number of sexual acts, their duration and piquancy), you would be shaken by how low it would be. After all, it's more words than deeds in this area. There are so many words, in fact, because there are so few deeds.'

'Of course,' said the Candidate, 'you're not going to go far on kasha and macaroni.'

'Moreover,' said the Old Man, 'they put something in our food to suppress the urge.'

'So that's why we're a bit sleepy all the time,' said the Associate Member. 'The swine! But that should be denounced! Where are your dissidents, then?! They rabbit on about all sorts of human rights and similar nonsense, but not a word about this!'

'Why denounce it?' said the Spiteful Maiden. 'This is exactly in the spirit of communist ideas. The best way of making people equal is to deprive them of whatever it is you're equalising.'

Everyone was in a bad mood after that. Conversation came to an end and the residents drifted back to their dormitories, looking at their watches every five minutes during the tedious wait for dinner.

'I'd like to know,' said the New Friend, 'whether in Paradise they pour bromides into the Holy Spirit and give all the saints a watch so that they can at least scratch the surface of boredom while they wait for lunch and tea. And in general, I think that I am beginning to understand what is at the root of all our problems: there has been an epidemic of schizophrenia raging in our people for centuries. And now we're infecting everyone around us with it. It is not we who need the "iron curtain" now, but the people on the other side of it.'

THE TRIP TO GORKI

An excursion to Leninskiye Gorki was a compulsory part of the holiday and one could only get out of it under very exceptional circumstances. A string of buses arrived at the grounds in the morning. The guests filled them to bursting point. The very fact that the excursion was free of charge created a festive atmosphere. And the news that there would be free tea and sandwiches at Gorki was met with a resounding hurrah. The All-Rounder, who had been drunk since he got up, pinched all the women in turn, breathing wine fumes all over them, and they squealed with delight. JRF managed to slip out of the clutches of the Little Lady (by apparently getting on to another bus by mistake) and make up to a brunette. But when they arrived in Gorki the Little Lady got rid of the brunette by saying something nasty to her. She in turn threatened to report her.

First they did a tour of the park, then Lenin's house itself. The guide led the guests from room to room showing them where the dining room had been and the sitting-room and the office and the bedroom, recounting a mass of interesting details. In every room the All-Rounder swore rather loudly and said that, in such smart surroundings, he, too, wouldn't have minded running the government. Hearing the All-Rounder's mutterings, the guide said that Vladimir Ilich had been a very simple man and that now even an average minister or academician or marshal had a more luxurious flat and dacha. The guests nodded approvingly.

JRF wandered along at the tail of the group, not listening to the guide and picturing to himself the events of that terrible night when the lorries had surrounded the estate, how Stalin and his men had gone into Lenin's study after pushing Krupskaya aside, how he had told Lenin of the Central Committee's, i.e. his, Stalin's, decision. Although historical fact, common sense and the psychology of the participants of that epoch militated against his vision, he had just as much faith in it as he would have had in a self-evident axiom. For a moment he imagined himself in Stalin's place. And he realised, not so much intellectually as with his whole being, that he would have acted in precisely the same way. If you want to know the truth about a person's behaviour in a difficult situation, put yourself in his position and trust your common sense, he thought. Yes, I would have acted in precisely the same way.

Afterwards they ate free sandwiches and drank free tea, walked around the grounds of the estate, sang songs and told Lenin jokes. There turned out to be an enormous number of them, with Lenin appearing as either laughable or stupid.

'Notice,' said the Old Man, 'that there have been few Stalin jokes, even to this day, and he never appears stupid in them. Why is that, do you think?'

'If you can laugh at someone, it means he's still a person,' said JRF. 'But if you can't laugh at someone, then he's not a person but a super-person or a non-person. Which is one and the same thing.'

THOUGHTS ON THE WAY BACK

On their way home JRF made an important sociological discovery. One has to distinguish, he thought, between voluntarist or despotic power and bureaucratic power, operating within a legal framework. In addition one has to distinguish between power coming from above and power coming from below, i.e. from the people. In the Stalin epoch there was a combination of extreme despotism and extreme ochlocracy. In the epoch of Khrushchev and Brezhnev, despotism and ochlocracy were held in check simultaneously. It is now becoming very evident the people themselves are more interested in destroying ochlocracy than power. The bureaucratic authorities, for their part, are interested in preserving it, for that is their stronghold, as it were, but in a restricted form which is under their control. But imposing limits on the power of the people and supervising it, has the inevitable consequence of weakening despotic power and increasing bureaucratic power. The resurrection of Stalin is impossible without a resurrection of the power of the people. But the people doesn't want that. There will never be another Stalin!!

NIGHT-TIME CONVERSATIONS

'What is the starting point of civilisation? It starts from the principle: in the sweat of thy brow shalt thou earn thy daily bread. And if what we have is civilisation, then that principle is at the root of it. But what does communism promise? In veiled form it promises a paradise of inactivity. Work is recognised, but what kind of work? It is seen as a development of some capabilities or other in man, as pleasure and creativity. There is even the prospect of its being considered as a rational way of spending one's time off work(!!) And we are moving towards that ideal. But in what fashion? By shockingly poor workmanship, eye-wash and idleness. Only the lower strata do any work, and they do that any old how. And they dream about how to get out of it, find some "clean" work, "set themselves up". And for the life of me, I can't see any other way out apart from forced slave labour. And they will breed people who will find that this slavery suits them. And if the sort of concern is shown for them that a solicitous farmer would show to his cattle, they will deify that system and its leaders.'

'But they'll still work badly.'

'That's obvious. For the moment we are living off the creative juices of the West. And as a result we just about keep going. But what's going to happen when the West is destroyed and goes the same way?'

'A period of unrestrained degradation could set in or stagnation lasting many centuries.'

'Let's not think about that. If we go on like that we'll end up with the destruction of the solar system and even the galaxy.'

'What's it all for, then?'

'If it's a question of "all", then the concept of goal is devoid of sense.'

TABLE-TALK

'What does "according to need" mean?' asked the Old Man. 'Let's take women, for example. Who among us doesn't get enough? No one? And who among us is completely satisfied? Again no one? That's strange. And the All-Rounder's no different.'

'Why should I be any different?' said the All-Rounder. 'We do have enough women. More than enough, even. But what kind of women are they? I'd like to find something really worthwhile. A woman who . . . who . . . well, would make you not want to run after another one. They tell me there are such women. And you read about them in books. Now and again you meet one in the street whom you'd give up the rest of your life to spend a night with. But none of that has anything to do with us. As with everything else, we get the second-rate, second-hand ugly ones. If you'll pardon the expression, we fuck the way we eat, drink and clothe ourselves.'

'Sometimes something worthwhile comes along,' said the

Candidate. 'But we are used to shit and don't notice them. And we don't believe that they really are worthwhile. We're frightened to stop. We hope for something better. But there will never be anything better.'

'And are we any better, then?' asked the All-Rounder. 'Do you know what the women say about us? I once had occasion to get an earful.'

'And what do they say?'

'That there are almost no real men left. Men are cowardly, deceitful and unreliable. They try and set themselves up at the expense of the woman. They have no sense of responsibility. Nothing is sacred. With them it's nothing but drunkenness, abusive language, dirty talk and meanness. Will that do?'

'That sounds about right.'

'But you get decent men as well now and again. For instance, you wouldn't deny that dissidents are courageous.'

'Have you seen them up close? Have you been in their company?'

'All the women who are physically worth anything use their charms to improve their situation, and there's nothing left of that woman we all dream about.'

'The men are no better.'

'Everyone wants to have a better life. And on their way to that better life they lose their most valuable qualities – femininity and masculinity in the elevated, romantic sense.'

'It's the only way of making it.'

'Well, I don't see any problem. You just have to be satisfied with what you've got.'

'That's right. Here we are eating kasha and macaroni. But we know that elsewhere in the world there are kebabs and chicken tabak.'

'You see,' summarised the Old Man, 'it's not so simple, this "according to need". It's all hogwash. Mere verbiage. It would be a lot more pleasant in a resort in the south. And the women there are in a different category.'

'What do you want with women, anyway?' sniggered some character in glasses. 'You've probably forgotten how to do it.'

'My dick', said the Old Man, 'is still in good enough shape to bounce off the skull of a mongrel like you.'

'Here, just a minute! I'll show you who's a mongrel.'

'Go ahead and show me! Do you want a bet? If I can't give you a good hammering with one hand tied behind my back, it'll cost me a bottle of cognac. Are you on?'

'You must be joking.'

'Quiet, you pair. We'll have people complaining in a minute.'

'And yet, I'd pay a lot for a real woman! I'm sick and tired of doing it like the cats or dogs.'

THE LAST DAY

After breakfast the guests were weighed. The doctor, with one eye on the person on the scales and the other on the book in which the person's weight had been noted on arrival at the rest home, gave him the good news: he had gained (if he was one of the thin ones) or lost (if he was one of the fat ones) so and so many kilograms. Then the doctor took the guests' blood pressure and told those with high blood pressure that it was down and those with low blood pressure that it was up. And everyone was pleased, both that the holiday had been so healthy and interesting and that the boring, tedious sojourn on a reduced diet was at last coming to an end.

The final supper was truly astonishing. The main course was sausages and buck-wheat kasha. And there was an apple each. And wine, the money for which had been collected earlier. The director made a warm-hearted speech. An expression of thanks on behalf of the guests was given by the Toothless Doctor. Then there was a do-it-yourself concert. The Little Lady sang. This time she sang badly and everyone felt very sorry for her. But they applauded her just like they applauded everyone else. The Candidate recited some of his own poetry. Two fat, slovenly cleaning women did a Russian song and dance number. The New Friend played a Rachmaninov prelude and a rhapsody by Liszt on the piano. Then there was a dance with prizes. JRF and the Little Lady won first prize for the waltz – a packet of cigarettes and a bottle of eau-de-cologne. Then everyone went for a walk in the fields. They swore to meet again in Moscow. The mood was melancholy.

'It's a strange situation,' said the Old Man. 'We're fed up

here, yet we don't want to go home. And we've got on each other's nerves, yet we don't want to part.'

'We don't want to get back into our everyday routine,' said the Candidate.

'Shall we see each other in Moscow?' asked the Little Lady.

'Better not to,' replied JRF.

'I see. Well, take my phone number just in case. Maybe you'll suddenly feel like giving me a call. You know, you only have to say the word and I'll come running.'

'Thank you. I wish you all the luck in the world. Take care!'

'Thank you, too. I won't forget you. You're a good sort. And that's a rarity, nowadays.'

THE SEND-OFF

They had violet-coloured potatoes for breakfast. 'Why not kasha?' he asked. 'We're short of groats,' replied the waitress. As he was leaving the dining-room he glanced at the newspaper-stand and saw a face he recognised. Beneath the photograph was an obituary, signed by all the leading members of the Party and government.

'A great epoch has passed away,' said the Old Man. 'It's time for us to be on our way, as well.'

'Where to?' he asked.

'Home, for the moment,' said the Old Man. 'For the moment . . .'

When they had vacated their dormitory, a cleaning-woman spread a dirty sheet on the floor, shook the contents of the waste-paper basket on to it and began to go through them. She put some of the bits of paper back into the basket, others she put carefully into a cellophane packet, including a letter which JRF had not sent to Herself.

As they were leaving the main block, after getting their passports back, the child part of the 'Happy Family' sculpture fell off in one lump and blocked the exit. They had to leave by the backdoor. When they were in the bus, they heard that the Associate Member's fur coat had been stolen after all. This news immediately raised everyone's spirits. They set off for the station singing and telling jokes. Dissident bounded along behind the bus, keeping pace with it all the way. And he sat on the platform until the train took the guests off to Moscow, a place he knew not of.

BACK HOME

His flat-mate's wife gave him his keys. 'Your latest ¯beauty dropped by,' she said. 'She said she was going off somewhere for a while.' His room was empty. Something familiar and important was missing. He didn't bother to work out what it was precisely. He lay down on the ottoman and stared at the dirty ceiling.

> Get ready! Soon your hour will come.
> With no superfluous delay
> You'll shuffle of this coil, in sum,
> You'll snuff it, croak, die, pass away.
> No longer will you eat bad chops
> And rotten gruel with nauseous juice,
> Nor with your beard pull out the stops
> And into bed the birds induce;
> No more in someone else's work
> Write someone else's trivial quote,
> Nor end up legless like a jerk
> On some official day of note.
> No more three times the price you'll pay
> For jeans already down-at-heel,
> Nor with the masses march for aye
> Towards the glorious ideal.
> This world again you'll never see,
> Nor all its horrors apprehend,
> Nor from the darkness soon to be
> Into the world of Light ascend.

Himself appeared.

'Where are all the others?' asked JRF.

'I've got rid of them all,' said Himself.

'You did right. I was sick and tired of them myself.'

'I knew that you would interpret my behaviour correctly. Tell me, what happened to Petin's notes?'

'He destroyed them all.'

478

'The so-and-so! And I trusted him. I spared his life, hoping that in time he'd write the truth about me.'

'He deceived you. In general he was a semi-literate, stupid man.'

'That's a pity! And I thought that he was acting like a fool to save his life.'

'If he'd acted like a fool, you would have decided that he really was a fool.'

'Perhaps you'll carry on where he left off? It'll soon be the hundredth anniversary of my birth. It would be very appropriate.'

'There's no point. If Petin had done it, it would have been all right. They would have published anything he wrote. Anything I wrote wouldn't get further than the KGB.'

'What's to be done, then? I want the world to know the truth about me.'

'It's a bit late for that. The world will never learn the truth about you now. Petin was your last chance.'

'What will these scoundrels do to me?'

'It's not difficult to predict. They'll rehabilitate you officially. They'll admit, of course, that you committed the odd error and occasionally went a bit too far, but in general you were a faithful follower of Lenin, resolutely carried out the general line of the Party and earned a lot of merit with your collectivisation, industrialisation and your conduct of the war. On the other hand, critics will howl about your crimes. But there won't be another revelation à la Khrushchev. Incidentally, there was a rumour to the effect that the speech which Khrushchev gave was really prepared by Beria. Is that true?'

'Not quite. It was prepared by Beria, but for me. I was intending to make the most sensational speech in history, something along the lines of "On Dizziness from Success", in which I was going to touch on certain errors and excesses being committed at local level and even by the leadership. It was going to be a pretext for removing Molotov, Voroshilov, Kaganovich and others. And Beria, of course. But I didn't have time.'

'Did they get you first?'

'No, that's nonsense. These cowardly jackals are only capable of having a go at the dead.'

'It's a pity that all this is going to remain unknown.'

'What about literature, then?! It can all be reconstructed in literature!'

'No. The writers who are prepared to do the "reconstructing" are all untalented chancers. The ones who are talented and honest know that it's beyond them. They would have to reveal a lot of things and in actual fact there is nothing to reveal.'

'What about science?'

'The same, only more so. There are even fewer intelligent and talented people among academics than among writers. Academics oscillate between two extremes – between the need for your existence and the chance nature of it. The least talented of them are trying to find a dialectical mean: chance as a possible form of necessity! But these categories have long since become vacuous.'

'What's going to happen, then?'

'There'll be the evaluation of history, i.e. a boring, mediocre account.'

'I am going away now. But as a farewell gift I want you to give me honest answers to the following questions. If you had been on the threshold of the revolution and had known what it would lead to, would you have been for the revolution or against it?'

'For it.'

'Would you have been on the side of the "Whites" or the "Reds"?'

'The Reds.'

'Would you have sided with me or with the others?'

'With you.'

'So what is it, then?'

'Re-fashioning the past is not my concern.'

'That means we were right, then?'

'No.'

'But we acted from the force of necessity. We had no other solution.'

'Yes, you had.'

'What was it?'

'Not to exist.'

'That's all right for the future, but not for the past. Let me give you a warning: watch out for yourself; They've got on to you. But don't think that They are any better that I was. I was a lion, or a wolf at least. But they are rats, or lice at most. Farewell!'

AT THE INSTITUTE

No one at the Institute showed any sign of being pleased to see him back. They didn't of course, have any time for him, since they were preparing themselves for Petin's funeral and the ensuing changes at the top in the Institute management. But there was more to it than that, something connected with him personally. There was something in the way people looked at him when they greeted him or spoke to him which he found vaguely disconcerting. Even Trollop only nodded to him and slipped past quickly. He was surprised at that, and offended.

Having stood for a few moments with raised eyebrows and mouth half open he lowered his head, shrugged his shoulders and wandered off to Tvarzhinskaya's office. Tvarzhinskaya greeted him curtly and did not offer him her bony prehensile claw nor invite him to sit down. He stood. And waited. He looked at her and wondered how this ugly, semi-intelligent old woman could have accumulated so much power over people's lives and futures. She leafed through the pages, holding them up to her beak-like nose, as if smelling them. Although JRF sensed that she was pleased with his work, she gave no visible sign and didn't even thank him. When she had looked through the manuscript she told him that he could go and that she wouldn't detain him any longer.

He stopped for a moment in front of the office where Herself ought to be. Should he go in and ask what was wrong? No, it wasn't worth it! Where should he go now? He didn't feel like phoning his new lady friend from the rest home, he was tired of her complaining. He didn't want to drink either. And he had no one to drink with, anyway. Nor the wherewithal. He thought of looking in at *Questions* but thought better of it. If they were going to publish his article, they would publish it without his visiting them. And if they didn't want to publish it, dropping in on them wouldn't help.

He stopped on the upper landing and lit a cigarette. He

skimmed through the wall-newspaper which had been put out in connection with the forthcoming public holiday. There was a picture of Brezhnev on the front page dressed in marshal's uniform and with all his decorations. He was portrayed as a handsome thirty-year-old. Then he read an announcement that there would be a briefing session that day at such and such a time for those marching on the right flank of the May Day parade. Previously their names had been published. This year they had decided to keep them a secret, just in case.

What next? Drop into the personnel department and sign himself out on some pretext, or just go out anyway? The Teacher came up to him.

'What are you thinking about?' he asked him.

'About what is better – to be an independent, single-cell organism, or a cell in the arse of a thinking creature,' replied JRF.

'What's your preference?' asked the Teacher.

'My preference is to go off without signing out,' said JRF.

A cleaning woman latched on to him on the staircase. He didn't know what the matter was but she kept shouting at him. 'The louse', he thought, 'has probably picked up something. What a race we are! As soon as we see that we can safely attack someone, we throw ourselves on him like a pack of dogs and bite where we can.'

He came out on to the street and took his normal route home – past the Lenin Library, the reception building of the Presidium of the Supreme Soviet, the university, the 'National' hotel and the Council of Ministers. He stopped at the statue of Marx. A mass of pigeons near the monument were frenziedly gobbling up the food which old-age pensioners were feeding to them from little packets. 'Despicable, capricious creatures,' thought JRF. He glanced at Marx but the latter responded with granite indifference.

At the Lubyanka the majestic Iron Felix, an island in a stream of traffic, looked off into some unknown future. No plain clothes agents were to be seen. 'Surely they can't have been removed?' thought JRF. 'Hardly. It's more likely that I'm not used to them any more and have lost the knack.'

A group of young lads were drinking in a children's playground. They broke the empty bottles on a little stone 'mushroom'. The fragments fell into the sand. One lad left the group, came out on to the street and fell across the pavement.

'Get him inside, lads,' said JRF, 'or he'll be taken off to a sobering-up station.'

'So what?' they replied. 'Bugger off before we pull off your beard.'

'No,' thought JRF. 'There is nothing romantic about boozing. Boozing produces scum. The romance of boozing is merely the invention of sober blather merchants. I must give it up.'

PETIN'S FUNERAL

As they wrote afterwards in the Institute wall-newspaper, Petin's funeral was a 'clear demonstration of the monolithic unity of Soviet philosophy'. From morning onwards the whole building of the humanities faculties, the courtyard in front of the building and the stretch of street as far as the editorial building of the journal *Communist* were crowded with workers in the field of ideology who had come from all over the country as well as from countries of the socialist fraternity. There was a whole delegation from Kiev, headed by the very progressive philosopher Nepeivoda, who, despite that fact, was pursuing a very successful career. After Krushchev's secret speech, when it looked like Petin's goose was about to be cooked, Nepeivoda sharply criticised Petin's philosophical errors, on the strength of which he became known as a progressive. Later on, when the storm in the Moscow tea-cup abated before it even got started, Nepeivoda, who had managed in the meantime to miss out a couple of rungs on his way up the career ladder, asked Petin to be an opponent at the defence of his doctoral dissertation. Petin agreed, of course, and praised the dissertation very much, thanks to which Nepeivoda moved yet another rung up the ladder. Arriving in Moscow, Nepeivoda met up with the progressive philosophers in the capital (Smirnyashchev, Subbotin, Tormoshilkina and others). Justifying his surname, which in Russian means 'don't drink water', Nepeivoda drank only vodka. In a burst of drunken candour, he confessed that he had come in order to see with his own eyes that 'that dreg and scoundrel' (he meant Petin) really had coughed it. The next day, however, he made a moving speech about the deceased at the official mourning ceremony.

There was a large number of police in attendance and an even larger number of plain-clothes agents to maintain order during the funeral proceedings. There were fears that some of Petin's victims who had survived, or their relatives, might turn up and provoke dissident disturbances of the peace. 'It's stupid to fear any such thing,' thought JRF. 'Petin's real victims are standing in a guard of honour beside the coffin or making laudatory speeches or patiently watching and listening. There are no victims, only accomplices.' JRF was right. The victims came and brought . . . a wreath. They wanted to write on the ribbon that the wreath was from the victims of occasional errors and excesses. But they were told that would be tasteless and so they wrote: from your comrades-in-arms in the struggle.

An orchestra thundered out continuously. Even one of the secretaries from the Central Committee came and stood for a few minutes in the guard of honour. The unity really was complete. Tvarzhinskaya appeared, flanked on one side by the openly anti-semitic Rabinovich and on the other by the secret zionist Sidorov. Tormoshilkina stood leaning against Professor Vaskin from the Higher Party School, who had written a secret report on her to the Central Committee, and nodded her head in agreement with her post-graduate student from the university, about whom she herself had written a secret report. Bulyga lent his handkerchief to Academician Evchuk, who couldn't restrain his tears when he remembered how Petin and he had repulsed the attack of the 'Menshevik idealists'. Smirnyashchev and Barabanov accompanied Academician Kanareikin, and Subbotin walked in front of them, demanding that the way be made clear for the academician. The Teacher whispered to JRF that, if the truth were told, Petin was not such a swine, fool and ignoramus as they thought. And they still didn't know whether the new director would be any better. Incidentally, there was a rumour that the director would be Nepeivoda. The Ukrainians were now dominating the leadership and slipping their people in everywhere. 'It's all the same to me,' replied JRF. 'The Chinese can dominate it, for all I care.'

'You're right,' said the Teacher, and went off to join Smirnyashchev, Sazonov and Subbotin.

484

Having been jostled about in the auditorium and having noticed several familiar plain-clothes agents, who recognised him and winked at him, and having found no one to keep him company (i.e., get out of there and celebrate the occasion in a more suitable locale), JRF extricated himself from the crowd and followed his nose. 'Anything to get away from this madhouse,' he thought. 'You can tell from Petin's funeral the extent to which Stalin will be rehabilitated and stalinism restored. The funeral is obviously a compromise affair. The Novodevich'e cemetery is not the Kremlin wall. And the secretary for ideology is not Suslov. The rehabilitation and restoration will be purely formal and superficial. In the first place, our present leaders regard themselves as no less important figures than Stalin and his crew. In the second place, no one wants to take the risk of declaring themselves Stalin's disciple and successor. Disciples and successors of Lenin, that goes without saying. But not of Stalin. In an hour or so they'll throw the last sod into Petin's grave and from that moment on even Petin's toadiest toadies will cease to mention his name. A great epoch is vanishing into the past, taking its secrets with it and leaving the stage to the lies of history.'

'Well, could you have declared yourself Stalin's successor?' asked an unidentified inner voice.

'Yes', he thought. 'I'd like to burst into someone's flat in the middle of the night, just once, to see the faces go pale and the hands tremble, and order them to "follow us". I'd like to carry out an important assignment just once, "at any price". Just once . . . Wait a minute! What are you talking about?! My God, look at the depths to which even someone like myself can sink! So why are we surprised?! Any of us is capable of any despicable act not only outwardly, but inwardly as well, so long as it is officially deemed to be in the name of, for the sake of, for . . . And inwardly to a greater extent. Outwardly our average bloke can be a layabout, leadswinger or dissembler, even when committing a despicable act. Inwardly, never. But that's enough of that. The problem of Stalin has died with Petin and I am free!'

But was that really the case. What if he had just now lost any freedom he might have had? After all, when he was making his plans, he was only a factor in someone else's plans. He was struck by this thought and stopped in his tracks. Plain-clothes agents bumped into him from behind and nearly knocked him down. 'Excuse me,' he said. 'I was thinking about something.' And he continued on his way, no longer thinking about anything.

IN HOLIDAY MOOD

The May Day celebrations were approaching. Queues grew in the shops and all essential goods vanished. 'Holiday parcels' were distributed in institutions of the top rank. In slightly lower ranking institutions such parcels were given to the most senior staff and in all the others a few parcels were distributed per department, and the staff either drew lots for them or shared them out. Moscow cleaned itself of its winter refuse, psychologically unstable individuals and unreliable elements. In district committees of the Party, leaders of columns of marchers in the parade were receiving their instructions and would in turn instruct those marching on the right flank. There were three times more policemen than usual in the streets and public places, and ten times more members of the voluntary people's militia. Agents in plain clothes were everywhere in such numbers that even a sudden move of a hand into a pocket to get a box of matches resulted in one's documents being scrutinised at a police station and enquiries being instituted. The strictest instructions had come from the top that there were to be no excesses and these instructions were carried out to the letter. At a secret meeting of the Politburo, news of which was immediately all round Moscow, the head of the KGB and the Minister of the Interior were told to their faces that if there were a political scandal, their jobs would be on the line. From the way plain-clothes agents regarded JRF with apparent indifference, he realised that they were keeping a close eye on him. What would that be for? He wasn't a dissident, after all. Nor was he yet a mental case. Surely They weren't still concerned about all that other nonsense?! It was absurd!

As the holiday drew nearer, the number of drunks on the streets increased daily in geometrical progression. A strictly scientific explanation of this phenomenon has been discovered. In the first place, the number of drunks is growing anyway, as are all the other indices of growth in our country. Secondly, as warmer weather approaches, all the drunks crawl out on to the streets and no longer lie around at home or in the entrances to blocks of flats. Thirdly, the numbers taken by the police to sobering up stations fall as the holidays approach, since the authorities are paying heed to the expectations of the workers (on the one hand) and all the places in police stations and sobering up stations are long since fully taken (on the other hand) – which is an example of the extraordinary unity of the Party and the people. Fourthly, particular causes become intertwined with the general causes. Last year, for instance, the authorities did the workers out of Easter. And they, particularly the non-believing Party alcoholics, began to drink twice as much as a sign of protest. This year, on the other hand, Easter fell on the Sunday before the May Day celebrations and the workers, at the prospect of four days off in a row, began to drink ten times as much as usual a week before. Moreover, as always, communist atheist alcoholics were to the fore, leading the rest of the non-Party and ignorant believing masses, which nowadays consist mostly of refined intellectuals who know foreign languages and listen to enemy Western radio stations.

SATURDAY

On Saturday he went to see his parents. They were not particularly pleased to see him. His mother complained of illness, about rising prices, the absence in the shops of things she needed, and queues. She scolded him for not yet having come to his senses and for wasting his talents, referring to others who were candidates, and even doctors. His father gave him all sorts of wise advice. He had stopped drinking completely because of his liver and consequently there was not a drop of spirits in the house. Money, they said in unison, was tight. His father had acquired a vegetable plot. A long distance away, mind you. But it was a good allotment and they wanted to build a little house on it and that cost a lot of money nowadays. For their part, they hoped that he would defend his thesis and . . . but his mother gave in and 'lent' him fifty roubles 'of her own'. He came away from his parents in confusion. And for the first time in his short life he was frightened. There was nowhere to go. There was nothing to do. There was nothing he wanted to do.

He spent the afternoon drinking. In the evening he got in tow with some drunken crew. 'We're one bloke short,' they told him. A drunk and rather slovenly 'girl' gave JRF the once-over and said: 'I'll take him. Wrap him up!' Things calmed down about three o'clock in the morning and they dossed down where they were and got into the love-making (those who were still capable) without switching off the light. He had a dream in which a voice spoke to him out of the darkness: 'If no one pays you any attention and you feel that you are alone in the world, there is only one way of overcoming that loneliness – you have to care about other people. If you want people to be nice to you, you have to be nice to them.'

'Who are you?' he asked.

'I am you,' answered the voice. 'Remember: the world appears to us as we project it. And there is no other wisdom on this earth.'

Then he had another dream, which was full of marxist quotations. They were all thread-bare, old, ugly, insolent and lewd.

A HYMN TO THE MARXIST QUOTE

There is a law holds o'er us sway,
Our birth cry scarce escapes our throats
When both our ears ring night and day
With crude bombastic marxist quotes.
You go to school, they're there as well,
Eternal and infallible,
These quotes instruct, demand, compel,
With every single syllable.
When later childhood you forsake,
Like beard and 'screw Them' anecdote
Where you go, there goes in your wake
The insep – er – able marxist quote.
You have to work then, like a horse,
But daisy-fresh and grandiose,
And thundering all day long, of course,

That marxist quote gets up your nose.
And when you try to celebrate
Some festival or day of note
E'en then you can't eradicate
The ubiquitous damned marxist quote.
When homewards from the pub you go
And dreaming, maybe, of your oats,
You stop dead in your tracks, for lo,
The night sky's flashing marxist quotes.
You fall into your lonely bed,
Whacked by the daily routine drear,
But even in your sleep instead
Of dreams these marxist quotes appear.
The first's the first one ever heard,
He's hairy, fat and, oh, so wise,
The next is small with ginger beard
And slanted, tartar-looking eyes.
But both of them quite soon give way
To a quote with large mustachio
Who leads quote armies to the fray –
'Tis the quotes' generalissimo.
But he in turn goes off forlorn
And, belching out vituperation,
Emerges from an ear of corn
A funny little round quotation.
But squashing it just like a tank,
With bushy brows and gaze remote,
In uniform of marshal's rank,
Goes lumbering on an endless quote.
The years will pass on by and when
You're ready for retirement too,
Don't think that's that, for even then
Those quotes will still watch over you.
And when you've played out life's last notes
And you must cross that Great Divide,
You'll meet the authors of those quotes –
They'll all be there on t'other side.

JRF'S HOLIDAY DREAM

He drank again. And again he slept. And had a wonderful
holiday dream. Suddenly everything was suffused with pink and
blue light. He was pushed into a large hall. He realised at once
that he was in the main assembly hall of the Institute. But why

was it now so large and magnificent? When he looked at the platform he saw what had happened. In place of the plaster bust of Lenin there towered a gigantic bronze statue of Brezhnev with his eyebrows raised. To the right of it was the old bust of Lenin and to the left, a similar bust of Stalin. There was a slogan covering the whole wall which read: 'Remember, you scoundrel, that you're not just anywhere, but in the realm of full communism!' Lower down there were excerpts from the Moral Code of Communism: 'The penalty for any sign of discontent is death', 'The penalty for needing more than you're supposed to need is death', 'The penalty . . . is death' . . . The Examination Board sat round a table on the platform, presided over by Tvarzhinskaya. On one side of her sat the third generation cretin Barabanov and on the other the third generation paranoiac Smirnyashchev. Along both sides of the table and in the second row of seats on the platform sat the members of the board: Subbotin, Tormoshilkina, Sazonov, the Teacher, Tatyana, the Old Man, Trollop, the Guru and all the others. They were awaiting the arrival of the representatives of the 'flying saucers'. The Representatives appeared from nowhere precisely on time in the place which had been reserved for them. In front were three ugly little green dwarfs and behind them three handsome giants of athletic build.

'These are our servants – bio-robots,' said the chief green dwarf, pointing to the giants. 'We bred them over a long period on one of our experimental planets. Ten thousand zillion similar humanoids perished before we managed to produce these specimens. As you can see, the results aren't bad. Well, I suppose you can begin.'

Tvarzhinskaya opened the special session of the Examination Board.

'There is one item on the agenda,' she announced, 'and that is the question of renewing JRF's appointment for a further similar period. Bring him in!'

Agents in plain clothes twisted JRF's arms behind his back and pushed him up to the table. Tvarzhinskaya's unblinking gaze fixed itself on JRF's forehead and he began to shrink and sink into the floor until only his head was visible. The cretin Barabanov read out JRF's curriculum vitae and the paranoiac Smirnyashchev gave an opinion of his academic work, stressing in the process his own contribution to world science. After that it was the turn of the members of the board. Dobronravov said that JRF was intending to blow up the Palace of Congress in the Kremlin. The Teacher said that JRF was planning an attempt on the life of the Chairman of the KGB. Trollop said that JRF had wanted to seduce her and had called Tvarzhinskaya a bitch. Tatyana said that JRF had set up an anti-Soviet organisation and that he was a drunkard and a womaniser. Adopting the pose of a naked fat woman in a Rubens painting and addressing the Representatives rather than the Board, Doctor Subbotin asked whether JRF had the KGB's permission to wear a beard. JRF babbled out something to the effect that he had wanted to make the appropriate application but had encountered certain difficulties. In the first place, he was not allowed to wear a beard without the KGB's permission, but to apply for such permission he was required to appear with a beard. Secondly, in order that the KGB could come to a decision about the propriety or otherwise of a beard, the applicant was required to appear before it wearing a beard according to one of the instructions and without it, according to another. Thirdly, according to a resolution of the Central Committee on beard-wearing, all citizens were required to remain as they were at the time the resolution was promulgated. And he, JRF, now didn't have the right to shave his beard so that he could appear without a beard before the KGB in order to apply for permission to wear a beard. Finally, now that communism had arrived, the state and the KGB had withered away, so that he, JRF, didn't know to whom he should apply. Tvarzhinskaya said that the KGB wasn't the state, but an initiative of the population. All those assembled applauded. The plain-clothes agents trod on JRF's head and stamped him into the ground. The Representatives said that they approved of the Board's decision, that they had been watching JRF for a long time and considered that he did not conform to their designs.

'I'll show you, you scoundrel, what kind of bitch I am,' hissed Tvarzhinskaya.

HIS DREAM ON MAY THE SECOND

On the second of May he drank and slept again. And had another dream in which a stranger appeared.

'It all boils down,' he said, 'to how and when a person is protected and when he is unprotected. In our part of the world a person, in the interests of self-preservation, has to be resourceful, cautious (i.e., cowardly), unprincipled, unreliable – he has to be precisely what we are ourselves. We don't need to fight a duel to protect our honour or the honour of our family. If someone does us wrong, there's the collective, the Party bureau, the courts. We don't have to show any personal initiative and risk our career. We're not in danger of being fired. On the other hand, we are powerless against the flea-bites of our flat-mates, public transport, queues. We are powerless against shop assistants and petty bureaucrats. At work we are in the power of the collective and the management at every single step. I haven't yet mentioned the KGB. It would be possible to draw up a complete list of the qualities of an individual and a complete list of his contacts with other people and with the environment in general. Then we could look to see which qualities were in practice unnecessary and which ones were regularly reinforced. And we would unerringly come up with ourselves. And we could work out all the deviations from the norm. For instance, if a person is courageous, open, straight, we all think that he's touched. That's true, isn't it? There is an unwritten rule among psychiatrists whereby they regard as a deviation from the norm "excessive" boldness, or a "heightened" awareness of what is just or unjust, and other qualities which used to be regarded as positive (and still are in our mendacious literature). And they are right, that's what's so terrible about it. We are not at all surprised by evidence of cowardice, hypocrisy, toadying behaviour, greed or lack of principle. And if some courageous, unselfish, honest person appears in our midst, it causes resentment. We won't rest until we have either reduced him to our level or got rid of him. As you see, everything is trivially simple.'

'Where will it all end?' asked JRF.

'Nowhere,' said the Stranger. 'But everything is going to be wonderful.'

And God will come to triumph and Eternal Peace will dawn
And we will love each other in that communist utopia.
And side by side, nay, hand in hand, our troubles long since past
                                                    and gone,
We'll sit together, feast upon an everlasting cornucopia.
And then will speak the higher one who o'er all this presides,
Explain that torments past have ceased for all, both young and old,
That exploitation, sickness, misery and a lot more else besides
Have been dispelled for ever more as marxist doctrine had foretold.
And, therefore, we should, all of us, make sure we understand,
Completely, once for all, from A to Z and first to last,
That there's no room for faces sour in this, the promised land,
And any such will be destroyed as they're a remnant from the past.

THE VIGIL

He didn't sleep on the night of May the second. And he remembered about the Representatives. And they appeared. But this time the handsome giants were in front again and the ugly dwarfs behind them.

'We didn't finish our conversation,' they said.

'I'm tired of talking to you,' he replied. 'Moreover, reason is incapable of convincing rational creatures. However, if you really want me to, I'll tell you what I think.

'The study of our society by the method which I have already sketched out for you allows us to predict all the essential trends within this society for as long as it exists. I am speaking about predicting trends, not concrete details. For instance, it is not possible to predict fashions, clothes, types of furniture, hair-styles, the names of our leaders, although no doubt appropriate specialists would be capable of some kind of foresight in these matters. Moreover, the prediction of basic trends within a society presupposes some rather major assumptions and leaves out of account such things as natural disasters, wars and epidemics.

'Everyone in the population will be strictly confined to a certain territory and within that territory to a particular institution. Movement from one place to another will only be permitted as and when the governing authorities see fit. The population will be rigidly stratified and membership of a particular stratum will become hereditary. An exception might be made for the intelligentsia, which won't have any heirs, will always emerge from the working class, will be the flesh of its flesh, a substratum and, in fact, the tradition and continuity of the intelligentsia will be eradicated. A bureaucratic hierarchy will be preserved. A certain part of the population will regularly be drafted into an army of slaves for particular types of unpleasant and dangerous work and for work in unhealthy regions. Not only will the working day be strictly regulated, non-working time will be as well. The system of ranks will reach the level of the divine. The head of the Party will be treated as a god. All creative activity will be depersonalised. The products of creative processes will bear the names of directors, chairmen, heads of departments and Party leaders. There will be no opposition. There will be complete unanimity of thought, desire, aim and action. A special system of amusements will be created for different strata of the population. Art will be entertaining and soulless. All the achievements of science and technology will be used by the privileged strata for their own ends. The remaining strata will have to make do with the crumbs that fall their way. The difference in the way of life between the ruling strata and the rest, will be similar to the difference in the way of life between the inhabitants of a modern cattle-farm and the animals which they breed. The "workers" will be cared for on the level of these farm animals. The sway of ideology will be horrific. Mendacity, coercion of the individual, despicable behaviour will permeate all levels of society. "Temporary difficulties" will occur regularly, i.e., specifically communist crises, a way out of which will be mass repressions, foreign adventures, wars. The population will be destined to struggle for every little necessity of existence to such an extent that it will have no possibility of thinking about its condition. The punitive organs will choke at birth the slightest hint of disobedience and criticism. Need I go on? Well, what do you say to that?'

But they had gone.

'Stop!' he shouted after them. 'I haven't told you the most important thing. Communism is a false solution to the problems of civilisation and that's why it's so tempting. It is a cancerous

494

growth on the body of civilisation. If you have come from Down
Below, I don't acknowledge you. But if you are sent from Heaven,
watch out! Even gods are powerless against Man at his worst.'

DREAMING OF A HAPPY END

'Well,' thought JRF, 'it's time to round things off. It's time to
think about a happy ending. And why shouldn't there be one?
All the ingredients are there: a handsome, educated, intelligent
young lad, with a beard, dressed in jeans, speaking a foreign
language and with his own separate room. So he's not a senior
research fellow? So what? I'll be patient for another five years
and I'll become one. Other people wait longer. I can find a wife
with a flat of her own and a good salary. I could marry that
Toothless Doctor, for instance. She has a two-roomed flat. We
could exchange her flat and my room for a three-roomed flat in
the South-West district. Many people do that nowadays. You
don't like the Doctor? How is she worse than anyone else? Give
her some teeth, a wash and some new clothes and she could pose
for *Playboy*. If the worst comes to the worst I can divorce her and
she can get shot of me for the price of a one-roomed flat in a co-
operative. Many people do that nowadays. But no one is going
to exchange a luxurious three-roomed flat. All right, if I really
don't like the Doctor (you can't tell your heart what to do!), I
can always marry Trollop. She has an eight-metre room in her
parents' two-roomed flat. We'll carry out some kind of complicated exchange and acquire a one-roomed flat somewhere on the
outskirts of Moscow. What's wrong with that? What more do I
want? I'm not the first and I won't be the last. And before I
know where I am, another eight or ten years and I'll make it to
doctor. And go abroad. I'll participate in an international . . .
oh, dream of my youth . . . symposium, or even colloquium. I'll
bring back a suede jacket! Is life not wonderful?! Nowadays all
sorts of critics and slanderers are crying out about there being no
idealism, no meaning to life. How can they! These critics can't
know what an international symposium is, or a suede jacket.
Why that same jacket Over There (i.e., in Their Part of the
World) only costs fifty roubles and Over Here (i.e., in Our Part

495

of the World) only four hundred. And you mean to say there's no meaning in that?! No ideal?!'

JRF had every reason to dream about a happy ending. There have been more serious cases which ended happily. There was a nightmare of a case in the Institute a few years before JRF's case. But even it had a happy ending. Tvarzhinskaya, delivering a speech on the occasion of the happy ending to this nightmarish incident, extracted a general theoretical conclusion from it, making thereby a significant contribution to the treasure house of marxism-leninism: she declared that unfortunate incidents weren't excluded under communism but that they all had happy endings.

And the case in question was the following. There was a Party secretary in the institution, a true marxist-leninist who resolutely carried out the general line of the Party. He had one small weakness: he liked changing his women frequently. As a result he contracted a nasty dose on one occasion and made a present of it to a dozen or so female colleagues. All of them were also true marxist-leninists who resolutely carried out the general line of the Party. Fearing discovery, the secretary committed suicide. Since it was impossible to cover up the suicide it was made to look as if the secretary had been poisoned by irresponsible critics of the regime. All twelve of his victims spoke at his funeral and declared that, although he had made the occasional little mistake, the secretary had been a true marxist-leninist who resolutely carried out the general line of the Party. Everyone gathered at the funeral felt uplifted and radiant. Even an outstanding mood-dampener like Dobronravov couldn't dampen the mood. He grunted spitefully that the mistakes hadn't been all that occasional. There had been at least twelve of them. And they hadn't been all that little. A young corresponding member of the CPSU might be forgiven for sleeping with women of long standing in the Party, moreover in working hours, but not an old experienced communist with a flat of his own who had access to the Institute in non-working hours. But even Dobronravov agreed in the end that the secretary had been a wonderful chap and that he (Dobronravov) was very pleased that the affair had turned out so well for him (the secretary).

THE ROAD TO THE MADHOUSE

On the way to the Madhouse he met Shubin, who was going in the same direction after a festive drinking-spree.

'I too was a junior research fellow for many years,' said Shubin in a burst of candour. 'My life was permanently dangling on a thread. I was often on the point of being led off to you-know-where. But I was lucky: that "liberal" epoch was beginning, with which the powers that be to this day have been unable to come to terms, supported by the "people", with whom they (the powers that be) would like to be able to come to terms. And instead of being taken to you-know-where, I was summoned at a moment when I was playing the fool on the lower landing, proposing new slogans along the lines of "Our people loves its people". The deputy director in charge of personnel was waiting for me. He stood up, walked towards me, gave me a welcoming smile, held out his hand, clapped me on the shoulder, winked at me as if I were a close friend, sat me down on a soft armchair beside his, placed one hand on my knee and with the other latched on to a button which was dangling, like I had been up till then, from a thread. I am describing these details not from a desire to be a realist and continue the best traditions of Russian classical literature, but as important elements in the procedure of the social behaviour of homo sovieticus i.e. I am acting as a conscientious and painstaking sociologist. For me, as another homo sovieticus, this behaviour was deeply significant. If, for example, the deputy director had walked towards me, smiled, shaken me by the hand and clapped me on the shoulder, that would almost certainly have meant that he was about to ask me to prepare some material for him on such-and-such a question, i.e. write a chunk for an article or a book of his. But in conjunction with the other details of this meeting, the aforementioned actions of the director meant that there was about to be a significant change in my life. I humbly lowered my skinny (at that time) frame into the soft armchair, again in a manner which conformed to the required ritual of behaviour, i.e., on one buttock, half-turned towards the director, ready at any second to leap up and exclaim rapturously: "It will be done!" I didn't even care that the deputy director was about to rip off that button, the like of which was not to be found in the whole of Moscow. To hell with the button. I'd survive without it. The way things were going, I'd have been prepared to sacrifice the jacket. "You're a good lad," said the deputy director in some new accent matching the spirit of the new age. "We're going to promote you. There has been a decision to bring our young people" (I was approaching forty!) "to the fore. We've been looking at your record. You've got the odd black mark, why hide the fact. But basically you're one of us. So we've decided to promote you to senior research fellow and set you on your way towards doctor. The Party is showing great trust in you and you will have to justify it."

'I was in seventh heaven with joy and swore to justify the Party's trust in me and to be exactly as my dearly beloved bosses wanted me to be. I promised not only not to spend any more time on the lower landing engaged in the sort of chatter that undermines our doctrine, but not even to appear in the Institute except on pay-day and for meetings, occasions when I couldn't not appear. And I promised to give up drinking. Naturally I didn't keep that promise and that very day engaged in the most grandiose drinking bout imaginable. But all I had been asked to do was to *promise* to stop the "scandalous behaviour", not to stop the behaviour itself. The deputy director told me at the time: "Cut out the drinking. Drink at home, in secret, in the bosom of your family. No one forbids you to do that. Drink as much as you like. But in a way that doesn't attract attention. And without these 'conversations'. Understand? Otherwise, drink as much as you like."

'The waiter in the restaurant where we celebrated the management's decision to promote its "talented young people" was one of our graduates. When he discovered the reason for our merry-making he disclosed that he had just been promoted to captain in the KGB and added twenty-five roubles on to our bill in addition to the normal swindling amount he usually added on. But we forgave him, for he was one of us as well. And in fact I soon did make it into the senior category, after only eight years as a junior. I was lucky. Your position is worse. Why? Because the liberal epoch could only start once. And once it had started it couldn't afford the kind of things it got up to with me and many others. Now it has learned to recognise that people like us represent the beginnings of something which is alien to our society and to take prophylactic measures against us.'

JRF wanted to ask Shubin why he thought that he, JRF, was an alien phenomenon in our society. But the latter, having said his piece, had already forgotten about his insignificant interlocutor and had nipped into *Questions of Ideology* to borrow fifty roubles till pay-day.

THE FINAL JOKE

There was the usual female conversation going on in the Department – prices were rising, you had to spend hours chasing round the shops for the most basic items, public transport was so overcrowded and you wasted so much time, it was difficult getting a place in a kindergarten, where should one try to go on holiday to, the debts . . . JRF sat down on a dirty settee and immersed himself in his thoughts. No one paid him any attention. The telephone rang. 'They want you in the director's office at once. Everything has to be at once for Them!'

There was the usual male conversation going on on the lower landing.

'They've just brought out a new toothpaste. Naturally with the quality symbol. And at twice the price. Do you know what it's called? BAM! And there's a little poem on the advertising slip:

> Try our great new toothpaste BAM,
> It socks you in the teeth, Wham! Wham!

I can't make my up my mind whether that's subtle humour or the absence of it. And after that there's a list of all the ingredients. It would astound you! It's got more vitamins in it than lemons and grapes. When you clean your teeth, it's a pity to spit the stuff out.'

'Do you know who the greatest harvester in the country is?

Brezhnev, of course. He was in the Little Land* and look what a harvest of medals and decorations he gathered in!'

Tormoshilkina, who had just returned from a symposium in Paris, was giving her impressions outside the research department.

'Oi, girls! You should see the slips they're producing over there now! Imagine, here . . . hee-hee-hee! . . . there's nothing at all. And here there are just little strings. You pull one of them and it's at your feet. The effect is stunning. Come and see me and I'll show them to you. And the panties! They would turn your head! Look, I bought a couple of pairs.'

'Oi, Nelka, let me have a pair!'

'I'll think about it. I've put on a little weight and they're beginning to tear just here. If they won't stretch, I'll let you have them. But, mind you, they won't be all that cheap.'

On the upper landing high politics is the subject of discussion.

'Carter, you know, has come unstuck with his human rights.'

'Shchipansky is attached to the CIA.'

'How could he not be? If his friend Lupansky is a spy, it would be strange if Shchipansky wasn't one as well. Imagine you and me living in the same room, getting drunk together, chasing the women and hanging around the foreigners together. Let's suppose I'm a CIA agent. Surely I would have a go at trying to turn you?'

'Naturally.'

'I take a very optimistic view of Brezhnev's trip to the German Federal Republic. You can't leave economic ties totally out of account. They are what count in the end.'

'Absolutely! Brezhnev is not so bad. All these awards and medals and so forth are laughable, of course. But I'd rather they gave each other awards and inflated each other's egos than put each other in the camps.'

'They don't seem to be putting people in the camps these days. For some reason you don't hear much about that.'

'What about the "Workers' group"?'

* *The Little Land*: a peninsula in the South Crimea where Brezhnev served during the Second World War as a political instructor in the Soviet Army. Much effort has gone into inflating the importance both of the place and Brezhnev's contribution to the war effort and *The Little Land* is the title of the first (slim) volume of Brezhnev's memoirs. (*Translator's note*)

'That doesn't count. They're just a bunch of head-cases. No, my friends, there will be no return to the past. Gradually we'll get this so-called "democracy" as well. With our people, it can't be any other way. It has to be gradual. And not for everyone. At first just for the people in education and business circles.'

In the corridor leading to the director's office JRF bumped into a girl from the research department. She slipped past with eyes lowered and without greeting him. The director's secretary nodded silently to JRF to go into the director's office. The head of the first section was there with two strangers whom JRF at once recognised. One of the men said that they had to have a talk with JRF, but not there. JRF shrugged his shoulders and turned to go without saying a word. As he crossed the upper landing he thought to himself: 'This time I'm leaving the Institute by the Escort method. It's a pity that no one will be able to appreciate the joke.'